PRAISE FOR REYNA GRANDE'S
ACROSS A HUNDRED MOUNTAINS

"Grande's spare, elegantly written tale of a young Mexican girl searching for her farmworker father, missing since he left to seek his fortune in 'el otro lado,' is a timely and riveting read."

—*People*

"A breathtaking debut."

—*El Paso Times*

"Grande's heartfelt novel addresses a worthy subject—the desperation of illegal immigrants and the families they leave behind."

—*Entertainment Weekly*

ALSO BY REYNA GRANDE

Across a Hundred Mountains

A través de cien montañas (Spanish)

DANCING WITH BUTTERFLIES

a novel

REYNA GRANDE

WASHINGTON SQUARE PRESS

NEW YORK LONDON TORONTO SYDNEY

W Washington Square Press
A Division of Simon & Schuster, Inc.
1230 Avenue of the Americas
New York, NY 10020

First Washington Square Press trade paperback edition October 2009

WASHINGTON SQUARE PRESS and colophon are registered trademarks of Simon & Schuster, Inc.

For information about special discounts for bulk purchases, please contact Simon & Schuster Special Sales at 1-866-506-1949 or business@simonandschuster.com.

The Simon & Schuster Speakers Bureau can bring authors to your live event. For more information or to book an event contact the Simon & Schuster Speakers Bureau at 866-248-3049 or visit our website at www.simonspeakers.com.

Designed by Kyoko Watanabe

Manufactured in the United States of America

10 9 8 7 6 5 4 3 2 1

Library of Congress Cataloging-in-Publication Data

Grande, Reyna.
    Dancing with butterflies : a novel / Reyna Grande.—1st Washington Square Press trade paperback ed.
        p.   cm.
    1. Women dancers—Fiction. 2. Women immigrants—Fiction. 3. Mexicans—United States—Fiction. I. Title.

    PS3607 .R3627D36 2009
    813'.6—dc22   2009004192

ISBN: 978-1-4391-0906-9
ISBN: 978-1-4391-4960-7 (ebook)

For Eva, mi mariposa

In loving memory of my grandmother, Jacinta Benitez.
I'm sorry I got there too late.

Happiness is a butterfly, which when pursued, is always just beyond your grasp, but which, if you will sit down quietly, may alight upon you.

—NATHANIEL HAWTHORNE

DANCING WITH BUTTERFLIES

CHAPTER ONE

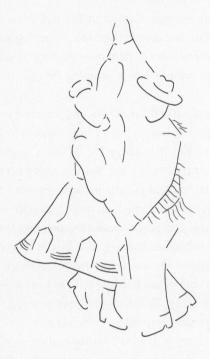

A dancer, more than any other human being, dies two deaths: the first, the physical when the powerfully trained body will no longer respond as you would wish.

—MARTHA GRAHAM

THIS is what it comes down to.

The sweat. The blisters on your feet. The aching of your arms from practicing the skirtwork. The hours and hours rehearsing the same song until the music buries itself so deeply in your brain you hear it even in your sleep. The constant need to coax your body to move past the hurt, the frustration, the exhaustion, and convince it that it can do more . . .

All that is worth this moment.

To be up here onstage, bathed in the red, blue, and yellow stage lights. A thousand eyes look at you, admiring your flawless movements. Your feet seem to float over the floor as you twirl and twirl around and around before jumping into the arms of your partner.

Applause erupts out of the darkness, and you close your eyes and listen to it, let it envelop you. It gives you strength. Three seconds to catch your breath before the next polka, "El Circo," begins, and your heart beats hard against your chest, but you can't hear it above the sounds of the norteño band playing upstage, the musician's fingers dance over the keys of his accordion as quickly as your feet stomp on the floor. As you and your partner move together, you feel the heat of his body, the intensity of his dancing. You look in his eyes and don't let him see that despite the adrenaline rushing through you, you're becoming more aware of the stabbing pain in your knee. You force yourself to keep smiling. He'll know for sure you lied—to him, to yourself, thinking that you could perform like this.

The stage is a flurry of dancers whirling and stomping. The audience breaks into a rhythmic clapping as they follow the lively song in 2/4 beat. On the fourth spin your knee buckles from under you and suddenly you're on the floor, the eleven other couples try not to step on you because after all, the dance must go on.

You try to get up and continue, but your legs no longer obey. You stare at the audience, yet all you see is darkness. The Exit signs like evil red eyes mock you. How is this possible? How did it get to this point? Your partner scoops you up into his arms and whisks you off the stage. Despite the pulsing pain in your knee all you can think about is that you've ruined the choreography. There will be a gap where there shouldn't be.

The dancers waiting in the wings rush over, looking beautiful in their black Chiapas dresses embroidered with big colorful flowers. You want them to go away, to stop looking at you with pity. You're used to the awe, the admiration, the envy. But not their pity.

"What happened?" they ask.

You take a deep breath, trying to come up with something, anything except the truth. "I'm okay, I'm okay. Don't worry. I landed on my ankle the wrong way. Now stop fussing over me and go back to your places."

"Is it your knee?" your partner asks as he helps you to the dressing room.

You shake your head no, glad that your Nuevo León skirt is long enough that he can't see your right knee has swollen to the size of a grapefruit. You find yourself unable to tell him the truth, even if he's your husband. Because once you admit it to him, you will have to admit it to yourself as well.

The pain will go away. It has to.

Yesenia

We've just finished warm-ups and are now taking a short break before moving on to the Azteca danzas, but I'm at the barre doing tendus. I need to believe warming up longer will help. That and Advil should help me get through practice, but lately that hasn't been the case. I feel my kneebones grinding against each other, and I've started wearing a brace and keep it hidden under my sweatpants—which I've been using now instead of my Lycra pants—and although the brace relieves some of the pressure, my right knee still stiffens and swells.

My son, Memo, comes to stand by me and stretches as far as he can, yet his fingertips are two inches shy of his toes. It makes me feel better that at twenty, Memo isn't that much more flexible than I am.

"I'm making chile verde for dinner," I say.

"Ah, Mom, I'm going out with my friends tonight."

"Where are you going on a Sunday night? Don't you have school tomorrow?"

"To the Arclight. The director is going to be there for a Q and A after the movie. I'll come straight home afterward. Besides, my first class isn't until eleven."

"You can have the leftovers tomorrow, then. That is, if your father and I don't eat it all."

Memo laughs and runs his fingers through his long hair. I brush it off his forehead, wishing he would cut it. He won't, though, no matter how much I complain that it doesn't look good onstage. The audience could think he's a girl dressed up in men's clothes.

"Guess what?" Adriana, one of my dancers, says as she joins us at the barre. "I got a job!"

"Great!" I say, suppressing a sigh of relief. Finally, Adriana will start paying her dues and stop begging her sister for rent money. "How about I take you to La Perla to celebrate?"

My husband, Eduardo, picks up the atecocolli and brings it to his lips. When he blows into the shell the dancers peel themselves off the walls or get on their feet and head to the floor. "Tomorrow after work, okay?" I say to Adriana. As Eduardo pounds on his drum, the studio comes alive with movement. Memo remains by my side, and as we dance I can't help but remember the child he once was. Three years old, and already he had learned to do a zapateado. And now, he dances flawlessly. Gives in to the music of his ancestors, and when he turns to me and smiles, I feel a rush of pride. This tall young man is my little boy, whom I taught to walk, to dance, to love Folklórico.

I look at the dancers around me. In the row in front of me is Stephanie, who at seventeen is the youngest in the professional group. In the row behind me is Olivia, who at thirty-six is the second-oldest dancer, six years younger than me. The women always leave. Start getting married. Having children. Pursuing a career. Little by little letting go of their passion for Folklórico.

I've been the co-director of my own dance group for nine years. Eduardo and I have worked so hard to get it where it is now. There are about a hundred Folklórico groups in Los Angeles, and Grupo Folklórico Alegría is one of the best. We have forty-five dancers, and in every one of our big shows there are always at least twelve couples on the stage.

When we finish practicing the Azteca danzas, I put on my dance shoes and my red practice skirt, which is made of fourteen yards of poplin and falls right below my ankles. Lately, whenever it's my turn to teach I focus on the skirtwork even more than the footwork because it gives me a chance to rest my knee.

"You hold up your skirt like this," I say, standing before the female dancers, my back to the mirrors. "Stop holding it as if it were a rag you clean your kitchen counter with! Veracruz is supposed to be danced with grace. You hold up the skirt delicately, as if it were sea foam, light in your hands. But your feet are fast, like the current."

Even though our next performance isn't one of our big shows but rather an adult school assembly, I won't let the dancers go until I'm pleased with what I see. "This isn't the time to learn but to perfect," I say. "Last year we gave an excellent show at this school and this year I want it to be even better."

We do another run-through of the Veracruz Cuadro Eduardo and I choreographed, except I don't finish the suite. At the beginning of "Coco," the last song of the cuadro, I step to the side and pretend my skirt has become loose. I wrap one strap around my waist, and then the other, slowly, breathing in and out. Eduardo glances at me, and so does Memo, the same worried look on their faces. I stand on the side and watch the dancers do the complex combination of steps. Sweating bodies flow in graceful rhythms, turning and turning, feet tapping faster and faster. I listen to the joyful music: the harp playing the melody, the jarana marking the rhythm, the requinto providing the counterpoint. To hell with my rebellious knee! I quickly pick up the sides of my skirt and join the dancers again. But by the end of the song, my feet hardly move. I do the skirt movements and hope no one can tell I'm only marking the steps the way some of the lazy dancers do, the way Adriana is doing now. How often have I told her she must dance at practice the way she would dance onstage?

I don't correct her today. How can I? My feet aren't as fast as the current anymore.

After practice I go home and head straight to the freezer; I sit on the recliner with an ice pack on my knee. Eduardo comes out of the shower with a towel wrapped around his waist. At forty-two he still has the body of a young dancer, slender and agile, so much like Memo's. I've always been jealous that he can eat anything he wants without gaining weight. Unlike me, who puts on pounds just by looking at food.

"I'm worried about you, Yessy," he says. He isn't a tall man; at five feet five he stands two inches shorter than me, and his thin body makes me feel like a beluga whale when standing next to him, but his deep, booming voice makes him seem larger than life. His poise conveys confidence, power. That's what attracted me to him the first time we met when we were kids. He isn't a good-looking man, but the way he carries himself always makes women turn to look in admiration.

"I'll be fine, you'll see. It's nothing to worry about," I say.

"You've let it go on for too long now. It could get worse." He comes to stand behind me and massages my neck. "Dancing isn't forever. When our time comes, we have to let it go."

"What are you talking about? I'm not ready to let it go. This will pass. It always does." I stand up and put the ice pack back in the freezer and begin preparations for a lonely dinner without Memo.

After a shower I tuck myself under the blankets and wrap my arms around Eduardo. "I'm scared," I confess. "I don't know what's happening to me."

He squeezes my hand and says, "I know, honey. I know. But you have to do something about it, Yessy. If you keep pushing yourself the way you've been doing, it could get worse."

"It can't be that bad, can it? Maybe if I take it easy these next few days . . ."

"You need to see a doctor. Even though the pain does go away, it always comes back—and it's worse."

I turn around to face the wall and sigh.

"No matter what happens, you'll always have Alegría," Eduardo says. "The group will always be yours."

I dreamed of starting my own group for a long time. When Memo was in sixth grade, Eduardo and I finally got serious about it and began to look for a studio to rent. Eduardo had just inherited his father's electrical business and didn't have much time for the group. Teaching and choreographing was all he could do, so I devoted myself to recruiting dancers, acquiring the costumes, looking for performance venues, hiring the musicians. I spent day after day writing grant proposals to get funding. Before finally forming a committee and assigning responsibilities to some of the other dancers, I was the one who spent countless hours on the phone trying to book performances, receiving the dancers' dues, making deposits, paying the rent for the studio, worrying about the constant shortage of money. Grupo Folklórico Alegría is mine as much as it is his.

I sigh in the darkness, trying to fight the nostalgia that lately has been visiting me at night. I get out of bed, careful not to wake him. Eduardo can fall asleep within minutes, whereas I have a hard time getting my mind to stop thinking. As I make my way to the kitchen to get a drink of water I notice the light seeping through the crack under Memo's door. I wonder if he had a good time tonight, but just as I'm about to knock I hear him talking on the phone, laughing once in a while. He's graduating from Pasadena City College in a few months, and in August he's moving to Riverside before the school year starts at UCR. I move away from his bedroom door. As I walk down the dark hallway, I try not to think about life without Memo at home.

Mondays at the AAA office are usually busy. By the time lunchtime comes around I've sold three new auto policies and five memberships. As I'm getting ready to finally take my lunch break, a client comes into the office. From the corner of my eye I see him checking in at the front. I want to rush out the door and later claim I didn't see him. But his name appears on my computer screen, and I have no choice but to get up and call him to my cubicle. He walks toward me with determined steps, and I notice that his right arm ends right above the elbow in a stump.

"Hi, my name is Yesenia." I awkwardly shake his left hand and offer him a seat. I sit at my computer and say, "How can I help you?"

"I want to get a quote for car insurance."

I ask him a series of questions that will help me determine his premium. I try not to glance at the stump and hope he can't see the disgust I feel. He should at least wear long-sleeve shirts to hide it.

"Does it bother you?" he asks.

"No, no, of course not."

He chuckles. "It's okay; I'm used to it by now."

"Were you in a bad accident?" I try to keep my eyes on my computer.

"No, actually, I was bitten by a cat."

I turn to look at him. "You serious?" I was imagining different scenarios; maybe he lost his arm in the war or performing some heroic deed, like Antonio Banderas trying to save Salma Hayek in that movie about a mariachi.

As I write his policy he tells me what happened—he didn't pay much attention to the bite, cleaning it with hydrogen peroxide, thinking the infection would go away, but it kept getting worse. Soon, his arm was so swollen he couldn't put it off any longer and went to see the doctor.

"Why didn't you go sooner?"

"Because I thought a cat's bite was no big deal," he says. He'd been hurt worse before. Stepped on a rusty nail once when he was walking around his yard barefoot, and nothing happened to him then, although his wife kept telling him he might get tetanus. So what was a bite of a stray cat going to do to him?

"The doctor said a cat's bite is much worse than a dog's bite," he says. "Cats have a lot of bacteria in their mouths because they're constantly licking themselves, even their butts. So the bacteria had spread so much there was nothing he could do but cut off my arm."

"I'm sorry."

"You know what the worst part is?" he asks. I shake my head. "Sometimes I wake up and reach for my glasses, thinking my arm is still whole. And I see this instead . . ." He lifts up his arm so that I can see the stump up close.

I pick up Adriana after work and we head to El Mercadito in East L.A.

"How long was it this time?" I ask.

"Three months, two weeks, and three days," she says as she lowers the window. She's wearing a hot pink blouse with lace around the collar, purple ribbons on her braids, silver chandelier earrings, and bright red lipstick. Every time I see Adriana outside of practice I think of an overly decorated Christmas tree, like the kind Eduardo and I put up in the living room every year. We never know when to stop with the decorations. Neither does Adriana.

"Let's hope this one lasts," I say. She's had more jobs than anyone I know. This time she's waitressing. Her last job was cleaning offices at night. The job before that I think she was a cashier or a parking lot attendant, or a pizza delivery person, I've lost track.

As we drive to El Mercadito, I tell Adriana about the man with the missing arm. "That's pretty fucked up," she says.

The whole day I haven't been able to put him out of my mind, wondering how one can deal with being incomplete.

Adriana likes the stores on the lower level because they sell typical Mexican clothes—blouses with ruffles and lace, peasant skirts and shawls, her usual attire.

What I like about El Mercadito are all the goodies sold there: corn on the cob lathered with mayonnaise and sprinkled with grated cheese and chili powder, or mango with chili and lemon, tamarind pulp, chicharrones, buñuelos, pumpkin and yam in syrup, and my favorite of all, churros, real churros, not that previously frozen crap sold elsewhere.

After browsing through the stores and sharing a bag of churros, we go up to La Perla restaurant on the third floor and order a bucket of Coronas. I can't decide what to order; everything looks so good—but I can't stop thinking about all those calories. I settle for a shrimp cocktail, one of the least fattening things on the menu. My New Year's resolution is to lose the extra pounds. Even though I'm so active with my dancing, I'm still at least thirty-five pounds over my ideal weight. The huge floor-to-ceiling mirrors at the studio shamelessly remind me of all the tamales I stuffed down my throat on Thanksgiving, Christmas, and New Year's. Right now my goal is to lose five pounds before our next performance. Five pounds isn't an impossible goal, but these last few years it's been getting harder to keep my weight down.

"Your knee still bothering you?" Adriana asks after she takes a big swallow of beer.

"The pain comes and goes."

"You seen the doctor? I mean, after you fell at the performance—"

"I fell because I hurt my ankle," I insist. The thing about lies is that once you say them, you have to keep saying them. "Anyway, it'll pass." Yes, the pain will pass and I'll continue to do what I've been doing since I was six years old. Folklórico is my life. It's all I know.

"You haven't been dancing as much during practice. You stand there with Eduardo and watch us instead. That's so unlike you."

"I just thought I'd help him out a bit. The show is coming up and I've been noticing some mistakes that he hasn't. Being a dance instructor isn't easy, you know?" I don't hold Adriana's gaze for long. It bothers me to stand there watching. Every year I teach a few dances and help Eduardo choreograph a cuadro, but my passion is for dancing, not teaching. "Anyway, here's to your new job. Hope this one lasts."

"Ha, ha," Adriana says.

I love the murals that cover the walls of La Perla. One is of a landscape of a beautiful Mexican village. Little houses are scattered alongside a lake, with a fisherman casting a butterfly net in the middle of it. The mural on the other wall is of a beach framed with straw huts on one side and large puffy clouds in the sky above. The multicolored track lights on the ceiling shine on the murals. Every time the color changes from blue, to red, to yellow, the time of day in the paintings changes, too. It goes from being a sunny afternoon to twilight, and the little lights inside the houses turn on, and even fireflies appear among the reeds on the lakeshore. In the other mural, the moon peeks from between the clouds, and the rays of the moon make the ocean water shimmer.

Right now it's nighttime; the sleepy town seems so peaceful, idyllic. The kind of place one could live in and be happy. A few minutes later, the lighting is red and the dawn comes, then slowly the lights change to blue and it's daytime and soon the sleepy village is awake again.

I've always been curious how the artist did this. What special technique did he use to have his murals change from morning to nighttime? As curious as I am, I've never asked because I want to believe it's magic. I want to believe the little village is real. That it's another world and if I walk up to it and touch it, I'll be magically transported to that little village by the lake.

I feel the alcohol warming me. The mariachi come out to the stage and begin to set up. I can't wait to hear them play those depressing Mexican songs about love gone wrong, betrayal, vengeance, disappointment, solitude, and regret. Because of the cat story, I'm already in the mood.

I check out the guitar player, the one who looks like the Mexican singer Pepe Aguilar. Nice ass. I imagine myself in his arms, or him holding my hand and blowing my worries away as if they were dandelion seeds. He would look at my body, my sagging breasts, the wrinkles on my face, and the magic of his words would make me feel like a girl of sixteen, not a woman in her early forties.

In the murals, time stands still. Morning and night come and go but the town never changes. Nothing changes. I wonder about the artist again. Wouldn't it be great if he could design some props for one of our shows? Maybe even paint the backdrops for Michoacán or Nayarit . . .

Adriana is looking at me with eyes half closed, leaning back against the chair, every bit of her succumbing to her third beer. As always, it amazes me how much Adriana looks like her mother, Cecilia, their lips forming a half smile that makes you feel as if they're laughing at you, as if maybe you have a piece of cilantro stuck between your teeth.

"You'll be an aunt soon," I say, thinking about Elena and the very big belly she's now carrying around.

Adriana shrugs. "Yeah. So what?"

"So, Elena is going to need you by her side. You don't know how hard it is after you have a baby."

"She has plenty of people to help her out. You, for instance."

"Elena is your sister. It's your place to be there for her."

Adriana drinks her beer in one big swallow and then wipes her mouth with the back of her hand, saying nothing.

"Any luck with your father?" I ask.

"No. He didn't want to talk to me last time I saw him."

"You should just forget about him, Adriana. Stop going to his house. A man like that isn't worth the heartache."

"He's my father. I'll decide if he's worth it or not."

Twelve years ago Cecilia died in a car accident, leaving her two daughters alone at the mercy of their father. I open my mouth to say more, to make Adriana realize the man she calls father is an abusive asshole who treated her like an animal. But the mariachi begin their first song. The music enters my body and makes me tremble. I lean back against my chair; there's nothing like the sound of violins and songs about a lost love to dig into your soul and make you bleed.

We sing along with the mariachi, Adriana and I. She with her perfect voice like that of her favorite Mexican singer, Ana Gabriel, and me with my off-key raspy voice that's sexy when talking but not when I'm singing. But who cares? I'm here to enjoy myself.

Our food arrives as we finish a song about wanting to go back to the arms of an old lover. One of the men sitting at the tables nearby gets up and walks up to the band. He tells them something I can't make out. The musicians nod and the man takes the microphone and gets on the stage. He's so drunk, he can hardly keep from falling.

My God, this guy makes me wish I were deaf! He sings "Mujeres Divinas." There's nothing for us to do but sing along with him and hope when the song is over, he'll go back to his seat. But no. He takes a liking to the mike and follows up with "El Rey." *With money or without money, I do whatever I want, and my word is law. I don't have a throne or a queen, or anyone who understands me, but I'm still the kiiiiiing!*

When the song is over he takes out a huge wad of money and hands several bills to the guitar player with the cute ass. Satisfied by the generous tip, the musicians pick up their instruments, and to my dismay, the man lifts the mike and sings "Tristes Recuerdos."

> El tiempo pasa. Y no te puedo olvidar.
> Te traigo en el pensamiento constante, mi amor.
> Y aunque trato de olvidarte, cada día te extraño más.

The customers shake their heads in disapproval. The guy is butchering this song, which happens to be one of Adriana's favorites.

"This is bullshit!" Adriana says. She looks at the bucket on the table. It's empty now except for the melting ice. She picks it up and looks back at the guy as if seriously considering throwing the ice water on him. She puts the bucket back down and heads to the stage. I stand up, fearing Adriana will do something rash—like slapping the man or kicking him in the balls. Instead, she grabs the microphone from him and begins to sing.

If only she could dance as beautifully as she sings. Every time I hear Adriana sing I can't help thinking she's in the wrong profession. I sit back down, mesmerized by her powerful voice, so strong and yet so tender, so full of something that makes you want to bare your soul to her. Hers is the voice that shakes you, that turns you inside out, that penetrates your most intimate thoughts, that uncovers your innermost fears, so that you admit you're scared shitless of getting old, of giving up the most important thing in your life. Folklórico.

Adriana

Me and Elena don't look like sisters. If you saw us walking side by side, you would think we were just friends. No, not even friends, maybe two people who know each other by chance. The woman doesn't need to put on lipstick; her lips are naturally pink and shiny. Her hair is shoulder-length and it's the dark brown color of piloncillo. I swear she must be someone else's kid. My mother was no saint.

As for me, I'm as dark as a Chocolate Abuelita bar (okay, maybe not *that* dark). And my hair, like my mother's, is black and straight. When I dance Azteca, and I wear the traditional indigenous costume, the headdress of long colorful feathers like a halo around my face; I'm a real Aztec princess come to life.

I imagine that's how Mom must have looked to my father when he first saw her dance.

An Aztec princess.

My father's a pocho. Born of Mexican illegals who came to this country to have a better life. He's never been to México, unlike Mom, who was born and raised there. I guess he'd figured Mom was as close to México as he'd ever get. Mom's Aztec princess glamour didn't last long, I think. Just long enough for Dad to get her pregnant with Elena. Or long enough for Mom to pin the pregnancy on him.

But even if Elena and me are not full-blooded hermanas, there's one thing that binds us—we were both left motherless the night Mom crashed her car into a fire hydrant and the telephone pole behind it. In my mind I can see the water shooting up like a geyser, while inside the car my mother lay with her head against the shattered windshield.

My mother's name was Cecilia Adriana Alvarez, and we never knew much about her except that she was from Chiapas, had come to the States at seventeen, worked at a factory sewing bathing suits, and had a passion for Folklórico. She lived with an aunt before hooking up with my dad, but then the aunt went back to México and my mom stayed in this strange country and the only family she had left was my father.

She was thirty-three years old when she died. Nine years older than I am now. I have my mother's face. I inherited her name. Sometimes I wonder if I'll also inherit her place against a shattered windshield.

Sometimes on my days off, I go to Highland Park to look for my father, and that's where I'm heading now. Since my car broke down on me again, I take the bus. I start feeling light-headed as the 81 bus speeds up Figueroa Street. As soon as we pass Sycamore Park my hand reaches out to ring the bell to request the stop. Avenue 50 gets closer and closer, but my feet are stuck to the floor. The bus pulls over right in front of a McDonald's. The front door swishes open. People look around the bus for the person who asked for the stop. The bus driver looks at his rearview mirror and, when he sees that no one is getting off, closes the door. He merges back into the traffic and I exhale.

Fuck. You're such a coward. I look out the window, see the familiar shops pass by. My back begins to tense up at feeling the helplessness and the anger and the hurt emerge as I think about my dad's parents, and the hellhole I called home for the two years I lived with them. It was Elena's damn fault I was sent to live with my grandparents after Dad went to jail.

It wasn't enough for her that we didn't have a mother. She had to go and make sure that we lost our father, too, that he hated our guts so much, he didn't want to see us again.

She had it easy. She was already eighteen, in her last year of high school. And she was only there for three months before the summer ended and she took off for San Jose to go to school. But me, I was sixteen, and she doesn't know what a hell it was to go live with my abuelos. To have to lock myself in my room because whenever I came out to shit or eat they'd come down on me like vultures. They said, over and over again, that me, Elena, and Mom had ruined Dad's life. It was because of us that Dad hadn't become a lawyer as they'd hoped. Because of us, Dad was thrown in jail.

"We came to this country so that our children could have a good life," they said. "So that they could get an education and have a great career." They would look at me and point an accusing finger. "How dare you send your own father to jail, like some common criminal?"

The bus pulls over at the next stop, on Avenue 52, and two people get off. I yank my feet off the floor and dash out just before the doors close. The bus pulls out into the street and leaves me standing by the curb. For a moment I feel like running after it, but the light has already turned red. I turn back and see the golden arches of the McDonald's down on Avenue 50.

Chingado. Just get it over with, Adriana. Why should you be afraid?

I make my way to Avenue 50 and cross the street. I walk across the train tracks, past the Laundromat where Grandma and I used to do laundry, the liquor store, and Fidel's Pizza, the little pizza place that sells great ham and cheese sandwiches. Up the street I go.

Then I see the beige house on the corner. I cross to the opposite side of the street, not wanting to be seen. What would Grandma say if she saw me standing outside her house? What would Dad say? Would he welcome me with open arms, or would he yell at me like he did the last time I had the guts to knock on the door and ask for him?

As I get closer to Granada Street I can see someone standing outside the house, in the yard. No, not standing. Watering. He's watering the grass. My father. He's hunched over, holding on to the hose, and even from here I can see the way his lips are pressed together, like they always do when he's lost in his thoughts.

I stand on the corner across from Grandma's house and hide behind my red sunglasses and straw hat. I stay near the bus stop so that it seems as if I'm waiting for the bus, not spying. I look at him, afraid he'll look my way and see me, and at the same time wishing that he would.

Look at me, Dad. I'm right here.

I can picture him looking at me, then tossing the hose to the ground, walking to the gate, and sprinting across the street, calling out my name. "Adriana! Adriana, I love you!" Then I shake my head. Shit like that only happens in Mexican soap operas. I've watched enough of them to know.

I remember feeling a stinging on my neck, and then Dad froze; the belt he was hitting me with was suspended in midair. Elena screamed. I touched my neck where I felt the stinging and my fingers got wet with something sticky. Dad tossed his belt on the floor and just stood there staring at me. Elena rushed to the phone, but when Dad yanked it out of her hand she ran out of the house. I don't remember what happened after that, but the next time I opened my eyes I was being carried on a stretcher to the ambulance.

A white woman walked alongside me, and Elena walked on the other side, holding my hand. I knew that the next day I would be black and blue everywhere. I bruise easily, like Mom. I asked her where Dad was and when I saw the cop car outside the apartment, and the guilty look in Elena's eyes, I knew why they were there.

"How could you?" I yelled at Elena. "They're going to lock him up and then we'll have no one."

"It's all right," the cops said later in the hospital when they were asking me what happened. "Everything's going to be all right now."

"He didn't mean to do it," I said. They told me the cut on my neck where the belt buckle sliced through the skin needed seven stitches. The artery got slightly cut. They said I was lucky the buckle hadn't cut any deeper because if it had, I would've bled to death before help arrived. "He was drunk, and he got angry with me because I didn't turn off the stereo when he told me to," I said.

"Everything is going to be all right," they said again. Cops are such fucking liars. Nothing was ever right again. Not with Dad, not with Elena. It was just a little blood. It would've stopped eventually and I would've healed and no one would've ever known about it. And then we wouldn't have been taken away from Dad. We would still be a family. It wasn't always bad with Dad. Sometimes he would be nice, too, especially to me. Once, for my fifteenth birthday, he even took us to Magic Mountain because we'd never been. He drove us there and came back to pick us up when the park closed, except by then Elena and I weren't speaking to each other and all we wanted was to go home. She didn't want to go on the roller coaster rides with me because she said they made her sick, and it wasn't fun to go on them by myself. I told her it was my birthday and how could she make me ride them by myself? We spent the rest of the afternoon and evening just sitting at the entrance of the park waiting for Dad.

She just wanted to ruin my birthday, just like she's always wanted to ruin everything for me. She spied on me constantly, especially when I had finally gotten Dad to teach me to play the guitar. She would be there, sitting on the couch pretending to be reading while I sang and played guitar with Dad. He would sit me on his lap and tell me what a beautiful voice I had, and Elena would sit up, the book forgotten, and look at Dad as if she hated him.

Now that she's about to have her baby, I tell myself maybe it's time to let things go, to kiss and make up. But it isn't in me.

When I look at her, I remember.

Dad is oblivious to me. He's whistling now, probably thinking about things that have nothing to do with me. Grandma comes outside and says something to him. I notice she walks much slower than she used to. Dad waters for a few more minutes and then turns off the faucet. He looks around the yard, as if satisfied with his watering, and then looks across the street. At me.

I hold the metal post of the bus stop and wait.

It's me. Adriana.

My fingers reach up to touch the thin scar on my neck. *It wasn't my fault you went to jail. I know you didn't mean to hurt me. Deep down, you love me, don't you? It was Elena who called. Not me. Not me . . .*

Just like I knew he would, Dad turns away without seeing me. He goes inside his childhood home without knowing I was there. The 176 bus pulls over in front of me and I jump, startled. I hadn't heard it coming. But now it looms above me, its doors wide open like the mouth of a great beast. I step inside and let it swallow me.

I don't know where this cold comes from, but for the next two days I feel like shit. Today is the worst. I can't go wait on tables with snot running down my nose, watery eyes, and chills that keep running up and down my body like electric shocks. So I stay in bed and quickly hang up on the manager of La Parrilla because I don't want to hear him tell me how irresponsible I'm turning out to be. I don't care if I get fired. I wasn't born to wait tables. I'm a dancer. Even if Elena thinks I dance like a damn horse.

In the evening I go downstairs to Ben's to hang out with him and use his computer. We've been neighbors since he moved into the apartment right below mine three months ago. I told him it was strange for him to live in Boyle Heights, an area full of Mexicans. He's probably the only gringo for miles around. But he teaches art to kids with emotional problems at a hospital here in East L.A., and he said it was nice not to have to drive through L.A. traffic to get to work. He likes to paint, and once in a while he also makes sculptures and clay pots.

The day we met, I was standing in the middle of the street yelling at my ex-boyfriend Manuel as he took off in his old Mustang. He was pissed at me because I wouldn't stay home to screw him till the wee hours of the night instead of going to my dance performance. He left me without a ride, standing like an idiot in the middle of the street, weighed down by my costumes inside the garment bags, and the duffel bag with my hairpieces and makeup and shoes. I walked over to my piece-of-shit car and kicked it. Damn car had broken down on me just when I needed it. Ben was outside watering the plants by his door. I didn't know what else to do. I asked him for a ride. I don't know if he accepted because I put him on the spot, but the point is that he drove me all the way to Northridge where the performance was and even waited around till the show ended and drove me back.

Ben walks into the apartment carrying a bag full of medicine. I told him I don't like taking medicine. He says I like to suffer—what was the word? Oh, yeah—"needlessly."

"Did you buy the whole pharmacy?" I ask. I laugh, but soon my laughter turns into a painful cough I can't stop. When I'm calm again, Ben gives me some cough syrup and goes to the kitchen to make tea. "I found some good-looking chicks on Myspace," I tell him. "Come check them out." I click on another woman's picture and read her profile. "Hey, she likes to paint and sculpt, just like you. Come look."

I told Ben he needs to hook up with someone. In the time I've known him, I've yet to see him go out with a chick. At first I thought he was gay because besides me he only has one friend—Dave, who he met in grad school. Actually, now that I see him walking toward me carrying a steaming cup of tea, I still wonder if he's gay.

"You'll make a good husband," I say as I grab the cup. "All those sisters you have must have trained you well." Ben has four sisters and three brothers. I tripped out on that when he first told me, because gringos don't usually have such a large family. He's from northern Wisconsin. Ben says there's nothing there but trees, lakes, and cranberry marshes.

"You'll feel better soon," he tells me as I drink the tea. "You need to be careful about losing your job. It's hard to find a job nowadays."

I know he's right. I don't want to have to job-search again. And it's embarrassing asking Elena—Ms. Perfect—for money, but I tell myself that she owes me anyway.

Soledad

Solitude. Loneliness.

This is what *The New World Spanish/English Dictionary* says my name means in English. Ma says she named me Soledad because I was born on December 18, on the day of Nuestra Señora de la Soledad. She says it was my destino. God knows what He is doing, and if He chose for me to be born on that day there's a reason. But if that is true, I say to her, then why didn't she name my half sister Francisca Javiera? She was born on December 22, on the day of Santa Francisca Javiera. But no, Ma named her Stephanie Elizabeth. Not one but *two* American names, so that everybody knows her youngest daughter was born in America, with all the privilegios and rights of a U.S. citizen.

Was it my bad luck to be born in a little pueblo in México, where some people follow the old tradition of naming their children according to the day of their birth? My mother was born on February 14 and has the name Valentina. My brother, in México, was born on August 10. His name is Lorenzo.

When the midwife put me in Ma's arms for the first time and Ma saw the red spot on my face, the spot she says looks like the fingers of the devil, is this why she decided to name me Soledad? Did my mother know I'll be forever alone? Did she feel in her heart I would never be held by the arms of a man, feel his lips on my lips, hear the latidos of his heart whenever I rested my head on his chest?

Tell me, Mother, why did you give me that name? A name that in seven letters describes what I'm most afraid of. Soledad.

The alarm clock rings in the living room where Ma and my step-father sleep. Ma turns off the alarm.

"Soledad, it's time," she calls out to me in Spanish. She doesn't speak English. I can speak some English, but I understand it a lot more than I can speak it.

Ma enters the room and turns on the light. I cover my face with the blanket. The light hurts my eyes.

"Get up, floja, it's time to get ready," she says. Today is Saturday. This day and Sunday we go to sell at the Starlight swap meet in Montebello. Tuesdays we go to the San Fernando swap meet. Wednesdays and Fridays we go to the swap meet in Pomona.

I shake Stephanie to wake her up.

"Leave me alone," she says, and then turns around to face the wall.

"Levántate," I say to her.

"I'm tired; let me sleep," she says in English.

"Do as she says," Ma tells me.

"But she always takes forever to get ready," I say to Ma as I get out of the bed. My shirt doesn't cover my legs. I take off my pants at night because I sweat too much. I see the cellulite on my thighs. Ma sees it, too. She shakes her head and goes to the bathroom. I lift up my shirt, look at the balls of fat, the purple lines Stephanie calls stretch marks. I let my shirt fall down. I look at my face, see the red birthmark that covers my cheek and part of my neck. I turn around but I don't forget the image in the mirror.

Tomás, my stepfather, is honking at us to hurry. He usually sleeps in the van because he's scared someone will steal the merchandise in it. I brush my teeth and braid my hair.

"Wake up; we have to go," I say to Stephanie. She doesn't move. "Come on."

My stepfather honks again. Ma looks at me. "Let's go, Soledad, Tomás is waiting."

Stephanie smiles and like a turtle, hides her head under the blanket. I follow Ma out of the apartment. I sit in the back with the cardboard boxes filled with cosmetics from Jafra, Mary Kay, and Avon, metal tubes, gray and blue tarps, wooden shelves, and milk crates filled with roll-on deodorant, Victoria's Secret lotion, and hair oil.

The van doesn't have seats in the back because my stepfather took them out to make space for the merchandise. I sit on the floor and hold the crates stacked up next to me, scared they might fall on me. The van goes side to side on the street. We go to the drive-through at McDonald's before heading down to the 60 freeway.

"Why didn't Stephanie come with us?" Tomás asks.

"She's tired, poor girl," Ma says. "Folklórico requires a lot of energy. She needs to rest so that she can be ready for school. My little girl works so hard."

I want to tell her we know that isn't the truth. Stephanie doesn't go to school all the time. She doesn't care about anything but the $300,000 she'll get on her birthday this December. "Dios sabe lo que hace," Ma always says. God knows what He is doing. She says this to Stephanie sometimes, when Stephanie doesn't feel good. On those days Ma holds Stephanie's fingers up and kisses them. She gives a bigger kiss to the finger my English teacher says is called index, and she tells Stephanie that is her lucky finger.

"Soon you will be rich," Ma says to her. "You could've just been another poor girl, but because God knows what He is doing, He made this happen, so that one day you would be rich!"

Stephanie smiles and doesn't feel bad anymore. She makes her right hand back into a fist and hides the lucky finger away. The lucky finger that doesn't have a nail. The doctor by accident cut off the tip of her finger when he was cutting the umbilical cord. Thanks to that little piece of finger, my sister will receive a fortune. The money is in the bank now, but the insurance company won't let Stephanie get it until she's eighteen.

We get to the Starlight swap meet and I thank God for getting us here okay. Tomás gives the security man the ticket and drives into the swap meet. Some sellers have already finished setting up their booths. Now they're drinking their morning coffee and waiting for their first customer. Others are putting together the metal frames or unloading their merchandise. Some vendors sell socks and underwear, women's clothing, kitchen things like pots and blenders, toys, plants, used lawn mowers and vacuums, Mexican candy, tools, fresh fruit and vegetables, music and movies. The lady next to me sells parakeets, doves, canaries, and little turtles and goldfish. Tomás drives down the aisles. We get to Line 14, where they take out my boxes, the metal tubes, and two tarps. I watch the van leave. Tomás and Ma are going to Line 19. Then I remember that because Stephanie isn't here, I have to set up the booth alone. I remind myself that Stephanie always drives the customers away, and if she was here today, I wouldn't sell much. Last week, a lady asked for the price of a face cream and when Stephanie told her, the lady said, "In Tijuana I could get it for half that amount." Then Stephanie said, "What the hell are you doing here? Go to Tijuana, then!" The lady walked away, buying nothing.

It won't always be like this, I tell myself. Soon, things are going to change. I'm a seamstress. I like to sew dance costumes and dresses for weddings and quinceañeras. I didn't have a quinceañera, and this is why I made sure Stephanie had one. Some of the dancers from Alegría were the godparents, and they helped with the cost of the party. Eduardo and Yesenia paid for the cake. I made Stephanie her dress. Everybody said she looked like a princess or a queen. Ma, she doesn't understand the swap meet isn't for me. I like to make costumes for Alegría, even if I don't make too many because Alegría doesn't have much money for new costumes. But what I really want is to have my own dress shop, make my own designs. This is my dream, and soon it's going to come true.

After we get home from the swap meet I go see my friend Rubén. He lives in Huntington Park with his parents. I met him when we were getting our certificates as clothes designers at the Escuela de Arte y Confección in East L.A.

"Quihúbole, Sol," he says to me when I come into his house. His mom says hello to me from the kitchen where she's making enchiladas. I say, "Cómo está, Señora Sofía?" but Rubén pushes me out the back door before Doña Sofía greets me back. and takes me to the garage. I envy Rubén because his parents' house has a big garage where he does his sewing. He makes quinceañera dresses, prom dresses, wedding dresses; once, he even got to work for a beauty pageant and designed all the dresses for the women. There's a big cutting table in the middle of the garage with a tray of scissors, buttons, and some pincushions. His industrial grade sewing machine is in the corner next to a garment steamer. By the door is a bookshelf with fashion design books and a basket full of magazines.

"Want to see my latest creation?" he asks. He takes me to the mannequin by the sewing machine. It's wearing black pants, a bustier, and a bolero jacket covered in rhinestones. There's a plastic bag of rhinestones and a bag of ruby cabochons on the floor.

"It's beautiful," I say. "Who's it for?"

"Me," he says. "Want to see how it looks?" He starts to take the pants off the mannequin. "I made it for my show at Arena. I've decided to do a tribute to Selena."

I say to Rubén to wait for me to go outside, but he doesn't listen. He takes off his pants in front of me. I feel my face get hot when I see him in his underwear. When I see the bulge between his legs I want to close my eyes but at the same time I want to keep looking. The pants he made are really tight, but he's thin and has nice legs. He stuffs the cups of the bustier with scraps of cotton fabric and then puts on the bolero jacket. "What do you think?" he says as he twirls around.

"You look very nice." I feel a knot in my throat. To me he's a man. I don't like to see him wear women's clothes. When he lived alone in his apartment he used to wear women's clothes a lot. Now that he lives here with his parents, they won't let him. He hates living here, but he needs to cut down on expenses to pay for therapy sessions. He says the fire that burned down the apartment building where he lived traumatized him.

"You gotta come see my show, Sol. Arena is an awesome club. You'll have fun."

I don't answer him. He knows I don't go to clubs. Besides, he has a lot of friends he goes out with. I don't like the people he meets at clubs. Sometimes they hurt Rubén. They make him sad. Sometimes Rubén calls me on the phone to come visit him. He cries and tells me he hates his life. He doesn't want to live. Then I hold Rubén for a long time until he feels better. When I don't hear from Rubén I know he's okay.

"Ay, Sol, when are you going to get your hair styled?" he says as he picks up my long braid hanging down my back. "You look like an old-fashioned woman from a little pueblito."

"But I am from a little pueblito."

"Come, let me put some makeup on you, at least. How can you even step outside your door with nothing on? Not even a little lip gloss?"

He sits me on a chair and grabs the container of makeup by the large mirror on the wall. I close my eyes and let him do what he wants. I've learned to let Rubén treat me like this. I know he just wants to help me, but I wish things weren't like this. Rubén is the only man I'm comfortable with. The only man that will listen to me, who doesn't laugh at my dreams, who doesn't think I'm crazy. Even if he forgets about me when he's happy he's still a good friend. He has offered to help me with the dress shop.

I feel his breath on my face and for a moment I forget he doesn't like women. "Have you talked to Mr. Johnson about the lease?" Mr. Johnson owns the space on Pacific Boulevard Rubén and I want to rent. I have tried to save all the money I can, and last month Rubén got $25,000. When the apartment building where he lived burned down a few years ago, all his things were lost in the fire. All the tenants got money.

"No, I haven't talked to the old man," Rubén says. He's putting eye shadow on me now and I can't open my eyes to look at him.

"Didn't he say that you would be signing the contract sometime next week?"

"I guess so," he says. The lease will be under Rubén's name because he has a good social security number and he's a U.S. citizen. Mr. Johnson said I can't be in the contract because I don't have my papers.

"Now, open your eyes, chica."

I look in the mirror and touch my face. It isn't my face I see. It is a stranger's face. A stranger with seductive, smoky eyes and red lips full of promises. The birthmark on my cheek is there, but it isn't as hideous when buried beneath all that makeup. "Mira qué chula te ves," Rubén says.

I wish he would look at me the way Eduardo Yáñez looks at Adela Noriega in my favorite soap opera, *Fuego en la Sangre*.

"Rubén, come eat," Doña Sofía says from the door.

"How many times am I going to ask you to call me Ruby?" Rubén says, putting his makeup back in the container box. I grab a tissue and start to wipe off the red lipstick.

"A million times," Doña Sofía says. "Can you believe it, Soledad? What's happening to my son?" She turns to him and says, "Your brother and father are home now. Come and eat dinner and cut it out with that nonsense. What kind of example are you giving your brother? And for heaven's sakes take those clothes off!"

Rubén sticks his tongue out at his mother as she walks back into the house. "She's going to have to get used to it," he says. "They all are."

"They will," I say, but I don't think Doña Sofía and Don Pablo are going to get used to Rubén being this way. They wish he was already married and had children, like his sister. I rub off the eye shadow before we leave the garage. Rubén tells me to leave the makeup on, that I look good like that. But even with makeup I can't get Rubén to feel something more for me.

On Wednesday I go pick up Stephanie at dance practice after my English class. I sit in the practice room in a little corner and wait. The dancers practice "El Alcaraván," a dance from the region of Chiapas, for a Folklórico competition in Dallas this summer. The women move their shoulders so sexy, their hips side to side. I see how the men look at them. I know in this dance they have to look like two birds who are courting, but I think the way José looks at Adriana is real. Like she's his woman. Like he wants to marry her and have children. See how Angel looks at Stephanie? How he puts his face close to her like he's kissing her? Stephanie says that Angel is a joto. Gay, she says. But he can't be gay when he looks at her with love in his eyes, just the way I wish Rubén would look at me. And Laura, the way she moves her shoulders and smiles at Memo. Then the song ends, and the men run after the women, wanting love.

Eduardo shakes his head and tells them to do it again. I think the dance was beautiful.

When practice is finished, I drive Stephanie home. In the backseat are dance dresses and charro suits Eduardo asked me to fix. Some of the silver buttons running down the outside seam of the pants fell off. Some of the pants are torn at the crotch. These pants have to fit really tight on the men but they tear sometimes. The men look so handsome in their charro outfits—white long-sleeve shirts, the silk tie in butterfly style, the black jacket and pants decorated with silver embroidery and botonadura. I wish Alegría had the money for new charro suits. I could make them out of poly-cotton stretch instead of gabardine, then I wouldn't have to be fixing them so often, and the men would be more comfortable.

Stephanie talks and talks about the dancers. She says Laura isn't a good dancer. That she's better than Laura. "I want to do 'La Bamba,'" she says, "but Eduardo won't let me. He says I always get confused about how to make the bow with my feet, and it comes out all out of shape, but it isn't true. He just likes Laura. But she isn't all that great, you know? When I get my money I'm going to start my own dance group and I'm going to dance the best regions, choose the best partner. Maybe I'll choose Memo. He's so cute."

Stephanie talks bad about Adriana. Says she stomps her feet like she's killing cucarachas. And Yesenia, she says, she's too old and too fat to be dancing.

I stop listening to Stephanie. She always says bad things about the dancers. I think they dance good. I wish I could dance, too. I wish someone would hold me in his arms, hide me under a big sombrero, and kiss me. But I look like the mother of my father. She died when she gave birth to my pa. She suffered much. Her name was Dolores—pain, sorrow, grief.

Elena

Now that I'm thirty-six weeks pregnant, I go to the clinic once a week. I schedule the appointments in the afternoon because I still have two more weeks of work before I officially go on maternity leave. Richard, my husband, says I should go on leave now. "You don't need all those brats you teach taking away the last of your energy," he says.

He's a teacher, like me, but he works at UCLA. I teach remedial English at a high school. Not an easy age to teach. What makes the job more difficult is the fact that I'm twenty-six years old but don't look much older than my students. Once, the principal asked me for my hall pass before realizing I was part of the faculty.

I co-direct a Folklórico group at the high school. The class is offered after school and the students don't receive credit for it. Due to budget cuts, we can't offer many electives to the students, and I feel that sharing my love for dance with them is one way to expose them to the arts. I tell Richard that as soon as I'm finished teaching my dancers the polkas from the state of Chihuahua I've added to the repertoire, I'll go on leave. He doesn't like the idea, but he knows me well enough to not pressure me.

Richard doesn't understand my desire to share with the students the beauty of my culture. Through dance I can teach them about our history, the richness we've inherited from our ancestors. Most of my students are first-generation Mexican-Americans, and they're learning to dance so they don't lose their culture. Through Folklórico, they learn about México's ancient and contemporary traditions and customs. But I also teach them the history of Folklórico here in the U.S., emphasizing its contributions to Chicano identity and art. Unfortunately, they aren't quick learners, and I worry they won't be ready by the time Cinco de Mayo comes around in two and a half months.

My next checkup is today. Soledad comes over to the school to measure the students for the Chihuahua costumes she's going to make. The students have to do fund-raisers such as car washes on the weekends or selling chocolate bars to pay for the costumes since the school won't provide the funds.

Soledad is giving me a good deal, and I tell her how much I appreciate her taking the time to make the costumes even though the money isn't very good.

"It's good for the kids to dance Folklórico," she says, "instead of joining gangs and getting into trouble."

I watch in admiration as she measures the girls' hips, waists, shoulders, even their necks and fists for the long-sleeve high-collared blouses. When she's done with all fourteen measurements for each student I dismiss them and ask her if she wants to come with me to the clinic. Richard has a class in the afternoons and usually can't come.

I'm used to the routine of my visits. Blood pressure is fine. My weight isn't bad; I've put on about twenty-five pounds. Blood sugar level is excellent. Slight puffiness, especially on my feet— I've gone from being a size seven to a size eight and a half. Soledad squeezes my arm in anticipation as we follow the receptionist down the hall.

"There's the baby!" Dr. Franco says as soon as she places the transducer on my belly. She knows Richard and I don't want to know the baby's sex so she just points out the different body parts to Soledad, who's never seen an ultrasound done before and is all smiles, as if she were the beaming parent. I can't help thinking what a pretty woman she is, although most people can't see past her birthmark. "And here is the baby's heart," Dr. Franco says, and then there's a catch in her voice. The screen shows the area of the thoracic cavity where the baby's heart is. Except there's no movement there.

"When was the last time you felt any movement?" she asks in her doctor's voice.

I tell her I felt the baby kick this morning during nutrition. After that I felt nothing. During lunch I lay down for a little bit on the couch in the teacher's lounge and didn't feel anything. I panicked and called Richard, but he reminded me that the pregnancy book we've been reading said it was normal and I shouldn't worry. Maybe the baby was sleeping. Maybe she (because I hope it's a girl) was just getting ready for her big day and was resting. I didn't tell Dr. Franco I was ready to burst into the main office and ask the secretary to call in a substitute so I could go to the clinic right away, but Richard said I was overreacting. My appointment was that afternoon, and it was probably nothing to worry about.

"Is something wrong?" I ask.

She asks me to get dressed and to come to her office; a coldness envelops me. Soledad steps out of the room, and as I get dressed I tell myself nothing is wrong.

I knock on Dr. Franco's door even though it's ajar and I can see her sitting at her desk. Her face is pale and she's twirling her pen absentmindedly. She says, "Come in," and when she smiles at Soledad and me it's simply out of reflex; she catches herself and her smile disappears completely.

"Sit down, Elena," she says. She's been my doctor since my first checkup, and I've heard nothing but good things from her. But now she tells me she has something serious to discuss with me and asks if Soledad should wait outside.

"She can stay." I reach for Soledad's plump hand and hold it tight as I listen to Dr. Franco tell me my baby isn't moving. The heart isn't beating.

"I'm so sorry," she says.

I shake my head. "This can't be happening." I take off my glasses and everything becomes a blur. I wipe them with the corner of my maternity blouse, not because they're dirty but because I need to do something, anything. *It isn't true.*

Soledad brings her hands up to her mouth and gasps.

"Your body will take care of it naturally," Dr. Franco says. She tells me that if I notice any bleeding or cramping I should go to the hospital immediately. But for now, I should go home and rest. I'll need my energy when the time comes to report to the labor and delivery unit at the hospital in West L.A.

I hold on to Soledad as we leave the clinic. We sit on the bench outside, and she asks me if I want to call Richard. But I can't speak. I can't even dial his number. She's the one who makes the call, who tries to explain in the best English she can manage what the doctor said. Then she walks me to my truck and takes the keys from me.

Why? What did I do wrong? I had the flu two weeks ago, was that it? I tried the best I could to do things right. I didn't smoke. I didn't drink. Never did drugs, either before or after I got pregnant. I was careful not to lift heavy objects. I ate the right things. I swam at the gym three times a week, if not more. Was it because I had a cup of coffee the few times I was too weak to resist? Was it our cats, even though it was Richard who fed them and cleaned their litter box just like the doctor said for him to do?

"Maybe the doctor has made a mistake," Soledad says to break the silence. "Those machines aren't perfect. They're machines. They can malfunction."

When we get home Richard is already there, having canceled his next class. Soledad excuses herself, knowing that Richard and I need privacy. Richard tells her we'll call her if we need anything, and before she leaves she gives me a soft kiss on the cheek and says she'll go and pray for us.

I lie down and put my head on Richard's lap, and he makes me tell him what the doctor said, what I saw on the monitor screen. He scratches his head and curses. "This can't be happening," he says. He picks up the phone to call his parents, but I tell him to wait. Wait. Because maybe Soledad is right. Machines can malfunction. They can be wrong.

I rub my belly, feel the baby's knee, but when I push it she doesn't push back like she usually does. She doesn't wiggle and play within me. There's only silence in there. *Wake up, little one.*

I stand up so suddenly I lose my balance. Richard holds me steady. "Let's go," I say, walking to the nursery to grab the bag we packed last week with baby clothes.

"Where are we going?" Richard asks, rubbing his eyes, but I have yet to see him cry.

"To the hospital." It must be a mistake.

I press my sweater tighter against me, my body shuddering. Hospitals are always so cold, and the labor and delivery unit of the West L.A. Kaiser is no different. I feel a blast of the A/C vent above my head and move closer to Richard. He pats my hand and tells me that everything is going to be okay.

The fear that seizes my body begins in my stomach, a painful burning sensation that spreads and spreads in waves. *Please, God, let her be all right. Please let it be a mistake.*

"Elena Sánchez?"

At hearing my name, Richard jumps to his feet and helps me get up. I put a hand over my swollen belly, poke it gently, but again, just like before, I feel no movement inside. *But last night all she did was kick.*

We're escorted into a room, and the nurse asks me to remove all my clothing and put on a hospital gown. She informs us the doctor will be with us shortly and hurries out of the room. There's a chair next to my bed, but Richard decides to remain standing. He scratches his head, pulls on his goatee, and begins to pace. When he notices me looking at him, he forces himself to smile.

"Everything will be fine," he says again. "The baby is fine."

The doctor comes into the room and introduces himself as Dr. Heller before pulling the ultrasound machine from the corner and bringing it closer to me. He lifts my gown to expose my belly and covers it with the conducting gel. The coldness of the gel makes me shiver. I turn to look at the monitor screen, but because it's facing the doctor, I can't get a good view.

If it's a girl, I want to tell him, Richard and I are going to name our daughter Xochitl, the Aztec word for "flower." And her middle name will be Kamilah, after Richard's mom even though she doesn't like me because she would rather her son had married a black woman. Xochitl Kamilah Davis. That will be our daughter's name.

The doctor's face is unreadable, although there's a flicker of pity, so quick I think I must have imagined it.

"The baby's okay, right?" Richard asks him. "Dr. Franco made a mistake, didn't she?"

"Mr. Davis and Ms. Sánchez . . ." Dr. Heller's face softens as he looks at me. I shake my head in denial. In the doctor's eyes I've seen what he's about to say. "Your baby—"

"It's not true," I say.

Dr. Heller looks at Richard, and I wonder if it's easier than to look at me. "I'm sorry. These things happen sometimes. There is nothing you could've done," he says. He turns the monitor screen so that we can see. "This is the fetal heart," he says. "And as Dr. Franco pointed out this afternoon, it is not beating."

"But how?" Richard says, his voice rising. "How could this happen?"

"These things happen sometimes," Dr. Heller says again.

"And now, what do we do now?" Richard asks in a voice so soft I can barely hear it.

"We can induce labor." Dr. Heller takes a deep breath and then looks at me and says the same thing Dr. Franco said earlier. "Or we could wait until your body goes into labor on its own. In about a week or two." Two weeks more. Two weeks more to keep her with me.

"You mean she could still carry the baby even though it's— it's . . ." Richard's voice trails off and then he looks down at the floor. I do the same.

When I don't say anything Dr. Heller says, "I'll give you a few moments alone," and exits the room.

"Elena, I don't know what to say," Richard says. He clears his throat a few times. It sounds strained, as if he'd been yelling, the way he sounds after watching a football game.

I look at him, and I'm glad I'm not wearing my glasses because I don't want to see the expression on his face.

"There's nothing to say," I tell him. "We hoped to hear something different, but there's no mistake, Richard. There's no mistake." He leans his head down on my lap and we both weep.

In the labor room the IV is begun and a suppository that'll make me dilate is inserted. After having labor induced, I'm to spend the rest of the night at the hospital. Richard dozes on and off on the recliner by the window. I begged him to ask his parents not to come, and despite feeling bad he's going through this alone, at the same time I get angry to see him there, sleeping as if this weren't happening.

Six hours later the contractions still haven't started. There are no cramps. No bleeding. I'm not allowed to eat anything except juice, Jell-O, crackers, and ice chips. Hunger is the last thing on my mind. I close my eyes wishing for sleep, but it doesn't come. I'm in the place halfway between sleep and awareness, where everything looks blurry, as if my head were covered by a black veil.

Another suppository is inserted. Another shift in nurses. Once in a while, I hear a baby crying. In my half-dreaming state I think it's my daughter who's been born. I open my eyes with a start and look around me. The monitor continues to beep, Richard continues to snore, and my swollen stomach tells me my baby has not yet passed from my body. I turn to my side, being careful not to get the tube attaching me to the IV tangled up. I lean my forehead against the chilly metal rail as I feel my first contraction begin.

The contractions are mild at first, like menstrual cramps. Little by little they intensify and I think of my mother, of Adriana, writhing in bed every month because their periods, unlike mine, are a source of excruciating pain. The next contraction begins and my body becomes tense. I take deep breaths, wishing my mother were here, or my sister. Somewhere in the labor ward, another baby shouts its first cry. A mother cries, victorious. I await the next contraction.

Fifteen hours after having labor induced, the contractions grow and grow and grow into a tremendous urge to push. When Richard wakes up, the doctor and the nurses are already in place. Richard holds my hand, and I try to push when Dr. Heller tells me to, but I lack the strength to do it. My body doesn't want to let the baby go. It clings to her. Perhaps if she stayed inside me, if I closed my eyes and slept, I would wake up tomorrow and this would've been just a bad dream.

But my body finally succumbs. It lets go with one final push, and I am drenched in sweat, spent with the effort of trying to hold on and at the same time having to let her go.

The cry doesn't come.

"It's a girl," Dr. Heller says.

This is the part when they were supposed to smile and congratulate me on my beautiful baby girl. Richard and I were supposed to hold each other while gazing upon the face of our child. Instead, they're looking down at the floor, as if ashamed at their helplessness. The doctor silently hands me the baby.

I reach out for her, afraid to hurt her. She's so tiny, so fragile.

I hold her close and look at her face, her small fingers curled into a fist, the umbilical cord still connecting her to me. Her eyes closed, mouth slightly opened. Did she cry out? Did she try to ask for help?

Richard stands up abruptly, rushes to the corner of the room, and vomits in the waste basket.

"What are you doing?" I yell, shaking with anger. "Get out! Get out! All of you!"

They all leave, one by one. Dr. Heller and Richard linger at the door. Richard wipes his mouth with a paper towel.

"I want to be alone with her," I say, calmer now. "Just give me a minute, please."

I know I'm asking Richard for too much. Isn't he the father? Isn't he part of this family? But he vomited, as if our child disgusts him. He nods and leaves the room with Dr. Heller.

I look down at her again, press her closer, touch her feet, count the toes, look at the perfect little nails, the curly black hair. The bluish tint of her dark skin.

Why didn't I listen closer, pay more attention? If I had, this wouldn't have happened. I reacted too late, got to the hospital too late to save you. When you kicked so hard it hurt, were you trying to warn me?

Forgive me, my daughter, for mistaking those kicks I joked so often about. "My baby is going to be a dancer."

Now you'll never be anything but boxes of baby gifts, black and white photographs of you growing in my womb, the tiny black dance shoes I bought for you in Tijuana, faint stretch marks on my belly, an empty crib that will be used by a child that will never be you.

Xochitl, my dead flower.

We stay in the hospital overnight and the baby stays with us. At first Richard is afraid to hold her. And when he finally holds her he doesn't cry. All night we talk to her and sing to her. The next morning after a quick exam, I leave the hospital on Richard's arm with nothing but a box containing my baby's footprints and handprints, her ID bracelet, and some pictures the nurse took for us. On the way home I feel a strange sensation in my breasts, and I realize my milk has come in. I take off my glasses and hide in my blindness.

My in-laws and Yesenia are at the house when we arrive. I know Richard needs his family by his side, and he thinks I need Yesenia, but I resent their presence. My back still hurts from the epidural and I have a slight fever and my stomach keeps cramping. Yesenia tells me it's normal, my uterus is shrinking, but the cramps take me back to the labor room, and I feel as if I were having my daughter all over again.

For the next three days I stay in bed. Richard takes care of all the arrangements, and Soledad keeps making coffee and hot chocolate, piling pan dulce and bolillos in baskets for all the people who come and go. I wish they'd go away. I especially want Adriana to go away. I don't want my sister's pity. Nor do I want to hear her tell me, like she did last night, that I can still have another child. That I'm still young.

∽∾

The day of the wake, some of my colleagues from work show up to pay their respects. Mrs. Rodríguez brings along the students in the dance group she and I put together at the high school. They shift from one foot to the other.

I sit across from the white coffin. Richard wanted an open casket so our friends and family could say good-bye to our baby girl, and I was too tired to disagree with him. Didn't he know how hard it would be to see her there, lying so still? Didn't he know I would want to pick her up and hold her in my arms? People come and go, give me kisses and hugs. Pat my back, squeeze my hands, whisper how sorry they are. But my mind is numb to their words and their touch. They say they feel my pain, and I want to scream at them. What do they know about what I've gone through? They don't know what it's like to go into a hospital to deliver a baby that won't be coming home with you. To feel her come into this world and the only cries you hear are your own.

Adriana comes to sit beside me and says, "Pobrecita, my niece, she'll never get to dance with Alegría." She stands up and leaves when the mariachi enter the room and begin to set up their instruments.

A few minutes later, the dancers come out in pairs from the opposite side of the room. Adriana is with them. They're all dressed in Jalisco outfits—the men with black charro suits and the women with dresses adorned with colorful ribbons. The men don't wear hats. It wouldn't be appropriate.

Eduardo, as the director of the group, comes to the microphone. He clears his throat and asks the people to be silent.

"I have known Elena since she was born. I saw her grow up. Had the honor to be her dance teacher and see her become the wonderful dancer she is. Tonight, I would like to express how sorry I am about the terrible tragedy that has befallen her and Richard. The group and I would like to dedicate these dances to Xochitl."

The mariachi begins to play "La Negra."

Richard comes to sit by me and puts his arm around me. We watch them dance, Yesenia with Eduardo. Adriana with José. Stephanie with Angel. Olivia with Memo. Laura with Felipe.

I put my hands on my belly, feel its emptiness. My breasts engorged with the milk my daughter will not be drinking. The music doesn't resonate inside me like it's always done. My body doesn't vibrate; my feet have no desire to move, to get up and dance. I realize it isn't just my daughter that I have lost. I take off my glasses, and now I can't see the dancers' faces, can't see their feet stomping on the floor, but I can still see the blur of beautiful dresses swirling around as the women turn in place. I stand up to leave.

"Where are you going?" Richard asks, holding my hand.

I pry my hand from his.

Richard thinks he knows what's best for us. "In a few weeks, once you've healed, we'll go to Europe. We can go to Spain, take a train to France. We've been talking about this since we started dating. Why not do it now?"

I throw away the books some of the dancers gave me.

"Why are you tossing those?" Richard asks.

"I don't need books to tell me how to grieve for my child." I pick up the corn husk doll Yesenia gave me after the funeral. A dancer dressed in a white Veracruz dress. Yesenia is an obsessive collector of these Folklórico dolls. "To remind you of Alegría," she said. "I hope you come back to us soon." I toss the doll in the wastebasket.

"And why are you throwing the doll away?"

"You know I hate decorations. They make the house look cluttered."

Richard stands up and puts his arms around me. "It will take time, Elena. But we have to try to put this behind us, get over this."

I think of Richard vomiting at the hospital. He said it was the sadness, the helplessness, the anger that made him vomit. Not disgust. But still, anger rises within me, and I embrace it because at this moment I would rather feel anger toward him than nothing at all. "You get over it," I say, and I push him away from me with all the strength I can muster.

CHAPTER TWO

While I dance I cannot judge, I cannot hate, I cannot separate myself from life. I can only be joyful and whole. That is why I dance.

—HANS BOS

You drop off the costumes at Yesenia's garage. You love coming here. You love to see the racks of costumes from every region of México. The mountains of plastic containers filled with rebozos, braids, jewelry, shoes, and machetes.

You go to the rack where the Chiapas dresses hang. Beautiful Chiapaneca dresses, the long skirts made of five flounces embroidered with big flowers of brilliant colors. You unzip a bag to touch the material, run your fingers over the shiny colorful thread of the flowers. You pull down the zipper of another bag and take out a China Poblana dress. The green and red skirt is almost entirely decorated with beads and multicolored sequins that form a design of the eagle and the serpent. You've seen the Alegría women do "El Jarabe Tapatío" hundreds of times, and it still takes your breath away.

You come upon the Sinaloa dresses. You close your eyes and picture the Alegría women dancing "Vuela Paloma," moving their shoulders up and down so sexy, batting their eyelashes and smiling as they do the waltz steps.

You look at yourself in the mirror, at the mark on your face, the double chin, the big round eyes Stephanie says are like frog eyes. You lock the garage door from the inside and take off your clothes. You put on the dress from Sinaloa Costa. The white satin blouse has a wide ruffle around the low-cut neck and small bell-shaped sleeves decorated with black rickrack and edged with bolillo lace. The skirt fabric is hot pink and is made of three connected ruffles. You pull the blouse down so your shoulders are bare. You put on the straw hat adorned with flowers.

You stand in front of the mirror and look at yourself. You want to pull up the blouse, to cover your shoulders, but you don't. You stand back and admire the dress. You move your shoulders up and down, like you've seen the dancers do. You think about Rubén. What would he say if he saw you like this, with your shoulders bare, a hat with flowers on your head? You picture the two of you walking around the plaza in your hometown, holding hands.

"You look so beautiful, querida," Rubén says to you. You bat your eyelashes, but say nothing. Instead, you lean forward and close your eyes. You kiss the mirror, and you try so hard to pretend it is Rubén you're kissing.

But you know his lips wouldn't be this hard and cold.

Soledad

When I'm finished sewing for today, I go visit Elena. I take her a hydrangea for her garden, a bottle of Victoria's Secret lotion I sell at the swap meet, and a card inside a white envelope. She has a pretty garden with many flowers. It reminds me of my home in México. My grandmother, Abuelita Licha, likes to plant flowers and herbs.

When I see Elena's garden I know it's different. Like Elena is now, the garden too is sad. It doesn't have as many flowers, some are being eaten by snails, others are dying. They need water. They need love. Like Elena.

She gives me a glass of lemonade and we sit on the patio. I watch a butterfly flutter near a rose. It looks like it is dancing Folklórico. Its wings white, like a Veracruz dress. So delicate. It reminds me of Elena dancing onstage.

"Elena," I say to her. "Why you no come back to Alegría? You need be with your friends."

She doesn't look at me. She looks at her hands.

"I can't."

"You're the best," I say, switching to Spanish. I don't know enough English words to say the right things. "I will pray for you, Elena, so that one day soon you are free of your sorrow. You weren't born on the day of Our Lady of Solitude, like me. You don't have an ugly mark on your face. You were born in the same month as San Martín de Porres. He's the saint that takes care of all the little animals. He will help you." I tell her to open the card I got her. She picks it up from the table and takes it out of the envelope. In the front is a picture of a monarch butterfly resting on a purple milkweed flower. "In my town we believe these butterflies are the souls of our dead. So you see, Elena. Your daughter isn't really gone."

Elena begins to cry. Her tears fall on the card and she keeps saying the word "butterfly" again and again. I don't say anything to her because sometimes the best thing to do is to keep quiet.

I close my eyes and feel the stinging of my own tears. Last year when she got married to Richard, I made her wedding dress. I used chiffon, a very soft and delicate material that is almost weightless. And this is how Elena is now. But I think of the other Elena, the one made of a sturdier fabric, and I see her onstage, her feet tapping fast, her colorful skirt fluttering around her. And I remember her smile, a smile so big it'd make me smile, too.

I have $5,356 in a box I keep in a secret place. It isn't much, but I don't want to start a business with Rubén with no money of my own. It wouldn't be fair to him. The money I save comes from the swap meet, making quinceañera dresses, Alegría's costumes, and selling cans and bottles at the recycling center down the street every week. After I pay the bills and send some money to my grandmother and brother in México, I save what is left over.

I have my own shopping cart from the Food4Less. I don't like to steal things, but I need a cart to pick up my cans. Because tomorrow the garbage truck is coming, tonight I go with Ma to walk around the neighborhood and look in the big bins lined against the curbs outside people's houses. I look in the blue recycling bin. Ma looks in the black trash bin.

"People throw away good things," Ma says to me. It's dark. There's only a little piece of moon tonight. A little moon like a sleepy eye.

Cars drive in the street too fast. From their cars, people call Ma and me trash pickers and laugh. I don't care what they say. We get $50 or $60 when we sell cans and plastic bottles. I push the cart down the street. I can see people inside their houses. They're watching TV, listening to music, eating dinner together.

Ma says to me she doesn't think I'll ever have my own family. The mark of the devil on my face is too scary. "Men get scared when they see you, Soledad," she says. "You're marked. And you're getting old. I was seventeen when I married your father, and you're thirty-three already. I worry about you, mi'ja." She says men don't want an old woman. She says it's a good thing Stephanie will be rich soon. She'll take care of me, too.

I don't remind Ma that soon I'll be the co-owner of a dress shop. I don't tell her I'm going to work hard so one day I can buy my own house. My own house, not like the shack of sticks and cardboard I lived in with my grandmother, not like the small apartment full of roaches we live in now, but a pretty house with three bedrooms and a large backyard I can turn into an herb garden. I want to have money to pay for health insurance. I want to have money for emergencies. Things Ma never thinks about.

We walk far away from our apartment and get many cans and bottles. Ma also gets a pot for cooking, a pair of shoes, a clock, a mirror with a small crack, a used candle, and a leather purse. "These are in such good condition," she says. "In México people don't have anything. But here, in America, people throw away good things."

We talk about Michoacán. I miss my town sometimes. My grandfather and father died when I was eight when they were trying to cross the border to come here. They crossed the border many times to come work in the fields. It was easier then. Now, crossing the border is more difficult. But back then, they would go back to Michoacán in the winter and then leave right before the spring began. I always knew it was almost time for them to come home when the monarcas, the monarch butterflies, arrived at the Oyamel forest close to my hometown.

But one day my grandfather and my pa didn't have luck crossing the border. They were found dead, with a big bump on their forehead as if someone had hit them with a rock while they slept. They had no money in their wallets, their watches were gone, and the golden chain with a cross each of them always carried around his neck was gone, too. When la migra found them, part of their bodies had been eaten by coyotes. When they died, Ma had to come to the U.S. to make money because we sometimes didn't have anything to eat. She left me and my brother, Lorenzo, with Abuelita Licha. She met Tomás a year later and she fell in love with him and they had Stephanie. After many years, Ma said to me to come help with Stephanie and the swap meet. So I came to help Ma, but Lorenzo didn't want to come. I was twenty when I came to America. I didn't go to school then because I had to take care of Stephanie. When Stephanie was in middle school, I got my certificate in fashion design. Now I'm taking English and citizenship classes because maybe one day I'll finally qualify for a green card, and I want to be ready. I need to learn English. How can I run my business without speaking English? My teacher at the adult school says to me, "Soledad, you can get your high school diploma, go to college, and earn a BFA degree in fashion design."

We come to a taco truck on the corner near El Sereno Park. Many young people are eating there. Kids that go to Wilson High School, like Stephanie.

Right now she's at her friend's house. She doesn't like to bring friends to our little apartment. She says the apartment is ugly. Mountains of boxes everywhere, mountains of things Ma won't throw away. Roaches and mice running across the floor, the bathroom walls covered in mildew, the carpet full of stains as ugly as my birthmark.

We look inside a trash can near the taco truck. There are so many cans and bottles there, I can't fit them in my cart! I'm happy I'll get good money tomorrow when I sell them.

"Hey, lady, you want my bottle?"

I turn around. A big kid looks at me and shows me his Coke. The bottle is half full. He and his friends laugh at me. I turn around and don't look at him anymore. I get the cans from the trash can. I don't care that they laugh. I'm not stealing anything. This is honest work.

Suddenly I feel a pain in my leg. The kid threw the bottle at me. Soda seeps through my pants. His friends laugh and call me names. I look at Ma. More kids laugh at her. A boy throws a bottle at her, too, and it hits her back.

I see Stephanie then, hiding behind a girl in the back. She looks at me and puts a finger on her lips. She doesn't want them to know I'm her sister. "Diles que paren," I want to say to her. Tell them to stop. But the words don't come out. I look at her again and she hides behind her friend.

"Let's go, Ma," I say. I push my Food4Less shopping cart and walk down the street. I hear them laugh. I wonder if *she* is laughing, too.

"Trash pickers, trash pickers," they sing.

I feel a pain in my heart. Like if Stephanie was dancing on my heart with her Folklórico dance shoes. Tap, tap, tap.

Ma doesn't say anything to me. I think she saw Stephanie, but she doesn't say anything on our way home. When she opens the door to the apartment, I say, "Ma, take the clock and shoes and the mirror inside." I pick up the pot and try to give it to her but Ma shakes her head and goes inside.

I don't go to the swap meet today with Ma and Tomás. Ma gets angry, but I need to get the costumes ready for the show this Friday and do last-minute repairs, and I need to work on the Veracruz dresses for the Cinco de Mayo performance. "I've told you many times you shouldn't make costumes," Ma said. "You should just make party dresses. They're less complicated and you get more money for them."

Ma doesn't understand the difference between making costumes and party dresses. Party dresses are what I do for work. I make costumes out of love. She doesn't know how good it feels to create something that preserves the traditions of my people.

I don't have a big garage like Rubén. My work space is the dining room. In here I have my sewing machines, a garment steamer, bolts of fabric in a corner, and my containers with threads, zippers, sequins, lace, ribbon, elastic, and everything else I need. We don't eat in here. We eat in the living room. I use the dining table to cut the fabric. When Stephanie gets home from school she comes to see what I'm doing and tells me she thinks the Veracruz dresses are beautiful. She makes a big fuss about them and I know what she's trying to do.

"You shouldn't have that kind of friends, Stephanie," I say to her in Spanish. Last night, Ma didn't say anything to her. Sometimes I feel so angry at the way Ma spoils Stephanie. Angry and jealous. Ma left me when I was thirteen years old, and for seven years I was without a mother. Stephanie's had a mother for all her seventeen years of life. She doesn't know what it's like to have been left behind by the person you love most.

She looks down at her lucky finger and doesn't say anything to me. I wish Stephanie didn't have to try so hard to fit in. When she was little the popular kids would laugh at her because of her lucky finger, and Stephanie tried so hard to have friends, she would help the popular kids make fun of others.

"You don't understand because you don't have friends," Stephanie says to me. She gets up to go to our room and doesn't come out.

Yesenia

At the studio, the death of Elena's baby is on everyone's mind. We dance because that's what we're trained to do, yet we don't give in to the movements; the music doesn't penetrate our muscles to make them go. None of us are in tune with our bodies. The mirrors magnify all our imperfections. There's no fluidity of movement. We are clumsy. Our steps sloppy. We forget to breathe, to come in on the right beat. Today, I can't tune out the stabbing in my knee. Today, I cannot conquer the pain.

After having canceled the last two practices, I thought Eduardo and I would make the dancers rehearse until their bodies could no longer take it. The performance is in two days, after all, but instead, when we get tired of painfully going through the motions, we linger around the studio, talking about the tragedy that befell Elena. It felt so strange to dance at Xochitl's wake. I welcome every invitation to perform at weddings, quinceañeras, even baptisms. Always when I dance I feel as if I'm floating on air, my heart racing inside my chest, my body completely surrendering itself to the music. But the few times I've danced at wakes, my feet felt heavy, as if I were dancing in a pool of mud.

Adriana, as Elena's sister and Xochitl's aunt, gets pats on the back and the dancers' pity. But not once have I seen her cry or express some kind of emotion.

During another long break I have the courage to bring up the subject.

"This is a good time to patch up the relationship you have with your sister," I tell her. "She's hurting right now, and she can use all our love and support."

Adriana takes a long drink of water and says, "There isn't anything she can do about it, so why doesn't she just get over it?"

I fight the urge to slap her. Sometimes, my patience with Adriana's attitude runs out. "This isn't the time to let your misplaced anger toward your sister get between the two of you. She needs you."

"Look, I know you've always tried to be a mother to us since Mom died, but it's not your place to tell me what to do or how to feel about my sister."

Stubborn as her mother. How many times did I try to get Cecilia to leave Gerardo? But Cecilia said she loved him and nothing I ever said was going to make her leave him. And instead of leaving him the first time he beat her, she went ahead and got herself pregnant with Adriana.

When break is over, the dancers start to form lines. I forgot to bring my bottle of Advil, and for the rest of the practice I stay in the last row. Every time the rows rotate I stay behind, as far away from the mirrors as possible. I grew up looking at myself in large mirrors, the objective eyes in which I studied my own body. The mirrors never lied to me. Throughout the years they showed me the dancer I was becoming. Now what they reveal is something I don't want to see.

Soledad comes over to the house to show me the new Vera-cruz costume she's designing for Alegría's Cinco de Mayo perfor-mance. With the exception of the Chiapas dresses Soledad made a few months ago, most of our costumes are falling apart. Right now we have only enough money to replace the old Veracruz costumes. The dresses are made of organza and lace, very fragile and delicate materials, and they get torn by the hangers when the dancers carelessly hang them back on the racks, or the dancers' heels get caught on the fabric during the performances, or when they walk around with their costumes on and aren't careful.

Soledad chose a shiny, transparent material with a silvery sheen that captures light like a prism—I can just imagine how the dresses will look under the stage lights. The skirt is made of three over-lapping flounces, which are decorated with row after row of lace and white ribbon. Soledad says it took about two hundred yards of each. I quickly put on the dress, excited to be the first to wear it (as co-director I'm always the one to put on the sample costume)—and rush to the mirror. I feel like the goddess Venus emerging from the sea. I extend the sides of the skirt and hold them up, then let them fall around me, like a cascade of white froth.

"Wow!" I say. Soledad's beautiful creations astound me. Before she came to Alegría, we used to buy costumes that were mass-produced in Tijuana. Soledad came and changed that. "Maybe we should do Veracruz instead of Chiapas for the competition." In the summer, twelve couples are going to compete in Texas. I love it when the group travels. Although the expenses add up—sometimes as high as $7,000 for bus rental, hotel, and meals—the trips are always memorable.

I pick up the Chalina, the white triangular shawl, and the velvety black apron adorned with flowers embroidered in satin stitch, and picture myself and the rest of the dancers all dressed up, ready to perform. I imagine us at a beach—like the one painted on the wall at La Perla—the blue sparkling sea behind us as a backdrop, the white jarocha dresses floating in the breeze.

"How is your knee?" Soledad asks, breaking my reverie.

There's something about Soledad that keeps me from telling my usual lies. I look at her eyes, a deep brown like the color of wet earth, and tell her the truth. "It's getting worse."

"I brought you some rue," Soledad says, taking it out of her bag. The branches are wrapped in a sheet of newspaper. "I grow it in my garden."

"What's it for?"

"My grandmother uses it when her arthritis gets bad."

"Just put it over there, will you?" I say, as I take off the dress.

"I didn't mean . . ." Soledad blushes. The birthmark on her cheek and neck turn a dark red, looking uglier than usual. It reminds me of a candle that was left out in the hot, scorching sun to melt.

"No, no, thank you for thinking about me, Sol. Now, let's get back to the costumes. Remember, the dresses need to be ready in six weeks," I say, desperate to change the subject. "Get all the help you can get from the volunteers. And remember, all the lace has to be carefully sewn onto the fabric. Make sure you measure the dancers correctly so that the dresses are a perfect fit. I don't want the dancers to look fat because their dresses don't fit right. And make sure you use the overlock. I don't want to see the threads start to unravel, and remember the headpiece has to be beautiful to complement the dress . . ." On and on I go, telling Soledad everything she should and shouldn't do. I know full well that Soledad wouldn't do sloppy work. Soledad is a professional. An award-winning costume designer, in fact. But my eyes keep looking at the rue on the table and I just can't stop myself. Her grandmother used rue. Does Soledad think I'm an old woman, like her grandmother?

Soledad keeps nodding, and as soon as I'm done talking she puts the dress back in the garment bag. "I'm sorry, Yesenia. I didn't mean to make you feel uncomfortable."

I put a hand on Soledad's shoulder as I walk her out. "Perdóname, Soledad. I know you're just trying to help." I hug her good-bye and watch until she drives away, then head to the kitchen and put the rue in a glass of water. I sit at the dining table wondering when Eduardo and Memo will be home. The mail lies unopened on the table and I start sorting through it. I pick up an advertisement with pictures of trees and beautiful green grass and a weeping willow, and I get goose bumps as I read the heading: "Beautiful burial plots available, buy yours today! Deciding where your body will spend the rest of eternity . . ." I stop reading and glance down at the address box. It is addressed to me.

"What the fuck is this?" I tear the cemetery advertisement to pieces and toss it into the wastebasket. Then my eyes catch a glimpse of the rue on the counter, and I rush to it and throw it in the garbage disposal and listen as the blades chop it up and make it disappear.

I visit Elena and bring her a peach cobbler and two sweet potato pies. I drove all the way to Pasadena to the Cobbler Factory, which Memo discovered near PCC. The cobbler there is so delicious I don't mind the drive.

When Elena opens the door I'm taken aback at seeing the pale face, the circles around the bloodshot eyes. Elena was thin already, but now she looks like a deflated balloon.

"Hi, mi'ja, I brought you some goodies." I walk into the house and ask her where Richard is.

"At the beach," Elena says. "For a bike ride."

I bite my tongue and don't ask what the hell Richard is doing at the beach instead of being here with his wife. Since Elena makes no attempt to take the paper bag, I put it on the dining table, grab two plates, and boil water for tea.

I sit down at the dining table and look at Elena, who's staring at her hands. I remember her as a little girl, such a great dancer she even made some of the adults look like donkeys dancing on their hind legs. Elena is the dancer directors dream of. At practice, whenever Eduardo tells her how he wants a certain step or movement to be executed, she does it exactly that way, sometimes even better. Unlike Adriana, who's lazy and usually has a bored expression on her face; her body can never seem to project what I want. Once onstage, Adriana blooms and dances well enough, but at rehearsal she's a pain in the ass. But Elena is always perfect—her grace, her projection, the coordination with her footwork and skirtwork is flawless.

"You must come back to Alegría," I say. "You shouldn't be here alone like this. You need to be with your friends, with the people who love you. Why don't you come to the show tomorrow? Being around Folklórico will surely make you feel better." I grab Elena's hand and almost recoil at the touch. Her hand is ice-cold and the skin feels like the skin of an uncooked turkey.

The kettle goes off suddenly and Elena jumps in her seat, her eyes wide with fear. I pat her on the back as I stand up. "It's just the kettle," I say, rushing to the stove to turn off the burner. I grab two mugs and fill them with the boiling water. In the pantry I find an array of teas.

"What kind do you like?" I ask. When Elena doesn't answer I pick up two chamomile tea bags and dump them in the mugs.

"I'm not coming back," Elena says when I put the mug in front of her.

"I'm not saying to come back this very minute. You need to rest, get your energy back. Let your body heal. But it isn't healthy for you to be cooped up in here, mi'ja. Let us help you get through this. If your mother was here she would tell you the same thing."

A noise escapes Elena's throat. Like a gurgle, like a painful intake of breath, as if someone had suddenly grabbed her by the throat and cut off her air supply.

"I think you should leave," Elena says.

"All right." I put the lid back on the peach cobbler and debate whether to take it with me or not. I decide to leave it even though I know she won't eat it.

I stand to leave and head to the door. I glance back at Elena, and seeing her like this fills me with shame. I wish so desperately to take back the things I told her when she confessed she was pregnant. "Why weren't you more careful?" I said. "You aren't in a position to have a baby. You're my top dancer. You just finished your first year at UCI. What were you thinking?"

"It was an accident," Elena said.

"What are you going to do now?"

"I don't know."

"It's a ball of cells," I said.

"No, no, it's not. It's a baby," Elena said, all of a sudden standing up straight, thrusting her chin up into the air. "It's *my* baby. And I want it." She walked out of the studio looking so determined, her eyes sparkling. I was sure that up until that moment Elena hadn't made a decision about whether or not to keep the baby. But when she walked out of the studio, whatever fears and confusion she might have felt had vanished and were replaced with love and a fierce desire to protect that baby. But in the end, she hadn't been able to.

I had no right to say those things to her, but I was sure she didn't want the baby, and all she needed was for someone to tell her it was okay not to want it. That no one would think less of her.

I look at Elena and wish I could see that look on her face once more. I want to see the defiance in her eyes. The determination. Something, anything but this dullness, the lifelessness, the look of a person who has nothing to live for.

After the performance, when all the dancers, the musicians, and the audience are gone, I make my way out to the stage. My heels echo against the silence of the auditorium, so quiet like a church. I stand center stage and look at the rows of empty seats. The janitors are sweeping the aisles. Soon they'll come and sweep the stage, too. Erase the remnants of the performance—the streamers under my feet, sequins that fell off the China Poblana dresses, a fragment of a broken cachirulo, a flower petal, a feather.

I close my eyes, and despite the silence, I can still feel the heat of the blinding lights above, hear the applause, the whistles, the porras of the audience urging me on. I can still hear the music of the harp behind me, feel it pierce me with its melody as it played "La Bamba." I can hear the blaring of the trumpets in Jalisco, the gentle sounds of the marimba in Chiapas. And I can see Eduardo, there in the back, pounding on the drum.

My heels clack as I walk around. I know I should be leaving, making my way to Angel's house for the after-party. Even though everyone is exhausted they'll be there getting drunk, talking about the performance, what they did wrong, what they need to work on, what went well and what didn't. They never stop talking about Folklórico. And neither do I.

I wonder what they'll say about me. Will they talk about the fact that I didn't make it? That in the middle of "Toro Rabón" I realized I didn't have the willpower to dance through the pain. I had no choice but to tell Stephanie to take my place, and I even helped her get ready. In the wings, I died a small death; I experienced a kind of hell watching someone else dance in my stead with my partner, my husband.

I like the sound of my heels against the wooden floor. I put my gym bag down and take out my Miguelito dance shoes. When they're on, I do un zapateo. The janitors look up, startled, but they go back to their cleaning. Flat-heel-flat, flat-heel-flat.

I can hear "La Negra" in my head. The last song I was supposed to dance. My feet become more demanding. I still have more to give. I can still hold on . . .

Then a searing pain shoots up my knee, and my feet stop. I stand there, alone, breathing in and out, fighting the stinging in my eyes as I realize that my body—the body I have cultivated for years—can no longer be trusted. My movements are no longer clean. My steps are no longer precise.

I pick up my gym bag, throw it over my shoulder, and exit stage left, my dance shoes scraping against the floor.

Dr. Brown points to an X-ray of my knee and tells me the same thing Dr. Weiner told me two days ago. I have osteoarthritis. He points to the space between the bones and says the cartilage there is thinning and the bones are getting thicker and growing something called spurs.

"What about surgery, Doctor? Isn't that a possibility?" I ask, hoping to hear a different answer than Dr. Weiner's.

"First of all, you're too young for knee replacement. And even if you had knee surgery, you wouldn't be able to continue dancing. The prosthesis wouldn't be able to take all that pressure on the knee."

"But—"

"Ms. Alegría, I've watched Folklórico performances before. My wife is from México and she loves going to dance shows. I know exactly what I'm talking about."

He turns off the machine and puts the X-ray back in the manila envelope.

"Isn't there anything else I can do?" I clasp my hands together to keep from grabbing his shoulders and demanding for him to say yes, that there's a way I can keep on dancing.

"Ms. Alegría, at this point there isn't much to be done . . . the only thing you can do is to stop dancing . . ." He pauses and his eyes soften, probably because mine have become wet with tears. "Look, don't let this condition affect your life completely. Be happy it isn't so bad that surgery would be required. All you need to do now is do moderate exercise, get plenty of rest, and keep your weight down." He looks at the chart and adds, "You're thirty-five pounds overweight. Maybe we should start there. You will also need to do thigh muscle exercises. Your quadriceps muscles are becoming weaker, so try not to put too much weight on that leg. And another thing," he says, looking disapprovingly at my Carlos Santana stilettos, "buy yourself some pumps."

He writes a prescription for a pain reliever and anti-inflammatory tablets, then hands me a pamphlet about how to take care of my knee.

I go straight home after seeing Dr. Brown and feel the need for sugar. I eat the flan I was saving for dessert. But even after I've scraped the last sweet, soft custard from the corners of the dish, the bitterness in my mouth is still there. I spend the rest of the afternoon watching videos of my dance performances. I flip through my photo albums, look at pictures of myself getting ready to dance, putting on makeup, my younger sister, Susy, braiding my hair. For a second I feel like picking up the phone and calling her and my mother in Arizona, where they now live. But what could they tell me that would make me feel better? My mother would probably tell me it's time I stopped with the dancing and concentrate instead on being a wife and a mother. To her, Folklórico was just a hobby, something to occupy my time and keep me out of trouble since she was too busy working two jobs and couldn't be there to take care of her daughters. But now that I'm forty-two, I'm too old for hobbies, she would say. "Look at me. Did I ever waste my time on such things?" She would bemoan the death of my father, of having to raise two young girls all by herself on minimum wage. "I gave you girls my best years," she would say. "And look at me now, only sixty-two but already look as if I have one foot in the grave."

And my sister, what would she say? She, who married a lawyer and had three children, who loves being a stay-at-home mom and has no desire to do anything else in her life but be a good mother and wife and a dutiful churchgoer.

No, I will not call them.

I look at the pictures of Eduardo and me on prom night, our wedding day two years after high school, the birth of Memo six months after the wedding, the celebration of the day Eduardo and I leased the dance studio and the group was born—named after me—Grupo Folklórico Alegría. And there's picture after picture of us dancing together since we were teenagers, me batting my eyes at him during "El Gavilán," him picking me up at the end of "Chicha," kissing underneath his charro hat at the end of "La Negra." Me, alone onstage performing a solo from Michoacán.

I gaze around the living room and look at the dolls displayed everywhere, which I've been collecting for years. Dolls dressed in costumes from every region in México. Dolls made of clay, corn husk, papier-mâché. My favorites are the Day of the Dead dolls, skeletons in white Veracruz dresses.

I walk around the room, touching each doll with my finger-tips. Perfect little dancers. They have no thoughts about getting old, about having to give up dancing. My fingers caress the skirt of a doll made of clay. My father gave it to me for my birthday when I was six years old after he took me to see the Ballet Folklórico de México at the Shrine Auditorium. It was the last present he gave me before he died of cancer. That was when I asked my mother to take me to dance lessons, as a way to remember that special day my father and I saw that magical performance and I fell in love with Folklórico. The doll is wearing a Jalisco dress and is leaning toward her partner, as if they were about to kiss under his sombrero. It reminds me of Eduardo and me, and I realize that by giving up Folklórico, I'll never dance like this with him again. I'll never again lean into him and hide behind his hat, see the sweat trickle down his face, see his eyes glowing with the love of the dance, with love for me, for the group we worked so hard to put together.

I send the doll shattering against the wall.

I tear the corn-husk dolls to pieces with my bare hands, as if I were tearing off my own skin. Spasms of pain go up and down my body, but I can't stop. Can't stop until the papier-mâché dolls flutter down to the floor like confetti, until the clay dolls lie shattered on the floor and the Day of the Dead dolls are broken pieces of skeletons.

Eduardo finds me among the shattered dolls. He gathers me in his arms and holds me while my crying begins anew.

I sit on the couch while he sweeps up the ruined dolls. I look down at my hands and cringe as if they were covered in blood. Soon, the only telltale sign of the massacre is the bareness of the living room. How different it looks now without my colorful dolls. How barren and sad.

My stomach growls, and I realize I haven't eaten anything since the flan. Eduardo goes to the taco truck down the street and comes back with carne asada burritos, tacos, and tortas. Memo arrives just in time for dinner. As soon as he walks in he looks around the room and frowns, as if trying to figure out what's missing. And then he turns to us and asks, "Where are the dolls?"

Eduardo grabs my hand. "Well, mi'jo, you see—"

"I destroyed them," I say, and the words weigh on me like a sinful confession.

Memo doesn't ask why. They both know today I was going to see another doctor. They both know what the result was without my saying it. The broken dolls have said it all. Memo sits at the table and we eat in silence. I devour my burrito and eat one of

Eduardo's tacos and still feel hungry. The void seems to keep getting bigger. Even after I eat the pan dulce I bought the day before and drink a glass of milk, I still feel hungry. Once in a while Memo attempts to talk, to shower me with optimistic words. He hugs me like he used to do when he was a little boy.

How could I tell them their hugs and kisses go unfelt by my skin? How can I describe to them the emptiness I feel inside? The emptiness that grows and grows with every breath I take? I'm numb all over. And I wonder if this is how it feels when a part of yourself is dying.

The numbness, the emptiness, the pain buried deep in your insides. The knot in your throat that keeps you from swallowing. The burning in your eyes brimming with unshed tears.

Elena

Two years ago I got an eye infection the day of a show and couldn't wear my contact lenses. It was a difficult performance for me. My balance was gone, and I didn't have time to adjust to dancing without being able to see well. It's hard enough to establish a focal point in a dark auditorium, let alone trying to dance when even the stage is a blur. The way I feel now is similar to that feeling I had onstage.

Now that everyone has left, it's just Richard and me. With all the people coming and going we hadn't been alone much. I hated their presence, but now I wish they were here so Richard and I wouldn't have to face our aloneness. Being with him reminds me of what we've lost. Everything reminds me Xochitl is gone. My body reminds me of this fact constantly. There's no movement inside. I still remember the first time the baby moved inside me, like the fluttering of butterfly wings, and I grabbed Richard's hand and placed it on my belly and said, "Feel her, feel her! Our little butterfly."

I grew accustomed to taking baths, but now that's impossible to do. I was used to seeing the outline of her body protruding from my stomach. And at night, I lie awake wondering if I'd gone to the clinic when I called Richard, if the outcome would've been different. The doctor said the autopsy hadn't revealed anything. Everything was normal. No congenital abnormalities, and therefore the cause of death couldn't be determined. In his records it'll go down as an unexplained stillbirth. But for me, the stillbirth will always be a source of too many questions and no answers.

The TV is a constant source of pain. On every channel there's always a commercial for baby products. "Change the channel," I say to Richard, and he does, although sometimes he's too slow and the image of the baby lingers on the screen for a second too long.

Who's to blame? I ask myself. The doctors? Richard? Me? Yes, me, because I was her mother—I *am* her mother and I couldn't help her.

Richard spends all his time grading papers or going to the gym, watching TV, surfing the Internet, and I get angry, so angry, because he's moved on and I'm still here, in this dark place. Sometimes I think I hate him. Sometimes my love for him overwhelms me. Sometimes I feel neither hate nor love.

I've gotten into the habit of taking naps in the rocking chair in the nursery. Those naps are brought on by exhaustion. When I wake up it starts again. I've never been the praying kind, but now that's all I seem to be doing. Praying. Praying for the pain to lessen a little so that I can breathe. Praying for my daughter to be happy, wherever she is. Praying for our hearts to be healed, hoping they weren't completely shattered by her death. Praying for Richard and me to stop drifting apart.

But that isn't all I pray for.

I pray to have my daughter back. I want to have her inside me again. I want to hold her in my arms again. I want to turn back time.

I want to bring her home.

❦

"I think you should go back," Richard says one Sunday morning over breakfast. He's dressed in sweatpants and a UCLA T-shirt, his alma mater and current employer. He finishes his orange juice in one big gulp and stands to leave. "You've refused to answer the dancers' calls. Locked yourself in our room when they've come to visit. Right now, we need all the love and support our friends and family want to give us."

I play around with my scrambled eggs, having hardly touched them. I'm dressed in workout clothes, too. My gym bag sits by the door with my dance shoes, practice skirt, a bottle of water, a banana and granola bar for me to eat during the break. Dancing always makes me hungry. It was Richard who put everything in the gym bag. It was he who said that instead of going with him to the gym I should go to practice.

Now I play with my food, my stomach beginning to hurt just at the thought of walking into a room full of my friends, who would probably be glancing my way throughout practice, asking me how I'm feeling, pitying me. Or even worse. What if I can't make my feet dance? What if what I felt at Xochitl's wake was real?

Richard leans over and kisses my forehead and then asks me one more time what I want to do. "I'll go to practice," I say. He nods and says I've made the right choice. He grabs his keys and leaves for the gym. I sit there for another twenty minutes before I have the courage to dump the scrambled eggs in the trash, brush my teeth, pick up my gym bag, and drive to El Sereno.

Because I took so long to get out of the house, I arrive late. They've just finished warm-ups, but some dancers are still lined at the barre stretching ligaments, doing breathing exercises, getting the blood circulating through their limbs.

Just like I knew would happen, everyone stares when I come in. From across the room I see my own sister leaning to whisper to Olivia while looking at me. Adriana has never been discreet. And despite myself, I wonder what she's saying about me. But why should I care? Let Adriana talk. Still, I cower in the back of the studio and try to hide in a corner, pointing and flexing my feet, doing a few pliés. Warm-ups begin with the feet, then the knees, the hips, stomach, and back muscles, and they end with the head, eyes, elbows, wrists, and fingers. Eduardo is very adamant that everyone warm up thoroughly before doing the strenuous movements Folklórico requires. Yesenia, on the other hand, was never this careful. She was always too impatient, rushing the warm-ups to get to the Folklórico part of practice. And no matter how much I warned her about plastic sweatpants, she insisted upon wearing them once in while to make her body perspire profusely and sweat out the fat. These kinds of pants make the body feel it's warmed up and ready to dance when it really isn't. How strange it feels not to see her here. I can't remember a day when she wasn't at the studio. Her constant presence was reassuring. After my mother died, Yesenia made my mother's absence more bearable.

Some of the dancers come to hug me and ask how I'm doing. Even Eduardo, instead of continuing with the Azteca danzas, holds on to his drumsticks and walks over to me, drawing more attention to my presence. He tells me how happy he is I'm back, but the more I hear it the more I want to run away, out the glass doors, to the safety and loneliness of my truck.

Eduardo returns to the front of the room and begins to play the drum. I look at the dancers in the large mirrors and skip over my own reflection. Instead, my eyes fall on Adriana dancing in the row in front of me. Every time she turns to look in the mirror, she frowns. She misses a step. Our eyes connect for a moment, and I feel a stabbing pain in my abdomen to see her disdain toward me.

When we are done with the Azteca danzas, Eduardo tells us we'll be rehearsing the cuadros for the Cinco de Mayo performance and the competition in Texas.

The first number is "La Bruja," from the state of Veracruz. I'm to dance the part of the witch, but as the music begins my mind becomes a total blank and I can't remember where I'm supposed to go. Eduardo starts the music again, encouraging me. This time, I don't think. I let my body do the movements automatically—recalling the knowledge stored in the memory of every muscle, every nerve, every cell in my body. My feet, legs, torso, arms, they all remember what to do; they all respond immediately to my commands. I glide and weave in and out of the lines of dancers, just like I've done so many times before, but I'm only a body in motion, empty, meaningless. When the music is over I stand to the side, feeling nothing.

I look at the mirrors, and they confirm what I already knew. I'm only going through the motions.

"That was great, mi'ja," Eduardo says. At hearing Eduardo call me that, I think about my father; he never knew I made him a grandfather. He never got to see his granddaughter before she was buried. "Elena?"

My stomach begins to hurt, and I wish I had brought my bottle of Tums.

"Ready to continue?" Eduardo asks.

When a dancer loses faith in the act of dancing, to keep dancing would be a lie. I know there's nothing in this studio for me now. "No. I think I've made a mistake," I say. I rush to pick up my gym bag and run out into the sunlight, away from the thing I once loved most—Folklórico.

When I come home I find Richard in the nursery, clutching the crib. I ask him what he's doing, and he tells me he thinks it's time to get rid of all the furniture in there. "Let's turn it back into an office," he says.

"Don't you dare touch anything in here!" I yell. "Just because you've moved on with your life doesn't mean I'm ready to forget my daughter."

"Elena, it isn't like that—"

"Get out, get out!" I push him but he doesn't move. He stands there while I hit him with my fists, while I yell at him and bury my face in his chest, my tears soaking into his shirt. He stands there with his hands in his pockets and all I want is for him to hold me, hold me, hold me, but when he does I push him away from me as if his hands had burned me.

I lie in bed listening to the airplanes fly above my house on their way to LAX. I try not to move and wake Richard. He'd know I wasn't sleeping when he walked into the bedroom. He'd know I willed myself to be still, to close my eyes so that he wouldn't ask me for something I can't give him. He wants us to make love, he says. He thinks it'll help us to bond again, to begin to heal our relationship.

But how could I tell him the feel of his hands on my body reminds me of what we've lost?

I think about the day I found out I was pregnant. Richard and I weren't married then, not even living together, and he came over that night with a bouquet of red roses and a bottle of sparkling apple cider.

"What's this?" I asked.

"We have to celebrate," he said excitedly. He took me into his arms and swooped me up and spun me around, laughing. "I can't believe we're having a baby."

I once read in an encyclopedia that the female red kangaroo of Australia has an extraordinary reproductive system. It has the ability to stop the development of an embryo until better conditions exist. I didn't tell Richard that, as I sat in the doctor's office, and my pregnancy was confirmed, I'd wished I was a red kangaroo. I wasn't ready to have a baby. I had just finished my first year of graduate school. Richard and I hadn't been together long enough.

Is this why this happened? I wonder as I sit up in bed. Was it a punishment for thinking such thoughts? To be like a red kangaroo. That's what I wished.

☙❧

When I tell Richard I've decided to return to work, he seems surprised. "Are you sure you're ready?" he asks me while I comb my hair up into my usual chignon. When I don't answer he adds, "Well, maybe you're right. You need to get out of the house, keep busy. Being cooped up in here doesn't help." He puts his arms around me and kisses the nape of my neck.

"I'll go get my lesson plans ready," I say.

Because May is right around the corner, and once May is over the end of the school year will be upon us, I walk into the classroom determined to have my students catch up. Substitutes can sometimes be too easy on them. But throughout the day the students ask me questions about the baby, and I can't progress with my lesson the way I planned to. I find myself having to take deep breaths and swallow my tears. Once, I'm too harsh and tell them it's none of their business. But they're undaunted, and they tell me about their aunts, mothers, cousins, who have gone through what I've gone through. One girl tells me that now I have a little angel in heaven and I shouldn't be so sad. And I want to shake her and tell her I don't want an angel in heaven. I want my daughter, here on this earth, with me.

During lunch I seek out Mrs. Rodríguez to tell her the dance group is now hers, but I don't find her. After school, on my way out to the parking lot, I stop at the doors of the auditorium.

The music coming from within calls to me. A danzón.

I enter the darkness of the auditorium and watch a young man dance with one of the group members onstage. Mrs. Rodríguez stands to the side, instructing them on how to move. Becky looks awkward in his arms, as if the young man were dancing with a rag doll, not a flesh and blood person. She can't guide her feet to the music, can't do the sensual movement of the hips.

Slow, quick-quick, slow, quick-quick, I say under my breath.

Mrs. Rodríguez sees me and motions for me to come over.

"Poor girl can't get it right," she whispers.

"Who is he?" I know all the students in the Folklórico group, but I don't recognize him. It's been eight weeks since I was last at the school.

"Isn't he great?" Mrs. Rodríguez asks. "Mr. Espinoza found him for us. You know that we needed one more boy to complete our four couples and Fernando volunteered. I was scared, too, because he's never danced before and I wondered how we would ever get him ready to perform in two weeks for the Cinco de Mayo assembly, but the boy is a natural."

I nod.

"I'm so glad you're back. I think I'm doing something wrong," Mrs. Rodríguez says. "I know I shouldn't have chosen 'Nereyda,' but danzón is so beautiful, so elegant. I wanted Fernando to do a duet with one of the girls—you know, to cover some time so the others can change costumes—and I wanted it to be something the audience would really enjoy. But it just isn't coming out right."

Fernando looks at me and smiles. Becky drops her arms in exasperation.

"I can't do this, Mrs. Rodríguez. It's too difficult," she says in a whiny voice. "I hate danzón. Why are we dancing this anyway; isn't it from Cuba?"

"Yes, but it was brought to México in the twentieth century," Mrs. Rodríguez says.

"Are you going to teach Folklórico again, Ms. Sánchez?" Becky asks. "Mrs. Rodríguez said that she thought you might not come back to finish the year because of your baby."

Mrs. Rodríguez pulls Becky aside and says something to her. I walk over to Fernando. His hair is wet with sweat and the tendrils curl up at the base of his neck. Beads of perspiration cover his upper lip.

"You're doing very well, Fernando," I say, putting out my hand to shake his. "I'm Ms. Sánchez."

"It feels weird," he says as he shakes my hand. "Something's not right."

It's not because of you, I want to say. "It'll be fine. It just takes practice."

"Why don't you try one dance with him?" Mrs. Rodríguez asks. "I think it would really help both of them out."

I open my mouth to tell her I've given up dancing, but Becky runs over to the CD player and the song begins again. Fernando shyly takes my hand and pulls me close to him.

His hand is on my waist, in a traditional ballroom embrace. He steps forward, and because I don't move, he steps on my foot. He mumbles an apology. I move away from him and turn to Mrs. Rodríguez. "I'm sorry, but I can't do this."

"I understand. I'm sorry I put you on the spot like that."

I excuse myself and head down the steps. The music begins again just as I walk out the door. The spot on my waist where Fernando held me feels warm. I can see his eyes looking at me still, as if he could lay bare the unspoken need inside me.

To dance Folklórico again.

Adriana comes over later that day. As usual, she's dressed as if she just stepped off the stage after a dance performance. She's wearing a Mexican peasant blouse (one of those tacky imitations), a long flowered skirt, and green and pink ribbons weaving in and out of her black braids. Her golden hoop earrings complement the outfit. Adriana often says she's proud of her Mexican roots, but she doesn't need to dress like Frida Kahlo to prove it.

She's come to drop off two tickets for Alegría's Cinco de Mayo performance at UCLA.

"Too bad you aren't coming with us to Texas in the summer," Adriana says. "You know how much fun traveling with Alegría is. Remember last year when we went to New York what a blast we had . . . ?"

I busy myself by opening a can of food for my three cats. They rub their purring bodies against my ankles as if they could sense my irritation. I know Adriana derives pleasure in the fact I no longer dance. And she will remind me of it any chance she gets.

I look at her, at the makeup caked on her face, the coral red lips, the mascara layered on too thick.

"Well, I'm outta here. Gotta go catch the bus."

"Where's your car?"

"That piece of shit broke down on me again and I'm totally broke." She bites her nails and tries not to look at me. She looks down at her feet instead. She turns her face a certain way so I can see the thin scar on the right side of her neck peeking beneath a layer of makeup.

She spits a nail onto the floor and then moves on to the next. I watch my cats eat. They're oblivious to the silence, to the guilt I feel when Adriana's around.

"How much do you need?" I say, looking away from her scar.

"I don't know, maybe two hundred."

I walk to the dining room and grab my checkbook from my purse. I write a check for three hundred dollars.

Adriana looks at the check but says nothing. She grabs her green shawl and flings it over her shoulders as she turns to go. "Well, I'll be seeing you then."

"Good luck at the performance," I tell her. I bend down to pick up my cats' empty food bowl to conceal my jealousy. Yet there's one thought that makes my jealousy diminish, that chases it back into the darkness. Adriana is a good enough dancer, but we both know she'll never be a great one.

Adriana smiles. I dislike her forced smile, the unnatural redness of her lips, the slanted eyes that look at me so indifferently, so uncaring.

If only she didn't look so much like our mother. Just looking at her hurts.

CHAPTER THREE

Dance is a song of the body. Either of joy or pain.

—MARTHA GRAHAM

You know that somewhere in the darkness beyond the blinding
stage lights, Elena is out there. You know that out of the thousand
eyes now watching you, two of them belong to her. You know the
audience won't notice the slight hesitation of your feet, the quiver
of your lips, the sudden drop of the elbow as you struggle to lift the
skirt, the small bead of sweat sliding down your temple. But Elena

will. Did she notice that step you just missed? Of course she did. Can she tell that your arms are tired now, and that this Jalisco skirt is so damn heavy, you can hardly twirl it anymore? Of course she can.

You try to forget that her eyes are watching you, but how can you forget? It's like trying to forget the mirrors at the studio that day after day show you how incompetent you are. How impossible it is to reach that perfection you desperately desire. For a second, you wish she was here onstage, too, so that at least then she wouldn't be watching you. You always enjoy dancing onstage because this is the only time you aren't judged by the mirrors. The only time when you're free. But if Elena will no longer dance, then you must take pleasure in the fact that you're the one who is dancing.

"Breathe, breathe," you tell yourself. You look beautiful. Your makeup is flawless. Your hair is perfect.

The lights blind you for a second. You look down at your skirt, watch the purple, pink, orange, black ribbons swirling and spiraling around you. José's crooked teeth gleam under the lights as he smiles. Veins stand out on his forehead and neck. You circle around each other as if you were courting. You come together as if to kiss, then pull apart. You keep an eye out on the thirteen other couples and make sure you keep up. You force your lips to match their smiles. You make your feet keep the rhythm of "La Negra." You let the strumming of the mariachi guide you. Why is it that your feet drag behind? Why is it that they slow down for a moment, unsure of themselves? Your fucking feet. They refuse to do what they're supposed to.

You give José your hand and let him twirl you around into his arms. You hide behind his big sombrero, your costume soaked with sweat, your chest heaving as you try to catch your breath now that the song is finally over. The clapping thunders out of the darkness like the sudden flapping of bats who have just gotten spooked. It scares you for a moment.

As you take a bow at the footlights, your eyes search for Elena in the blur of people who are waving, clapping, shouting. You wonder if she liked the performance. You tell yourself you did good. You were great. You let José guide you off the stage as you swallow the sour taste in your mouth.

Adriana

When I come home I see Ben's little Honda parked in front of the apartment building. The lights are out in his apartment. I hiccup as I go up the stairs to my place. I hold on to José's hand because I feel like I might fall. I shouldn't have drunk so much tonight. But the after-party was good. They always are. These dancers are crazy. Too bad that twelve out of the eighteen male dancers are gay, and they're so fuckin' cute, too. It's a waste. That's why I asked José to bring me home. *His* dick is available. Even if it's so fucking small. I swear even my middle finger is bigger.

"Thanks for the ride," I say.

"Es un placer," he whispers close to my ear. A pleasure. I smell the alcohol on his breath and I feel a rush of desire. Alcohol makes me horny. As I fish in my purse for my keys I notice a bundle right outside my door. I bend down to grab it, even though the movement makes me want to barf.

White roses. I breathe in the pungent scent and feel sick again.

"Secret admirer?" José asks.

"Nah." I open the door. I throw the roses onto the coffee table and turn on the light. "My neighbor."

José laughs and walks over to the coffee table to pick up the card that came with the roses. He reads it. "You were wonderful tonight, Ben."

I grab José's hand and pull him with me onto the couch.

"Did you like how I danced tonight?" I ask him.

"Ah, yeah." he says. He looks at the card from Ben and reads it again. "You were wonderful tonight." Then he bursts out laughing. A little bit of his spit sprays my cheek. I look at my guitar leaning against the wall next to the night table, so lonely in the shadows. I look at my Frida Kahlo prints hanging on the walls. None of them speak to me now. The Fridas are quiet. They don't like José being here.

I feel his hand rubbing the inside of my arm. He traces the tattoo I have on my right shoulder and asks me again why a moth. Who the hell gets a moth tattoo?

"Most girls I know would've chosen a butterfly," he says.

"Fuck butterflies."

He slides closer to me, his breath on my cheek. I look at the Two Fridas, afraid to turn his way. His tongue slithers over my earlobe like a snail, leaving a trail of saliva.

"C'mon, Adriana, why do you always pretend you don't want it?"

I hear a voice inside my head. It's the other me, the other Adriana telling me I should've listened to her and asked Yesenia for a ride instead of this baboso that wants to screw me. But my hand reaches out to touch him, to feel his warmth. José's lips suddenly latch on to mine, and he drools all over me, like a friendly dog. But I hold on to him because I'm afraid of the loneliness of my apartment and the memories that come creeping out at night. I tell myself that at least for tonight, José is here to chase all those memories away.

Elena was fourteen when Mom died, and I was twelve. Unlike me, she was born a perfect dancer. She didn't have to spend long, frustrating hours trying to learn a step. The story goes that when she was about three years old, Ms. Perfect surprised the whole dance group when, in the middle of practice, she walked up to the dancers and did the step they were doing.

That's the way Mom would tell it. I don't know if she was exaggerating—she had the tendency to do that—but I remember how she would hug Elena and her face would beam with pride because even at fourteen Elena was already a better dancer than most of the women in the group, including Mom. Mom used to say Elena was born a good dancer because the first time she saw El Ballet Folklórico de México perform, she was pregnant with Elena. She said she remembered feeling Elena's feet moving inside her belly from the moment the show started. Whatever.

I didn't understand why she even had me. She didn't need another daughter. Especially one who couldn't dance.

And this is why I don't understand why Elena tries to act as if Mom never existed. That ungrateful bitch just plain forgot she ever had a mother. She hardly talks about her and she hates it when I ask her about Mom. Dad used to hate it, too.

"Why do you need to talk about your mother?" he would ask.

"Because I can't remember what she looks like," I would tell him.

"Look in the mirror, girl. There you'll see your mother. You have her fucking face!"

Slap.

When Dad would hit me harder than he meant to, and I would get a bloody nose, or a cut lip, or a black eye, I would stand in front of the mirror and know he was right.

I did see my mother in the mirror. For some reason, I would forget I was actually looking at myself. I remember how much the longing for her overwhelmed me then, and that was when I cried. Dad would think I was crying because of what he did to me.

But no, you asshole, I cried for her.

Because in those moments of anger when you punched my face, you helped me see my mother again.

Yesenia

Today I'm out in the field doing inspections instead of working all day at the office. I have to drive around the city and take pictures of people's houses for insurance purposes. As I drive, all I can think about is how much I miss going to the studio.

My next inspection is in Lincoln Heights, where I grew up. I drive down Broadway Street and turn on Daly. I pull up in front of a house I recognize from my youth. Despite the weeping willow that wasn't there before, and the new blue paint, this is Sam González's house. Sam González, my high school crush.

I never admitted the crush to anyone. All my friends knew Eduardo and I were a couple, had been so since we met at Danzantes Unidos, when the festival was held at UCLA. We were thirteen, and even at that age I knew I would marry a dancer. From watching the older dancers around me, I learned how hard it was to have a relationship with someone who doesn't dance. It's disastrous. Sooner or later the other person will start to resent the presence of Folklórico in your life. So many of my dancers have left the group because of this. But Folklórico is the strongest tie between Eduardo and me. So no, I never confided to anyone I once wondered what it would be like to be with someone other than Eduardo.

I wonder, for the first time in a long time, whatever happened to Sam González.

That was so long ago, but I can't help feeling disappointed his isn't the house I'm to inspect. That house is two doors down. I get out of the car and look back at his house. A wooden sign, the kind you can get at Disneyland with your family name on it, reads, "Casa de la Familia Rodríguez." Not González. It seems he no longer lives there.

I make my way down the street and knock on the door. The owner of the house went into the office a few days ago to apply for home insurance. I greet the woman and step inside the house. My camera dangles from my wrist. The woman shows me around her house, which is littered with all kinds of religious books and dozens of cats. Cats everywhere.

"That's the mother," the woman says as she points to a big black and white cat, which happens to be very, very, pregnant.

"She's the mother of all these?"

"Yes. She just won't stop! As soon as she gives birth she's pregnant again."

"Why don't you get her fixed?"

"Oh, no, that's inhumane. I don't believe in things like that, and I'm totally opposed to abortions, as well. God meant for all his creatures to procreate, and . . ."

I stop listening. I pick up the camera and take pictures of the kitchen, trying to not think about what the woman said. But she follows me around, going on and on about her beliefs. She shoves a religious magazine, *Awake!*, into my hands and tells me I should ask Jesus into my heart. That He will forgive my sins.

The house is filthy. There's trash everywhere. The kitchen floor is covered in boxes of canned food and old newspapers and clothes. Grime layers the linoleum. The bathroom walls are covered in mold, and the bathtub drain is clogged with hair balls. The toilet rim is splattered with feces. The faucet has a leak that has stained the sink with a yellow streak. More boxes are stored in the bathroom, too. *What the heck does she have in there?*

Seven litter boxes are in the woman's bedroom, and I'm there for only ten seconds snapping a few pictures of the second bathroom before my head begins to reel from the smell.

"Unfortunately, after completing the inspection of your home, I am sorry to say that under our guidelines your home doesn't qualify for insurance at this time."

"But why?"

"Lack of maintenance of your property could result in potential losses to us," I say. *Do I really need to spell it out? You live in a shithole, lady!*

I run out of the house as soon as I can. I lean against my car, thinking about what the woman said and about the baby Cecilia aborted with my help. A boy? A girl? It had been too little to tell. But the fact is that Cecilia almost died from the poisonous tea she asked me to buy her on one of my trips to Tijuana. If Elena and Adriana knew, they would never forgive me for that.

Cecilia wouldn't tell me why she wanted to abort the baby, and I wasn't about to convince her to keep it. I myself chose to have only one child because I didn't want to stop dancing. I knew that between work and Folklórico, I wouldn't have much time to devote to children, and I wanted to do a good job with Memo. The times I saw Elena standing behind the stage with her big round belly, I felt sorry for her because I could see in her face how desperately she wanted to dance.

A woman pulls up behind me, gets out of the car, and makes her way up to Sam González's house.

"Excuse me!" I yell after her. "Does Sam González still live here?"

The woman opens her mailbox and takes out the mail. "I bought the house from him about five years ago, but I don't know where he lives now."

I sit at the dining table and listen to the silence in the house. The clock above me reads 8:06. Right now, they're probably doing a run-through of the cuadro the group's going to perform at the competition. I wonder if they miss me. When I told them I was taking a break from the group because of health reasons, no one was surprised. I admitted to them I have osteoarthritis and they pitied me. I want them to remember how I danced before my knee betrayed me.

I walk over to the garage and spend the rest of the evening looking at all the costumes and wishing we had more money for

Soledad to make new ones. When the group first started we had to put up the money to rent the theaters where we performed. We did so many performances for free as well—weddings, quinceañeras, conferences, school assemblies—just for the exposure, hoping to start getting hired for events. And once we established ourselves, we were hired by the theaters to do performances. Now we get $10,000 or $12,000 for big shows, and in October we'll be getting $20,000 to perform at the Mondavi Center in Davis! But all that money goes toward the production of the show. Sometimes Eduardo and I have to put up our own money to cover some costs. We have a responsibility to our audience to give them a great show. So every year we add at least one new region to our repertoire, have a set of new costumes, new props. I don't want the group doing the same show over and over again. Every show has to be different. Have a different theme. I want the group to be recognized nationally. Not just in Los Angeles but all across the U.S. I want Alegría to do more performances, get hired by top-notch theaters like the Orange County Performing Arts Center or the Kennedy Center in D.C. I want critics to review the shows, to have articles about Alegría printed in magazines and newspapers. I have so many plans for the group.

Alegría.

After years of watching it grow and learn, now it's moving on without me. Like Memo.

Eduardo suggested I teach the little kids taking classes at the studio. It wouldn't be as demanding, especially the beginning or intermediate class. Memo is in charge of those classes, but now that he's moving to Riverside he wants someone else to take over. It'll be hard enough driving to El Sereno for Alegría's practices. Eduardo also said now I could spend more time writing grant proposals and scheduling performances, recruiting dancers and teachers. But none of that interests me if I can't dance. That's the part he doesn't seem to understand. If I can't dance, then what's the point of being part of the group? What's the point of putting up with a bunch of irresponsible people and their bullshit?

Like at the last performance, for example, when one of the male dancers decided he had to quit the group because his grades were suffering. A day before the show he quit the group, as if he couldn't wait until after the performance. But it always happens, especially before a show. Someone has too much schoolwork and can't make it. Another has an ingrown nail he didn't take care of and on the day of the performance—voilà—his toe is too swollen and he can't perform (even though every good dancer knows you must cut your nails to the shape of the toe to prevent ingrown toenails). Another person is sick, or can't get the day off from work. And then what am I and Eduardo to do? Do they think dancers fall from the sky trained and ready to do the show? No. I have to recruit them. I have to train them. I have to turn them into professionals. Alegría isn't like many other groups whose style is so easy to learn that I can borrow dancers from those groups.

Sometimes they bitch and complain about the hours. Three days a week we rehearse—Wednesday, Friday, and Sunday, for three hours each day. And on Saturdays the female dancers have an extra class where Elena taught the skirtwork. Right now Olivia is teaching the class until Elena decides to come back.

It's too demanding, the young members say.

How much do you love it? I ask them sometimes. How much do you love Folklórico?

Maybe it's better this way, right? I'll simply cut Alegría off of me. Like an infected arm.

Soledad

Our neighbor, Doña Esther, comes to the house with her daughter, Nancy. She wants me to make Nancy a dress for her quinceañera. They show me a picture of a dress in a wedding magazine.

It looks like Cinderella's dress. Lots and lots of tulle and satin. A big bow in the back. I take Nancy's measurements and then they leave. Doña Esther gives me $150 so I can buy the material. I'll get another $250 when the dress is finished. Two-fifty that will go into my savings for the dress shop.

I drive to the fabric district downtown. On the way I stop at El Pollo Loco on Broadway and order the Wing Lover's special, my favorite. Across the street is a place for rent, next to a travel agency and a bakery. I think about my dress shop. I'm happy Rubén and I finally found a place that isn't too expensive and is in a good location. The rent will be $2,000 with utilities included. It's a big rent payment, but I have faith in Rubén and me.

I love all the fabric shops here on Ninth Street. Bolts of linen, cotton, poplin, taffeta, lycra, crêpe, velvet, organza, lamé, rayon, all leaning against the outside walls of the shops or safely stored on shelves inside, waiting to be touched and admired. Waiting to be turned into something beautiful.

I don't buy anything right away. I hold on to my money, resist the urge to buy the cloth I see. Because Alegría has a small budget I've gotten good at finding the lowest prices for the best fabric. I walk slowly from shop to shop, stopping to touch the satin that feels like cool water in my hand, or the cotton that's as smooth as a baby's cheek. I think about all the costumes I would make with all this fabric, dressing up my dancers, seeing them on a stage under the bright lights.

All the colors reach out to me, and when I close my eyes they form a rainbow in my mind. A big, giant rainbow, and if I lift up my hand I can grab it and cover myself with all its colors.

I go visit Rubén, but he isn't home. Doña Sofía is embroidering the bodice of a wedding gown Rubén has made. It's a beautiful dress, very simple but elegant.

"One day you'll get to wear one of these," Doña Sofía says. Her eyes are a little red, and I wonder if she's tired from embroidering little flowers with silver thread. She puts the dress down on her lap and looks at me. "I've given up hope, Sol. I thought my son would change. I thought maybe you would help him to change, but now . . ." She starts to cry.

I walk up to her and take the dress away before she stains it with her tears. Then I bend down and hold her hand. "What's the matter, Doña Sofía?"

"My son, he's come up with some crazy idea that he wants to become a woman."

"What do you mean?"

"He wants to have his thing cut off."

"What thing?"

She looks at me as if I were a little child. "You're so pure and innocent, Sol." She starts to cry again. "You're the daughter-in-law I wanted to have, and now, now . . ."

"What's going on, Ma?" Rubén says as he comes into the house. I stand up and say hello.

"I'm telling Soledad about those blasphemous ideas you're getting!" Doña Sofía says.

"Ay Dios. Don't be so scandalous. I'm supposed to be the drama queen around here, not you, Ma."

Doña Sofía gets up and goes to her bedroom, crying even louder.

Rubén stands there looking at me. I gulp, blushing under his gaze. He's so handsome. His eyes are so big and his hair curly. How can he be gay? Even though he's wearing a hot pink shirt that fits him really tight on his chest and has the word Sexy printed on it, I see him as a man, and I can't help looking at the muscles on his arms, the strength of his square jaw.

"Stop staring at me like that, chula. You're barking up the wrong tree."

"I'm sorry, I—"

"Forget it. C'mon, let's go to the garage." He picks up the wedding dress his mom was embroidering and carefully takes it with him, making sure it doesn't get dirty.

"So, did Mr. Johnson tell you when the shop is going to be ready for us to move in?" I asked. "He's taking such a long time, don't you think? We should have at least signed the lease by now."

Rubén puts the dress inside a clear garment bag and turns to look at me.

"Sit down, love," he says. I sit on a chair and look up at him. "Listen, Sol, I know you're going to hate me forever and ever after I tell you this, but I decided not to lease the shop."

"What do you mean?"

"I'm not leasing the space, Sol. I really want to, you know I do. But there's something else that I want more than anything, and now it's my chance to do it. Now, with the money I just got."

I wipe my eyes dry and stand to go. "You don't have to explain. I know it's your money, and you can do whatever you want with it."

"Sol, Sol, don't be mad at me, chula, please." He walks behind me and grabs my hand.

"I wish you had told me sooner."

He drops onto a chair and throws his hands up in the air. "I know, Sol. I know. I'm such a jerk. I just didn't want to hurt your feelings. I know how much you want this shop. I know what it means to you. And I really was going to do it. I really was. But I finally got approval for the surgery. After all the hoops I had to jump through to get approval I didn't think it was going to happen, but see . . ." He takes out an envelope from his bag and shows it to me. "My therapist thinks I'm ready."

"Ready? For what?"

He takes a deep breath and says, "I'm going to become a woman, Sol. Can you believe it?"

"I don't understand."

He says all those therapy sessions he's been going to since two years ago were a requirement to get approval for surgery. He's also been taking hormones for almost a year now.

"You told me you had to see a therapist because you were traumatized from the fire, from the fact that you almost died. And I don't understand why you need hormones."

He says they're hormones like women have, like what I have. Estrogen, he says. He sticks out his chest at me and says, "Notice anything different?"

I say to him no, nothing looks different. He walks to the mirror on the wall and sticks out his chest like a rooster. "I could've sworn they were a little bigger. Yes, I think they are a little bigger now." He says the estrogen he's been taking for the last twelve months will make his breasts grow bigger. "Of course they'll never be as big as yours, but still . . ." He turns back to the mirror and looks at himself. He rubs his chin and says the only bad thing about it is that it won't make the hair on his face go away. He hates shaving.

I say to him I need to go. I don't want to hear this anymore. I rush out of his garage, and before I close the door I see him still standing there looking at himself in the mirror, wrapping a measuring tape around his chest.

Stephanie wants Ma to buy her a $250 dress from Macy's. I say to Stephanie it's too much money for a dress. She cries to Ma. She wants the dress so much because it's beautiful and she wants to wear it to the prom in two weeks. A football player asked her to go with him, she said, and she has to have the most beautiful dress or she'll die of shame. I tell her she still has next year to go to her prom. Next year she'll have her money and she can buy whatever dress she wants.

"I want this one," she says. "This one is so amazingly beautiful."

She says the truth. The dress is beautiful. The taffeta is woven with cross-dyed yarns; the weft is blue and the fill is green. It changes colors when it's moved. It reminds me of the sea, the light above our heads like the rays of the sun shining on water. Stephanie says to Ma she has to buy the dress. She says to Ma that soon she'll get her money, and she'll give back to Ma all the money she spends on her. "I'm going to be rich, soon, remember that, Ma," Stephanie says. "I'm going to take care of you when you are old and wrinkly, when you can't work at the swap meet anymore, I promise."

Ma doesn't have money. I know it. But she takes out her bag of money and says to Stephanie, "Okay, mi'ja, I'll buy you the dress you want."

"That's the rent money," I tell Ma. "We need to pay it tomorrow. There's no need to spend so much money on this dress. I'll make one for you," I say to Stephanie.

"I don't want a homemade dress."

I remind her she thought the quinceañera dress I made her was beautiful. She looked like a princess. Ma agrees.

Stephanie says, "Okay, fine." I take her hand and we go away from Macy's, away from the dress that is too beautiful, but we need to pay the rent.

I go to the Bank of America by my house to fill out an application for a loan. I asked Mr. Johnson to give me a chance to lease the place. My mother can sign for me. She has a social security card and a green card. Mr. Johnson says I still need to give him two months of rent and a security deposit. And I don't have that much money.

Things don't go well at the bank. The loan officer says they can't give me the $10,000 loan. I need a social security number—a good one, not the one I got by MacArthur Park for $120.

To make things worse Mr. Johnson calls me and says he checked Ma's credit score. I think about the many times the bank has threatened Ma about taking away the van because she doesn't make the payments on time. I think about the credit cards she never pays. Jafra and Avon won't sell her merchandise anymore because she never pays. Now we have to get the merchandise from her friend at a more expensive price. I'm not surprised when Mr. Johnson says to me, "I'm sorry, but I can't let you have the space. I've waited months for you and Rubén, and both of you just wasted my time."

I'm at home trying to think of another plan when I get a phone call from Macy's.

"Are you Mrs. Valentina Durán?" they ask.

I lie and say to them yes. They say Stephanie was trying to steal something. I need to come pick her up. I call Ma to tell her what happened. She says that she and Tomás are downtown buying our merchandise for the swap meet and can't go get Stephanie right now.

"But this is important, Ma. You need to go talk to those people and deal with what Stephanie has done."

"Ay, Sol, they're probably going to speak English to me. I think you should go. You go and you tell those people my Stephanie is a good girl and if their merchandise wasn't so damn expensive I could be able to afford it and she wouldn't have been forced to steal it and—"

"Ma, you need to take care of this."

Ma hangs up on me, and when I call back she doesn't answer.

I drive to Pasadena to get Stephanie, wondering what she tried to steal. It's Ma's fault. She lets Stephanie get away with too much. I think about that one time when Stephanie was ten and she stole a handful of balloons from a party supply store. I told Ma Stephanie put balloons in her pocket before we left the store. Ma asked me, "Did anyone see her?" When I told her no Ma shrugged and said, "Then it's okay. Let her keep them."

I try not to think about the other times.

I park and make my way up the escalator. Stephanie is inside an office. Her eyes are red from crying.

They give me papers to sign and call me Valentina, my mother's name. They say I need to pay a $1,000 fine because Stephanie is a minor and I'm responsible.

"But I no have a thousand dollars," I say.

"We understand that, and we aren't expecting you to pay it right away," the blond lady says. "But you'll need to send it in payments, or otherwise she'll be arrested."

They show me a list of the things Stephanie was trying to steal. A pair of $40 earrings and a $250 dress. I look at the blue dress they have hanging there.

"She was trying to hide it in her backpack," the man says. "We found the price tag in the dressing room where she tried it on."

I sign my mother's name, promising to pay the $1,000, and Stephanie and I are free to go.

"Stephanie, why—?"

"Save it, Soledad. Despite what you think, you're not my mother."

I turn around and I feel angry, so angry. The mark on my face feels like it is burning. Stephanie looks at me with so much hatred. I don't understand it.

"I told you I was going to make the dress for you."

"And I told you I didn't want a homemade dress, okay? I hate being poor, I hate it. And I hate your homemade dresses and I hate all of you!"

We get to the car and she doesn't say anything anymore. I look at her lap, see her right hand in a fist, hiding the lucky finger away. I try to make her see that what she did was wrong, but she tells me she doesn't understand Spanish and I should speak to her in English.

In my broken English I tell her we aren't poor. Poverty is what you see in México. There, people don't have water, gas, or electricity. There, people don't have food to eat.

"Blah, blah, blah. I can't understand what you're saying. Is that Chinese you're speaking?"

She laughs. I try to concentrate on driving my little old Geo Metro over the curves of the 110. Because I'm not legal, I don't have a license, and I don't want to get in an accident. My eyes are blurry, but I wipe them and then they're okay.

Tomás and Ma don't say much to Stephanie. I leave them in the living room and I go outside to tend my little garden. It isn't much. Just a little patch of dirt in front of the apartment building. But still, it's nice to dig my hands into dirt, to forget I'm in Los Angeles, in a city made of concrete. I pull out the weeds growing around the chili plants, epazote, cilantro, mint, rue, and oregano. I check the ten cornstalks for worms, and I run my fingers over the silky hair of the corn growing on the stalks. I remember my grandmother, and how she would give me a little baby corn to play with. I would pretend it was a doll with blond hair. An American. I tear off a leaf of epazote and inhale its scent, and the yearning for my country swells inside me. Thirteen years without going to Michoacán, without seeing Abuelita Licha or my brother.

Stephanie comes out of the apartment and passes by me to go to the gate.

"Where are you going?"

"None of your business, you tattletale." She sticks out her tongue at me and then goes down the street. Ma and Tomás are in the living room watching the news.

"Where did Stephanie go?" I ask.

"To her friend's house," Ma says. "Why?" I don't answer her. I go to the dining room wondering how I could make her understand Stephanie needs to be punished for what she did. I pick up the satin cloth of the quinceañera dress I'm making and sit at my sewing machine, letting the click-clack of the needle make me forget my frustration with Stephanie and Ma and the $1,000 we need to pay.

Adriana

Eduardo decides to serenade Yesenia on her forty-third birthday, a few days shy of our trip to Texas. She won't be going with us, and he asked us to come, so that she knows Alegría will always be there for her. In the evening, the dancers gather outside their house. The mariachi shows up, but they have to tune their instruments inside the garage first and keep quiet. We don't want to spoil the surprise. I follow behind them and sit on the floor in a corner in the garage and listen to them play. It's hard to keep quiet. The trumpet players don't even bother to play. I watch Rogelio—the mariachi director—play his violin. I close my eyes and listen to him, the music reaching inside me, finding its way inside the dark corners of my mind.

When I open my eyes I see him standing in front of me, smiling. He sits down next to me and plays for me. I listen, humming the lyrics to "La Malagueña." I sing softly, too embarrassed to let all of them hear me. Only Rogelio can hear, and when the song is over, he leans over and whispers in my ear, "You're beautiful."

He says those magic words, and for a moment I stop looking at him the way I've always looked at him whenever he plays at our performances. *Chaparro, gordo y feo.* Yuck. Short, fat, and ugly. His eyes take me in, hungry, lustful. I look at his hands, the firm yet gentle grasp he has on his violin, as if he were holding a child. I try to picture him holding me in that same way; the man who comes to mind is not him but my father. I remember the way Dad would hold his guitar. His hands knew how to be gentle, although not with me.

"What's the matter?" Rogelio asks.

I shake my head. "Nada," I say. Eduardo comes into the garage to tell us it's time. I go back out and join the other dancers gathered outside Yesenia's bedroom window. Rogelio winks at me. "Let's hook up later," he says, and then goes to join the mariachi.

While we sing "Las Mañanitas," I look around me, at the couples hugging, at Rolando and Maricela, even Soledad sharing her sarape with her sister, Stephanie. It gets me pissed to be standing here alone. So fucking alone. With no one to hold me and listen to me sing.

After the serenade is over Rogelio comes up to me and walks me to my car, which I've finally gotten fixed.

"I didn't know you could sing like that," he says.

"How?" I lean against my car and shiver as I feel the cold metal against my back.

"Your voice is like flan. Sweet and smooth. One can never get enough."

"You're full of it. And don't start getting any ideas, 'cause I know you . . ." I open the car door, yet despite myself, my lips form into a smile. I hide my face so he won't see it.

"Have you ever thought about joining a mariachi? I've never thought about having women in my group, but for you—and your beautiful voice—I would make an exception."

"Thanks but no thanks," I say. I want to keep dancing Folklórico. It's the only thing I have left of my mother. When I'm dressed in a China Poblana costume, or any costume for that matter, and my head is adorned with a big braid with colorful ribbons, I can see her in me, and I remember her so clearly, as if she were on the other side of the mirror looking back at me.

"So what are you doing now?" he asks above the noise of the engine.

"Sleep," I say, feeling my stomach tighten the way it always does when I think of her.

"The night is young. Let's do something."

"Don't you have a wife to go home to?"

He laughs and clutches his belly. The silver in his hair gleams under the streetlight. "I'm divorced."

Chaparro, gordo y feo. I tell myself, not interested.

"Don't look at me like that," he says. "You remind me of Cecilia."

"My mother?"

"Who else? She was good-looking, too, but mean, just like you. She played me real good, your mother. Real good."

"Don't tell me you went out with her?" I turn off the car. I don't want to be wasting what little gas I have left. Could my mother have gone out with Rogelio?

"Why don't you and I go get a bite to eat and we can talk about your mother all you want."

I lock my car door and walk with him to his truck, a big motherfucker truck with huge wheels. He has to give me a lift to climb inside.

"Don't you need a stool?" I ask him. He lifts himself up and gets in. We stop at a taco truck and he gets out to buy some tacos. When he comes back he starts driving away.

"Aren't we going to eat here?"

"No, there's a place I want to show you," he says. While he drives he tells me stories about my mother. He tells me what a good dancer she was, how all the guys in the mariachi had the hots for her. He says how one day she tripped on someone's foot during rehearsal and sprained her ankle when she fell. She cried backstage because she couldn't be in the performance and he was there to comfort her.

Somehow we end up somewhere in a different part of the city I've never been to. He says we're in Mount Washington. That's right by Highland Park. He goes up a hill on a road that curves forever. He pulls over at a place where we can see downtown L.A. spread out below us. The sight is amazing. I take in the red, yellow, blue, and orange lights below. It's so quiet up here I can even hear the crickets chirping in the bushes around us.

Rogelio pulls out a bottle of tequila from the backseat and takes a swig. We munch on our tacos and take turns drinking from his bottle. He says when I was a little girl I would sit so quietly in a corner of the studio and watch the dancers rehearse, and I would clap for my mother, only for my mother, telling everyone that my mother was the "bestest" dancer of all.

Tears well in my eyes, and downtown L.A. becomes a shiny blur. I tell him how much I miss my mother. I wish I could steal his memories and put them in my head, so I could remember her the way he remembers her. His memories are so clear, so crisp, but mine are just pieces.

He holds me the way he held his violin, like he's afraid that if he lets go I'll fall to the floor and break.

I press my lips against his. But he turns and shakes his head no.

"I brought you here to do just that, Adrianita. But what kind of man would I be, to take advantage of you now? Right now you're nothing but a little girl who wants her mami."

He starts the truck and heads down the hill. I ask him to drive through Highland Park, just for the hell of it. And when he drives by my father's house I poke my head out the window and yell a loud-ass "FUCK YOU, GERARDO!!!" But it only makes me cry even more.

As I lie on my bed, thinking about all the things Rogelio said about my mother, I suddenly feel ashamed, because deep inside I know Elena tried to fill the gap our mother left in my life. I think of that Elena, the sister who brushed my hair into a French braid. The one who brewed mint tea for me when I got my period, who held my hand in the dark when I dreamed of Mom's death. Who patiently went over the dance steps I just couldn't get.

But she walked out on me. She broke up our family and then left me to fend for myself at my grandparents' house. The day Elena left for San Jose was my first day of sophomore year in high school. She got up with me that morning and watched me get ready for school, then walked me up the hill on Avenue 52. At the top of the hill she said good-bye. The Greyhound bus was leaving at ten a.m. and I knew when I got back from school, she would no longer be there.

She gave me a hug and told me to take care. "I'll call you," she said.

I looked down at my shoes, because I knew if I looked at her, I wouldn't be able to hold back the tears.

"I'm doing this for the both of us," she said for the hundredth time that week. "I'll work hard at school, try to be done in three years so by the time you finish high school I could get a good job and be able to take care of you."

I nodded and said I was going to be okay. I could handle our grandparents.

"Just stay out of their way," she said.

I watched her walk back down the hill, once in a while stopping to wave good-bye to me. Once she was far away where I knew she wouldn't see them, I let the tears come out. One more person walking out of my life.

That day I got into a fistfight with a girl in my class. Why, I can't even remember anymore. But it felt good. And that was the first of the many fights I was in. That day I disobeyed my grandparents' rule about coming straight home after school and instead hung out with friends behind an alley, smoked my first cigarette, had my first kiss, and got locked in my room without anything to eat because I came home at eight o'clock in the evening.

Elena's side of the closet was empty. She left behind a dress I often borrowed from her. A parting gift. I burned it two months after that, because my grandparents were right. "That sister of yours doesn't care about you, girl. People who care don't leave." Over and over they said that to me, until I stopped crying for her. Until I stopped acting as if there was a way out for me. Until I began to accept that because of Elena I had ended up in that hellhole and there was no way out.

Today after work, I decide to take my guitar over to the cemetery where Mom is buried. I take my songbook along with me and sit by her grave and play her favorite boleros. When I get there I'm told I only have one hour before the cemetery closes.

I always begin with "Déjame Llorar," because it's about a person who's lost someone she loved. "Déjame llorar. Desde que te perdí. Queriéndote olvidar, me acuerdo más de tí." I don't finish the song. I get choked up and start to cry even though I told myself that this time I wouldn't. I try to dig up all the happy memories I've forgotten, like how she loved to eat gummy bears, especially red and green ones, because the colors reminded her of her beloved México.

I remember her in her coffin, lying so still and beautiful. She was buried wearing a red Jalisco dress. Her hair made up in a bun, the braids woven with colorful ribbons. Her black dance boots.

I dry my tears and pick up my guitar again. I sing a couple more songs and then I pack up to leave. I still have half an hour left before the cemetery closes. And even though I hadn't planned it, I begin to walk down to where my niece is buried. Not too far from Mom. Her grave is still fresh, and there are many bouquets of flowers on it. I wonder how often Elena comes here. I stand by her grave, and I have no idea what to say to her, except that I would've liked to see her grow up and become a dancer, just like her mom and aunt and her grandmother, and her great-grandmother. Because I don't know any children's songs, I sing "Cielito Lindo" for her. I put my guitar away and as I walk through the gate I tell myself I should buy a book of children's songs so the next time I come, I'll be prepared.

Elena

Richard reaches out for me in the dark and I don't move. He whispers words of love in my ear. His hands on my body, asking for something it can't give.

"When, Elena?" he asks, his hands sliding down to the mattress, away from me.

"I don't know."

He curses under his breath and turns around to face the wall. When his breathing changes pace I know he's fallen asleep. I lie on my back, looking up at the shadows on the ceiling, feeling nothing. Not even a twinge of guilt.

Because I can't sleep I get out of bed and go to the nursery. I sit in the rocking chair caressing the small dance shoes I once bought for my daughter. One pair of girl shoes, because I was sure it would be a girl.

I close my eyes, listening to Don McLean's "Starry, Starry Night," willing myself to relax, to let sleep come. But it doesn't. Instead, I stay awake thinking about Alegría's performances, the competition in Texas. Just like I knew would happen, they placed first, like they did last year. Except I wasn't there this time, and I can't help feeling they don't need me after all; Yesenia was wrong to have held me in such high regard.

Although I was asked to teach a summer class, I decided to stay home. Richard has taken on a full load of classes to teach.

This is why tonight he doesn't come home when he's supposed to. He calls to tell me he has too many papers to grade and will stay in his office until he's done with the entire stack. He always brought home his students' work. I don't ask him why he doesn't do so now.

I finally succumb to sleep, and tonight I dream about a serpent crawling in through the bedroom window, slithering across the floor up to the bed, entering me through my vagina and tearing off my ovaries. I awake with a scream stuck in my throat. I lie awake in the dark, touch the empty space where Richard should've been, and listen to the silence.

In the morning Richard asks me if I want to go to the beach for a walk. I tell him I want to stay home. He says he'll be back soon and puts his bicycle in the car and leaves. But he doesn't come back right away. I drive to La Placita Olvera in the afternoon. It was one of my mother's favorite places. A little piece of México in downtown Los Angeles. I eat a plate of carnitas with cactus salad while staring at the empty seat across from me. People glance my way, and I wish I had a book to read so I wouldn't feel so awkward eating alone. I think about Richard, and for a moment I have an overwhelming need to hear his voice.

I pick up the plate and toss it in the wastebasket, the spiciness of the salsa burning a small hole in my stomach. As I walk from stall to stall and look at the leather sandals, embroidered blouses, little girl dresses with the colors of the Mexican flag, I remember how my mother would tease me about not being able to eat chile, while she and Adriana could bite into an habanero as if biting into an apple.

I sit on a bench watching people walking around. Their faces blur in front of me, as if they've just been painted on a canvas with broad strokes. This is how the world looks when I take off my glasses. Like a large oil painting done by an Impressionist artist.

I sit near the kiosk and try not to think about the many times I danced here with my mother and sister.

A woman passes by me and I can't take my eyes off of her. She seems to be in her thirties and has long black hair. But it's her laugh that makes me shiver, a deep throaty laugh that begins with a giggle. I remember that laugh.

I should keep looking at her without my glasses. Her face is blurry, indistinct, and I can pretend it's her, if only for a little while.

With my glasses on the woman's features come into focus, and she doesn't look at all like my mother.

I begin to sleep until noon, after spending the better part of the night roaming around the house. Sometimes, when I feel guilty, I go outside to water my dying plants. The hydrangea Soledad gave me has shriveled and died in its container, but I don't have the heart to toss it in the trash. As I water, I look up at the sky and watch eight airplanes make their way toward LAX, their lights shining like stars, forming a constellation in the otherwise starless L.A. sky. I wonder what the chances are that a plane would fall on my house and crush it.

Snails slowly crawl over the garden. How quickly they've overtaken it. I don't remember the last time Richard and I weeded, fertilized, or sprayed the garden with pesticides.

One night, on impulse, I decide to clean out the garage. I take out the boxes of baby gifts Richard put away despite my protests. As a compromise he put away only the gifts we received at the surprise baby shower the Alegría dancers held for me at the studio. But he promised he would leave the things we ourselves bought for Xochitl, including the nursery furniture we fell in love with at JC Penney's.

I throw all the gifts in black trash bags. Baby blankets, booties and socks, pajamas, stuffed toys, rattles, clothes. I load them in my truck. Even though it's one in the morning I head over to the Goodwill donation station in Long Beach. Perhaps another mother can make better use of these things. I unload the bags quickly and without another glance I drive out of the parking lot, without a specific destination. I end up at the beach, and because I'm not yet tired, I decide to park and go for a walk. The cool ocean breeze plays with my hair, and I wish it would blow away the heaviness inside me. Like a cleansing. I close my eyes and imagine the wind seeping through my body and blowing away everything that weighs heavily on me until I could be light and free. But when I open my eyes the heaviness is still inside me, and I drag it with me back to my truck, like chains tied to my ankles.

On my drive back home, I pass the exit that leads to Goodwill, and the thought of giving away all those gifts meant for my daughter is suddenly too overwhelming. I exit the freeway, drive back to Goodwill, and like a thief, I quickly load the bags back into the truck and speed away.

Soledad

While downtown buying some accessories for a wedding dress I'm making, I run into Rubén at the corner of Ninth Street and Maple. He's carrying a bolt of cream-colored satin and says he's making another wedding dress. "The bride-to-be wants me to make this horrendous dress, something straight out of the nineteenth century," he says. "I tried to get her to see reason, but she wouldn't listen."

I say to him it isn't his wedding and he must do as the bride says. I don't say it to be mean, but Rubén thinks so.

"Ay, chula. Why the attitude? Are you still mad at me because of the dress shop? Don't be mad at me, Sol. Please, chula. You're my only real friend. What would I do without you? C'mon, I'll buy you a diablito." We walk down the street and he buys me one from the vendor on the corner.

"Notice anything different, Sol?" Rubén asks as he hands me the cup full of crushed ice topped with tamarind syrup, chili powder, and pieces of mango.

I look at him and notice his curly hair is longer, an inch and a half below his ears. He's dyed it, too. Brown, like cinnamon, with blond highlights. His eyebrows are thin and shaped like a "V" that is upside down.

"Look a little lower," he says. He smiles and sticks his chest out. I see his T-shirt—a white one with Princesa printed on it with hot pink letters. And then I see them.

"What do you think?" he asks. "They finally started growing."

He has small breasts, like the size I had my breasts when I was twelve.

"And here, touch this." He picks up my hand and puts it on his cheek. "Feel anything?"

I shake my head. "No, what am I supposed to feel?"

"Nothing!" he says. "Thank God for laser hair removal!"

He says in a month he's going to have his surgery, something he calls SRS.

"My mother insisted on going with me to see the doctor," Rubén says. I tell him I need to go back to my shopping. The hot chili powder in the diablito is making my stomach hurt now. He walks with me back to Ninth Street and keeps talking. "And you know what she said to him?" I shake my head and we cross the street. I forget now what I needed to buy.

"She asked the doctor if—after my surgery—he could give her my pecker so she could keep it as a keepsake! Can you believe that woman?" He pulls my arm and yanks me back to the sidewalk. Cars honk at me. I didn't notice the light was red.

"And you know what the doctor did?" Rubén says to me when the light turns green and we start to cross the street. My stomach is hurting me and I can't talk.

"He turned a deep, deep magenta color and said, 'Ma'am, I can't do that.' And my mother said, 'But why not? I want to re-member I once had two sons!'" Rubén laughs. "Oh, my God, Sol. I could've died of embarrassment . . ." He stops and looks at me and asks if I'm okay.

I nod and tell him I must do my shopping, but he keeps going. "What my mother doesn't understand—and I've tried to explain it to her a million times now—is that the doc isn't going to cut my pecker off. He's just going to shape it into a vagina."

I see the people giving us weird looks. Rubén looks at them and says the word "vagina" really loud so everyone can hear. I wish I could run into the closest shop and hide my humiliation among the bolts of cloth. I say to Rubén I really need to do my shopping now, but I don't feel like shopping. I want to go home.

He kisses both my cheeks and tells me to take care. I wave good-bye to him and turn to look at the bolts of cloth outside the stores. They spin around me, like if I was on a merry-go-round, all the colors blinding me. I run to the curb and throw up the diablito. The spiciness of my vomit makes my throat and mouth burn.

After the swap meet, Ma and I go to Western Union to send money to my Abuelita Licha and Lorenzo. It feels so good when I give the cashier the two hundred-dollar bills, still warm from my hands. "I wish we could send more," I tell Ma.

"When Stephanie gets her money, I'm sure she'll start sending some to your grandmother," Ma says.

"We should bring her here. Life in México is too hard," I say to Ma on our way home. I see an old lady walking in front of us, wearing a black shawl over her head, just like Abuelita Licha likes to do. All these years I've worked hard to send money to her and my brother. Ma and I finally finished building a house for Abuelita Licha four years ago. It isn't a big house. Just a small house with two bedrooms that replaced the shack we lived in. But it's made of brick and concrete. And there's a brick wall that goes all around the property to keep the river water out when it floods. With the money we sent, Abuelita Licha bought herself a few pigs, a goat, and some chickens. She tends her little garden and from there she gets tomatoes and chiles, squash, watermelon, corn. I haven't seen the new house, but my brother describes it to me when we talk on the phone. One day, when I finally have my dress shop, I'm going to build my grandmother a bathroom. A real bathroom with a toilet that flushes and a shower.

"She doesn't want to come, Soledad, you know that. How many times have you asked her to? She is afraid. After your grandfather and father died crossing the border she got even more scared. I had such a hard time convincing her I should come. And the only reason why she let you come is because I promised her I wouldn't let you cross the border the hard way. I told her you would cross with a borrowed birth certificate, and then she was fine with it."

"But maybe when you become a U.S. citizen you can petition to bring her here," I say. "That's one of the benefits of being a U.S. citizen."

"I don't qualify to do the interview in Spanish, Sol."

"Well then, study English, Ma. Come to school with me and then you can do the interview in English."

"Ay, mi'ja. English is too hard. No se me pega nada."

I'm glad when we get home. Ma gets me angry. If she only tried I wouldn't get angry. Ma goes inside the house and I stay outside to tend my garden, thinking about my grandmother.

When I first came to the U.S., it was very hard for me. I missed my grandmother very much. I missed sitting outside our little shack, embroidering napkins with colored threads. Abuelita showed me how to make all kinds of stitches. During the holidays people asked Abuelita to make dance costumes for their children so they could be in the parades or the school's celebrations. When she was young, she was a sewing girl for El Ballet Folklórico de México. But when she got married my grandfather took her to Michoacán to be with his family. In Michoacán she tried to make a living by sewing school uniforms, quinceañera or wedding dresses, but she loved making dance costumes, like me.

She and I, we were always together. It was so hard to leave her behind when I came here to be with Ma. After so many years of Ma being gone I'd started to see my Abuelita as my mother. Sometimes, I asked myself why I even came. Abuelita started to go blind, and she was making dresses less and less. I started to do more of the work. When Ma said to come to the U.S., Abuelita didn't like the idea. But then she realized that there was nothing for me in Michoacán. Abuelita wanted me to go to school. She wanted me to be someone important, like a teacher. In México everybody loves teachers. Here, they aren't appreciated like they should be. Abuelita Licha said for me to come, that I had a lot of potential and she thought one day I would be somebody.

But I came here and Ma didn't want me to go to school to learn English. Because I was twenty, she said I was too old to learn anything, anyway. She wanted me to work and baby-sit Stephanie. Working at the swap meet didn't make me feel good. I wanted to work with my hands and make beautiful things. I missed the colored threads, the sound the scissors make as they cut the fabric, the feel of cloth against my fingertips. The click-clack of the sewing machine.

So I bought a used sewing machine at the swap meet and started to make dresses for Stephanie. She was little then, and she didn't mind the dresses I made at home.

One day I walked far from the house. I never went far because I was afraid I'd get lost, but I hated being locked up in the apartment. That day was beautiful, and I forgot about my fears and just kept walking. I heard music I recognized right away. When I looked up I was standing in front of a dance studio. I went inside and found dancers practicing "La Danza de los Viejitos," a popular dance from Michoacán. It made me so happy to find something from my state in this city. I sat in a corner and watched the young men dancing bent over, holding a cane, and shaking their bodies to imitate old men. I laughed so hard watching them trip over one another.

That was the day I stopped being so unhappy being in this

country. Eduardo and Yesenia were nice to me. They let me come to watch the practices and gave me tickets to their performances. I took Ma, Tomás, and Stephanie. Then Stephanie said she wanted to dance because she liked the pretty dance costumes. I started to bring her here, and she was good, but this place was special to me, and now I had to share it with her. But I was happy with Alegría, very happy to make costumes like my Abuelita taught me. A little piece of México, that's what Alegría is to me. A little piece of México.

CHAPTER FOUR

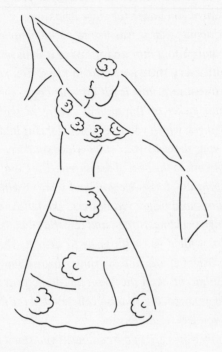

Then come the lights shining on you from above. You're a performer. You forget all you learned, the process of technique, the fear, the pain, you even forget who you are. You become one with the music, the lights, indeed, one with the dance.

—SHIRLEY MacLAINE

As you watch the performance, the beauty created by the costumes, the music, the lighting, the props, takes your breath away.

You allow yourself to remember, for just a moment, what it was like to be up there, cut off from the world. There onstage, nothing exists beyond the curtain. There are no drunk abusive fathers, no dead mothers to mourn, no sisters who despise you. No stillbirths. Nothing can harm you under the stage lights.

You think about what it was like to put on your makeup, pinning up your hair into a bun and spraying it with several coats of hair spray until every stray wisp was in place. You remember the beauty of each costume, how it felt on your body. The tight-fitting suede skirt and jacket of Tamaulipas decorated with floral arabesques and fringes, which you wore when dancing huapangos from Tamaulipas, your arms at your sides while your feet did the tight huapango footwork to the beat of the jarana. The Chiapas dress—so much like a princess dress—elegant and vibrant with its fuchsia, turquoise, yellow, and bright red flowers. The Jalisco dress with its long sleeves, high neckline, ruffles, and colorful ribbons, so emblematic of México, it filled you with pride to wear it. The Michoacán dress with its bright colors and swirling ribbons, magical and yet demure and innocent. And the Veracruz dress, your favorite, the white lace and organza, the Spanish coin jewelry, the fan, the velvet apron, made you feel regal, sensual.

You remember the rush of adrenaline as you stood in the wings, waiting to begin. You moved your body to keep the blood circulating, to keep your muscles warm and supple, and then, at last, you burst out onto the stage and became enveloped with bright lights, and you felt the music flowing through you, felt every part of your body working together to make the right movements, felt each muscle contraction, your lungs expanding with each intake of breath.

You miss the lightness you felt onstage. You miss the purity it made you feel inside your being, as if you had gone to church and taken communion. You miss the fluidity, the efficiency with which your body moved. But all that is gone now. Here in the audience, you can't escape reality. You're a mere mortal in this world. So there's nothing to do but lean back in your seat and succumb to the

darkness pressing in around you, while onstage, under the bright
lights, your sister is the one who is dancing.

Elena

For Alegría's ninth-year anniversary performance, I help Mrs.
Rodríguez drive the dance students to the Ford Amphitheater.
I couldn't bring myself to say no when she asked; it's the least I
can do, now that I've left her with all the responsibilities of the
group. But the thought of having to sit through another Alegría
performance is overwhelming.

We meet in front of the school at five thirty in the evening on
Saturday. The performance will begin at eight. There are ten of us.
Mrs. Rodríguez, myself, and eight group members. Fernando is
one of them. Mrs. Rodríguez takes four students with her. I take
the other four. The three girls choose to sit together in the back.
Fernando shyly slides into the passenger seat. I haven't seen him
in four weeks, since the start of summer vacation. I don't know if
it's because I haven't seen him recently that he looks older to me.
His voice sounds deeper, his chest looks fuller, and the peach fuzz
above his upper lip has turned into thicker, coarser hair. He'll be
shaving soon.

I grip the steering wheel tighter and look at the road ahead,
reprimanding myself for thinking such thoughts. The moisture
on my palms rubs onto the steering wheel. I see Fernando looking at me out of the corner of his eye. My truck feels too small, its
space presses in around me. As if to break the silence, Fernando
tells me he's excited about the show. He's never been to a dance
performance before.

"You'll enjoy tonight's performance," I say. "Alegría is a great
group."

"Mrs. Rodríguez said you used to dance with them before."

I nod but don't elaborate.

He remains silent for a moment, and then changes the conversation. "Have you been enjoying your vacation, Miss?"

"Yes," I lie. "What about you?"

"I miss Folklórico practice."

I ask him about his family. The girls in the back lean forward to hear better. I notice how they look at him. Fernando tells me his mother works cleaning houses and his father passed away seven years ago after he was thrown off his horse in México. He has a younger brother and sister who've recently arrived in the U.S.

"How long were you separated from them?" I ask.

"Four years," he says.

"That must have been hard."

He nods and then asks me about my family.

"My mother died in a car accident when I was fourteen," I say.

"I'm sorry, Miss," Fernando says. "I know how that feels."

"I miss her a lot," I say, wondering why I even said that to him.

"And then you lost your baby, too?" one of the girls says. "That really sucks, Ms. Sánchez. First your mom and then your baby."

I don't respond to the girl's comment, thinking about my mother, wondering what must have gone through her head when she was dying. I can still hear a twelve-year-old Adriana whispering in my ear, asking me: Why did this happen, Elena? Why did she leave us behind?

Because it's Richard's thirty-third birthday, we go out for dinner at Houston's. It's Richard's favorite restaurant, and the thought of having barbecue ribs, he says, makes his mouth water. It wasn't easy finding a gift for him, but while driving down the 405 yesterday I saw the golf course where he's played with friends before, and I decided to buy him a $200 range card.

It's the first time we have gone out since our daughter died.

We both seem to realize the significance of this, and as we drive to Houston's our conversation remains light. He tells me about the students in his class, the things they try to get away with, and I find myself laughing, hardly recognizing that the sound is coming from me.

We order a bottle of red wine with our meal, and I'm surprised at how relaxed I feel, so relaxed that when Richard kisses me to thank me for the gift, I return it as if it were the most natural thing to do, to kiss one's husband. I don't recoil at his touch, at the feel of his lips against my own, the softness of his goatee against my skin, the warmth of his hand on my leg.

After dinner we drive to City Walk. It's one of the places we frequented when we first met at a teachers' conference two and a half years ago. We walk side by side, and I'm grateful that it's crowded with people. For once being in a crowd doesn't intimidate me. We lose ourselves in the throng and pretend we're like the hundreds of couples walking by us holding hands. We reach for each other's hands in an attempt at normalcy.

Because it's after ten there are no couples with children, at least, as far as we can see. During the day you see families here on their way to Universal Studios or back. But now, thankfully, it's safe. Or so I think, until we pass by Bucca Di Beppo's and we hear a child's cry. We turn to look and see a family emerging from the restaurant, the mother holding her son's hand and the father carrying a little girl in his arms, a sleepy little girl who is too tired to walk.

I think this is what makes Richard and me decide to end our walk. I claim that I'm cold, although it's a pleasant summer night. Richard says his new shoes are bothering him. In silence we make our way to the parking lot.

When we get home Richard pours us another glass of wine, and we sit in the living room. I look at him sitting on the love seat, his burgundy shirt halfway unbuttoned. He stares at a spot on the carpet, but I know he isn't really looking at anything. I see him then, in that instant, through my dancer's eyes, and as I see the slight twitching of his mouth, the constricted breathing, the curve of his spine, the tensed muscles, the stillness of his body, I remember what my years of dancing have taught me: the body expresses that which we can't express with words. I realize now that if I'd been looking closer, I would've seen that his suffering was as great as my own. This is why I put my glass down and go to him. When I reach him he presses me so hard against his chest I feel as if I can't breathe. He scoops me up in his arms, and when he drops me on the bed I tear at his shirt. He pulls off my underwear and enters me without reservation, without waiting for me to be ready. I cry out in pain, but I beg him not to stop, not to stop because the pain helps me remember that I'm still alive.

In the morning, I wake up to the sound of whistling. I smile. When Richard is in a good mood he likes to wake up early and make us breakfast. Usually scrambled eggs, grits, and bacon. Sometimes, if he's especially in a good mood, even waffles.

I stand up and put on his burgundy shirt. I roll up the sleeves on my way down the hallway toward the kitchen, and then I realize there's no smell.

I follow his whistling, and even before I enter the nursery I know what he's doing. I find him with a screwdriver in hand, disassembling the crib.

"Get out! Get out!" I yell, rushing toward him.

He grabs my wrists and rolls me onto my back. He pins me with his body, trying to explain, but I struggle beneath him, hit him with my knees, try to free my arms so that I can lash at him, hurt him.

"Sweetheart, please, please," he says over and over again. When I'm spent, I lie still beneath him. It's hard to breathe with his body on me. He brushes away the strands of my hair stuck to my lips with saliva.

"You can't do this," I say. "You can't do this."

"Listen to me, Elena. You're turning this room into an altar, and as long as this nursery is here we will never heal, don't you understand?"

"No, no, no, you can't do this."

"Sweetie, please. Last night I thought that finally we would be able to put the past behind us and save our marriage and move on with our lives. And this morning I saw the crib, and everything inside this room, and I knew that it had to go. Every time I pass this room the pain comes back again and I just can't take it, Elena, I can't take it anymore."

He loosens his hold on me and I push him off. I crawl to the crib and grab hold of it so tightly, as if we were out in the open sea and this crib was the only thing that could save me from drowning.

"It's over," I say to him. "It's over."

His side of the closet is empty.

I walk around the house, hear the door open and close as Richard fills his car with his belongings. I go out to the patio and sit under the avocado tree, looking at the garden, the plants withering under the August sun. For an instant, my fingers itch to dig into the earth, to pull weeds, to prune rosebushes, to watch things grow. The feeling lasts for only a second, because flowers no longer mean anything to me.

I tell myself it's better this way. A missed pill. A dead child. A failed marriage, and now I sit here, hearing the back door open, and I know that the time has to come to end it.

"I'm gonna get going," Richard says. He puts his hands in his pockets and fidgets from one foot to the other. I'm afraid to look at his face. What if I can't let him go after all? What if I'm making a mistake? He agrees it's for the best that he leaves. He says we need time to think, to make a decision, but I've made my decision and time won't change it.

I stand up and face him, recalling the scene in the nursery. It gives me courage. What right did he have to decide for both of us? "Well, I guess this is it," I say. How stupid it sounds, but I don't know what else to say.

He nods. He looks up at the tree. "I'm sure gonna miss the avocados," he says, smiling.

I take off my glasses. "Richard, I know that—"

"You don't have to make me feel better. I love you, and you love me, but for now love just isn't enough. That's the way things go sometimes."

"I'm sorry." I look at his face, see past the mask, hear the pain in his voice, the sadness he's trying hard to conceal.

"Me, too," he says. He pulls me against his chest, and for the last time, I press my ear against his heart and listen to it beat. For the last time I feel his breath upon my face, his lips against my lips. He lets me go and turns to leave. I stand by the lavender bush and watch a beetle fly around. I listen for the sound of a car starting. The beetle flies over the fence and disappears. I look around the patio, searching for any sign of life. A trail of ants, a mosquito, a snail, a fly, a bee, a butterfly. Anything. But there's nothing here. Only me, and my pain, and the bittersweet taste of Richard's lips.

Yesenia

I started bringing Memo to dance practice when he was only six weeks old. I put the stroller in a corner of the dance studio, and there Memo lay still, listening to the music, the tap-tap-tapping of the dancers' shoes putting him to sleep. He got so used to the sounds that even at home I had to play Folklórico music to get him to sleep. One day when he was almost three, I found him in his room looking at himself in the closet mirror, and to my surprise, my little boy was trying to do un zapateado. My love for him pushed against my chest until it hurt, until I couldn't breathe.

When I had Memo at twenty-two, the first year was very hard. I didn't know how lonely motherhood could be. I still remember those endless nights I spent sitting in the nursery room at one, two, three, five in the morning. While the world was sleeping—while Eduardo snored in the next room—I had to comfort that baby and find a way to keep his cries down so his father wouldn't wake up. I remember those moments of sitting on the carpet with Memo thinking about all the things I wanted to do with my life besides just stacking blocks and making sure my little boy didn't get hurt. My days at home had become a time of just trying to get through. Of having no one to talk to but a little baby because Eduardo was gone all day long working to support us.

But that day when I discovered Memo trying to dance, all those sleepless nights and lonely days suddenly didn't matter anymore. I started teaching him some steps and began to take him to dance classes and later, to his dance performances. How proud I was of my son when I saw him perform! Memo never danced clumsily like little kids do—their hands dangling at their sides because they would forget what they were supposed to do with them, their feet not following the music, their lips forgetting to smile, their hats falling off their heads. Even from the start he was a professional.

Instead of watching cartoons, Memo would watch dance videos with me, and he would tell me about his favorite dances. He would clap at the end of each dance and would get up and imitate the dance positions. He always liked tagging along whenever I went to Tijuana to buy accessories for the costumes. My little boy.

Now he's leaving me.

I stand in front of the dryer letting the heat coming from it warm my knee. I've always hated folding laundry, especially pairing socks. Eduardo and Memo's dress socks are so hard to match.

They all look the same, but upon closer inspection the differences in the pattern or color become obvious. This time, though, I'm doing Memo's whites, and his socks are easy enough to pair up, although part of me would rather throw the socks away, for no matter how much bleach I used the dirt didn't come off. Socks get dirty from dancing shoeless at the studio, no matter how hard we try to keep the floor clean.

I take the clothes out of the dryer and head to the couch and begin to fold. I take my time folding his shirts, enjoying the feel of them. I think about the many times I complained about having to do his laundry and made him wash his own clothes. "Your future wife will thank me for teaching you to take care of yourself," I would say. But now I don't want the pile to go down. I want to sit here on the couch and keep folding his clothes. I want him to spend the night in his bedroom, even if it means he'll be hours on the phone with his friends. I want to wake up early in the morning tomorrow and make him his favorite breakfast of pancakes and eggs sunny-side up, crispy bacon, and a licuado of bananas and Choco Milk. I want to keep making Jell-O for him because ever since he heard that it's good for bones and elasticity, he eats it every day, claiming it helps him dance better.

He and Eduardo keep going in and out of the house carrying boxes out of his room. Finally there are no more boxes, no more laundry to fold. With a sigh I finish folding the last shirt and put it inside the basket with the rest of his clothes. It's a little heavy, and my knee hurts as I walk out of the house carrying the basket.

"Are you sure it wouldn't be better if you stay here?" I ask Memo as he rushes over to take the basket.

"I think it's better if I live near campus, Mom. You know how L.A. traffic is. And it's far driving from Riverside to El Sereno."

We walk together to the driveway where Eduardo's truck is parked. Eduardo comes out carrying a nightstand.

"Is she still trying to convince you?" he asks. They both laugh the same hoarse laugh. "You gotta hand it to your mother, Memo. She's persistent."

Memo puts his arm around me. "Mom, I'll see you after practice. I'll make a quick stop and visit." He leans down to kiss my cheek. I take off my slipper and touch the grass with my toes. I shiver and wish the sun were out, but the sky is a dirty gray. It reminds me of the old beggar woman asking for alms at the freeway exit on my way to work. The woman's eye is covered by a grayish film.

When they finish loading up the truck Eduardo uses for his electrician job, Memo gets into the Toyota Prius we gave him as a graduation present. It's another bill Eduardo and I will have to pay, but Memo deserved it.

"You ready?" Eduardo asks as he starts the engine.

"I think I'll stay," I say.

"You sure?"

"Yeah, my knee is bothering me, and you know, all those stairs in his apartment building . . ."

I walk over to Memo's car to tell him good-bye. But when I look at him, full of excitement, ready to begin to live his life away from home, I become furious. He could at least pretend to feel bad. He could at least shed a few tears. Isn't he hurting as much as I am?

"How could you leave now when you know that I need you?"

Memo looks down at his hands and begins to crack his knuckles just like he always does whenever Eduardo or I scold him for whatever mischief he gets himself into. He hides under his long hair and doesn't say a word. I swallow my tears and turn on my heel, walking back to the house as quickly as my knee lets me.

"Mom!" Memo yells.

Eduardo puts the truck in gear and begins to back out of the driveway. He waves at me. I stand on the porch and watch them drive away. How could I say that to him? I feel the bile in my mouth and spit on the ground the way I've seen Mexican men spit, hard and unapologetic. If I could let go of Alegría, I could let go of Memo. I repeat this like a mantra, but still, when the truck and Memo's car disappear down the street, my son's departure leaves me feeling empty. I fight the urge to spit again and instead swallow hard and fight the tightness in my throat. I walk back into the empty house and go inside Memo's room. It's barren now, the ever-present mess gone. His posters of Alegría's performances that once covered the walls are gone. As I lie down on his bed, my eyes burn with tears, and I cry for my boy, and for Alegría.

Now I know why some people sometimes have so many kids. It's so hard to watch them leave home. For a brief moment, I think about the children I chose not to have. I wonder if another child would have made Memo's absence more bearable.

I wish that time would stop, that it stopped months ago, right before my knee began to stiffen and swell up, right before Memo decided he was old enough to be on his own. I know I should be happy my son is going to university. I should be proud. But I can't help wishing there had been a way to keep him with me.

They all show up unexpectedly. Eduardo opens the door for them and pretends he's surprised to see them, but I know that he isn't. As some of Alegría's female dancers walk into the living room bathed in perfume, their hair all done up and their faces heavily painted, I become conscious of how red and swollen my eyes are from crying, and how my hair is a tangled mess. I'm wearing my favorite pair of old sweatpants and a UCR sweater Memo gave me.

"What's going on?"

"It's Saturday night, Yessy, and we wanna take you out dancing," Olivia, Alegría's accountant, says, her smile so wide, and yet I can see she's nervous by the way she keeps jiggling the bangles on her wrist. Erika, Laura, Adriana, Olivia, and the two Teresas stand by the door, all dressed in tight, glittery dresses with spaghetti straps. Hoochie dresses young girls like to wear, that reveal everything and leave nothing to the imagination. I would've never worn short dresses like these when I was their age. Thinking about myself when I was young makes me feel old.

I throw my arms up in the air, "I wish you had called first," I say, a little too harshly. They look at each other and then at Eduardo still standing by the door.

He coughs, embarrassed. "I tried to get her to change," he says.

And I now know why after returning from Memo's new apartment he kept offering to take me out, saying I needed a distraction, and he kept insisting I put on that burgundy dress he likes so much and wouldn't give up when I told him I didn't feel like going out, putting on makeup, brushing my hair, pretending everything is okay when nothing is. I should've known what he was trying to do. I can't remember the last time he and I went out, just the two of us. Almost every weekend "going out" for us meant going to perform at weddings, quinceañeras, or some other party.

Laura walks up to me and puts her arm around me, hesitantly. "The girls and I want to take you to Acapulco's for drinks. The others are meeting us there. We know that it's been rough lately—"

"But we're here for you, Yessy," Erika, the only gringa in the group, says.

"Ándale, mujer, no te hagas del rogar," Adriana says, and she grabs my hand and takes me into my bedroom. She looks through the closet and takes out two dresses. "Which one do you want, the blue one or the burgundy one?"

I sit on the bed and don't answer. Adriana puts the dresses on the bed and looks through my shoe rack. Now I understand why Elena locked herself in her room the night we showed up at her house. How hard it is to keep myself from yelling, to make them understand I want to be left alone. Out of the eighty high heels I own Adriana chooses a pair of Carlos Santana stilettos studded with crystals of different colors and holds them up for me to see. "These would look nice with either dress."

Even though Eduardo is so short, and I tower above him with heels on, I love wearing heels. At five seven, my Carlos Santana stilettos raise me up to five ten! My father was six feet. Most Mexicans are short, but in the state of Jalisco, where my parents are from, tall people are common. I remember when I last wore those heels. It was at the Christmas party Eduardo and I had for the dancers, here at the house. It was a great party, and I stuffed myself silly with the buñuelos and champurrado Soledad made. I remember the little sugar crystals falling on my shoes as I ate the buñuelos.

Ever since the doctor said to buy pumps, I haven't worn my heels much. So I ask myself why not? Why not get dressed up, put on these shoes that show off my pretty feet. That's my favorite part of my body, isn't it? No matter how much weight I put on, my feet are always the same, thin and shapely. Besides, a few Long Islands and margaritas don't sound bad at all. "Fine," I say. "Hand me the blue dress."

"Ajúa!" Adriana claps like a silly girl and rushes over with the dress. She sits on the bed and watches me dress myself. We've dressed and undressed in front of each other for so many years at our performances, but now I feel uncomfortable under Adriana's gaze. I stand in front of the mirror with just sweatpants and a bra, the dress in my hand. I look at the bulges of fat all around my waist. My breasts are supported by the bra but otherwise would be sagging like water balloons dangling from a child's fingers. I see the wrinkles on my face, especially the laugh lines and the one across my forehead. My hair is a mess; it has been a while since I went to the hairdresser, and I can see a few gray hairs peeking out.

Behind me, Adriana talks and talks about a performance they had a few nights ago. Eduardo himself couldn't stop talking about it. Last week he went to do some electrical work in a mansion in Malibu. He was talking to the owner, and the owner told him about a party he was having for his wife. When he found out that Eduardo had a dance group, he offered him $1,000 for the dancers to come and entertain his guests. Eduardo had eight couples ready to go by the next day, Adriana among them. They went to the man's party, and not only did they earn $1,000 for a twenty-minute performance but the man gave them a $250 tip as well. Eduardo split the money and gave each dancer his or her share. Now Adriana was talking about the luxurious mansion. How the walk-in closet, which they used as a dressing room, was even bigger than her own bedroom! I look at Adriana's image in the mirror, her dark skin that looks so beautiful with the turquoise dress and the red coral necklace she's wearing. Her hair isn't braided as usual; instead, it's draped around her shoulders, shiny and black like obsidian. Adriana glows with the radiance of youth. "And you should have seen all those purses that lady had. And the shoes, beautiful designer shoes that just took your breath away. I swear, if they'd been my size, I would've walked out with a pair. The lady has so many—ten times more than you—she wouldn't even have noticed . . . !" She giggles and covers her mouth, making her seem even younger than her twenty-four years.

"I can't do this," I say, throwing the dress on the floor.

"C'mon, Yessy. It'll be fun," Adriana says.

I pick up my UCR sweater and put it back on. "I don't feel like going anywhere."

"But—"

"I said no, don't you listen?"

"Jeez, don't get all pissed off. What's gotten into you? We just wanted to be nice. Fine, have it your way." Adriana walks out of the room. After a few minutes the door closes, and I lie down on the bed. Eduardo comes into the room and asks if I'm okay. He puts the dresses Adriana took out back in the closet, the shoes back in their box, and it's as if nothing ever happened, as if the Alegría women weren't here at all, wanting to take me out to drinks, following the tradition we've always had—when one of us is feeling like shit, we must do our best to cheer that person up.

Eduardo puts a blanket over me and bends down to kiss my cheek. He leaves the room and I close my eyes, thinking about the girls. How could I explain to them that their mere presence hurts me? To see their youth, the many years of dancing still in their future. They're the ones whose faces have not been blurred by too many years of living. Like Laura. Eighteen years old. Fresh and supple like clay, eagerly awaiting someone's hands to shape her. I imagine them now, drinking margaritas or piña coladas at some club, being asked by young men to dance, and because they're awesome dancers, they will have everyone gawking at them as they twist and twirl across the dance floor. And their knees will feel no pain.

Soledad

Today Rubén calls me and asks me to come to his house. I know something must be wrong. He wouldn't call me if everything was fine. Still, when I get to his house I'm surprised at how I find him. He's wearing a dress he tried to tear off his body, and his face is smeared with makeup. Streaks of black mascara are under his eyes. The red lipstick smeared high up his cheeks makes him look like an evil clown.

His mirror is shattered into a million pieces, and I'm careful not to step on the glass as I walk into his room.

"What happened?" I ask, closing the door behind me. The house is empty, and since it's midday I know Doña Sofía is at the school where she works in the cafeteria, Don Pablo is also at work at the auto shop, and Junior is at school.

Rubén holds up his arms to me and I go and hold him while he cries. He tells me he's afraid. Terrified of the surgery, of everything that could go wrong.

"Everything is going to be fine," I say as I clean his face with the hem of my dress. I wipe away his tears but more come.

"What if I'm making a mistake?" he says. "After the surgery there's no going back. And my father, last night he told me the most horrible things, Sol. He said he's ashamed of having a two-faced son like me. That he can't understand how I could be a man on the outside and a woman on the inside. He said I'm an abomination, and if it weren't because of my mother he would've kicked me out a long time ago. He said—he said that if I went on with the surgery I would be dead to him."

I don't like to see Rubén like this. But what can I say to make him feel better? Like his parents, I wish Rubén would change his mind about the surgery. I wish he would wake up tomorrow and feel different. But I know people are like fabric, we cannot change their nature. They are what they are and the only thing we can do is use them well. God made him how he is and I must love him. Not as a man, but as a person. As a human being. I tell him that sometimes it's hard for parents to accept their children as they are. I tell Rubén to follow his dream and to not let anyone make him feel ashamed to be who he is. "Think of the combed cotton twills brushed and printed on both sides, we use to make reversible garments. There's no right or wrong side to those fabrics. They're beautiful either way."

I help him change out of the torn dress and he puts on a T-shirt and jeans. He washes the makeup off his face, and then we sweep the room and put all his things back where they belong. When Doña Sofía comes she doesn't see anything wrong. She asks him if he's still planning on having the surgery tomorrow, and when he says yes she doesn't say anything. She just makes the sign of the cross and then goes into her room.

The next day Rubén goes to the hospital. I don't go with him because he doesn't want anyone to go. He's coming back home the day after the surgery because he says staying in the hospital is too expensive. He's hiring a nurse to take care of him at home, even though I told him I could take care of him. "You don't have the stomach for it," he said. "You'll freak out."

I visit him in the evening, when he returns home. The house is full of people. His sister and her husband are there, and so are some of his cousins and aunts and uncles. They're all drinking. Doña Sofía offers me a Tecate but I shake my head no. She's so drunk she almost falls to the floor. Even Rubén is drinking on the couch where he's lying. The nurse tells him again and again he shouldn't be drinking because he's taking medication, but Rubén doesn't listen.

"Hey Rubén, so like, are you going to be able to have children now or what?" one of his cousins ask.

Rubén throws a pillow at him. "It's Ruby now, dude. And no, it isn't like that."

"How are you going to have orgasms now, man?" another cousin asks. "I mean, now that you don't have a—"

Don Pablo yells at them to shut up. He takes another beer and finishes it in three swallows.

I look at Rubén; he's so pale and so sweaty his hair sticks to his face. I glance down there, even though I can't see anything. I feel my face get red and I look away. How can doctors make a penis into a vagina? It's like trying to make a dress using a pattern for a pair of pants. I ask him if he's okay, if it doesn't hurt too much, and he says it's just a small, dull ache.

Doña Sofía puts a Tecate in my hand. She starts to cry and says that yesterday she lost a son.

"But you have a new daughter," one of the cousins says, laughing. This makes Doña Sofía cry even more.

I open the can of beer. I've never drunk before but right now I feel this loneliness pressing in around me, enveloping me like a thick wool blanket. After the first swallow the beer goes down much easier. It tastes like cat pee to me and I wonder why men are so addicted to this drink. After a few swallows I feel like I just drank a ray of sunshine and it's warming me from the inside out. I laugh at the jokes people make even though I don't really understand what they're saying.

When I wake up it's morning already and I realize I fell asleep on the floor. Someone put a blanket over me during the night. Doña Sofía is in the kitchen putting water in a plastic bowl.

"Rubén has a fever," she says. My head hurts so much, and the room feels like it's moving around.

I get up slowly and go inside Rubén's room. His eyes are open wide and he's moaning. I touch his face and my hand pulls back right away. He's as hot as a comal when heating up tortillas.

"Where's the nurse?" I ask Doña Sofía.

"I sent her home last night. I'll take care of my son from now on." Doña Sofía sits next to him and puts a wet cloth on his forehead. I ask him if I should call the doctor but he says no, that he's okay.

"I shouldn't have drunk last night," he says. "Qué estúpida."

I reach for his hand while Doña Sofía drains something Rubén calls a catherer. He says it'll be a while before he can pee the "right way." He says that he needs to get back to work. He has to finish the bridesmaid dresses he was working on before his surgery and now he won't be able to sit down for several days at least. I don't tell him he shouldn't have taken the job so close to the date of his surgery. I know he needs the money as much as I do and it's hard to pass up work. I hold his hand until he falls asleep, and then I go to his garage, and even though I haven't eaten breakfast and my head hurts from too much drinking, I sit at his sewing machine and get to work.

I don't leave Rubén's house until all six dresses are finished. He had already cut the fabric, and all I needed to do was guide the cloth through the machine and sew all the pieces together and watch them become a whole. It felt strange to be sewing something not measured or cut by me. I love cutting cloth. I love the long sweeps the scissors make across the fabric. But I love sewing, too, the power of creating something beautiful. I think of God having this power. I see Him sitting at a sewing machine making humans out of cloth. But I wish when cutting me out of the cloth,

His hand had been sure and steady. You can't hesitate when you're cutting. You can't be afraid or you'll make a mistake. When I look at the mirror sometimes and see the ugly red mark, I wish God's hand hadn't shaken.

I go to Rubén's room to say good-bye. I tell him the dresses are finished now and he shouldn't worry about them anymore.

"Ay, chula," he says. "What would I do without you?"

When I'm walking out of his room he calls me back. He tells me he's high on morphine and he's going to say something to me he'll never say again. I tell him not to say it then, because it'll be the morphine speaking, not him. But he shakes his head and says no, he wants to say it. He has to say it.

"If I'd been born a straight man I would've fallen in love with you, Sol."

I don't say anything to him, but I feel my eyes start to burn with tears, and I don't know if it's the pain or the anger I suddenly feel that's making the tears come.

"Take care, Rubén," I say as I walk out of his room.

"It's Ruby now, Sol. Ruby!"

I know what his new name is but my mouth refuses to say it. It's so hard for my lips to form the word, as if it were one of the many words in English I just can't pronounce, no matter how hard I try.

When I come home I find Ma crying.

"Where have you been?" she yells. "You were gone all night and all morning, and I don't even have a way to reach you!"

"I'm sorry, Ma. I'm sorry I didn't call." I want to tell her about Rubén, but she starts crying again and says Lorenzo called to tell her Abuelita Licha is very sick. She got bitten by a scorpion, he said. She didn't tell anybody. She felt okay for two days, then she started to feel sick. She's too old to fight the venom. The doctor said she might not get better.

I think about my grandmother. She took me to church, taught me to pray. Now I pray for God to cure her.

Ma calls Lorenzo. We have to wait because the owner of the store where we call has to send someone to the house to tell Lorenzo he has a call. It's hard to hear what Ma tells him, she's crying so hard. She hangs up before I can tell her to let me speak to him. She says, "She's getting worse. I need to go buy a plane ticket to México, Soledad. I need to see my mother."

"But Valentina," Tomás says, "we don't have money to pay for a ticket. Where will we get it?"

"I don't care. Call your sisters. Call the neighbors, anybody. Ask them to let us borrow some money. I need to go see my mother."

Stephanie sits on the steps listening to music on her headphones. She doesn't care much for Abuelita Licha. She doesn't know her. She's never been to México.

Ma cries more. I don't like to see her cry. Tomás goes inside and calls his sisters. They sell tamales and don't make much money. They don't have papers, either. Tears rush to my eyes. My grandmother is dying.

I know what I need to do. That money was meant for my dress shop, and a part of me doesn't want to do what I'm about to do . . . all those years of saving. I hold Ma's hand and say to her that everything will be okay soon. "I have some money, Ma. I'll pay for your ticket."

"Money? Where did you get this money, Soledad?"

"I saved it."

Ma makes the sign of the cross and says, "Thank you, God."

I go inside and get my box. Maybe I don't need to spend too much.

The tickets are expensive because it is an emergency.

"We'll take two tickets," I say to the lady at the travel agency.

Ma asks, "For me and Stephanie?"

"No, for you and me," I say.

"But Soledad, you don't have papers. You can't go."

Ma looks at Tomás. "Think about it, Soledad," he says. "We'll need to find a coyote for you to get back, and that's going to be expensive and dangerous."

"Two tickets for me and my daughter Stephanie," Ma tells the lady.

"But Ma, school is about to start and she shouldn't miss it. We'll be gone for a long time and she will miss too much."

"She's her grandmother, too," Ma says. "She needs to go see her. And besides, she's a U.S. citizen and doesn't have a problem coming back. But you—you need to stay."

"I don't want to go," Stephanie says. "México is dirty and full of thieves. My teacher told us that kidnappings in México are on the rise. What if I get kidnapped or something when people realize I'm from the U.S.?"

"No, you must go," Ma says. "She's my mother—your grand-mother—you need to see her at least once. You must go."

"But I don't want to go. I don't even know those people. I don't even know that lady."

"Two tickets," Ma says.

"Three," I say.

"Soledad—"

"Three." I throw the money on the counter. Some dollar bills fall to the floor. "Three," I say again. The lady punches the key-board of her computer, and very soon the printer starts to print our tickets.

My tears roll down my cheeks, and I listen to the beeping sounds the printer makes. What if I can't come back?

"Ay, Dios mío, Dios mío," Ma says.

We leave the agency with two round-trip tickets and one one-way ticket, for me. I don't feel good. I start to feel hungry, very hungry. I say bye to them and walk to El Pollo Loco down

Soto Street. I need to be alone. I need to cry alone, for my grandmother, for my $1,700 I don't have anymore, for the journey across the border I'll have to make to come back.

The next day we go to México. Tomás takes us to the airport. He helps to take out our suitcases, then hugs Ma and Stephanie good-bye. He turns to look at me. He's never hugged me before, but now he pulls me against his chest. I close my eyes and pretend he's my real father.

"It's not too late to change your mind, Soledad," he says.

"It'll be okay," I tell him, but when we're sitting in the airplane, and I hear the doors closing, I feel like running out of there. The plane starts to move slowly. Ma looks at me, but she doesn't say anything. Stephanie listens to her headphones, but she looks at me, too. For a moment I feel jealous of Stephanie. I touch the ticket stub in my sweater pocket, and I feel angry about the injustice of it. It's not my fault I wasn't born here.

I don't like to fly. I'm scared the plane could crash or be taken over by terrorists and I'd die. I feel sick most of the time. I go to the bathroom to vomit. Ma has a rosary out and is praying. She doesn't pray much since she came to America. She says America took her religion away. She's too worried about money to survive in this country. She doesn't have time to pray. Now she prays for Abuelita Licha. I close my eyes and pray, too.

Stephanie looks outside the window at the clouds and the blue sky. She says when she gets her money, she'll buy a plane and fly all over the world. She likes flying, she says. But she doesn't thank me for buying her ticket. Ma doesn't thank me, either.

When we get to México City we take a bus to my town. Soon it's too dark to see anything, but I keep my eyes open and look out the window. We get to my town in four long hours. Everything is dark and quiet. Across from the bus station there's El Mercado, the big marketplace in town. All the booths are closed now, but in the morning I know everything is busy with many people coming to buy food. We catch a taxi and go to the colonia where my grandmother lives. My brother, Lorenzo, lives with her with his wife and four children. I told him not to have too many children. He can't provide for them. But he didn't listen to his big sister.

We pass over the bridge. Under the bridge there's a river, but now I'm surprised how smelly it is, like rotten water. When I was little the river had a lot of water. I would come to swim in this river. Lorenzo would come to fish. I hold my breath as we drive over the bridge. The train station is up ahead. It's abandoned now. Lorenzo said the government took away the train many years ago. People don't have work. Lorenzo doesn't have steady work. He used to work at the train station loading and unloading the freight trains. Now he works in the fields and whatever else he can find.

The night is so quiet. I remember the sound of the train at night when it passed by our house. Now all that's left is an abandoned train car rusting on the tracks.

My grandmother lives in front of the train tracks. I pay the taxi driver and get the suitcases. Ma knocks on the metal door. Lorenzo opens it. He looks different. I haven't seen him for thirteen years. He's too skinny and has a beard and long dirty hair that needs a haircut. He isn't wearing a shirt. He wears old pants with a rope tied around his waist as a belt. When he hugs me, I feel so fat as I feel his rib bones poking me.

"How's my mother?" Ma asks. She doesn't introduce Stephanie; she doesn't remember Lorenzo has never met Stephanie before. He offers her his hand but Stephanie doesn't want to shake his hand. She hides behind Ma instead.

"He's your brother," I say to her. I push her forward, but she holds on to Ma and doesn't move.

Lorenzo puts his hand down and looks at Ma. His eyes are red from crying.

"She's gone," he says.

Ma runs inside the house. Lorenzo helps with the suitcases. I feel something tight in my chest, and it hurts to breathe. I came back without papers and I didn't even get to say good-bye.

We go into the living room. I see the coffin there surrounded by candles and flowers called cempasúchil, big yellow marigolds.

Ma hugs her mother and cries and cries. Abuelita Licha looks so calm and peaceful. She changed so much from when I saw her last. Now her gray hair is completely white, and her face is full of wrinkles, like brown silk crêpe georgette. I sit on the couch and cry, not believing she's really dead.

"When did it happen?" I ask him.

"She died at six twenty-two," he says. At 6:22 we were on the bus.

"But I don't understand how she could have died," I say. I remember the three times I got bitten by a scorpion. I had nausea, headaches, vomiting. But I didn't die. "You should've taken her to the doctor right away."

"I didn't know. She didn't tell anyone she got bitten. She just asked for a raw egg and some onion and she didn't tell us. She didn't." Lorenzo leans against the wall and covers his face. Abuelita Licha believed if you eat a raw egg and rub onion on the bite, the poison won't harm you.

"You should've known," I tell him. Ma goes to him and hugs him. I let myself fall down on the sofa. Stephanie sits next to me and puts her head on my lap. She's tired, she says. She wants to sleep. I tell her to close her eyes. She doesn't want to look at our grandmother, she says. She's scared. "I can't believe you have a dead person in the living room. Aren't there any mortuaries?"

"México is different," I tell her. "People here aren't afraid of the dead. It's okay to have a dead person in your house so you can pray and say good-bye."

Stephanie closes her eyes and goes to sleep. I play with her hair. It's soft, like satin cloth, like a Jalisco rebozo. My little sister. She looks innocent, like Abuelita Licha. They have the same lips, the same eyebrows, the same nose. Ma was right in bringing her along. It isn't right Stephanie didn't have a chance to see her grandmother. It's sad she doesn't care for México. She has raíces here. Roots. This place is where her mother, her grandmother, her great-grandmother were born. This is where Folklórico is from. But Stephanie doesn't care. Her home is America. Her language is English. I like America, too, but I don't forget my country. I don't forget where I come from.

Ma refuses to be the one to change Abuelita Licha into her burial dress. She's scared she says. I tell her she's her daughter. Her only daughter. And it's her duty to do so, but Ma shakes her head like a chicken and says no, no, no. She makes the sign of the cross and walks away.

I ask Malena, Lorenzo's wife, for the dress, and she helps me to change my grandmother. I ask Abuelita for permission first. I tell her that I don't mean any disrespect by taking off her dress. Her skin feels like rubber. It's cold, and she's stiff and heavy to pick up. Malena and I struggle to lift her to remove the old dress and put on the new one. My grandmother. Only her hair feels the same to me. Soft, like rayon yarn for making the fringe on fancy scarves.

"She never wanted to talk to me on the phone," I say to Malena while I braid Abuelita's hair.

"She was afraid of phones, Soledad, don't take it personally. But Lorenzo always told her everything going on with you on the other side. She knew everything about you. She cared about you and loved you very much."

She puts a hand on my shoulder and leaves me alone with my grandmother. I put one stiff hand over the other and tie them with a ribbon. Then I wrap a rosary around her hands as if she's praying. This is how I remember my grandmother. Her praying hands, her gap-toothed smile, the scent of almond oil. On her right hand I search for the place where the scorpion bit her, but I can't see anything but wrinkles.

"I'm sorry," I say to her. I bend down and kiss my grandmother on her cheek for the last time, remembering her laughter, her kindness, the hours we spent sewing together, the sound of her voice. I think of her taking me out for walks along the river, to the cornfields, the meadow, pointing out the colors Mother Nature uses. "She has a great eye for color, Sol. Look to Her for inspiration. She makes a seamstress's job easier."

I think about the Jalisco dresses I designed using the colors of the monarch butterflies. I think about the Lester Horton Award I got two years ago for best costume design.

That award was Abuelita's as much as it was mine. But she never got to see it. And now she never will.

CHAPTER FIVE

Funny how I adore all those lovely "pretty things" called dancers, whose bodies and faces are sculpted and graceful, but the fact that I am such a creature means nothing to me.
—TONI BENTLEY

You rush down the street holding tight to your gym bag, a stabbing pain on your right side, your calves beginning to burn. As you get closer to the dance studio, the sound of drumbeats gets louder.

Sweating and panting, you run even faster. You stop short outside the dance studio to catch your breath. When you open the glass doors, you're surprised to see only one person dancing. A man you've never seen before. The other dancers are sitting around in a semicircle watching him.

You take small breaths to steady your heart as you lean against the barre and watch the stranger dance. For a moment you forget to breathe, drooling over the rippling muscles of his bare chest and back, his glistening brown skin, his black shoulder-length hair, and his face—the hard, calculating face of a man who's never afraid. You shiver. He dances as if he's dancing in a forest under the light of the moon, with no one to watch him but the stars shining above him and the wild animals creeping nearby. A real Aztec warrior.

You close your eyes, your heart pounding inside your chest, as if you were the one dancing. You know exactly how he feels. You know that the sound of Eduardo's tambor is speaking to his heart, his spirit, the way it speaks to yours. You know that at this very moment he feels pure, godly. He's in the place where nothing else matters but him and this moment, this music that mimics the rhythm of his beating heart. This music and dance that take you to another realm of being: the connection between the earth and the sky.

As the drumbeats quicken, you know his muscles contract and release, contract and release, faster, faster, the air whipping across his face as he turns in place. The danza ends with one last bang of the drum. The dancer is down on his knees, his chest heaving, his lips pressed together. His eyes look straight ahead, in your direction, but you know he doesn't see you at all. You clutch the barre with both hands. You don't know if it's because of all the running you just did, but you feel all your energy drain out of you and at the same time you're overwhelmed by the desire to be noticed by him, to be seen by him.

Everyone claps as he stands up. The dancers begin to get up from the floor and form the usual lines in front of the mirrors, as if nothing has happened. But you can't take your eyes off him.

*During break, you ask Eduardo to pair you up with the new
dancer when practicing Guerrero. But he pairs him up with Laura,
instead.*

*"Keep away from Emilio, mi'ja," he says to you with that con-
cerned fatherly voice of his. "He's not for you."*

*Por favor. Eduardo says that about all the guys in the group.
You take one last yearning look at Emilio and turn to go in search
of José. You don't care about his small dick. You just don't want to
be alone tonight.*

Adriana

Ben and I started watching movies together the night Manuel left
my sorry ass hanging. He was supposed to take me out dancing at
El Rodeo Night Club but didn't show up. He decided to go drinking with his buddies instead. I was so bored that night. I played
my guitar for a little bit, but I was in no mood to sing those heart-
wrenching songs I like to sing. They reminded me too much of
Mom. I tried to watch videos of Alegría's past performances, but
that just made me feel even lonelier. I tried to watch the Mexican
soap operas on Channel 34 to distract me, but if you aren't in the
right frame of mind you realize how pathetic the story lines are.
And all the female leads ever do is cry for their impossible loves.
Pleeease.

I went downstairs to see if Ben was home and found him
watching some weird Asian film with English subtitles. There
were daggers and people flying all over the place. I mean, c'mon,
people can't fly like that, even Asian martial artists.

"Why can't you be normal?" I asked him. I've never known
anyone who watches Asian films, or any foreign films for that matter. Well, maybe Elena. "No wonder you don't have a social life."

"Sit," he said.

And so I did, and this is how I found out that Ben has good taste in films, actually.

I grab my bottle of Tapatío sauce and head down to Ben's dressed in my pajama bottoms and a tank top because when the movie is over I crash into bed. Mine, not his.

As soon as I open the door (he leaves it unlocked for me), I can smell Ben has already made popcorn. I grab the bowl and start pouring Tapatío sauce on the popcorn.

Ben presses Play and grabs a handful of popcorn smothered in sauce. In the time I've known him I've gotten him to eat chile. None of that bland white-boy Taco Bell crap, I'm talking the real stuff. I've tried teaching him to dance, but he looks silly dancing.

Tonight's movie is an Italian film called *Malena*. The film makes me stop wishing I was beautiful and had a sexy body. How cruel people can be to a beautiful woman, I swear. For once, I'm okay with my lonjitas and my flabby tummy. But it does make me wonder if Ben chose this film because I was whining about the way I look a few days ago.

"I'm ugly," I told him. "I wish I was beautiful."

He didn't say anything then, and I suppose this film is his way of saying I'm not ugly or that I shouldn't wish to be beautiful, without actually having to say it. I curl up on the couch and try to forget it's September. I'll be turning twenty-five in two weeks, but that's not the reason why I don't want to think about September.

September is the month Mom died.

When the movie is over we sit in silence munching on the last of the popcorn. I look at Ben's hair; the light of the lamp streaks his blond hair with gold. He has a receding hairline, even though he's only thirty. But his big forehead makes him look wise, and the lines etched around his eyes make him look as if he's had a tough life. But Ben's childhood, as far as I know, was easy. Living a simple life in the woods, being babied by his eight older siblings and his loving old parents.

I suck my fingers clean of Tapatío sauce and get up to leave. "Thanks for the movie," I say. "It made me feel better."

"Good," he says. "Hey, do you want to go swimming tomorrow?"

I laugh. Won't he give it up? He's got it in his head I need to learn to swim. Everyone should know, he says, in case of an emergency. I wouldn't be surprised if the next movie is *Jaws*, or something like it.

"I don't have a bathing suit," I tell him for the hundredth time. "And I'm terrified of drowning."

He smiles like he already knew what I was going to say. "Have a good night, Adriana," he says as he gets up to walk me to the door. He unlocks the door and holds it open for me. I feel the chill of the September night on my bare shoulders. I shiver. I look at him and close the door shut.

"I don't want to go home tonight," I tell him.

He looks at me for a long time, as if trying to figure out what I'm really saying. Finally, he nods and says, "You don't have to. You can stay here." I grab his hand and he leads me to his bedroom. He pulls the blanket back and tucks me in. I look at all the canvases neatly piled up on top of a table. The canvas on the easel is a half-finished painting of a young girl looking out a window. It's as if she's leaning the weight of her sorrow on the elbow resting on the windowsill. She has a faraway look, as if wishing she were somewhere else.

"Who's that?" I ask.

"She's my older sister, but in the painting she's still a teenager."

"You've made her look like she's about to crack into a million pieces. Is that really how she looked?"

Ben stays quiet for a long time. He doesn't answer my question. Instead, he walks to his closet and takes out a blanket before heading to the door and turning off the lights.

"Good night, Adriana."

"Ben?"

"Yeah?"

"Come here."

I hear him take a deep breath, and for a moment I think he won't come. But moments later I feel the bed lean under his weight. "It's September," I tell him, feeling a tightness in my stomach, the memory of my mother like a clenched fist that won't let go.

"It'll soon pass," he says. I turn on my side to look at him. He runs his fingers through my hair. He traces the moth tattoo on my shoulder. In all these months I've known him I've never told him why I have that tattoo. Tonight, because it's now September, I would like to tell him, but the words just don't want to come out.

Instead, I close my eyes, feeling the darkness press around me. *Keep me safe from the darkness, Ben. Touch me the way I know you would touch me—with too much tenderness. I need that tonight.*

"Good night, Ben," I force myself to say. I turn to face the wall, and a few seconds later I hear him leave the room, closing the door behind him. *What the fuck are you thinking?* The other Adriana asks me. *The guy is too damn nice. Now Alegría's new dancer—Emilio—he's the kind of guy a gal like you needs.*

Because next week is my birthday, I have the guts to knock on the door this time. My grandmother opens the door and right away I feel like a stupid fourteen-year-old, scared shitless. She does this to me.

"What do you want?" she asks in Spanish.

"I want to see my father." I try to stand up straighter.

"He doesn't want to see you. Now go." She tries to close the door, but I'm a young woman and she's an old vieja. I push the door open and yell my father's name.

He comes to the living room, holding his twelve-string guitar. "What are you doing here?" he asks.

My mouth feels like it's stuffed with a rebozo. I can't speak. I look at my grandmother. She's holding the door, one hand on her waist, ready to shut me out. Talk, Adriana, talk.

"I—um. It's my birthday next week, and I was wondering if we could go out to dinner together."

He walks over to me. I can smell the alcohol on his breath. I look at him and see the anger in his eyes, the wrinkles that weren't there before, the gray hairs on the temples. I look down at the guitar, that special twelve-string guitar I always imagined would be my inheritance. A Rickenbacker, the most expensive thing Dad has ever owned. He wouldn't even let me come near it. He taught me to play using an ordinary six-string he bought for me at El Mercadito. Sometimes I loved that Rickenbacker and wanted it so badly it hurt. Other times I hated it and wanted to break it into pieces; didn't it receive all my father's most gentle, loving caresses and leave none for me?

"Don't look for him anymore, do you understand?" my grandmother says. "He doesn't want to see you. You and that sister of yours aren't his problem. Get out of here."

"It's okay, Mom. Let her come in." Dad opens the door wider for me, and my grandmother turns on her heel and leaves. He offers me a beer and I take it, hoping it'll help me relax, but my hands are trembling. I can't believe he let me come in.

Don't fuck this up, Adriana. Don't fuck this up . . .

"So, how old are you going to be now, twenty-two?" he says as he sits on the couch.

"Twenty-five," I say, taking a big swallow of beer.

"Goddamn, I'm getting old."

"You look good, Dad. You look really good."

He shrugs and picks up his guitar. He starts to play "Solamente Una Vez." I close my eyes, listening to my father sing. "Solamente una vez, amé en la vida. Solamente una vez, y nada más . . ." When was the last time I heard his beautiful voice? Too long ago. Halfway through the song, I get the courage to start singing with him. This is the only thing I inherited from my father. His singing voice. When the song is over he immediately goes on to the next song, one of my favorites. "Reloj no marques las horas, porque voy a enloquecer. Ella se irá para siempre, cuando amanezca otra vez . . ."

Grandma comes into the living room and scowls seeing me still here. She asks my dad to come to the kitchen to help her with something.

"In a minute," Dad says, and we keep singing.

"The water's about to boil and I need the rice right now," she says.

Dad stops playing abruptly and puts his guitar on the couch before disappearing into the kitchen. I reach across the coffee table and pick up his guitar. I strum a few chords, hoping that when he comes back we can keep singing, with me playing this time. I can show him how good I've gotten. But when he comes back I know there will be no more singing. The moment is gone.

"Listen, it's getting late and I have some things I need to do," he says.

"So, do you think we could go to La Perla on my birthday?" I say. Too late, I realize that La Perla was my mother's favorite place to go. I bite my damn tongue. Stupid, stupid, stupid. "It doesn't have to be at La Perla. We can go anywhere you want."

He shakes his head. "I gotta work."

"Couldn't you ask for the day off?"

"No, I can't. I don't want to jeopardize my job after all the trouble I had getting it." He looks at me and points his empty beer bottle at me. "Do you have any idea how hard it is to find work when you have a criminal record?" I shake my head; my body becomes tense again. *Shit. No, please, don't . . .* He reaches across the coffee table and yanks his guitar from me. I recognize the look in his face, the way his left eye twitches when he's pissed.

He grabs my arm and yanks me to my feet. He pushes me out the door and slams it in my face. I stand there and look at the wooden door in front of me for a few seconds. When the thunder hits the sky, I bounce off the porch and run out to the street.

Sin madre, sin padre, sin perro que me ladre.

This Mexican saying was created just for me, I swear it. Without a mother, without a father, without a fucking dog to bark at me. I rush down Avenue 50, rubbing my watery eyes so I can see where the fuck I'm going. By the time I get to the bus stop on Figueroa, it's pouring. I stand there and shiver in the rain, in the darkness, in my solitude.

Goddammit, why can't he forgive me? I'm his daughter.

The headlights blind me for a second. The beams shine on the raindrops. I watch them fall in front of me.

"Wanna ride?"

I look at the man waving at me from the car. I don't know how many of them there are. It's too dark to see. I wrap my wet sweater tighter around me.

"¿Sí o no?"

I look up the street. There is no sign of a bus. At this hour of the night, who knows if and when it'll come.

"¿Cómo te llamas?" the man in the driver's seat asks me as soon as I take a seat in the back with one of his buddies.

"Jennifer," I lie.

"Where do you want us to drop you off?" he asks in Spanish. The red light turns green. He pushes the gas pedal and the car lunges forward.

"Drop me off on the corner of Fourth Street and Mott, please," I say in Spanish. These guys don't speak any English. There are empty Budweiser cans on the floor and the car stinks of weed. The man sitting next to me looks to be in his late twenties. He's clean shaven but his hair is shaggy and badly needs a cut.

"I'm José," he says. I roll my eyes. The world is full of too many Josés.

"I'm Uvaldo," the driver says, then he points to the man next to him in the passenger seat, "and this here is Artemio."

I turn to look at the street in front of us. The rain is coming down harder now, and the wipers swish up and down trying to clear the windshield but failing. I put my cold hands in front of the back heater vent to warm them. My clothes are soaking wet, even my damn underwear.

Uvaldo takes a joint from his pocket and hands it to me to light it for him. I wonder why he didn't give it to Artemio or José. When I hand it back he refuses and tells me to take a few hits. The other Adriana tells me I shouldn't. She says I promised I wasn't going to do that shit anymore, and I've been good. But there's a pain in my chest I need to numb, and there are thoughts in my head I want to forget. I lean back in the seat and do what Uvaldo told me to do.

Artemio turns on the stereo, and Chalino Sánchez fills the silence with "Nieves de Enero."

"You like Chalino Sánchez?" he asks.

"Yeah." I think back on my high school years and remember how most of the ESL kids I hung out with were crazy about Chalino Sánchez, though the guy had been killed years before. I remember Héctor. That motherfucker took my virginity in the storage room under the bleachers and then never looked at me twice. The asshole loved Chalino Sánchez.

I feel warm all over. The heaviness I felt in my chest eases up, and now I can breathe. I feel as weightless as the smoke coming out of my mouth. "So where are you guys coming from?" I ask. They're all wearing tight jeans, cowboy boots, and long-sleeve shirts. I can see the brims of their Tejanas by José's feet.

"From a friend's house."

"Do you like to dance?" Artemio asks.

"Yeah," I say. "I'm a professional dancer." It's true. I mean Eduardo only pays us once in a while—and only a measly thirty or fifty dollars, if that—but that still puts me in the category of being a paid dancer, a professional dancer, right?

"Chale," Uvaldo says. "So do you strip dance?"

I laugh. "No, tonto, I dance Folklórico."

"That's too bad," José says. "I would've liked to see you strip for me."

The guys laugh. The car exits the freeway and makes a left turn. We're almost home. I hand the last of the joint to José, who quickly puts it to his mouth.

"So, you got a boyfriend, Jennifer?" José asks.

I try to sit up to look at him, but I don't have the strength to do it. "Why do you want to know?"

"I'm a curious guy."

"And what else are you curious about?"

"I'm curious to know how it would feel like to have your legs wrapped around me," he says.

The guys burst out laughing. "Chale, José, you don't waste any time with the ladies, do you?" Artemio asks.

We're now at the intersection of Fourth and Soto. The clock in the car reads 9:33. I tell Uvaldo to pull over as soon as he passes Roosevelt High School. I look outside. My apartment is right across the street. All the lights are out in Ben's apartment, like I knew they would be. He's coming back tomorrow from some artist retreat in Santa Fe. I sigh, feeling disappointed. Artemio opens the door and gets out of the car to let me out. The rain has now turned into a drizzle.

"I need to piss," he says.

I get out of the car and thank them for the ride.

"Hey, how about letting us use your bathroom?" José asks. "I really need to piss, too."

Even though my brain is numb with all that crap I just smoked, I'm aware of what they're really asking for. I look back at Ben's dark, empty apartment. There's no one there to talk to. "Okay." I sigh. They cross the street with me and follow behind me, drooling like dogs after a bitch in heat. My apartment is freezing, and it smells of rotten food. I've forgotten to take out the trash for a few days now. I light the candles and an incense stick while they take off their leather jackets and hats. Then they take turns using my bathroom. Fuck, I hope it's not too dirty.

"Do you have something to drink?" Artemio asks while he walks around my living room looking at my Frida Kahlo prints.

"Who's the ugly bitch?" José asks as he points at the frames.

"Frida Kahlo," I say.

"Oh," they say, but I know they don't have a clue.

"You know, I think she looks like Salma Hayek," Uvaldo says. "I remember seeing a picture of Salma dressed like this Frida woman." Uvaldo is messing around with my guitar. He puts it down carelessly on the end table, and my guitar topples down to the floor. Cabrón.

"You really have the hots for her," José says as he parts my Frida bamboo curtain and goes into my kitchen. "Mira la Jennifer, she has some good stuff," he says when he comes back. He holds my bottles of tequila and vodka I keep on top of the refrigerator. José hands everyone a shot glass and they all toast to me. Artemio turns on the stereo and starts dancing to Shakira. The guys start hooting and throwing coins at him. My apartment feels like a closet.

"What's wrong?" Uvaldo asks me. "You look sad."

I feel tears welling in my eyes. Damn alcohol. It's getting to me. "Nothing."

"Nah, you have a broken heart," Uvaldo says. "I recognize the symptoms."

"Yeah, you should," Artemio says, "all your girlfriends dump your sorry ass in a day or two."

"We'll make you happy, corazón," José says as he runs his hand over my arm. It is rough. It reminds me of my father's hands.

"Why don't we get going, guys?" Uvaldo says. He looks at me with tenderness, and I can almost see Ben in him.

"Nah. We can't leave her alone," José says. "Dance for us, Jennifer," he says as he pulls me up to my feet. I shake my head. I don't want to dance. José hands me his shot glass and I down its contents in a big gulp.

"Come on, Jennifer, dance for us." Artemio urges me on. Uvaldo stands by the door, as if he doesn't know what the fuck to do. Then the hombre in him takes over. He goes to clear the coffee table and puts the candles on the floor. Artemio pumps up the volume, and I let Shakira's voice take me out of myself. I see the way they look at me, see the hunger in their eyes.

The other Adriana tells me I shouldn't do this. I don't need to stoop this low. *Have some pride*, she tells me. *Don't do it. Don't do it.* I get up on the coffee table and begin to dance. My clothes come off one piece at a time. I see Uvaldo lick his lips. José puts his hand over his hardening dick. Artemio's nostrils are flaring, his chest heaving. I see their eyes, their unblinking eyes filled with lust, with want.

I let them hypnotize me.

Elena

After several days of serious heat, the rain arrives unexpectedly on my second week back in school. The students barge into the classroom soaking wet because they refuse to wear jackets or carry umbrellas. Their wet shoes squeak as they cover the linoleum floor with muddy streaks. They sit in their chairs shivering with cold, water dripping from their clothes. I take a deep breath and then exhale slowly, knowing that today will be a very long day.

I point at the screen.

"Remember, each paragraph needs to begin with a topic sentence." I look at them for a signal of understanding, for a hint that they're here with me, but their seventeen-year-old minds are somewhere else. One is doodling in his notebook. Another looks out the window, another twirls her hair around her finger, another giggles behind cupped hands, another passes a note to the girl behind him and pretends I didn't notice.

My fingers automatically reach up to touch the olive green silk scarf I tied around my neck this morning. My index finger twists the fabric around and around. I take a deep breath, trying to ignore the painful pounding in my right temple. I step behind the projector so that the light blinds me, and I hide in that blindness, not wishing to see the faces of the students who are completely ignoring the lesson.

I hold on to my scarf, grateful to have something to cling to. The door opens and a young man walks into the room ten minutes late. He walks over to me and hands me a registration slip. He stands too close to me, his eyes looking at me too intimately. I try to stand up straight, attempting to appear taller than five feet four. He towers above me, a good six feet tall. He looks me up and down and says, "So, you got a boyfriend?"

The students erupt with laughter.

"Please take a seat, young man," I say as I point to an empty desk by the window. I take off my glasses. The throbbing in my temple worsens. I turn off the overhead projector, write three topics on the board, and ask them to choose one and begin a draft. My voice resonates on the walls but falls on deaf ears.

Right now is our busiest time of the year. There are lesson plans to be prepared, classroom decorations to be put up, student schedules to be adjusted, parents to be contacted, and assignments to be corrected. There are many reasons to justify my presence in my classroom at five in the afternoon, when the janitor comes to clean the room and get it ready for the night school teachers.

But there's only one reason why I linger, why I'm afraid to go home.

It is September.

As I turn the corner onto Florence I see a group of students huddled at the bus stop. It's drizzling right now, but the dark clouds seem to be threatening us again. From the corner of my eye I spy a red bandanna on someone's head, and I turn to look at the young man who is doing a zapateo. I pull over and honk, smiling. There is only one young man in the school who would be practicing his dance steps at the bus stop. Fernando recognizes my truck and walks toward me. I see the other kids looking at me. Some of them recognize me. Teachers must not allow students in their cars, the union rep often warns us.

I lower the window. "Get in," I say, "I'll take you home."

He shivers in response. He's wearing a sweater that's too thin to keep him warm or dry. I turn the heater a notch higher as he settles himself in the passenger seat. He takes the bandanna off his head and smiles at me. "Thanks," he says. "I just missed the bus."

"Did you just get out of practice?" I ask. He nods as he puts his hands up to the heater to warm them. We don't say anything for a while. The traffic on Florence is worse than on non-rainy days, and on those days it's pretty bad.

"Are you okay, Miss?"

I know he's been watching me from his peripheral vision. "What do you mean?"

"I don't know. You look kind of down."

"Tough day."

"Yeah, I'm sure it was."

I turn to look at him. "Oh yeah, how would you know?" I smile. Why is it that he always tries to sound so grown up?

"The students were really out of control today. They thought it was funny to make squeaking noises with their shoes, interrupting the teachers' lessons. Some of the girls even walked around the classroom hitting us with their wet hair! And there was a food fight during nutrition *and* lunch. And there were a lot of kids standing out in the rain, jumping on the puddles and splashing water."

"Well, let's hope it doesn't rain tomorrow."

Fernando smiles. "Ah, it's supposed to rain all week."

"But it's September. It's not supposed to be raining yet!"

He puts his hand on my shoulder and says, "Don't be afraid of the rain, Miss."

My teeth clench. I feel a shiver go up and down my spine, and I blame it on the cold, on the rain, but when I turn to look at him and see the way his eyes look at me, I know it isn't either of those things.

I park in front of his house. The rain beats down on the truck and the sound reminds me of Eduardo playing his drum. I'm suddenly nostalgic for Alegría.

As if he can read my thoughts, Fernando says, "The raindrops sound like an Aztec danza."

I smile.

"I really liked Alegría's performance at the Ford," he says. "It just blew me away. All the costumes were so beautiful, and the dancers were so good. I don't think I could ever dance like them."

"Of course you can. It just takes practice and having a good teacher."

"Yeah, I guess. It's just that . . ." He stops and blushes.

"What?"

"I wish I could join Alegría, but El Sereno is far from Huntington Park, and my mom doesn't have a car."

"I understand. Maybe we can find a way to get you there."

He smiles and leans back on the seat. "What's your favorite region, Miss?"

"I don't have one. Each region has its own unique dance style, music, and costume. I like them all."

"But there has to be one, above all others, that you like best," Fernando insists.

"All right," I say. "Then I will choose Veracruz. I love sones jarochos."

"Why, Miss?"

"Because they're unique. The music and dance of Veracruz is a mix of Spanish, Indigenous, and African cultures. Besides,"

I say with a smile, "the beautiful jarocha dress and the intricate footwork has no equal." Talking to Fernando makes me realize how much I miss teaching Folklórico. Teaching dance isn't just about teaching a sequence of steps and choreography, it's also about exposing students to history, to their roots.

"My mother says she's glad I have a pastime to keep me out of trouble, but I don't think of Folklórico as a pastime, Miss."

"You're right, Fernando. Folklórico is not a hobby—at least for the true dancer it isn't. It's a big part of our lives, it defines who we are to a certain extent. It's something that requires sacrifices. It's about performing the dance with passion, love, and a great respect toward our culture."

"You know, Miss, when I was up onstage at the Cinco de Mayo performance at school, tons of emotions were running through me as I danced. It was almost as if all the emotions that I have in my heart were pouring out on the stage for everyone to see. It scared me a little."

I nod to let him know I know what he means and that I want to hear more.

"I wish I had learned to dance a long time ago. I feel so desperate to make up for all those years. I get so frustrated sometimes with myself for not learning the steps Mrs. Rodríguez teaches us fast enough."

"It takes years to learn to dance well, Fernando. Enjoy the process and remember that one accomplishment leads to another."

We say our good-byes and he waves at me from the sidewalk and waits until I drive away before going inside his house. My face is flushed, and my heart beats hard against my chest. I watch him get smaller in the rearview mirror, and I feel sorry that I have to leave, because I would rather stay and talk about Folklórico. I realize how different it was with Richard, who, no matter how he tried, could never really understand my passion for dancing. The loneliness of my house suddenly reaches out to me. Instead of turning on Central Avenue, I keep on going down Florence, then catch the 110 freeway and head to the cemetery to visit my daughter and mother, wondering if they, like me, feel just as lonely.

Yesenia

Even though I'm eating, my stomach is growling with hunger. A deep, desperate hunger intensified by the fact that I'm on a diet. I've put on twelve pounds since I stopped dancing. Twelve pounds. Most of the weight has gone straight to my stomach, making me look as if I were four months pregnant. So now I can't have anything on the menu except this nasty salad with no dressing on it. I shouldn't even call it a salad. It's just lettuce and lemon juice sprinkled over it. I put some in my mouth, force myself to chew it, to pretend that I'm eating a nice thick steak with mashed potatoes and gravy. It doesn't work.

I should've just stayed home and made myself dinner. But the house is so lonely now, with Memo gone and Eduardo being busy with work and Alegría's performances this month. They have at least fifteen shows this month because of Mexican Independence and Hispanic Heritage celebrations. I've hardly seen him at all this week. And when I do see him all he does is talk about the shows and how everyone had a great time; I just want to scream and tell him I don't want to hear it, but I don't say anything because I realize now that if we don't talk about Alegría or Memo, there's hardly anything for us to talk about.

To distract myself from the nasty salad I start flipping through a copy of *La Opinión* somebody left on the table. I flip through the pages of the newspaper, and I stop short at an advertisement for a clinic in Tijuana that specializes in liposuction, breast augmentation, face-lifts, and tummy tucks. I stare at it for a while, and all of a sudden I feel as if a burden has been lifted off me. Yes, this is the answer, right here in front of me! If the doctor said my weight put too much pressure on my knee joint, then surely if I got rid of all the fat on my body I might be able to heal and continue dancing. I think about the horrible stories I've heard about these kinds of surgeries, but right now, I'd do anything, anything, to be back onstage.

I stand up feeling elated, and right here and now I decide to abandon my diet. With one swoop I pick up the salad and throw it into the trash, and with determined steps I walk back to the counter and order a plate of nachos with lots of cheese and meat on top. When it arrives I sit back at the table, and right before putting a nacho loaded with melted cheese into my mouth, I tell myself that whatever weight I gain from this meal will be taken out very, very soon. Delicious.

During my lunch hour I call the clinic in Tijuana and make an appointment for a consultation in two weeks. When I hang up I make my way back to the AAA office, telling myself I made the right decision. How could I not have thought of it before? Instead I wasted my time and energy on stupid diets that didn't work! There's still hope for me.

After work, I'm in good spirits. Just the thought of getting rid of the fat on my body helps me deal with the fact that right now I would've been driving down Soto Street to El Sereno for Wednesday night practice. But not anymore. For now, at least. Not wanting to spend the evening at home alone, I drive to El Paseo Mall, despite the traffic, and waste my time looking at clothes and getting my nails done. I end up letting the salesgirl at the makeup counter at Macy's talk me into buying all kinds of things, like concealer and highlighter, a complete set of cleansing products to help my skin fight wrinkles, and some kind of mask—things I've never really used. I also buy two pairs of Carlos Santana stilettos because once my knee gets better I can go back to wearing heels.

When I get home I soak in a hot bath, drink a glass of champagne, and flip through my old high school yearbook. I stare at the glossy pictures of myself when I was young and carefree. And then I see him—Sam González with his hand stuck inside a soda machine. I remember that day so clearly. It was class time, and I shouldn't have been buying a soda, but on my way back from the restroom I thought it was a good idea to get it now because once lunchtime began the line would be endless. The machine took my money but the soda didn't come out. When I saw him standing next to me I stopped kicking and began to walk away.

"Don't you want your soda?" he asked.

I shrugged. "Ah, forget it. It just took my money."

He got down on the floor.

"What are you doing?"

"I'm going to get your soda."

I grabbed his arm and tried to get him to stand up, but he shook his head and put his arm into the machine where the sodas came out.

"This is crazy, Sam, it isn't going to work." I covered my mouth because all of a sudden I began to giggle. He looked ridiculous.

"I do it all the time," he said. "It's easy."

"You should be in class," I said.

He looked up at me. I was wearing a denim skirt, and I didn't know why, but I didn't move back to keep him from seeing up my skirt. Instead, I stood there, three inches away from his head, and let him look at me. My long legs were lean and muscular from dancing. My waist was small and my stomach flat, and my breasts pushed against the fabric of my blouse, rising up and down with each breath I took. Our eyes locked, and I didn't know if he was too distracted by me, but the next thing we knew his arm got stuck and he couldn't get it out. I thought he was joking, because the guy was never serious, but his face even turned red. Just then, the lunch bell rang and the students starting coming out of the classrooms.

"Come on, Sam, get your arm out."

"I can't."

The students began to make a semicircle around him, pointing fingers and laughing at seeing him on the ground with his arm stuck in the machine. Someone in the yearbook staff took a picture. Sam started laughing, too, and he looked at me and said, "I'll do anything for you, Yessy."

To this day I still wonder what would've happened between us, if Eduardo hadn't been in my life.

Eduardo opens the bathroom door and startles me out of my reverie. He sits on the edge of the bathtub and starts talking about practice, and this time listening to him go on and on about Alegría doesn't hurt at all. He's excited about a new choreography for Tamaulipas he's teaching the dancers for Alegría's tenth-year anniversary.

"Maybe we can get the Durfee grant this time," he says enthusiastically. "We'll need at least $4,000 to get new costumes made—once Soledad comes back from México, that is—and we'll need some money for new props . . ."

I fight the urge to tell him about the Tijuana clinic, about what I'm going to do. He would never approve and would try to talk me out of it. I've already made up my mind.

"And the dancers are coming along really nicely with Guerrero. I think they'll do great at the competition in New York next month. Laura already reserved the bus for us and—"

"Is there any news from Soledad?" I ask. Eduardo shakes his head no, saying he hopes everything turns out all right for her, before moving on to what he really wants to talk about. I nod and continue listening to Eduardo's plans for Alegría.

It isn't until we're in bed that he notices something is bothering me. It's hard sometimes, to keep things from him. I turn off the light before I tell him about the clinic in Tijuana. "Maybe that's the answer to my problems. The doctor said I need to lose weight. Maybe once I do that my knee will get better and I can go back to dancing."

Eduardo reaches over to his nightstand and turns the light back on. "Those surgeries are dangerous and expensive. I know how much you miss dancing, but—"

"I can't just sit here with my arms crossed and do nothing. I could at least look into it and go from there. Just a consultation."

"All right, Yessy. If that's what you want. But I won't be able to go with you. I have a big house to re-wire that weekend. Couldn't you reschedule?"

I turn off the lamp and tell him not to worry. I'll call Elena.

Elena and I meet at the Olive Garden in Downey. As always, the restaurant is brimming with people. "How are things with Richard?" I ask. I wonder if it must be difficult for her to be all alone now.

"I filed for divorce. Yesterday."

"Oh" is all I can manage. I was against their marriage from the start, having told her that just because she was pregnant didn't mean she had to marry the guy. Still, I feel bad about them splitting up, but I don't know what to say. "I'm thinking about having plastic surgery," I blurt out, ready to change the conversation. "Will you come with me to Tijuana? I have an appointment."

"I don't think this is the answer, Yessy—"

"Eduardo said the same thing, but I'm not giving up on this. Now, please, I don't need to hear how dangerous it is or how it isn't going to solve anything. I just need you to be there for me. Okay?"

Elena nods and says nothing. The waitress comes to clear our plates and asks if we want anything else. "Let me have the tiramisu," I say. When the waitress leaves I turn to Elena and ask, "So, are you going back to school at UCI?"

"I don't know. I've extended my leave of absence. Besides, I would need to quit my job with the district, and I really should finish out the school year with my students."

"Well, you know I've been against it from the start. You don't need to get a degree in dance to be a dancer. Nobody does. You either have it in you or you don't. You're either born with natural talent or you're not. When it comes to dance a diploma is meaningless. It's just a paper. And besides, what would you do with a degree that you aren't already doing?"

"I don't know. I wanted to take that extra step in my education, and I thought I should get a master's degree in the subject I love. But things have changed now . . ."

The tiramisu comes and I'm glad for the interruption. I offer some to Elena, but she shakes her head no and excuses herself to use the restroom. I devour the dessert with gusto and close my eyes, enjoying the explosion of tastes—coffee, a hint of liquor, chocolate. The tiramisu is so good it almost makes me forget about Alegría and the pain of its absence, and about Elena and her sad eyes, and about the nagging feeling I've always had whenever the dancers bring up college and education. Many of them are teachers, social workers, nurses. Whereas I ended up being just a sales agent at AAA with nothing to my name but a high school diploma. College was something I didn't get to do, and I briefly wonder what I missed out on.

Adriana

I notice him as soon as he enters the restaurant. He flings the glass doors wide open the way gunmen enter bars in movies. The two customers sitting by the entrance look up, startled at the noise. I stop pouring water into a customer's glass and stare at him. The guy is filthy—jeans covered with stains and torn around the knees, a T-shirt that looks like a baby's used bib, his hair matted and oily. I walk to the door, ready to kick out the beggar coming to ask for alms. But then I see his hand go up to his mustache, and I stop walking.

"We'll see if the caldo is as good as you claim," he says, winking.

"Emilio?" I ask, feeling a fluttering in my stomach. I can't believe he's here. Two days ago I barged in on a conversation he was having with Eduardo about seafood. Dumbest thing I could think of was to boast about La Parrilla's caldo de siete mares. It turns out this is Emilio's favorite dish. Eduardo rolled his eyes at me before walking away. I never thought that ridiculous boast would bring Emilio to my doorstep—I mean, to La Parilla's doorstep. "So you really are a truck driver," I say as I point to the red and blue cement truck parked out front in the red zone. Even from here I can hear the engine still running and see the drum spinning around.

"Well, are you going to offer me a place to sit or not?" he says. I take him to a booth by the window so that he can keep an eye on his truck.

"Why don't you turn it off?"

"If I do the cement will harden up like rock and it'll be hell trying to get it out of there," he says from underneath his hairy mustache. I look at his hands. They're rough and callused, mapped with bulging veins. His arms are covered in dark, fuzzy hair, almost like fur. A section of a tattoo peeks from under his sleeve. I catch a glimpse of claws.

"When did you get that?"

He pulls up his sleeve and reveals a panther pouncing on an invisible prey.

"Last week," he says, impatiently. "When did you get the scar?"

My fingers touch the rough area on my neck. I don't know what to say. He smiles to show he's just fucking around.

"My dad gave it to me," I say.

"Oh, yeah. Were you being a bad girl?" He runs his tongue over his upper lip. I catch him staring at my tits under the white lacy ruffles of my blouse. I smile, thinking how underneath that cockiness, my Aztec warrior is just like any other man. Horny.

I force myself to smile. "I was a *very* bad girl," I say. My throat suddenly feels so dry I want to take a sip of his ice water.

Emilio looks at me as if sizing me up. He nods. "Well, come on, lady, bring your famous caldo over so I can see if it's as good as you claim."

I rush to the kitchen and give Fat Pancho the order. I lean on the counter and take deep breaths, trying to get a hold of myself. Emilio is pulling on his mustache, twisting the hairs around. He seems like a man who could cause pain. The other Adriana feels like hiding behind the counter, frightened. She tells me to stay away from that man. *Stop being a chickenshit,* I tell her.

I hurry back to the table with his order. "It's my birthday tomorrow," I say as I place the steaming bowl in front of him, leaning down more than I have to so I can give him a good view of my tits. "Why don't you come to my house tomorrow night? We can go out to celebrate."

"Yeah, maybe," he says as he stirs the stew.

"Be careful, it's hot," I say. We both watch the steam floating from the bowl curling into the air.

He licks his lips, staring at my tits. "De veras?" he asks. "Show me how hot."

He picks me up after work and drives me home in a beat-up Tacoma that's covered in pigeon shit. The smell of the lemon-scented air freshener inside makes me dizzy. We walk past Ben's apartment, and I catch a glimpse of him through the kitchen window. Emilio follows behind me as we walk up the stairs, and I shake my ass a little more than I have to and show him the goods I've got. As soon as I punched out I changed out of my waitress uniform and put on a tight top with spaghetti straps and jeans.

"Nice tattoo," he says. I feel his fingers on my skin. I shiver. "Why a moth?"

I shrug my shoulders. "No reason," I say as I open the door to my apartment.

"So how long have you been with Alegría?" he says as he lets himself fall onto my couch. I go to the kitchen to grab some chelas.

"Since nine years ago, when the group started. But before that Eduardo, Yesenia, and my mom were in another group. I've been dancing since I could walk," I say as I come back to the room with the beer.

"Really?" he says, taking a drink.

I don't like the way he said that. "Yeah."

"You know, you still have a lot to learn."

"Like what?"

"You're what we call an hechicera. You know how to engatuzar the audience. People who don't know shit about Folklórico would think you're a great dancer, but people like me, who know everything there's to know about dance, can tell right away that you aren't that good."

I down the rest of my beer and go back to the kitchen to get another one. What the fuck is up with him? I didn't bring him to my house to be insulted. "And who named you the Folklórico Police?" I ask when I come back to the living room. I mean, just because he used to dance for El Ballet Folklórico de México when he lived in México City doesn't mean he's the big Folklórico caca.

"Come here," he says. I walk over to him and sit down by his side. He caresses my hair as if I were a little girl and pulls me close to him.

"I've been watching you," he says as his hand makes its way underneath the thin strap of my top. "I know what you need. I can clean up your technique, improve your rhythmic sense. I can make you a great dancer. Do you want me to do that?" He leans over me and starts to kiss my neck.

He has rough hands like tree bark, teeth that bite too hard, a dick too big to give pleasure, only pain. Yet I hang on to him with both hands. I like to watch the panther tattooed on his forearm, see its sharp claws, its menacing fangs. I can almost feel the bite, feel it tear through my skin and slice me open.

I listen to my bed squeaking.

Then I remember my bedroom is right above Ben's bedroom, and he can hear us. I picture him standing alone, painting. Emilio shudders then goes to the bathroom to clean himself up. I stay in the bed, feeling the emptiness between my legs now that he's gone. I cover my nakedness with a blanket and curl into a ball, my body unsatisfied. Emilio comes back freshly showered. I watch the lithe movements his body makes as he gets dressed. The muscles of his buttocks tighten as he slips into his jeans. I count the buttons of his shirt as he pushes them through the holes. He runs his fingers through his hair and lets out a deep breath.

"Well," he says, "I'll see you later."

I hold my breath until I hear the door close behind him. I listen to his footsteps as he runs down the stairs. His truck drives away. Then there's nothing but the faint ticktock of the clock on the wall. I get up and make for the shower. I sit in the tub and let the hot, steaming water soothe my sore body. My tits ache from his hard sucking, from his sharp teeth that bit my skin too hard, as if he had no control of them.

I think about his eyes, those eyes that looked past my face at some speck on the wall while he pumped into me. I wanted him to see me. But he never did.

Soledad

For nine days people came to the house every afternoon to pray for Abuelita Licha's soul. I spent too much money on milk for the hot chocolate and a lot of pan dulce and bolillos to give to our guests. I worry about how much money I'll need for a coyote to take me back to Los Angeles, but I know it's tradition to have a novenario.

On the last day of the prayers we made a big dinner for our guests. We made mole with chicken and rice. We had to buy ten chickens at El Mercado. This is where we're going now to buy food for our midday meal. I love to go walk around the stalls. It reminds me of the swap meet in Los Angeles. Vendors hold out the things they sell as we pass by. Leather sandals, belts, clay pots, paintings, pirated CDs, jewelry. Stephanie holds on to Ma. Vendors call her güerita and ask what she wants to buy. People always recognize those born in America.

We come to the meat section. We walk from stall to stall, looking at the chickens. The vendors shoo the flies away. Stephanie covers her eyes and doesn't want to look at the chickens hanging by their feet.

"This is disgusting!" she says.

"Remember when Eduardo was teaching the choreography for Nayarit?" I say. "How he explained about El Mercado—this is what he was talking about. This kind of place."

Stephanie looks around the marketplace, and I think I see her expression change a little, like if maybe she really understood what I was trying to tell her. Folklórico is all about reenacting the Mexican traditions and customs onstage.

We continue to walk to the next stall. Stray dogs lie down on corners eating bones and pieces of fat the vendors throw at them. Ma stops at a stall and looks at the chickens. I look at their heads, their empty eyes, their broken necks. The chickens dangle from a pole by their feet upside down, as if they were crucified.

"Let's buy trucha today," I say to Ma. And we move on to the next aisle, where the stalls sell fish fresh from the lake.

〰

Stephanie doesn't want to get out of bed. She got scared last night, when she almost stepped on a scorpion crawling near her shoe. I tell her to shake her shoes upside down and check there are no scorpions inside, just like every night I shake her bedcovers before she lies down.

"I'm scared," she says. "What if they sting me? What if I die in this place? Then I'll never get to spend my money, never see my friends again. And I don't want to be buried in that haunted cemetery."

I laugh. Stephanie thinks the cemetery where we buried Abuelita Licha is scary. It isn't like cemeteries in Los Angeles, with nice green grass and headstones all in straight lines. No, here our cemetery is full of trees and weeds and wild grass, with headstones of all shapes and sizes, old statues of La Virgen de Guadalupe, or Jesus, or little angels. There are big concrete tombs of people who had money, and there are dirt graves of the people who were poor. Abuelita Licha's grave is just dirt and a wooden cross with her name. Ma wants to buy Abuelita Licha a big headstone with the statue of La Virgen de Guadalupe to guard her sleep. Maybe someday we'll have the money.

I pick up Stephanie's shoes and shake them. Nothing but pebbles comes out. I hand the shoes to her and tell her to put them on. It's noon now.

"I don't want to go outside," she says. "My shoes got so dirty yesterday, and I felt so icky and slimy and this house doesn't even have a shower."

"I'll heat up water for you like I did last night; now get up." Finally, Stephanie gets out of bed. She puts on her shoes, all this time complaining about the way people bathe here. You heat up the water, carry it in a bucket to the bath area, and then throw the water over you with a plastic bowl. This is how things were when I was little.

"And the toilet, my God," she says. She walks behind me out to the patio where Ma and Lorenzo are talking. "I can't believe you have to throw a bucket of water in it to make it flush."

At least there's a toilet now. When I lived here we had to squat on the ground. Stephanie hurries to Ma and complains to her all over again. I sit with Lorenzo. He looks at Stephanie, and in his face I see he's confused at what she's telling Ma. She goes from English to Spanish, and Spanish to English. Even Ma has a hard time understanding.

"She's complaining about México," I tell him.

He nods and shrugs his shoulders. "I guess she misses her home."

Outside, Lorenzo's little children are playing with the dog. The oldest, who is ten, is working, helping people carry their shopping bags around the marketplace. When I lived here, Abuelita Licha would make tamarind pulp and candied guavas, yam, and pumpkin for Lorenzo and me to sell around the streets.

"Where's your wife?" I ask.

"She went to visit her mom. She'll be back soon."

Stephanie shrieks and hits her leg hard. "That really hurt," she said. "Look at my legs, they're full of bites."

"We need to buy more mosquito repellent for your sister, Soledad," Ma says.

I don't know what gets into me, but I say to Ma, "Or maybe Stephanie should go to the hills and gather cow poop to burn."

"That's gross," Stephanie says. Lorenzo and I laugh, remembering the days when we were young and would have to gather cow poop and burn it in the house to scare the mosquitoes away. The thought of Stephanie walking around with a bucket of cow poop makes me laugh so hard I almost pee my pants.

Little Lupita, who's three years old and is Lorenzo's only daughter, follows Stephanie wherever she goes. Stephanie sits near the water tank, washes her feet, and then spends the afternoon giving herself a pedicure. Lupita watches Stephanie's every move. Stephanie doesn't talk to her. She doesn't talk to our nephews either. They come to me and I give them money to buy candy. Lupita doesn't want candy. She stays in her little corner to watch Stephanie put makeup on, brush her hair, and put beautiful shiny pins in her hair.

When Malena comes home I ask her to go with me to the stores near the plaza to buy Lupita beautiful things for her hair and a pretty dress for her to wear instead of the old faded torn dress she's wearing now.

On our way to catch the bus, Malena stops to say hello to her friend Norma, who lives with her three children in a little house made of adobe. Part of the house has crumbled and the roof is caved in.

"Her husband is in the U.S. but he has a new family now and stopped sending money many years ago," Malena says when we walk away from Norma's house. "Now she has to work cleaning bathrooms at the school to support herself and her children."

On the way to the plaza Malena points out to me the pretty two-story brick houses we see through the bus window. She tells me that's how you can tell when someone has relatives in the U.S. and when someone doesn't—by the houses.

"But I'd rather be poor, as long as my husband is with me," Malena says. I look at Lupita sitting on her mother's lap and smile at her. Lupita buries her face in her mother's chest. She's scared of me, of the ugly red mark on my face.

After I buy Lupita two dresses and a pair of patent-leather shoes, we sit at the plaza and I treat Malena and Lupita to a bag of churros. I see women with babies on their laps. Little children playing tag or hide-and-seek, or riding their bicycles. Once in a while, an old man passes by on a horse. I don't see anyone I grew up with. Where are they? Is it that I don't recognize them?

"Where are the men?" I ask Malena. It is so strange to me to see women sitting alone with their children. I remember coming to the plaza here with Abuelita Licha and Lorenzo. There were always families here, fathers playing with their children, husbands walking hand in hand with their wives.

"They're gone, Sol. The men are all in the U.S."

This isn't how I remember my town.

Elena

I sit in the darkness of the auditorium and watch him surrender himself to the music. Cuerpo y Alma. The same music that makes his body vibrate enters mine in the same way. Just by watching him, my feet tingle. With each stroke of the harp, the twinkling of the marimba, the throbbing of the jarana, the strumming of the requinto, the high-pitched voice of the singer, I feel more and more connected to Fernando. There's something about him that reminds me of myself at that age. The way his eyes glow under the stage lights. The way he perspires. The sharp intake of breath. The feverish desire. It isn't a girl who makes him feel this way. It's this dance that seduces him.

I hum along to "Tilingo-Lingo" under my breath as I watch him. Then I notice his mistake. He's doing el huachapeado incorrectly. As a matter of fact, they all are, not just him. I wonder if this is how Mrs. Rodríguez taught them. I glance at her and debate whether to say anything or not. Why should I care how she teaches them? But I look at Fernando again, and the thought of seeing him doing things wrong bothers me. He could be a great dancer.

He listens to the music and can identify the beat and carry the rhythm throughout the entire song. Unlike the rest of his peers, he can remember the sequence of the steps the first time they're taught. He can keep his place in the choreography, and unlike the rest of the dancers, he's aware of his space on the stage. Ever since I met him, I've noticed how his posture improves day by day and how good he is at listening to advice and applying it right away. I remember the last performance, how I admired the way he came across as a true performer, not just a high school student who memorized a sequence of steps.

I approach Mrs. Rodríguez but don't take my eyes off Fernando. As if she could read my thoughts, she says, "Isn't he wonderful? Every day I'm amazed at how quickly he learns. Folklórico is in his soul."

"Yes, he is exceptional."

"I've been thinking about how great it would be if Fernando could go to Alegría. I mentioned it to him, but he says his mother doesn't have a car."

"Yes, I spoke with him about that, too."

"It's a shame. If I didn't live in Long Beach and have three kids to look after, I would take him myself." She turns and looks at me. "What about you, Ms. Sánchez? You live close to his house. Would it be something you could do, take him to Alegría? I could take care of all the paperwork."

I turn to look at Fernando. He's helping Becky correct the way she holds her skirt. He looks up and smiles at me.

Tonight I go to my sister's house. It's Adriana's birthday and I'm taking her to Benihana. A dark-skinned Mexican with a black, hairy mustache is sitting on the couch. He's dressed in cowboy gear: tight black jeans, a huge belt buckle in the shape of a horseshoe, a plaid long-sleeve shirt, and black boots. His eyes are red and watery, as if the smoke from the incense stick burning on the coffee table is irritating them.

"That's Emilio," Adriana says from her kitchen. Was that meant to be an introduction? A bamboo curtain with Frida's face painted on it separates the kitchen and the living room. When Adriana parts the curtain, Frida's face becomes misshapen until the bamboo sticks settle back into place. "He's coming with us," Adriana says, her voice laced with defiance.

I don't know how old this guy is, but I can see a few gray hairs sprinkled on his temples, the planes of his face lined with some wrinkles. But that's beside the point. Why in the world did she ask him to come?

"Mucho gusto," he says. I nod, not wanting to say that I'm glad to meet him, too, because I most certainly am not.

Adriana is walking around the living room blowing out her candles. She looks like a peacock dressed in a bright blue huipil embroidered with hot pink and yellow flowers. Her hair is parted in the middle, braided, and wrapped around her head like a crown. A canary yellow rebozo covers her shoulders and she wears a blue calla lily made of corn husk over her ear. But that's not what bothers me most. It's her makeup. I wish I could tell her she shouldn't wear stage makeup when she's not onstage.

Adriana puts her arm through Emilio's and heads to the door. I press myself against it and let them pass. Emilio is missing only his Tejana to complete the outfit. He probably left the hat in his car. Adriana sure knows how to find them. She should've worn a costume from Chihuahua, at least, to match his cowboy outfit. Or he should've worn white cotton calzones and leather huaraches, to match hers.

When we get to the bottom of the stairs, I turn to look at Ben's apartment. I've seen him only a few times, mainly after the dance performances or the few times I've visited Adriana since he moved into the building, but he's a nice guy, and I refuse to be alone with Adriana and this man.

"Where are you going?" Adriana asks, surprised.

"To get myself a date," I say. "Or were you expecting me to be your chaperone for the night?"

Adriana opens her mouth to protest but quickly clamps it shut. Music drifts out of Ben's open windows. Omara Portuondo, one of my favorite Cuban singers. Ben has good taste.

"Hi, Ben, I was wondering if you would like to come with us for dinner? It's Adriana's birthday today and we're taking her out."

I blurt this out the second he opens the door, not wanting to lose my nerve in midsentence.

"Sure. Let me grab my keys." He doesn't look at Adriana and her cowboy standing outside, but I know he's seen them. I'm bold enough to put my arm through his. Adriana pretends not to notice, but her eyebrows draw together as they always do when she doesn't like something.

"Let's go to Chalío's," Adriana says all of a sudden. "I'm craving birria."

I shrug and don't say a word. While I drive, I call and cancel the reservation I made at Benihana. Ben gives me a quizzical look. I follow Emilio's truck down First Street. My stomach churns at the thought of him with Adriana, at the thought of eating at Chalío's. Why can't Adriana get out of Boyle Heights? Why can't she try other food besides Mexican?

I turn to Ben and say, "Well, I hope you like goat meat."

It's an awkward dinner, but Ben and I make the best of it. For the most part, Emilio monopolizes the conversation. I can't help being jealous of Ben, whose lack of Spanish exempts him from having to listen to Emilio go on and on about having danced for El Ballet Folklórico de México when Amalia Hernández was still alive.

Adriana listens attentively, as if he were the messiah and she his disciple. She's hardly touched her birria, but there are plenty of empty Corona bottles on their side of the table.

Ben and I start our own conversation. He tells me about an art show he attended at UC Irvine.

"Elena had started her master's at UC Irvine," Adriana says. "But she dropped out after the first year."

"I didn't drop out," I say to Adriana. "I took a leave of absence when I got pregnant."

"Same thing, the point is that you didn't go back," she says and takes a sip of her Corona. She leans on Emilio's shoulder and looks at me, then glances at Ben. There's a flicker of jealousy, which she quickly tries to conceal.

"So, as I was saying," Emilio continues, "one time the group got invited by the president himself to perform at a dinner at his own house. And after our performance, he even came and shook our hands, and he congratulated me and told me how much he'd enjoyed my performance in La Danza del Venado . . ."

After a while, only Adriana listens to him.

"What was your master's in?" Ben asks, quietly.

"Dance."

"Do you think one day you'll go back and finish?"

"What for?" Adriana breaks in. "She's raking in the dough as a teacher."

I try not to snort. "Well, Adriana, then maybe you should try to get your degree and teach, too, so you can 'rake in the dough' as well." Even though Adriana denies it, I know her lack of education bothers her.

"I'm taking a, what's that you called it? A 'leave of absence.' A very long leave of absence." Adriana picks up a Corona bottle and makes everyone pick up their drinks for a toast. "Here's to leaves of absences." She takes a drink from her beer, then says, "First Mom took one. Then Elena *made* Dad take one. And now I wanna take one, too. What's wrong with that?"

Laughing, Adriana accidentally spills her Corona. It runs across the table and some of it lands on my pants. I stand and grab my coat. Once Adriana mentions our parents, I know what's going to come next—a barrage of accusations toward me, especially about Dad's arrest.

"Excuse me," I tell them. "But I think it's time for me to leave."

Ben gets up and offers to come with me.

"Where are you going? We haven't finished our dinner yet," Adriana says. "Or what, does hearing the truth bother you?"

I whirl around and face her. "What do you want from me, huh? You want me to stay here and listen to your accusations?"

"What accusations? I'm just stating a simple truth. It's your fault Dad is pissed off at us. Why the fuck did you feel obligated to make that call?"

"I thought you were going to bleed to death, what the hell was I supposed to do?"

She smirks. I take a deep breath, knowing that Adriana has gotten what she wanted.

"You were supposed to deal with it, that's what. Not go running to the fucking phone. So because of you I had to deal with all that shit our grandparents dished out. I had to be a prisoner in their home. Had to deal with feeling like I was trash, while you were off in some other place, having the time of your life."

I came back for you, I want to say. On impulse I reach up for my glasses but find nothing there. I forgot that tonight I put on contacts. I want so desperately to be in my oil-painted world, where Adriana's hatred can't reach me.

"They kept me from practicing with Alegría, and no matter how many times Yesenia begged them to let me go to practice, they refused. You don't fucking know what that was like for me."

"Adriana, why don't you talk to her about this in private?" Ben asks quietly. I can see some of the customers looking at us from under the brims of their hats.

I reach out to touch her, wanting to tell her that I do know how that was because I also was away from Alegría all that time. But Adriana shrinks from me, as if my mere touch burned her. "I have to go," I say. "Have a happy birthday."

"Fuck you, Ms. Perfect. And fuck you, too, Ben. You traitor!"

Ben turns around and looks at Adriana for a moment. I hold on to his arm, resisting the urge to pull him along. Emilio puts his arm around Adriana.

"Good night," Ben tells them, and we both walk out of the restaurant hearing Adriana's shouts above the voices of the customers and the Tigres del Norte song playing from the jukebox.

Yesenia

First thing I have to do is fill out a health questionnaire. That isn't so bad. Elena sits quietly by my side, although once in a while she asks if I'm sure about what I'm doing. "Yes," I say for the hundredth time.

On the drive down I felt a little apprehensive. I wasn't sure how much Tijuana clinics are to be trusted. México doesn't have the same regulations as the U.S., and I wondered what the clinic would look like. Would it be a hole-in-the-wall-type thing, or would it be located on the second floor, right above a bar or a strip joint? Would it be dirty, with mice running around and roaches scurrying across the walls?

As soon as we got here my fears vanished. The clinic is adjacent to a six-story hotel. It's immaculate—the tiled floors shine as if freshly mopped, the tall glass windows are clean and streak free, the white walls have no scuff marks. As we walked down the hallway to the lobby I spotted several women and a few men, most with blond hair and blue eyes. If I didn't know I was in Tijuana I would think I was in a clinic in the U.S. *Well, if gringos get their surgeries done here then it must be safe.*

I watch the receptionist and the doctor's assistants going in and out of doors. They all look as if they just stepped out of the pages of *Vanity Fair*. I wonder if they're naturally shapely or if they're walking advertisements of what the doctor can do. But I didn't come here to be turned into a model. I came here seeking a miracle.

I finish filling out the questionnaire and head to the counter. As the receptionist looks over the paperwork I can't restrain myself, and I ask her why all the employees look so good, their bodies and faces so perfect, as if chiseled by the hand of God himself. The girl laughs and say they've all been worked on, including herself.

"Just you wait," she says. "You'll be amazed at what Dr. Salas can do."

He has the power to help me. He has to help me.

When I'm called in, Elena stays in the waiting area while I go inside another room, where I'm handed a blue thong and a small top to cover my breasts.

"Please put this on. When you're ready come out through this door so that we may take some pictures," the doctor's assistant says.

I stand there for a long time, trying to muster the courage to undress myself. I hold up the thong and gulp. How can I come out wearing this? How can I allow this stranger to see me practically naked and to take pictures of my fat body, the cellulite on my ass that looks like craters on the moon? I sit on a chair and run my fingers through my hair. After a while, I stand up, take a deep breath, and begin to unzip my jeans. I didn't come all this way for nothing.

"Only one child?" Dr. Salas asks.

I nod. He looks at me, questioning. What? I want to say. Was I supposed to have five children like his mother probably did?

He writes something down on the health questionnaire.

"Ms. Alegría?"

"Oh, I'm sorry, Doctor, what did you say?"

"I was asking about your knee problems."

"I have osteoarthritis."

I look at the computer on his desk and see the pre-op pictures his assistant took about fifteen minutes ago without passing judgment or offering any kind words. She just asked me to turn to the left, to the right, bend at the waist, face the wall, so she could get a shot of every side of my body. I look at the bulges of fat on my midsection, my thighs, my back. The map of stretch marks on the area below my belly button, the sagging skin, the scar from the Cesarean section.

"So you want to do all these areas, is that correct?" Dr. Salas asks as he points at the pictures on his computer screen. Pictures, like mirrors, do not lie.

I nod.

"We'll need to do lipo first, and in three months, once the swelling goes down and I know how much skin I have to work with, we'll do the tummy tuck."

"A tummy tuck?"

"I strongly recommend it. Once all the fat is gone the skin will just sag," he says. "You won't like the look of that, trust me."

"I—I don't know, Doctor."

He looks at the screen again. I wonder what he's thinking. Is he used to seeing naked women? Does my body disgust him the way it disgusts me? I try not to look at the computer screen. "Well, you have time to think about it. Now, is there anything else you'd like to get done?" He glances at his computer screen again. "Facial rejuvenation, perhaps?"

Do I really look that bad? "I thought one needed to be older than I am to get a face-lift," I stammer. "I mean, I only just turned forty-three a few months ago."

He smiles. "Most rhytidectomy patients are between the ages of forty and seventy. But I apologize to you, Ms. Alegría, I didn't mean to hurt your feelings. Although may I suggest that you stay out of the sun and try to reduce your stress level?" He clicks on the picture of my face and enlarges it. "You have rhytids forming here, here, and here," he says as he points to my forehead, the crow's-feet area, and around my mouth. I look at the sagging cheeks and jowls, and the double chin. I stare at the computer and can't believe that I'm looking at myself. It's my mother's face that I see: my mother, who has always looked older than her true age. It's that trait inherited from her that I hate most. "Now, will there be anything else?" he says.

I suddenly wish I could run out of his office, that I hadn't taken those pictures. I force my eyes away from the computer and take a deep breath. "Well, I always did hate my flat butt," I finally say, trying hard to smile.

He smiles in return. "It's going to be thirty-five hundred for liposuction in the areas you indicated, and for a thousand more I can add the excess fat I'm removing to your buttocks."

"I didn't know you could do that! But I think I'll pass, Dr. Salas."

He looks down at his watch and says, "If you want to do the surgery today I have an opening in an hour. That way you won't have to drive down here next week, just in four weeks for your follow-up visit. You didn't have breakfast, did you?"

I was too nervous this morning to be hungry. But still, I didn't plan on having surgery this soon—if at all. "Today?"

"Sure," he says. "Why wait?"

"Yessy, don't do this," Elena says as I cover my naked body with the robe the nurse gave me. The doctor just left the room, having marked the fatty areas on my thighs, waist, abdomen, and back with a black marker.

"I want to do this," I say. I get back in the bed and wait for the nurse to come back.

"But your body—"

"My body has betrayed me."

"You pushed it beyond its limits, Yesenia. Our bodies can only take so much."

I wave her words away. Elena sits on the chair, holding the book she brought with her. I suggest she go drink some margaritas instead. We're in Tijuana, after all.

"This is dangerous. I really wish you would reconsider. Why don't we go back to Los Angeles? Give yourself an extra week to think about it. I mean, you just came for a consultation, not to have surgery."

I look down at the floor. "I know, but it's better this way. I'll just get it over with."

"But what about work?"

"I've hardly taken any vacation in the six years I've worked there. Believe me, I could take a year off if I wanted to. Besides, Dr. Salas says I should feel well enough to go back to work on Monday."

There's a knock on the door and the nurse comes in carrying a tray. She walks to the other side of the bed and inserts the IV into my wrist. Then she gives me two pills to take.

"Will it hurt?" I ask her after swallowing the pills.

The nurse laughs. "You'll sleep through the whole thing, don't worry."

She calls another nurse, and together they start to push the hospital bed out of the room. Elena walks by my side, threatening me that she's going to call Eduardo so he can put a stop to my madness.

"Don't," I tell her. "I'll be okay." I think I see her eyes become wet with tears, and I want to tell her not to worry. But the darkness is already pressing in around me. A sudden fear seizes me. What if something goes wrong? I try to force my eyes to open. I try to force my mouth to tell them to wait, that I do want to think about it after all. But it's too late, and my last thought is that I should've apologized to Memo for what I said the day he moved out. *Wait, wait . . . !* But the darkness washes over me.

I don't know how many minutes or how many hours go by, but sometime during the surgery I wake up to excruciating pain. I feel the doctor insert metal into me. I hear a sound, like scraping. I'm lying facedown and realize Dr. Salas must be working on my back. Wave after wave of pain comes, one after the other, and I can't speak, can't tell him that he's hurting me. Can't tell him to stop. The only thing I can do is lift my head, hoping he can hear my silent cry.

"Is it hurting?" someone asks. I nod and let my head fall down again. In a little while I don't feel anything, and the darkness starts to crawl back in. Like a stage curtain after a dance, it drops all of a sudden and blocks everything out.

In the evening, after I've had time to recover from the anesthesia, Elena walks me to the hotel adjacent to the clinic. I walk like a hundred-year-old woman, bowing to the ground and taking tiny steps while holding on to Elena all the way to the room. I think about "La Danza de los Viejitos," and how throughout the entire dance the dancers have to have their backs arched. That dance is hilarious, and it makes the audience laugh. But there isn't anything funny about the way I feel. My body hurts as if it was run over by a car, or worse, a bus.

Elena goes down to the restaurant and brings back some chicken noodle soup and quesadillas for dinner. I'm glad she's here with me.

"Is the food okay?" she asks. "It's not making you feel sick?"

"No, the soup is fine. I'm starving. All I got was apple juice and gelatin after the surgery." I don't tell Elena that I vomited at the clinic when I woke up after the surgery, that I passed out in the bathroom, and the next thing I knew I was lying on the cold floor and a nurse was asking if I was okay.

Elena helps me to change the bloody bandages. She tucks me into bed and gives me two pills and a glass of water. She gets into her own bed and turns off the lights.

In the darkness, I say, "Go back to Alegría, Elena."

Elena doesn't say a word, but after a while I hear the muffled sound of weeping.

"Elena?"

"I can't, Yessy. I just can't."

"Well, then that makes two of us." It hurts like a bitch, but I start crying, too.

Elena pulls up in front of my house and ends the torturous two-hour drive. Every pebble in the road made me want to scream. The lights are on in the living room. Elena opens the door, then she leans down so I can support myself on her shoulder as I get out of her truck. I try not to groan as I struggle to get out. I don't want Elena to know I'm beginning to regret not listening to her and giving myself more time to think. What the heck have I gotten myself into?

Elena opens the front door with my key, and I hear her say hello to Eduardo above the noise of the television. I stand behind her, and I hate myself for acting like a teenage girl afraid of her father. But the truth is I hadn't thought about what I was going to tell Eduardo. He turns off the television. "You're back!" he says and rushes over to greet us.

He gives Elena a hug, and then he comes over to me. "So did the doctor make you see reason?" he says as he leans to hug me.

I hold up my hand and say, "Don't touch me!" I didn't mean to say it that way, and I can see the hurt look on his face.

"What's going on?" Eduardo asks.

Elena holds my arm and walks me to the couch. As I struggle to sit down on the edge of the couch, I feel an intense burning sensation, as if my whole body is getting stung by a hundred bees. "I had lipo!" I blurt.

"What?" Eduardo looks from me to Elena, growing more confused by the minute.

"Liposuction," I repeat.

"You said you were going for a consultation, to get the doctor's opinion."

I turn to Elena and say, "Thanks for coming with me, but you should go now."

"Are you sure you don't need me to stay?"

I nod. Elena kisses my forehead and then tries to hug Eduardo, but he pulls away from her. She practically runs out of the house.

"Yessy, what were you thinking? What's happening to you?" he says.

"I don't know what you mean. Nothing's happening to me. I'm just tired of being fat, okay? I'm tired of dieting all the time, of killing myself at the gym. Now it's all gone and I'll be able to return to Alegría."

"First of all, you weren't fat. And second, what makes you think this is the cure? You didn't even talk to your doctor about it. And how did you pay for the surgery?"

"I took out money from our savings, but I'll replace it with my next check. I did really well this month. I sold more than thirty auto policies and fifteen home policies. I'll be getting a good commission . . ."

He shakes his head. "I just don't know what you were thinking, Yesenia. Things like that are dangerous. People have died doing—"

"Well, I didn't. I'm still here, vivita y coleando."

"What are you doing to yourself, Yessy? I love you just the way you are. I don't know why you want to do this. Those doctors are like butchers . . ." He walks up and down the living room, going on and on about the dangers of these kinds of surgeries and describing all the worst-case scenarios of what could've happened if things had gone wrong. When he's finally done venting, he looks at me again, and this time his face softens. "Do you need anything?"

"Water, for my pills."

He goes to the kitchen and comes back with a glass of water.

"I need to change my bandages," I say after I swallow the pills.

He helps me to the bathroom, and when he begins to unwrap the blood-soaked bandages, he groans. "Jesus Christ, Yessy," he says. He excuses himself and goes outside for a moment. When he comes back, I notice his eyes are red.

❧

Memo comes over the following day, and just like his father, he scolds me as if I were a child. There's an awkward silence during dinner. I can hear them grinding the tostadas with their teeth. In unison they each take a drink of water, set the glass down, and continue eating the pozole Eduardo picked up from El Gallo Giro.

"How's the show coming along?" I ask them, realizing that I really don't know what Eduardo is preparing for the performance up in Davis.

Eduardo nods. Memo grunts.

"Was that supposed to be an answer?"

"Mom—"

"Yesenia, please," Eduardo says. "Let's not get into arguments again. Let's at least try to enjoy our dinner."

"It's my body."

"I know, Mom, but Dad and I are part of your life. We deserved to know. This affects us, too."

"How in the world does my surgery affect you?"

"Yesenia, that's enough," Eduardo says.

"Mom, please."

"Please what?"

"What if something had happened to you?"

"Well, nothing did happen to me."

"But you could've died, Mom. People die doing that stuff."

"I could've died giving birth to you, young man. And that doesn't seem to bother you at all."

Memo stands up and puts his napkin down on the table. He looks at Eduardo. "I have some homework to finish," he says. He takes his jacket from the closet and puts it on. Eduardo stands up and picks up their bowls. I sit on the chair and don't move, trying so hard to keep my tears inside. I want to call out to him, to see him running toward me with his arms open, a smile on his face, like when he was a little boy and would forgive me anything.

Memo looks at me from the door. "Bye, Mom," he says. Eduardo puts his arm around him and walks him out.

Eduardo comes back five minutes later and begins to wash the dishes.

"I didn't mean it."

He continues washing.

"Did you hear me? I didn't mean it."

"I'm not the one who needs to hear that." He scrubs too hard, and one of the glasses breaks in his hand. "Goddammit!" he yells, letting the broken glass fall in the sink.

I stand up too fast, and my body suddenly feels as if an electric current is running through it. I lower myself onto the chair, cursing under my breath, while Eduardo stares out the window, blood dripping from his hand.

"I'm worried, Yessy."

"About what?"

"About us. Alegría."

"We're going to be fine, you'll see. Alegría is going to be fine, too." As soon as I get better everything will be fine. I'll return to dancing, and Eduardo can stop worrying about me and focus on the group. Next year's anniversary performance will be the best yet. I'll apply for more grants. And maybe we could get an NEA grant, or a Dance/USA award, or even the James Doolittle Foundation award. We'll stop worrying about money and put on a show worthy of the group! I want to tell Eduardo this, but he walks away and goes into the bathroom. The shower runs for a long time, and when he comes out he goes straight to bed and doesn't even say good night.

CHAPTER SIX

I don't want people who want to dance; I want people who
have to dance.

—GEORGE BALANCHINE

*IT starts with constant hunger. No sooner are warm-ups over than
you are looking through your gym bag for a snack, which you usually save for later. Halfway through practice, your energy begins to
lag, and it takes all your willpower to make it to the end. Your body
feels hot, as if it were burning from the inside out. And you can
never drink enough water to quench the unrelenting thirst.*

Then the dizziness comes. Your feet begin to cramp. Your timing is a bit off. Your body feels different somehow. Something has changed.

And when you know what this change is, when your fear turns into joy, the changes in your body no longer frighten you. You embrace them. The dancing becomes easier. The music flows through you, and your body is once again one with the beat.

Later, your center of gravity shifts, but your body learns where your proper balance lies, and it quickly compensates. Your arms, your legs, your shoulders, they know how to adjust to the changes. When you can't stretch to full capacity and can no longer dance full-out, you put your dance shoes in the closet, looking forward to the day when you can put them on again.

In the hospital, you realize how much dancing has prepared you for what's to come. You know how to breathe. Your body and mind are in tune with each other. Your muscles know when to relax, when to contract, when to release. Your body has given you years of joy, and now, it gives you this baby. This miracle. Xochitl.

The many years of twirling heavy skirts have made your arms strong and muscular. Perfect for carrying her around. Your feet are fast and steady. When you chase your daughter around the house, they dance to the music of her laughter. Dancing has given you proper body alignment. You know the right way to bend down to pick her up. Your back and abdominal muscles are strong. You twirl her around as if she were a Folklórico skirt, your faces mirror images of each other. Two smiles, eyes sparkling with joy.

When you wake up, you can still see her eyes. You can still hear her laughter, but your arms are empty and sadness floods your heart.

Elena

Fernando invited me to his little sister's birthday party at Roosevelt Park. I didn't promise him I'd go, even though the park is only ten minutes from where I live and I have nothing else to do.

I sit on the patio the entire morning looking at a snail crawl around the last of the surviving pansies. The petition for divorce is on the table. The copy I'm supposed to serve Richard is in an envelope, and even though I'm the one initiating the divorce, I can't help feeling as if Richard is abandoning me. He said he wouldn't contest it and that I could keep the few things we'd purchased jointly in the twelve months we were married, this house and some of the furniture. How easily he has let me go. I wonder, had Xochitl survived, if things would've turned out differently. Was Xochitl's death a test we both failed?

I glance up at the avocado tree and distract myself by counting the last of the fruit hanging from the branches. Many of them are on the ground, having fallen from high above and breaking open when they hit the ground. I've no desire to cut them down. Richard fell in love with this property because of the huge avocado tree. I think of him cutting the avocados down for me to make guacamole.

I seal the envelope with the papers, then grab a pole and begin to cut down the avocados. Because there are some that I can't reach, I work up the courage to climb up the tree. My heart pumps rapidly, and for a moment I feel dizzy. I hold on to a branch, and when I'm high enough where I can reach the rest of the avocados, I straddle a branch and cut, cut, cut, until they're all lying on the ground below. I put the avocados that survived the fall intact in a Trader Joe's paper bag and then take a shower and get dressed. I stop at CVS on the way to the park and look at the toy section, but I don't know what a young girl of nine would like. Instead I buy a birthday card and put thirty dollars inside.

❧

I'm not sure what to expect at the party. But as soon as Fernando sees me he comes to meet me with a big smile on his face.

"Hi, Miss." He takes the Trader Joe's bag from me.

"I brought some avocados for your mom."

He introduces me to his mother, Beatriz, a tired-looking woman in her late thirties with hands made rough from cleaning other people's homes. I think of Yesenia, of what she would say if she knew that this woman is four years younger than her and yet looks so much older.

I give his little sister, Bertha, the birthday card, and she wraps her arms around me and kisses my cheek. As soon as she lets me go, Fernando's mother hands me a plate of rice, beans, and carne asada. His young brother, Pepe, brings me a soda. I sit next to a woman who introduces herself as Fernando's aunt. It isn't until the woman gets up to grab another drink that I notice her belly. Five or six months pregnant, I think, judging from the way I myself looked around those months.

Fernando throws a rope over a branch of a tree and hangs the piñata from it. The little kids gather all around him, wanting to touch the piñata. Fernando laughs and tells them to line up, the smallest to the tallest. As the birthday girl, Bertha gets to go first. Fernando ties a handkerchief over her eyes and spins her around a few times, then leads her to the piñata. For a moment, I feel a pang of pity, seeing him take on his father's role at such a young age. He reminds me of myself with Adriana. And I wonder if his decisions, too, will ever be wrongly judged by his siblings.

"Thank you so much for coming," Beatriz says in Spanish. "Fernando talks so much about you I feel like I already know you." She sits next to me and begins to sing a traditional Mexican song as Bertha takes a swing at the piñata. "Dale, dale, dale. No pierdas el ritmo . . ." Beatriz glances my way and smiles. She claps as Bertha makes contact with the piñata. "Harder, mi'ja. Hit it harder."

There's something in the curve of her smile. The way her eyes light up when she laughs. "It's amazing how much you and Fernando look alike," I say.

She nods. "You know, I loved Folklórico when I was little, but I never got a chance to dance. I'm glad Fernando does."

"Me, too."

"I think that maybe next year I might be able to buy a car and maybe then I can take him to dance practice. But I won't tell Fernando yet. I don't want to get his hopes up."

I look at Fernando as he pulls on the rope, then slowly releases it, teasing the kids with the piñata. He drops the piñata down to the ground and lets a little girl hit it several times. She laughs with glee.

"Well, if it's okay with you, I can start taking him to Alegría in the meantime," I say.

"Are you sure this is what you want? Have you completely thought about it?" Adriana says, one hand on the handle of the truck door. I take a deep breath, then nod.

"Yes, this is what I want."

Adriana opens the door and slams it shut. She walks with unsure steps up to the duplex Richard is renting in Inglewood. She looks back at me and mouths the words *Are you sure?* I nod again and motion for her to ring the doorbell. I try to make myself small, so Richard won't see me sitting there in the truck.

He opens the door and Adriana serves him the divorce petition. He looks startled for a moment, then glances my way. I press myself against the seat, wishing to vanish.

Richard comes out of the apartment and heads toward me. He's barefoot, and he winces as he walks over the gravel on the driveway.

He knocks on the window and I lower it.

"This is it, huh?" he says, waving the papers in the air.

"You know it wasn't going to work."

He leans on the truck, looking down. I can smell the spicy scent of his aftershave.

"I don't know anything anymore, Elena. You just pushed me away, without thinking that maybe I was hurting, too. She was my daughter, too, you know?"

I stare at the steering wheel, part of me wanting to say sorry, that he's right. I buried my head in the sand and ignored everything else around me—his pain, his feelings, his needs. But the other part of me is still angry, and because I have nothing else to hold on to, I hold on to my anger.

"You said I was overreacting. You said that everything was going to be fine. You said to wait a little longer, why rush to the hospital? You said—"

"I know exactly what the fuck I said!" Richard says, slamming his fists on the truck. "I know exactly what I said." He walks away and goes back to the house.

"Thanks," I say as I start driving back toward the freeway. How embarrassing that Adriana had to witness that scene! Now I wished I had asked Yesenia, but I was embarrassed, thinking that Yesenia has made her marriage last for twenty-one years, whereas my marriage fell apart in one. And now Adriana is here instead, probably laughing at me on the inside.

"Marriage sucks, huh?" Adriana says.

I shrug. I hadn't been married long enough to really know what marriage was about. Maybe other people are luckier.

"I think it's better this way," I say, more to myself than to Adriana. "I mean, look at Mom and Dad. They were married for fifteen years and neither of them was ever happy."

"I guess not," Adriana says, looking out the window.

"I hated all that arguing, the hitting, the insults. How could she have put up with it for so long?"

"She loved him," Adriana says, softly, and then she repeats it again, with more conviction. "She fucking loved him. I can respect that, why can't you?"

"Maybe she would still be alive if she had left him," I say, realizing I'm treading on dangerous ground. At any given moment, this conversation could turn into an argument, and Adriana, as usual, will start throwing things in my face. Before she has a chance to reply I turn on the radio and raise the volume, hoping my sister gets the point that the conversation has ended.

"Sometimes love hurts," Adriana says, and thankfully, she drops the conversation after that.

It takes Mrs. Rodríguez a week to take care of the necessary paperwork for me to start taking Fernando to Alegría's dance practice. So the following Sunday I pick up Fernando at nine. Practice begins at ten. I want to give him extra time to introduce himself to the rest of the group.

I haven't been to the dance studio since I ran out seven months ago. Here, at least, nothing has changed. Dancers are scattered throughout the floor dressed in their usual tights, leotards, sweatpants, shorts, skirts, leg warmers. Some are stretching at the barre, others practicing a step in front of the mirror, while others are sprawled on the floor doing splits or massaging their legs and feet. There are some new faces, but I recognize most of them. I take the opportunity to introduce Fernando to some of the older dancers as I walk around greeting them. They kiss me on the cheek and ask me when I'll return. I make excuses. Adriana comes into the studio as I prepare to leave, now that I've safely delivered Fernando to Eduardo, who has promised to take good care of him until I return. Adriana has a collar of dark purple hickies. She's tied a red paliacate around her neck in an attempt to conceal them. She should've worn a scarf instead.

I suddenly feel uncomfortable in this place. It's as if Adriana's presence has evoked in me memories of all the years I spent in a dance studio. When Adriana tilts her head a certain way I can almost see our mother. I tell myself it's a good thing I've stopped dancing. This way, I no longer have to look at Adriana's reflection in the mirror. How many times did my stomach do a somersault when I would catch a glimpse of Adriana's face in the mirror, and it was like seeing Mom's ghost dancing before me? I tell Fernando I'll pick him up at two, when practice ends. Then I flee the studio as Eduardo hits the drum and the dancers peel themselves off the walls to begin "Águila Blanca," an Azteca danza.

I sit on the curb outside. In my mind I can picture myself onstage at my last performance over a year ago. The headdress of feathers on my head, the tenabares tied to my ankles, rattling with every step I took. I can still see Adriana dancing right next to me, my sister's eyes glowing under the stage lights, so happy, so carefree. And then she turned and looked at me and smiled, urging me on. Adriana loves Azteca. She's so athletic and has so much of that wild energy, no one can dance it like she can. I remember Adriana looking at me with no hatred in her eyes, no resentment. She loved the music that surrounded us, and at that moment while we danced, Adriana was free to love me as well.

I drive the short distance to Yesenia's house after calling to let her know I'm on my way, not wanting to show up uninvited. Yesenia's feet drag across the wooden floor as she comes to unlock the security door. She looks less pale now than when I saw her last week. She moves slowly, wincing once in a while.

"Lock the door, will you?" she says. We sit at her dining table. "Would you mind getting yourself something to drink?"

"I'm okay, don't worry about me. Are you in terrible pain?"

She shakes her head. "It's the headaches that are killing me."

"What headaches?"

"The medication must have triggered my migraines."

"That's awful, Yessy."

She waves my words away. "Small price to pay," she says. "So you brought Eduardo a new dancer, huh?"

"I think Fernando is too good a dancer to hold him back. He could learn a lot with Eduardo."

Yesenia smiles. "Yes, he probably could."

I look around the room and realize it looks different. My eyes roam over the numerous certificates and trophies displayed over the fireplace from Alegría's dance competitions and performances throughout the years, bookcases filled with books about Mexican history and traditions Eduardo pours over when preparing a new cuadro. Then it suddenly hits me. "Where are the dolls?"

"In the trash." She also looks around the room, but then she focuses on me again. "I heard you're going through with the divorce."

I know she's trying to change the conversation, and I indulge her. "He and I weren't meant to be together. Not like you and Eduardo."

"You're wrong, Elena. Eduardo and I were bound by our love for Folklórico. That's gone now. Memo is gone now. So what do we have left?"

When I get back to the studio, it's still a blur of bodies moving, jumping, spinning. They're dancing polkas from the state of Nuevo León. This region was one of my favorites. The history of all Folklórico dances is so rich. I think about the Germans arriving in northern México and Texas in the nineteenth century, bringing with them their polkas and their music. As I watch the dancers through the steamy glass doors, I'm witness to how the humble people of México made this European dance their own, making it livelier, rowdier, the movements more aggressive and intense.

I spot Fernando among the dancers and smile. He dances perfectly with Adriana. As always, I admire his sense of rhythm.

He understands that in order to stay right on beat one must anticipate it. One cannot dance to the beat but must be one with it.

Adriana looks like a pubescent girl of thirteen learning a new dance. She executes her steps a millisecond too late, as if she can't understand that by the time her brain identifies the beat, it's already passed. Because she's a musician at heart it puzzles me that Adriana sometimes has a hard time dancing, especially in the studio. In here she's distracted, thinking about who-knows-what. A dance movement can't be done correctly when one is thinking about something else. She glances at the mirror too much, and I wonder what the mirror reveals to her. When she's onstage and is focused, she dances well, but there's something missing in her dancing. Watching her now I'm reminded that technique is something that can be taught, but one can't be taught how to enjoy, and be passionate about, Folklórico.

But still, it's she who's now dancing.

My body aches from the desire for movement. My muscles yearn to be used. I miss the connectedness between my mind and body, the awareness of its inner workings—muscles, joints, nerves, bones—and how it always amazed me what my own body was capable of, how far I could push it. If only I could use it to express how I feel. To push my pain out through my torso, my arms, my legs, my head, my feet, until I was free.

At the end of the dance Adriana jumps up and Fernando catches her in his arms. I'm surprised at his strength. Ajúa! The dancers wipe the sweat off their foreheads and clap. They're back to reality now, no longer in that state where body and soul are vulnerably exposed, and so it's safe for me to go inside.

"Thank you for bringing me," Fernando tells me in the truck. His cheeks are flushed. His curly hair is still sweaty. I've never seen him more alive than now.

"You were wonderful."

"Your sister is a good dancer. She was very patient with me, too."

"She works hard."

"It was so cool to be surrounded by people who really love to dance. What about you, Miss? What do you love most about Folklórico?"

I don't tell him that I no longer love it because that would be a lie, and I've learned Fernando can see past the lies. "I love the variety of the dances. Each region—or state—in México has its own unique dance style. Like, for example, the dances of Oaxaca are so different from the dynamic jarabes of Jalisco with its mariachi band. Or the sones from Veracruz, which are influenced by the Africans and Spaniards who came to the area, are so different from the vigorous dances of northern México, which in turn are influenced by the polka, schottische, and redowa brought by the Germans and Polish to that region—"

"God, Miss, when I hear you talk like this I just don't understand how you can stand not dancing. It's in your soul. Why do you fight it? My dad used to say that life's too short not to do the things you like, or be with the ones you love."

I don't have an answer for that.

"I think your baby would have wanted you to be happy," Fernando says shyly.

I look at the road ahead. The heat of his body radiates against my skin. Eduardo worked them to exhaustion. As if he can read my thoughts, Fernando lowers the window—which was starting to get covered with steam—and leans his head out, letting the wind dry up his perspiration and cool his face. His black hair waves in the wind.

As the sun shines on his olive skin, I think that this is how one must look when one is free. When there are no dark nights, no longing, no loneliness or regrets. No emptiness. Only the sun, and the wind, and your body alive with dancing.

Soledad

Now that we've honored Abuelita Licha's memory to Ma's satisfaction, it's time for her and Stephanie to leave. Ma has to work hard to make back the money I spent because I need it to pay my smuggler. Ma says she can't miss another day of work or she won't have money to buy the merchandise for her booths.

"Tomás is already looking for a coyote for you," Ma says to me at the bus terminal. "Just be patient, Soledad, and if it is God's will, very soon you'll be back with us." Ma's eyes are puffy from crying. She gives me a hug and then climbs inside the bus. Stephanie hugs me, too.

"I'm sorry," she says. And even though she doesn't say why she's sorry, the way she looks at me tells me she feels bad I'm staying behind. She goes inside the bus and I'm left with Lorenzo at the terminal. The bus makes its way down the crowded street, and when Lorenzo puts his arm around me, I want to run after the bus and be with Ma and Stephanie again.

His hug feels strange to me. He was seventeen when I saw him last, and now he's thirty, a man I don't really know. I only know his voice from talking to him on the telephone, but not the face, not the arm that now holds me tight.

"I'm sure that Abuela Licha will watch over you from Heaven. She'll make sure you get back to America safe," he says.

We go back to his house and I help Malena with the cooking. I make blue corn tortillas, my favorite. I give a piece of dough to Lupita so she can play with the little tortilla maker I bought her. She says thank you, but I've yet to see her smile at me. I want her so much to smile at me.

"You're welcome to stay with us, Soledad," Malena says as she stirs the black bean soup she's making. "You and your mother built this house. It's yours. Besides, America is so far from here. This is your country. Michoacán is your home."

"But that's where my life is now," I hear myself say. And then I know this is true. I think about my sewing machine at home and my notebook with all my drawings of pretty dresses. I think about my booth at the swap meet, about Alegría and the costumes I didn't finish mending. And I think about my English class. I even miss my Food4Less shopping cart. I think about the dress shop I want to own one day.

I go outside and walk on the train tracks. I feel the sun on my back. The Paricutín volcano in the distance, its tip barely visible. All along the tracks are little houses made of sticks and cardboard, stone or adobe. There are piles of burnt trash because here there are no garbage trucks like in Los Angeles. I pass by the river that now has only rotten water and junk. When I get to the train station I sit on an old bench and I try to remember this place when the train would come by. But now it's so empty, full of trash, broken windows, and it makes me feel so lonely. So many years longing for my country, and now that I'm here I realize it no longer feels like home.

In the evening, Lorenzo and I sit outside the house listening to the crickets and watching the fireflies floating above the bushes. Dogs bark in the distance. I shiver. Lupita has fallen asleep in Lorenzo's arms as he gently rocked her. Now she's quiet, her face pressed against his chest, dreaming beautiful dreams.

Lorenzo has been very quiet lately. It's like he has too many thoughts in his mind and it's difficult for him to think. He has a frown on his face, and for a moment I can almost see my father in him.

"What's the matter, Lorenzo?"

He stares off into the darkness. Crickets sing their sad songs, and somewhere in the distance, I hear an owl's hoots.

"What are you thinking about?" I ask him.

"Tell me about America, Sol. Tell me again what it's like."

"I've told you many times what it's like," I say, remembering our phone conversations we've had throughout the years. There was even a time I tried to convince him to come to America with us so that he could send money home to his family, but he always said no. He didn't want to leave his wife and children behind. Now that I see my town, and how lonely it is without the men, I think Lorenzo was right to stay. His family needs him here. But he makes only $8 a day working in the fields. That's $48 a week, working Saturdays.

"America is a nice country. People there are poor also, but not the kind of poor you see here in México. You'll never go hungry or without clothes."

"What about the people?" He looks down at Lupita. "What are they like?"

"It is like here, some are nice, and some are not." I don't know what he wants me to say about America.

"Do you think I'll make good money there, enough to buy my children nice things, to feed them well so they aren't so skinny like me? And do you think I would be happy there?" He looks at me with his big brown eyes. He has long, long eyelashes, big lips, and dimples on his cheeks. I wish I'd gotten those lashes, and the dimples.

I think about the men in my ESL class. Some feel so sad living in America. Some can't find good jobs. Some work twelve hours every day and still make too little money for all their hard work. They aren't happy in America. They miss their country, their families, but they can't go back and be poorer there than in America. They must stay. At least in the U.S. they make $40 a day—not a week.

"I don't know, Lorenzo," I say. "I don't know if you'll be happy there, but you could make better money than you're making now, that's for sure. You can look into construction work. I hear that pays very well."

I look down at Lupita, sleeping like an angel in her papa's

arms. I sigh. "But do you think you would have the heart to leave your children?"

"It breaks my heart to see them go hungry." He stands up with Lupita in his arms and we go inside the house. Malena and the other children are all sleeping now, and I hear him in the darkness, getting ready for bed. I hug my blanket closer to me and try to find a good position on this old couch. I miss my bed. I miss feeling Stephanie sleep next to me. I look up at the ceiling, at the shadows from the candles on the altar. Out of the silence, I think I hear Malena crying.

Adriana

This morning, Ben's friends have come to pick him up. There's a white dude with sunglasses and a cap, and three white chicks wearing shorts and tank tops. I wonder where they're going. I lean over the rail and accidentally spill some water from my watering can on one of the white chicks.

"Eeeehhh," she shrieks.

"Sorry!" I yell. Ben comes out and looks up. He waves at me. He's wearing a T-shirt and shorts; a backpack and a water bottle hang on his left shoulder.

"Hello, Adriana," he says.

"Hi." I notice the white chicks don't like Ben talking to me. Tuff shit. "Where are you heading off to?" I ask as I water my red geraniums and pink amor de un rato hanging from the rail.

"Hiking at Malibu Creek," he says. "Want to come?"

Any other time, I would've said no. Hiking? Out in the wilderness where I can get bitten by a snake or some shit like that? Nah. But when I see the look the chicks give me, that "don't you dare come with us, wetback" look, I quickly nod.

"Sure, I don't have anything to do."

I pour the rest of the water into a flowerpot Ben made for me and don't stick around to watch the water drip out of it and land below. I just hope it wets one of those hoochie mommas.

I'm glad I'm a dancer. My legs are used to hard work. We walk endlessly under the hot sun. I look at my brown skin and I'm thankful for it. I know that tomorrow I'll look only a shade darker. But the gringas panting and complaining behind me will look like boiled lobsters.

"I need to rest," one of them says. I think her name is Stacey.

"Yeah, I'm beat. Let's sit down under that tree," the other says. What's her name? Oh, yeah, Rachel.

The third one, Kay, is too tired to say anything. She only nods. Ben looks at his friend Dave and shrugs. They both look at me. I stand up straight and try to look cool. I have not even begun to sweat.

"Let's rest for a minute," Ben says. As always, he's a gentleman.

We sit in the shade and drink water. I look at the stream below. The rays of the sun dance on the water. Ducks swim among the reeds. Birds chirp all around us. I feel the wind ruffling my hair and think that this isn't too bad.

Ben and his friends laugh at something. I crawl into myself, thinking they are laughing at me. The other Adriana tells me I shouldn't have come. One of the blondes removes a dry leaf from Ben's hair. They're talking about Ben's art. He wants to have an art exhibition sometime next year to finally start making a name for himself in the art community.

Then they talk about people I've never heard of, composers, I think. I recognize the name Beethoven. I'm not that dumb.

Dave is a musician. He plays for the L.A. Philharmonic. He tells Ben he'll give him some free tickets for their next performance at the Disney Concert Hall. Stacey says she'd "love" to go, too. With Ben, I suppose.

None of them look at me. I pretend to be looking at the butterflies fluttering around. I don't give a shit about butterflies.

"You should come spend a weekend at my house," Rachel is saying to Ben and Dave.

"Ojai is such a pretty place," Stacey says. "And Rachel has a gorgeous house there."

"Have you heard of the Pink Moment?" Kay says. Ben shakes his head. "It's when the last rays of the sun color the tops of the mountains purple. You would love to paint it if you saw it!"

"It only lasts ten minutes. And it's such a beautiful sight," Stacey says.

"But I don't get a view of the Pink Moment at my house," Rachel says. "But I do get a view of the gorgeous lavender sunrise."

Ben looks at me. I sit up straight and glare at him. What the hell are these chicks talking about?

"I think we should get moving," I say.

The chicks grumble their complaint, but Ben and Dave get up. We walk and I take the lead. My feet float above the rocks and over the roots protruding from the earth. I expertly climb over the bigger rocks, jump from one to another as we make our way alongside the creek. I'm a descendant of indios. I'm an Aztec princess. I'm a goddam chiva, a goat, an iguana. I was born knowing how to climb rocks.

I make my way up through the trees and realize that I've never felt so alive as I do now. My heart beats differently than when I dance. I stop to catch my breath and turn to look behind me. I see only one pair of blue eyes. I smile.

"Keep going, Adriana," Ben says. "I'm right behind you."

Ben and I make it to the top of the cliff. The creek looks like a tiny ink spill down below. We sit on a rock and watch a hawk gliding across the sky. My heart pumps less rapidly now.

"It was a good climb," Ben says as he wipes his forehead.

"What happened to your friends?"

"They headed down to the creek to cool down."

I feel the wind drying my sweat. I look at the blue sky above, the trees around me, the creek below, and Ben by my side. "This place is cool," I say.

"It reminds me of home."

"Oh, yeah? How come?"

He tells me again about the endless trees surrounding his childhood home. He talks about the lake behind it, how in the summer he and his brothers and sisters liked swimming and fishing in it, and in the wintertime they loved ice skating on it.

"And which is your favorite season?" I ask, trying hard to picture a bunch of little gringo kids skating happily on the ice.

"I liked them all. Every season has its unique beauty."

I can almost see the green colors he describes to me, the leaves of the trees turning a fiery red before falling and making way for winter. He describes the whiteness of the snow, and the way the cold wind stabs into your skin like pricks of a needle.

I wish I could stay up here until the sky turns dark and the stars are so close I could touch them. I wish I could lean on Ben, put my ear against his chest and hear the beating of his heart. I wish I could lift my fingers and smooth out his ruffled hair. Ben turns and reaches out to hold my hand. He looks at me with too much tenderness. With too much of something that overwhelms me. He leans toward me. My heart pounds in my ears.

Then I think of Emilio.

I pull my hand away and punch him lightly on his arm and tell him it's time to go. Mr.-Nice-Guy-Ben is just too sweet, too fragile. Like ripe guavas.

I go to Emilio's apartment when I get back from hiking. I've called his cell phone many times, but all I get is his voicemail. He lives by the projects. I take the bus down Soto Street and get off on Olympic. When I get to his place the first thing I hear is the sound of the television and male voices. A tall Mexican with too many pimples and a big nose opens the door. Emilio's roommate.

"Hi, Paulino," I say. As usual, the guy looks me up and down. I look past him and see Emilio sitting on the couch, surrounded by a bunch of guys, drinking Coronas. Emilio looks my way and then turns back to the TV.

Nice to see you, too, cabrón.

"Excuse me," I say to chorizo-face Paulino.

The apartment stinks of smoke, dirty feet, and sweat. The guys look at me with hungry eyes, like they haven't seen a vieja in a long time. Then they, too, turn back to the TV. I awkwardly step over the men sitting on the floor. I wish now I hadn't worn a denim mini skirt, but it looked so nice with my red embroidered blouse and my leather sandals. Emilio yanks my arm and pushes me onto his lap. He plants a kiss on my breasts and squeezes my ass.

"Hey, guys, this is my vieja," he says.

His friends grumble a hello and then turn back to the TV. They're watching a recording of an Oscar De La Hoya boxing match that took place God-knows-when. I remember watching the same fight with Manuel. Emilio and his friends act as if this is the first time they've seen this fight, but I know they've seen it before because once in a while one of them will say what's going to happen next. What a bunch of losers.

"How was work today?" I ask.

He shakes his head. "Not right now," he says, then he quickly turns to the TV and yells, "Pégale, pinche cabrón!" When Oscar De La Hoya takes a punch Emilio shakes his head and says, "Pendejo." Then he turns to look at me and lifts his empty beer bottle. "Bring me another one." He motions to the kitchen.

I stand up and jump over the men sprawled on the floor. I trip on someone's leg and almost fall. Somebody grasps my waist to keep me from falling. I look at the guy on the floor who's still grabbing my waist, and thank him, then I quickly make my way to the kitchen and get two Coronas out of the fridge. Man, I need a drink.

"So you're Emilio's lady?" someone asks behind me. I turn around and see the man who kept me from falling. His thin mustache makes him look like Cantinflas.

I nod.

"Listen," he says in a soft voice, "I don't know you, but what's a nice lady like you doing with a guy like Emilio?"

"Mind your own business," I tell him. I leave the kitchen and make my way back to Emilio. He glares at me for a second, then turns back to the fight. I let the Corona do its work. Someone brings back more and I take another. And another. I lean against Emilio and feel his rough hand tracing circles on my inner thigh. His hand goes up higher and higher. I try to push it away. Cabrón, does he have no shame?

"Relax, chiquita," he says in my ear. I grab his beer and quickly down it. I feel Emilio's finger thrust into me. And to my shame, I start to get horny.

After the fight his friends take the hint and get out of the apartment as quickly as possible. As soon as the last one leaves Emilio turns to look at me and slaps me.

"Pinche puta. What the hell were you doing flirting with that cabrón?"

I'm stunned into silence. My hand automatically reaches up to massage my throbbing cheek. My eyes become blurry with tears. "I wasn't flirting with him," I say. I look at his eyes, except now they are not empty but full of anger. For the first time, I feel that Emilio actually sees me.

"I saw you, cabrona. You were whispering to each other, smiling." He pushes me against the wall and thrusts his knee between my legs. "Don't you have enough with me? Huh?" I look at the gray hairs at his temples, see the wrinkles etched into his forehead. Feel his hands rip off my thong.

"Emilio, stop it. Stop it!"

I feel him push inside me.

He slaps me again. "You like having me inside you, baby? See, you have enough with me, right? Tell me you have enough." His pantherlike teeth bite into my shoulder. His fingernails dig deep into my back.

It's as if he wants to tattoo himself into my flesh.

Afterward, Emilio snores loudly by my side. Even in his sleep, his hand has reached out to grasp my breast. He leaves his hand there, and it's as heavy as stone. I lift up his hand and crawl away. I stumble toward the bathroom.

When I turn on the light I'm blinded for a moment, but I open my eyes and gasp. I look at the woman in the mirror. Matted hair, bruised and swollen cheeks, bite marks all over her neck and tits. I feel a rush of anger. Feel it sweep over me like a wave. Hear the roaring in my ears and I can't breathe. It's as if I'm drowning in my own shame, in my own anger, in my own hatred.

I recognize the face before me.

My fingers reach up to my shoulder to touch my tattoo.

"You were right, Mom," I say to the woman in the mirror.

Right before my mother died, I overheard her talking about me with Yesenia. We went to Yesenia's house, and Mom thought I was playing with Memo and Elena in the backyard, but I had come in for a drink of water. She and Yesenia were in the living room watching a video of a Folklórico performance at the Orange County Fair where I danced with Elena, Memo, and other kids. I peeked into the living room, and I saw myself on the TV screen, dancing Jalisco next to Elena.

"Look at those girls, they're as graceful as butterflies," Yesenia said.

Mom laughed. "Everyone but Adriana," she said. "She's like a moth compared to the other girls."

I know Yesenia saw me hiding behind the door. She knew I

heard and changed the conversation, but it was too late. A moth. My mother called me a moth. A dull brown moth dancing with butterflies.

Yesenia

Little by little, the swelling and the bloating start to go down. The stitches are beginning to fall off, but the bruises are still a yellowish purple. I hope the arnica montana pills the doctor prescribed will help them go away soon. It still hurts when I sit down or stand up, but I've learned not to make sudden movements. I've been going to the gym every day after work because the doctor said that light exercise—such as walking on the treadmill—will help me heal faster. Driving to the gym was painful at first. Every time the car went over a pothole my body felt as if Eduardo was banging on it with his drumsticks. Dr. Salas said it'll take up to three months for me to make a full recovery.

After I'm done taking my walk to nowhere, I sit in the steam room; it helps reduce the soreness. My skin feels numb to the touch, as if it weren't attached to my flesh at all. Since no one is in here I don't wear the girdle, and I drop the towel to gently massage myself. I feel lumps under my skin, and I hope they'll go away soon as well.

I close my eyes and find myself thinking about the argument I had with Eduardo last night. With everything that's been going on, I completely forgot to send in the $50 registration fee and the video, and now we're out of the competition in New York.

"We can try again next year," I said.

"What am I going to tell the dancers now?"

"Tell them it isn't worth going. Tell them that the prize money wouldn't even cover all the costs of the trip. And that's assuming if Alegría won."

"You wouldn't be talking like this if you were dancing. Dammit, Yessy, Alegría is still your group. You have a responsibility to it. You were the one who wanted this group, and just because—"

"Stop it. Stop it!" I yelled and ran to lock myself up in the room.

The discomfort after the surgery overwhelmed me; I couldn't think about anything else, and the throbbing in my forehead wouldn't let up no matter what I took. Now, thankfully, the headaches have gone away.

I stand up and leave the sauna. The cold air in the women's locker room stabs my head like a knife made of ice. I change quickly and leave the gym, suddenly feeling drained. Old.

Once I go back to dancing it'll all be worth it. The group is performing up in Davis next month at the Mondavi Center, and I'm planning on joining them. If I could just heal faster so I can get back to rehearsals . . . I imagine myself onstage, finally wearing one of the new Veracruz dresses Soledad made. I never feel old when I dance. Despite the differences in age, all the women look exactly the same—mirror images of each other—our faces painted exactly the same: blue eye shadow, rosy cheeks, red lipstick, our hair done up in buns. Onstage I'm not the oldest member of the group, I'm just another one of the dancers. Up there, no one can see the wrinkles. Up there onstage, I'm ageless, beautiful.

Tonight, as usual, Eduardo gives me a massage. Afterward he bends down to kiss my neck. "Better?" he asks. I nod and thank him. I wrap my arms around him. Run my hands down his back. Kiss his lips. How long has it been? He kisses me for a few seconds but then lies down next to me. "I don't want to hurt you," he says.

"You won't."

He shakes his head. "I just don't feel it's time." He closes his eyes and turns away from me.

"You won't hurt me," I say

Our lovemaking is a combination of pain and pleasure. No matter how careful he is, the rocking movement hurts me.

"You okay?" he asks once in a while. He is too gentle, as if afraid to touch me, as if I were one of those fragile corn husk dolls I once collected. "Yessy, Yessy," he whispers as he kisses the two quarter-inch incisions on my pelvic area. "You're beautiful just the way you are, mi amor." It takes him longer than usual to reach orgasm. He falls asleep holding me in his arms so tightly, as if even in his sleep he were trying to protect me, keep me safe.

The next morning I get up before Eduardo does. My knee feels a little stiff, and I sit on the bed and tell myself it's nothing, probably I slept on it the wrong way. I limp slightly as I walk to the dresser. Nothing is going to dampen my spirits. I've already made up my mind that tomorrow I'm going back to Alegría, put myself back in the show—especially the one at the Mondavi Center, which I've been looking forward to since last year—and this little discomfort in my knee isn't going to stop that. I grab my sweatpants and T-shirt and tiptoe out of the room. I change in the bathroom, put my hair up in a ponytail, and then go outside.

It's six thirty. Already the birds are chirping on the jacaranda tree in front of the house. The rosebushes that line the walkway are covered in dew. The St. Augustine grass seems greener and thicker to me than ever, a rich dark green color that reminds me of the rebozo I wear with my Chiapas costume. The thought fills me with pleasure. I walk the one mile from my house to the dance studio, feeling so good about getting my body back in shape, getting it ready for the rigor of dancing Folklórico. I'm too busy thinking about Alegría's tenth-year anniversary performance to really register the throbbing in my knee. I'm thinking about doing corridos, re-enacting the Mexican Revolution through dance,

emphasizing the role of the women soldiers in the war. I'm imagining the Adelita costumes I'll have Soledad make when she returns, and the props, and a block or so before I get to the studio I
feel as if a screwdriver stabs me in the knee.

I stop walking and grab on to a metal fence to keep myself
from falling. I stand there panting and close my eyes, waiting,
praying. I limp the rest of the way to the studio. I take out the key
from my pocket and go inside. I don't turn on the lights. Instead,
I lie down on the wooden floor and shut my eyes tight, listening
to the silence, trying to recall the laughter, the sound of feet tapping, the drums playing, the echoes of mariachi music. The musty
smell seeping into my body through my nostrils is intoxicating—
the scent of bodies in motion. My knee has stiffened now, and I
know I won't be able to walk the mile back to my house. I put on
a Folklórico CD and raise the volume as high as it'll go before
falling back on the floor again. With the remote control in hand,
I lie on the floor and feel the music vibrate in the wooden floor,
enveloping my body, my knee, until the pain goes away and I can
no longer feel anything.

"Losing weight helps, but it's not going to cure osteoarthritis" is
Dr. Lugo's response after I complain to her about my knee.

"You mean it was all for nothing?" I ask. "I spent all that
money and went through that pain for nothing?"

"Don't look at it that way. Although I personally wouldn't
recommend liposuction, now that you've had it—and you look
great—you can focus on other things besides dancing."

I shake my head.

"You can try swimming," Dr. Lugo says. "Swimming puts no
pressure on the knee joints and it's a great way to stay fit . . ."

I leave the clinic and stop at a pupusería to eat fried plantains
with beans and sour cream and two pupusas revueltas. I told myself I was going to watch what I eat because I don't want to gain

weight. But I want so badly to erase the bitterness in my mouth, as if I've been eating nothing but lemons all day long.

I drive back to work only to sit in the office doing nothing. Wednesdays are usually slow, but this is ridiculous. Two hours after I've been back to the office a client finally walks in to get a quote and decides AAA is too expensive for him. But what can he expect? He's only had his driver's license for three months. His name is Sam, and after he leaves I find myself thinking about Sam González.

We met at the beginning of the eleventh grade, second week of school, in Spanish class. He forgot his textbook at home and the teacher told him to share with someone. I was sitting on his left. Maricruz, the band's drum major, was on his right. Sam took one look at her and then one look at me, and he moved his desk toward me. I tried to keep my face from showing relief, and from the corner of my eye I saw Maricruz scowling. I put my textbook between us, and when the teacher told us to turn the page Sam reached over to do it and his hand grazed against my breast. He turned red, and I looked away, trying to suppress the tingling running through my body.

Sam. Where are you, Sam? You'd know how to make me feel better, wouldn't you? You'd know the right words to say.

I run his name in the AAA database and get a list of seventy Samuel Gonzálezes and ten Sam Gonzálezes. I spend the rest of the day at the office looking through those names, narrowing the list down one by one. When it's time to go home I haven't sold any policies—but I have an address. After all that work would I really go look for him? And what if I've got the wrong Sam? Even worse, what if it's the right one.

Adriana

For the first time in a long time, I don't go to practice today. I know Eduardo is going to chew my ass off for this, especially since our big show in Davis is coming up, but I just can't go. I lie in bed and listen to the rain falling outside.

I hate the rain.

I can feel the cold seep into my pores. I'm about to get up and turn on the heater, but then I remember that my gas was shut off two days ago. I've forgotten to send the check now for three months. Things like that escape me. I guess that's why I have such crappy credit. I can't remember when my bills are due. I'm not good with dates.

I throw my blanket over me and get into a fetal position. My feet are cold. I can hear music drifting up from Ben's room. I close my eyes and listen to the muffled sounds of the piano. I let it envelop me. Let it take me out of myself, where I can't feel the cold, or the cramps that seize my abdomen in spasms.

I've inherited Mom's problems with menstrual cramps. I remember her writhing in pain sometimes, cursing herself for being a woman. The first time I got my period it came with fever and shivers. I remember clutching my stomach tight and crying on my pillow. Mom was already gone by then. Elena was worried. She didn't know how to deal with my pain. Her body bleeds in silence, unlike mine.

I shiver under the blankets and try to force myself to fall asleep. In sleep I won't feel the cold, or the cramps. But instead I end up remembering the time my grandparents locked me out of the house after I had snuck out to go to Alegría's first show. Yessy had taken me home that night. I begged her to just drop me off in front because it was late and my grandparents went to sleep early and I didn't want to wake them. When I went in through the gate I waved bye to her and she left. In the twelve months I had lived with them, they had never given me my own set of keys. So I had no choice but to knock. I knocked and knocked. Waiting outside in the dark, hearing a gunshot somewhere in the distance, the sound of a helicopter. I knocked again. I went around to the back and knocked on their bedroom window, knocked so loud my knuckles hurt. But they wouldn't open the door. I knew they were doing it on purpose. This was my punishment for disobeying them.

I walked back to the porch and leaned against the door, shivering the whole night while I drifted in and out of sleep. Hours later, I felt something poking me to wake up. My grandmother stood above me with her cane. The sky was already turning a light blue, but the sun hadn't come out yet.

"Get inside," she said.

I kept sitting on the porch, wanting so desperately to go inside and warm myself in my bed, but at the same time not wanting to swallow my pride and let her see what they had done.

"I like it out here," I said. "Sleeping under the stars." I made a sweeping gesture and pointed to the sky.

"Suit yourself," she said, smirking.

She walked in and slammed the door shut.

I knew I wouldn't last that long outside. When my bladder felt as if it was going to burst, when I could no longer stand my cold feet and the chills running up and down my body, covering my skin with goose bumps, I opened the door and ran to my room, hearing my grandmother's laughter above the hissing of the frying pan as she made breakfast.

I finally drag myself out of bed, get my shawl, and rush down to Ben's.

His eyes widen slightly at the sight of the bruises on my face. I see his mouth quiver. He opens the door wider to let me inside. His hands are covered with clay.

"No practice today?" he asks.

I shake my head. Even if I didn't have these cramps, I still wouldn't have gone to practice. I'm not ready to see Emilio again. Even though he's left messages on my machine saying how sorry he was. He was drunk, he said.

"Have a seat," Ben says. "Would you like something to drink?"

I shake my head no and walk over to the heater and stand against it. My cramps seem to release their hold on me. I glance sideways and see Ben looking at me.

"What happened, Adriana?" he asks.

"Nothing, Ben. Forget it."

"What do you mean? You're covered in bruises. Who did this to you? Emilio?"

I head to the door. "I don't want to talk about it, Ben, okay? I'll see you later."

He comes over to me and closes the door. "You can stay," he says. "Tell me when you're ready."

He looks down at the floor for a moment and then returns to his seat at the kitchen table. He's making a sculpture. Or trying to. The ball of clay is refusing to take shape. I walk to the window and look outside. My breath gets stuck on the glass. I wish for the sun. I yearn to feel it on my back. I think of Malibu, hiking with Ben, and wish I was back there again, on top of the rocks, feeling the sun kissing my neck.

My cramps come back again. I clutch my stomach tight. Damn aspirin doesn't do shit for me.

"Come with me," Ben says. He throws a wet towel over his clay and walks me to the bathroom. He turns on the faucet in the bathtub and lights a candle that smells like cranberries.

"Am I that stinky?" I ask.

Ben looks at me with a scowl. "It'll help with the cramps."

Now how the hell does the guy know about that? As if he can read my thoughts, he says, "I have four sisters, remember? I learned a thing or two from them."

The water looks inviting. At least it'll take the cold away. I undo the belt of my robe and let it fall to the floor. Ben attempts to leave the bathroom, but I'm in his way. Maybe my body disgusts him. Hell, it disgusts me.

"Adriana," he says. I know there are no words he can say to express what he sees. I look like I was in a wrestling match and lost.

"It wasn't as bad as it seems," I tell him. "I bruise too easily, and they take forever to go away."

The look Ben has in his eyes makes me regret undressing before him. I hold Ben's gaze and feel myself drowning in the depths of his blue eyes. I lean against him, feel the softness of his shirt against my naked breasts. Smell the fresh scent of his aftershave. Touch the smoothness of his cheek. The voice inside me tells me I shouldn't be touching him now. Not like this. Our friendship is the only innocent, guilt-free thing in my life.

The tears I was holding back begin to slide down my cheeks. Ben reaches around me and I cry in his arms, all the time hating myself for breaking down.

Fuck me. What the hell am I going to do now? I look back behind me, can't see La Parrilla's door anymore. I kick a can out of my way. I hear the manager's voice inside my head: "You're fired."

"Fuck you," I told him, and then left. I looked like shit, I wanted to tell him. What was I supposed to do? Come to work all covered up in bruises?

I walk down Cesar Chavez Avenue, hear them honk at me. "Mamacita," they yell.

"Vete a la mierda!" I yell back. I can't think. All I know is that I haven't paid my rent this month or my dancer's dues, my piece of shit car still doesn't work, and my electricity got cut off. All I know is that there's five dollars in my purse, and there are three eggs, a dozen tortillas, a can of evaporated milk, and a can of jalapeños at home left for me to eat. All I know is, I can't get that motherfucker Emilio out of my head, my body is still bruised, and the stupid bus is taking forever to get here.

I have to find a job, I have to. I'm not going to lose my apartment. If I have to go prostitute myself, I swear, I'm not going to lose my apartment. It is my space. I still remember six years ago when I first moved in, how fucking great it felt to be able to come out of my room without anyone to yell at me, to make me feel like shit. I could be in the living room, in the dining room, eat at the table like a normal human being, no longer having to sneak food into my room and lock myself up. I could lie on my couch all day and night without anyone coming home to kick me out and tell me to get lost. Every piece of furniture, every dish, every article of clothing, is mine. I earned it, goddammit. And I'm not going to lose any of it.

He finds me kicking the shit out of my car. "Need a ride?" he says.

When I see that smile of his, the thick, furry mustache like that of Pancho Villa, I can't help but melt like a damn ice cube. I look away, though, and start heading down to the bus stop. I have thirty minutes to get to practice.

"Come on, Adriana, get in. We're going to be late." He drives slowly, following me down to Soto Street. "C'mon, corazón. I'm sorry. Okay? Perdóname."

I walk up to the car and get in. Only because I don't want to be late to practice, I tell myself, but I know I'm just bullshitting myself. He kisses me all over, and I look straight ahead and don't kiss him back. I ain't gonna make things that easy for him.

"Qué mala," he says, and then drives on. I put my gym bag between us, and I scoot all the way against the passenger door. He laughs. "I missed you," he says. He hands me a small box. "Ándale, take it. It's a present for you."

I've always been a sucker for presents. Carajo. My hands dart out and snatch the box from him. It's a bracelet made out of fifteen pieces of magnet, and on each magnet is a miniature print of Frida Kahlo's artwork.

"You like it?" he asks.

I don't answer him. I gotta pretend I have some pride, after all. But my heart is beating so fast as I put the bracelet on. I suddenly want to fuck Emilio. Make him want me so much he'll never want to let me go. When he pulls into the parking lot he jumps on me so suddenly it scares the shit out of me. He thrusts his tongue deep down my throat, his teeth biting my lips, his hands squeezing my tits so hard it hurts.

Then just as suddenly he lets me go. He says, "You go on ahead."

"Why?" I ask, and I wanna ask him if he's ashamed of me. I wanna ask him why he doesn't want anyone to know about us. But he points at his dick and says he can't go in like that. "Look what you do to me," he says.

I smile and feel the knot that was forming in my stomach start to disappear. I run up to the studio, happier than I've been in days.

After practice we come back to my apartment and drink the twelve-pack we bought on the way. He fucks me like there's no tomorrow, and I swear the guy just can't get enough. It isn't until the third time he comes that he's finally spent.

"Tell me how you got into Folklórico," I tell him.

"Why do you want to know?"

"Just curious. You never talk about your family."

"Maybe 'cause there's nothing to say."

"Come on, tell me."

"Fine," he says, taking his arm out from under my head. He puts both arms under his head instead and stares at the ceiling. "When I was young my mom left my dad for some second-class wrestler she met. My dad would come every day to the house, begging her to come back. Sometimes he would even start to cry, saying he couldn't live without her. But she said she didn't love him, and eventually he got the picture because he stopped coming. Anyhow, my life turned to shit after that."

"Why?"

"Let's just say the wrestler used to practice his wrestling skills on us. When I started fighting back, and actually managed to do some damage, he kicked me out of the house. I didn't have a place to go, and when I looked for my father I learned he had died, and I guess that's the reason why he stopped coming."

"What did he die of?"

"Who the fuck knows," he says. "His neighbors said he died of sorrow but who the hell dies of that? I mean, he must have been a real wimp or something. Dying 'cause a woman didn't love him back."

"Well, so where did you end up?"

"The old lady that would hire me to run errands for her hooked me up with a little room in the back of her house. Turns out her daughter had a dance company. And the old lady said that in exchange for my room and board I had to start taking dance classes because there was a shortage of male dancers in the class."

"And did you like it?"

"I was good at it," he says. "And it got me the hell out of that place. I went to live in México City and danced there for Amalia, and when I started making money I would send it to my mom, and in every letter I would ask her to leave that asshole, who had already knocked her front teeth out. But she refused, saying she loved him."

He gets on top of me and doesn't even wait until I'm wet. He just jams it all in and starts to pump into me with all his might. "Mujeres," he says. "Les gusta la mala vida." He flips me around doggy style so I can't look at him, but it is already too late. I've seen the look on his face. A look that resembles mine when I think of my mother.

Yesenia

It's going to be a long weekend with Eduardo and Memo gone. I could've gone with them to Davis, but I just couldn't imagine being on a bus full of Folkloristas who do nothing but eat and breathe Folklórico. I can't think of a worse torture than that. The show at the Mondavi Center was booked fourteen months ago, and I remember how thrilled we were to have gotten it. For the first time, Alegría will be earning $20,000 for a performance, although most of it will go to pay for the transportation, the dancers' meals, lodging, the musicians, the technician, the truck rental to transport the props, backdrops, and costumes. So much money goes into producing shows, but at the end of the performance, standing at the footlights, listening to the applause that comes at you in a roaring wave—that is worth every penny . . .

Stop it! I tell myself. *Stop thinking about Alegría.* I need to do something, anything, to help me forget. I grab my purse and take out the paper where I wrote down Sam's address. He lives in Alhambra, not far at all from El Sereno. We're practically next-door neighbors. In his policy he's a number 5, for divorced. Maybe he has nothing to do on a Friday night either, and wouldn't he be surprised if I showed up at his doorstep after all these years!

I spend the next hour picking out the perfect dress. Now that most of the swelling has gone down, I can fit into a size eight! The peach dress I finally pick emphasizes my small waist, and the push-up bra underneath makes my breasts spill out of my dress. I curl my hair, carefully apply makeup following the tips in a magazine on how to create a younger effect.

When I pull over in front of Sam's house, I breathe a sigh of relief at seeing the Harley-Davidson he insures with AAA parked in the driveway. But what if it isn't him?

I spray perfume on, reapply my lipstick, crunch up my hair to encourage the curls to stay bouncy, and as I head down the walkway that leads to the back of the main house, I caress the motorcycle with my fingertips.

I stop and take a deep breath, readjust my bra, and push up my breasts to give him a good view for when he opens the door. I make my way to the back, but just as I get to the fence that divides the front main house and the small back house where he lives, I hear laughter, and I stop. I walk slowly, careful not to make any sound with my high heels. Through the branches of a lavender bush I see Sam—and it is my Sam! (I would recognize that head framed with those gorgeous curls anywhere)—sitting in the patio with a young woman next to him. She couldn't be much older than Memo. Her hair is dyed black with a streak of red on the side. Her nails are painted blue or black—I'm too far to tell and it's too dark to see. The young woman laughs at something he says. He goes inside the house and comes back with two cans of Tecate beer.

I tiptoe back to my car and sit there for a while, wondering if I should leave or wait around until the girl leaves. But who knows when that'll be. It's eight o'clock already. It took a lot of guts to come out here, and all for what, just to confirm that indeed he is the Sam I'm looking for, but he's with a girl who's too young to be drinking?

Could it be his daughter? A neighbor? A lover?

I take out a crossword puzzle book from the glove compartment. Memo gave it to me for my birthday. I get frustrated too soon. What do I know about salami purveyors or who Boggs of baseball is? I skip from page to page, stopping when I no longer know the answers and then moving on to the next puzzle. A Colonial Dutch landowner? Scottish pudding? The state flower of Tennessee? By nine o'clock, I have twelve unfinished puzzles and the girl still hasn't come out. I start the car and go home to my empty house.

The next morning I drive to Tijuana for my follow-up visit with Dr. Salas. He checks my progress and says that everything is fine. "In a month and a half we can do the tummy tuck," he says. "We just need to wait for the swelling to be completely gone to see how much skin we have to work with."

"Is a tummy tuck really necessary, Doctor?"

"Why don't you get dressed and we'll talk about it in my office," he says.

He and his nurse leave me in the room. I put on my jeans and can't help loving the fact that I'm now wearing a size eight. The last time I fit into this size was before getting pregnant with Memo. Maybe Dr. Salas is right, maybe a tummy tuck wouldn't be a bad idea after all. I look so damn good, why let sagging skin on my abdomen get in the way? I look at myself in the small mirror hanging on the wall above the sink. I trace the lines on my face with a fingertip, pulling back the skin around my eyes so that it's almost the same face I had before Memo came. Fifteen years ago, when my sister, Susy, got married, I helped my mother with her makeup. It was when I did her eyes that I first got a glimpse of what awaited me. When I applied the eye shadow, the wrinkled skin on her eyelids would move from side to side with each stroke of the foam brush. The skin had completely lost its elasticity, and no matter how much I tried I couldn't smooth it out. I don't want to look like that. And why would I have to? Why let anything get in the way? Why should I let age triumph over the technology that can make me young again? Look at my body! It is a miracle, surely, to look this good. "Body sculpting" is what Dr. Salas called it. The term sounds so nice. It makes me feel like a piece of limestone in the hands of an accomplished artist whose loving hands have chiseled me into a work of art. Like Pygmalion and his Galatea. "Facial rejuvenation" is what he called a face-lift. The words are beautiful. Rejuvenate—to make young again. To live again. To get a second chance.

"How much would it be for a face-lift?" I ask Dr. Salas as soon as I walk into his office. "I mean, not that I've decided on it or anything, I just want to know."

"For you, $2,500," he says.

I think about my bank account. It's pretty low right now. These past few weeks I haven't been meeting my goal, and my paychecks have been terrible.

"We have an opening tomorrow," Dr. Salas says. "If you decide you want to do it."

As I drive across the border I get a call from Eduardo. They're getting ready for the performance, and he doesn't have much time to talk. But he wanted to tell me he misses me and to ask how it went with the doctor.

"Everything's fine," I tell him. "The doctor says I'm healing well."

"Good, good," he says. He tells me how beautiful the Mondavi Center is. How he wishes I'd come with them. In the background, I can hear the music of Veracruz playing. I hear laughter. Feet tapping on wood. The familiar sounds of a dress rehearsal. He tells me he has to go now. They have to get ready for tonight's performance.

"Break a leg," I say, and the last thing I hear is the twinkling sounds of the harp. I dial the clinic's number, and as soon as the receptionist answers I say, "I want that appointment for tomorrow, if it's still available." I exit the freeway and head straight to Bank of America. The bank is going to close soon and I don't have much time. I tell myself that what I'm going to do is wrong. Our account is pretty depleted, especially right now that Eduardo has been so busy with Alegría, he hasn't been working much. But there's another account I have access to. I think about the stress and strains and years of devotion to Alegría. The group is the reason my body and face are so beat up. Let Alegría pay for my face-lift—at least, until I can replace the money. It'll be a loan. A favor, for all my hard work.

"Tell me again what's going to happen?" I say as the nurse prepares me for surgery. She sits on the edge of the bed and pats my hand. She's overweight, even more so than I once was. I wonder why she hasn't done something about her weight, or about the crow's-feet, the double chin. Surely she could get a good employee discount.

"Don't worry," the nurse says, "everything will be fine."

"Tell me," I say, clutching her hands tight. Dr. Salas already told me, but I want to hear it again. I want to know that I'm not making a mistake.

"The doctor will make incisions around your ears and the hairline behind your ears," the nurse says as she traces her finger over the area. "He'll pull the skin and tighten the muscles that are sagging. He'll then remove extra skin. Oh, and he'll also perform liposuction beneath the chin—"

"And there'll be no scars, right?"

"Very little scarring, and the scars will be hidden above the hairline so no one will see them." The nurse is quiet for a moment and then says, "You can still change your mind, you know?"

"He'll fire you if he hears you say that," I say, smiling.

The nurse doesn't smile. "I just don't want you walking out of here unhappy."

"And do you think I'll be happy if I do it?"

The nurse shrugs, and for a second I think I see contempt in her eyes. She excuses herself and leaves the room. I'm wondering why the nurse looked at me that way, when three other nurses walk in and wheel the hospital bed out of the room.

In three and a half hours my face-lift is done. I sleep through the entire surgery. Feel no pain. Wake up in the recuperating room remembering nothing about the procedure. I touch my face, feel the dressing around my head and face, the rubber tube behind my ear to drain the blood and fluid accumulating beneath the incisions. Because I brought no one with me this time I spend the night at the clinic and have to pay an extra fee. I swallow the painkillers the nurse gives me and close my eyes, willing myself to fall asleep, to forget that I'm in a clinic, nauseous and on the verge of vomiting the gelatin I was fed earlier, so far from home, so far from anything and anyone I know.

Adriana

When we get back from Davis, I immediately get back to my job search. I find one at a fish market.

"You've got a pretty face," the guy says to me. He looks me up and down, stares at my chichis for a long time, and then nods. "Yeah, I've got just the thing for you."

This is my job: stand outside the fish market, hold a huge-ass catfish up in the air, and point its head toward the market. He tells me to make sure I make eye contact with all the drivers passing by.

"It works for the car wash up the street," he says. And I want to tell him that the guy up the street is holding a sign that says $5.99 Car Wash, not a goddamn fish that weighs a ton!

But I need the cash.

He gives me a fish and sends me off on my way.

"And please, tomorrow, wear something sexy," he says as he looks at my peasant skirt. "Sexy," he says again as I go out with the fish. It's so slippery, I almost drop it on the sidewalk. I stand as close as I can to the curb and raise the fish as high as I can lift it, which is just a little above my tits. If it wasn't for having strong arms from twirling heavy Folklórico skirts I don't think I would be able to even pick it up. I pretend I'm an Aztec priest raising an obsidian knife, about to do a sacrifice for the gods. But it doesn't work.

The damn fish slips from my fingers and takes a dive onto the street. Cars honk at me. I pick it up and raise it up again. Now that it's covered in dirt it's easier to hold. I smile at the incoming traffic, point the fish toward the market, but all the damn drivers do is whistle and honk as they drive by.

"Mamacita! Quiero tu pescado!"

"Come in and get some!" I yell back.

It's a good thing he isn't paying me commission only, because after a half hour of standing here with the damn fish, there hasn't been one person who's pulled over. And my fucking arms are so sore I can't even feel them anymore.

"How's it going?" The owner comes outside and stands by the door.

"Okay," I say.

He lights a cigarette and leans against the wall. He smokes silently, all the while staring at me.

He throws the stub on the floor and grinds it with his heel.

"Tomorrow," he says, "lose the skirt and those damn huaraches. And for Christ's sakes no braids. No braids."

"Lila Downs wears braids!" I yell after him. "And that hasn't hurt her career at all."

"Who the hell is Lila Downs?" he yells back as he goes into the store. "And she isn't here to sell my fish. You are."

"You stink," Emilio tells me when I greet him at the door of my apartment.

"Sorry," I say, my cheeks getting hot with vergüenza. Dude, I took a shower. I swear I did. I wrap my arms around his neck and kiss him. He doesn't kiss me back.

"What?" I ask.

"Nada," he says, his eyes full of disgust. I crawl into myself, hide in a little corner. "Just, that smells turns me off, what do you want me to do?" I follow him to the living room. I don't want him to look at me like that.

He sits on the couch and taps his fingers on his knees. I sit next to him, move closer, but he only looks straight ahead. He stands up.

"Where are you going?"

"To Tony's. My friends said they would be there playing poker."

I wrap my arms around his waist, trying to keep my hands away from his nose. "Forget the bar. Take me dancing tonight."

"Nah. I'm not in the mood."

I stay quiet, not knowing what else to say. Then I show him the tip of my middle finger, which is wrapped in a bandage. I tell him I cut myself when I was learning to gut fish and it took a long time for the bleeding to finally stop.

"I should sue them and maybe I'll get some good money," I say.

"Don't be ridiculous, why would anyone pay for you being careless?"

"I don't know, but hey, it worked for Stephanie. The doctor cut the tip of her finger off and now she's getting a big-ass fucking fortune."

"Really?"

"Yeah, ask her. She loves to talk about all that dough she's going to get. Anyhow, why didn't you go to practice yesterday?"

"I'm getting pretty fed up with Alegría."

"What do you mean?"

"Are you deaf? The group sucks, that's what. I mean, who the hell does Eduardo think we are? When I danced for Amalia Hernández we not only got paid for our performances but the rehearsals, too. And Eduardo drags us all the way up to Davis for the weekend, where half the group had to take at least a day off from work, and he wants us to do everything for free? Alegría got a lot of money for that performance. A lot of money. And where does it all go?"

"Back into the group, that's where," I say. "All the costumes, the props, the studio rental, hiring special instructors. All that takes money, you know?"

"What makes you so sure they aren't spending some of that money on themselves? Look at Memo, he's driving around a brand-new car that his mami and papi just bought him—"

"Eduardo and Yesenia would never do something like that, Emilio. Besides, Olivia is the group's accountant, and she'd know if something like that was happening."

"Whose side are you on? I'm tired of having to bring my own water to the performances—they should at least make sure we had something to drink and eat. And why should I be carrying my costumes around—isn't that what the volunteers are for? I'm sick of having to spend my own money on parking fees when we perform. Why couldn't Eduardo negotiate free parking for us? Anyway, I've been thinking about starting my own group."

"Really?"

"Yeah. I've got lots of ideas for good shows. And why not? I don't think it's that hard to start a group. And if I play my cards right, I might be able to take most of the Alegría dancers with me when I leave, and I'll shape them into the kind of dancers I think they should be."

I'm too shocked to say anything. Alegría breaking up?

"Don't look at me like that, chiquita," he says as he puts his arm around me. "If you're a good girl maybe I'll let you co-direct."

I smile and lean against him. Me? A director of my own group?

I straddle Emilio and press my tits against his chest. "I'll be a good girl," I tell him, thinking about what kind of costumes I'd choose for the group. And I wonder what we would name it. Just think, Emilio and me, co-directors. Like starting our own little family.

Emilio opens his mouth to say something, but at that moment there's a knock on the door. I forgot to lock it, and now Ben stands in the doorway. He freezes for a moment, and then apologizes before closing the door. I let go of Emilio.

"What's that gringo doing here?" he asks.

"He's my neighbor, remember?"

"And you just let him walk in to your place like that? Are you fucking him?" He stands up and pushes me off of him.

"Answer me!" he says and slaps me.

"Emilio!"

"Who does he think he is, walking in like that, huh?" He suddenly lets me go and heads to the door. I run after him. In my mind I can see him beating Ben to a pulp. The thought overwhelms me. I throw myself at his legs and grab him. He starts to kick me. "Puta," he says. I don't let go. My body keeps him from opening the door. He grabs me by my hair and the punches come, swift and cruel. I think about Ben, his blue eyes, the bathing suit he gave me that I've yet to wear. I picture myself in a deep blue pool, and I feel myself drowning, drowning.

I don't go down to Ben's apartment until four days later, when the bruises don't look as bad as they did before. He opens the door, and I see him hesitate before letting me in. Sometimes, I wish he would slam the door shut in my face and tell me to fuck off. But instead, Mr.-Nice-Guy-Ben goes to the kitchen to grab me some cranberry juice, and it takes him a whole ten minutes before he tells me that this thing with Emilio has got to stop.

"You can't let him keep doing this to you," he says.

I play around with the glass, not looking into his deep blue eyes. Instead, I put on my tough-girl face and tell him it's none of his business. He'll have none of that. He comes to sit beside me, and I can hear the genuine concern in his voice.

"Love isn't like this, Adriana. What you went through with your father gave you a distorted view of what love is. Whatever Emilio feels for you isn't love."

"Emilio cares about me. He just grew up with a lot of abuse in his home and this is all he knows. He never learned to express his love. He only learned to use his fists."

He takes the glass from me and then grabs my hands. I fidget under his gaze. "I don't want to hear it, Ben," I say just as he's about to open his mouth. "I'm not one of those fucked-up teen-agers you work with. I don't need therapy sessions from you. If you care about me, you'd drop it."

"It's because I care that I tell you this," he says. We don't say anything for a while, then he sighs. He pulls me to my feet. "I'm leaving for D.C. next week to visit one of my sisters, and I want to take you somewhere tonight for dinner. Would you like that?"

I nod, and the other Adriana snickers that the problem with Ben is that he's too damn nice. Shut up, I tell her. But she only laughs.

He takes me to a Japanese restaurant in Pasadena. As we get out of the car, I tell him that just a few blocks away we passed some Mexican restaurant called El Portal. "We should go there instead," I say. But he only shakes his head and says it's time I tried some-thing new.

When we enter the restaurant the hostess hits a drum a couple of times and welcomes us. She walks us to our table and hands us a menu. I look at it and nothing appeals to me. Ben takes the menu from me and says he'll do the ordering.

He orders all kinds of sushi, saying it so fast all I catch is rain-bow roll and Philadelphia something. He orders two miso soups and cucumber salad.

"I don't know about this place, Ben," I say, thinking that only a few blocks away I could've been ordering some mole or chiles rellenos at El Portal.

"Have an open mind," he says.

I glance around me and notice that everyone seems to be enjoying their dinner. Maybe it won't be too bad.

"How long will you be gone?"

"A week," he says. He goes on to tell me about how beautiful D.C. is. A little cold this time of year, but it's a city so rich in history. I listen to him describe the place. I notice how his blue eyes sparkle under the light. I wonder where Ben gets all his money from. I mean, I don't think art therapists, or whatever he is, make a lot of money, and I don't know how he can afford to be traveling all the time.

The sushi arrives and Ben shows me how to use the chopsticks. I've never used them before, and it takes me a whole bunch of tries before I'm able to grab one piece of the Philadelphia roll.

"You dip it in the soy sauce, like this," he says. He pops a whole piece into his mouth and closes his eyes as he chews. I laugh and dip my own piece in the soy sauce. Then I notice something green on the side of the tray. Is it guacamole? It sure looks like it. I put a whole bunch of it on my piece, and just as I'm about to put it in my mouth Ben opens his eyes and says "Don't!" but I don't know why he's saying that. The piece goes into my mouth and excruciating pain goes up my nose.

"That's too much wasabi!" he says. My eyes are watering and I spit the sushi into my napkin, but the pain spreads higher up my nose, to my fucking brain it seems.

"What the hell is this shit, Ben?" I say as soon as I can speak. Long agonizing seconds go by before the pain subsides. "I thought it was guacamole."

"I'm sorry, Adriana, I should've told you. This is wasabi, and well, you aren't supposed to eat it by the spoonful."

I notice people looking at us and whispering to each other. My appetite is suddenly gone, and I refuse to touch another piece of sushi.

Ben eats a few more pieces, but since I'm not eating he puts his chopsticks down and offers to order something else for me. "You'll like the teriyaki chicken," he says.

"I'm fine."

He asks the waiter to put the sushi in a container, and we leave the place.

We go play miniature golf because I've never done it before and Ben insists on making up for the wasabi. I tell Ben that if he really wants to make up for it then maybe we can go get some drinks down at a bar. But he shakes his head and tells me there are other fun things to do besides drinking. I tell him I don't believe it. What I love about dancing Azteca is the natural high I get, and when I don't dance I drink, just to get high.

"Okay, so how do you do this thing?" I ask him when he hands me my club. He puts his ball down and stands next to it. He explains to me how to position my feet, how to swing my club, how to hit it with just the right amount of force. He hits his ball and it goes in a perfect line all the way to the hole. He misses it by half an inch.

"Your turn," he says.

I stand just like he showed me, and then I swing. The ball goes up the ramp, then it stops for a second before sliding back down toward me.

"Hit it a little harder," he says.

I swing again, harder this time, and the ball flies over the ramp and I'm out of bounds.

Ben goes to pick up my ball and brings it back.

"I can't do this, Ben. Let's go buy a six-pack and we'll call it a night."

"Here, let me show you."

He stands behind me and puts his arms around me. We both hold the club, his hands over mine, hot and soft. I feel his breath on my neck, and I hold the club even harder.

"Ready?" he asks.

I nod, but all I can think of at that moment is the heat of Ben's body. His smell, his breath fanning on my skin. We swing the club, and the ball goes up the ramp and stops inches from the hole. He doesn't let me go. And I don't push him away. We stand there holding our breath for a few seconds more before we separate and become two people again. My back feels cold. And I look at him, wanting something, but I'm afraid of not knowing what it is that I want.

When the night is over, Ben walks me up the stairs to my place. I laugh. "That wasabi hurt, Ben!" He stands there with his hands inside his pockets and then does something that is totally unlike him. He leans down and kisses me. A soft kiss, hesitant at first, that becomes more the moment I respond, and then nothing matters but this kiss.

You'll hurt him, the other Adriana says to me. And then I feel the chilly breeze, hear the cars swishing by, a baby crying somewhere near. I break away. Emilio is wrong. There are people who die of sorrow. And Ben could be one of them. I'll disappoint him, I know it. He'll want things from me I won't be able to give him. Somewhere down the line he'd know that he made a mistake by loving me.

"I can't, Ben," I say, looking down at the floor.

"Because of Emilio?"

Because of everything, I want to say, but it's easier to just nod and not say anything when he begins to walk back down the stairs. I hear the door of his apartment close behind him. And I go inside my apartment, part of me wishing to go after him, the other part telling me that never in a million years would anything happen between me and Ben. We're as different as chile rellenos and a plate of sushi.

Yesenia

Dr. Salas said it would take three weeks or more for the swelling to disappear completely. Right now, the way my swollen face looks, somebody might mistake me for Quasimodo. But out of the bruises and the swelling a beautiful face will emerge. A younger face that tells the world I'm still here. This is what Dr. Salas says to me on my follow-up visit a week later to get the stitches removed. I'm not sure if I should believe him.

"I look like shit," I tell him as I look at myself in the mirror and notice the bruising—especially under my eyes, the puffiness, the numbness of the skin. Tears well in my eyes, and I take deep breaths to hold them back.

"Most patients are depressed during the first weeks," he says as he pats my shoulder. "It's quite normal. Now, remember you need to avoid strenuous activities. You can walk and do gentle stretches, but easy on the housework, and talk to your husband about going easy on the sex, too. Avoid alcohol. I know that you've been going to the sauna because of the lipo surgery, but now you should stay away from it for several months."

I make an appointment for my tummy tuck. Just after Christmas, so I can take advantage of the holidays and my vacation time to rest.

As I wait at the border inspection station, I look at the women and children walking around asking for alms. A woman knocks on the window. She has a baby wrapped around her back with a rebozo. She holds her hand out to me. I look at her hands, trying to avoid the woman's gaze. I remember the contempt in the nurse's eyes at the clinic. *Yes, it's stupid, isn't it?* I want to tell the woman. *That here I am spending thousands on surgery while you and your child suffer hunger, disease, and poverty I can't even begin to comprehend.* I glance up and see the woman still there. Damn this traffic! Damn the border patrol agents that take so long! I glance at the baby and notice the mucus seeping out of his nose in a steady stream. A fly buzzes around him. The baby wipes his mucus and smears it all over his face. I open my purse and take out a twenty-dollar bill. "Para su hijo," I say as I hand the bill to the woman, who kisses it before putting it inside her brassiere.

The traffic finally moves, and I drive away from the woman and child, thinking how difficult it must be to not be able to give your child something as basic as food and clothes.

After what seems like an eternity, finally, it's my turn.

"Reason for visit," the officer asks.

"A doctor's appointment," I say. He glances at my passport and gives it back to me. He waves his hand and wishes me a good day.

That was easy, I tell myself. I don't even look like the picture in my passport with this swollen face. Jesus, didn't he notice? I could've been using someone else's passport.

I come home to an empty house. I call Eduardo's cell phone, but it goes straight to voicemail. Where could he be on a Saturday afternoon? I told him I wouldn't be long. But since last week things have been pretty bad around the house. I'd never seen him so furious in all our years of marriage. I knew I should've told him about taking money out of Alegría's account, but I didn't have the courage. When Olivia spotted the withdrawal she rushed to Eduardo to find out where the money was spent. I promised him I would work hard to put the money back into the group's account, but he wouldn't hear it.

"You know that money isn't ours to touch. You know how important it is for the dancers to trust us with that money. And now you go and do this? What do you think is going to happen if they find out? They're going to question everything we own. They will look at this house. Our cars. The clothes we wear, the food we eat, and wonder if *they* are the ones who are paying for it all—"

"They won't find out," I said. "Olivia is very discreet, and I've talked to her already and she promised she wouldn't say anything."

He stopped talking to me then. The whole week he didn't say a single word to me.

I call Memo.

"Is your father with you?"

"No, Mom. I haven't talked to him today."

"Are you coming over tonight? I'll make you dinner."

"Thanks, Mom, but I'm going out with Laura."

"Laura? What Laura?"

"Laura from the group."

"Since when have you been going out with her? And why didn't I know about this?"

He's quiet for a moment.

"Well?"

"Jeez, Mom, Dad knows about us. It's just that . . . now that you . . . "

"Now that I'm not part of the group I don't get to find out what's happening, is that it?"

"No, that isn't it at all. I was going to say that now you've been doing all those surgeries you hardly even pay attention to me or Dad."

"I'll talk to you later."

"Mom, wait—"

I throw the phone down, get my car keys, and leave the house.

I dab at my eyes, which are stinging with tears. Even though I'm embarrassed about how I look, I go to the fish market where Adriana's now working.

"What's up?" Adriana asks, looking up from the fish she's gutting. There's a streak of fish blood on her cheek.

"I look like shit, huh?"

Adriana shakes her head, looking down at the fish. "Nah. It's not that bad."

Well, at least I'm not the only one with bruises. The bruises on Adriana's face have turned a sickly shade of yellow. At least I have a better excuse for the way my face looks. There's nothing wrong with having a face-lift. But to get beaten up by a man, now, that's something different. How can Adriana let Emilio treat her like that?

"When do you get off?" I ask.

"Half an hour. Why? Wanna go drink some chelas at La Perla?"

I shake my head. "Doctor said no alcohol."

"Well, that sure sucks," Adriana says.

I look down at the new fish Adriana is holding, its empty, dead eyes. Adriana cuts open its belly and then inserts her finger and mercilessly yanks out all its organs. The image of myself lying unconscious on an operating table, the doctor cutting me open, taking things out, removing excess skin, makes me sick. I suddenly can't breathe in this place. The smell of blood is overpowering. "You haven't talked to Eduardo today, have you?"

"Nope. Why, you lose him?"

"No, just asking. Anyway, I'll talk to you later." I walk away with quick steps. I don't even know why the heck I came. What did I want to see Adriana for, anyway? I get in the car and sit there for a long time. Where can Eduardo be? I pick up my cell phone and dial his number again. Voicemail.

I drive aimlessly around the city, not wanting to go home. When I finally pull into the driveway I sit there for a long time before finally getting out and heading to the garage to surround myself with the costumes, with my memories.

CHAPTER SEVEN

If I could tell you what it meant, there would be no point in dancing it.

—ISADORA DUNCAN

*H*ow *can you describe how it feels to see the Alegría dancers wearing your costumes onstage? It's the end of a long journey, beginning with Abuelita Licha teaching you the art of costume making. Each Folklórico costume comes with specific guidelines that must be followed. They've been shaped by history, custom, climate—everything that is unique to their particular region. The costume maker doesn't change these things but works with them and around them.*

Abuelita tells you about fabric—every cloth has its own movement, its own weight, its own texture. Touch this! Feel this! Look how it moves! Visualize the movement onstage. A costume cannot call too much attention to itself. The sweep of the skirt. The fluttering of the fan. The swirling of the ribbons—all must complement the dance, highlight the movement of the dancer. Think about the music. What's the style of the dance? How will the lights fall on the fabric? Choose the colors according to the mood you want to create. Listen to the music, let it enter your body, let it tell you what colors will enhance it and the movement. Remember that the dancers' movements will cause much stress on the costumes. Your sewing must be strong. But most of all, you must never forget that each costume you make, the colors and shapes you use, are filled with symbolism. They are links to your past. They are the continuation of your people's traditions. Your costumes must preserve the essence of your culture.

You lay the cloth on the table, smooth out the creases. Abuelita Licha stands beside you, guiding you. "Don't be afraid of the scissors. Don't ever be afraid of anything."

Soledad

The weeks have gone by and Ma still doesn't have good news for me. The sales at the swap meet haven't been good. She tells me she can't make the payment for the van on time, she can't buy the merchandise she needs. She can't save enough money for the coyote to take me and Lorenzo to Los Angeles.

I help Malena with the housework all I can, but Malena isn't so nice to me anymore. She thinks I'm the one who gave Lorenzo the idea to go to the U.S. with me. I feel sad for her. She cries at night, and in the morning her eyes are red and puffy. She puts slices of potato on them to make the swelling go down.

Sometimes when she's in a bad mood, I take Lupita to the hill behind the house and we lie down and watch for the monarch butterflies. They have to pass through the town on the way to the oyamel forest about an hour away from here. We lie on the grass and look up at the blue sky.

"Abuelita Licha said that the butterflies are the souls of our loved ones who return to us in butterfly form," I say to Lupita.

"So Abuelita Licha is coming back as a butterfly?"

I say yes. Abuelita Licha is coming back as a butterfly and we must keep looking at the sky to see when she comes. We look up again and the sun makes me squint. I tell Lupita about Alegría, about the bright stage lights hitting the multicolor dresses I made. I close my eyes and I can even hear the music of Michoacán accompanying the movement. I tell her it was Abuelita Licha who taught me to sew, and maybe one day, I will teach her.

When we come back to the hill we're lucky. We see ten butterflies in the half hour we're there. Lupita runs home yelling so loud for Malena and her brothers to hear, "The butterflies are here! The butterflies are here. Abuelita Licha is back!"

The next time, I take the boys to witness the coming of the butterflies. When we're leaving, Malena asks if she can come with us. I'm happy that she leaves the house and doesn't cry anymore. This time we count seventy butterflies. We lie together on the grass and I feel at peace, and for the first time in a long time, I feel at home.

Now that the butterflies are here we prepare for the Day of the Dead. I feel bad that Stephanie isn't here to see it. She would understand a little more about this special day; she would learn it's more than just performing a dance at La Placita Olvera. We have to prepare an ofrenda to honor our dead—especially to honor Abuelita Licha. The children and I go to El Mercado to buy marigolds. I buy sugar skulls, papier-mâché skeletons, and candles to put on the altar. We take the only picture we have of our grandfather and put it next to the pictures of Abuelita Licha and my father. We set out my Abuelita Licha's favorite foods, like calabaza en tacha, huchepos, and pan de muerto. I know that when we kneel before the altar and pray, Malena isn't praying for our dead but for the husband she's about to lose.

We go to the cemetery and visit Abuelita Licha's grave, my grandfather's grave, my father's grave, Abuelita Dolores's grave, the graves of the dead children Abuelita Licha lost to childhood diseases. Children are selling water at the front of the cemetery so that we can clean the graves. We build my grandmother an arch and decorate it with cempasúchil flowers. The people at the cemetery don't cry. This isn't a time to cry. This is a time to remember our loved ones and enjoy the brief time they've come to visit us.

Elena

Fernando will be performing today at La Placita Olvera for the Day of the Dead. It's his first performance with Alegría. I'm on my way to pick him up. I may not be Fernando's high school teacher, but I'm his personal chauffeur. The thought makes me smile.

The kid holds too much power.

They live in a shoe box. A closet-sized bedroom. A closet-sized living room. A closet-sized kitchen. In the living room, a tiny sofa along with a bunk bed makes the space look even smaller. Fernando sleeps there with his younger brother. His mother and little sister sleep in the bedroom. Boxes are everywhere, piled up on top of each other. Some are filled with clothes. I know this because this closet-sized house has no closets, and I've seen Fernando open up those boxes when he was once looking for a T-shirt to change into.

Even though they don't fit in this house, they own a dog. A

little Chihuahua. But I think it suits the house well. What other kind of dog can you have in a tiny house such as this?

The dancers are painting their faces like skeletons: white paint, with black around the eyes, nose, and lips. It's a tradition of the Day of the Dead. Fernando asks me to paint his face for him. It's the first time he's ever done this, and he's too nervous to try.

I wish I could say no. I'm afraid to touch him. I shouldn't get too close. I look around to see if anyone else could do this, but everyone is busy applying their makeup, inspecting their costumes, doing their hair, or polishing their shoes.

Eduardo is busy trying to get everything ready. I know how proud he must be for Alegría to have gotten hired to do this performance. He choreographed something special for today, and tonight the group will be earning a good amount of money. Maybe he'll finally have the money he needs for new Tamaulipas costumes.

I grab the paint and a sponge and bend closer to Fernando. His eyes widen a little before he forces them shut. I start with his forehead first. As I paint it I can feel his warm breath on my face. I see his eyeballs quivering behind his eyelids, as if he's trying hard to keep his eyes shut.

I put the black circles around his eyes and nose, and to paint the shape of skeleton teeth over his mouth I get closer, trying to keep my hand holding the paintbrush from shaking. I can't help but notice the fullness of his lips as I draw straight lines over them. Fernando opens his eyes before I can lean back. I remain still, looking at him, our faces only inches apart. He doesn't move.

"Are you done with that?" I hear someone say.

I peel my eyes away from his and look at Stephanie next to me. She stands there with one hand on her hip, the other hand reaching out for the paint. I blush under her judging eyes.

"Yes, here you go," I say slowly, trying to keep my jaw from trembling. Stephanie walks away and glances back a couple of times while she applies her own makeup in front of a mirror Eduardo set up for the dancers. Fernando stands up and puts a hand toward my shoulder, but I move away from him, far enough where his hand won't reach me.

After the performance, I tell Fernando I'll wait for him by the altars while he cleans his face and changes out of his costume. I squeeze my way through the crowd full of skeleton faces with glittering eyes. Even little children wear the face of death. It makes me shudder.

I enter the building where the altars are and walk around as I look at them. A few are dedicated to people who are famous still in death, such as Frida Kahlo and Diego Rivera. Reproductions of Frida's and Diego's paintings hang on the wall. At a dining table in the middle of the room, two skeletons are sitting. One wears a rebozo and a traditional Mexican dress; the other, pants and a painter's smock. Frida and Diego.

Many altars are dedicated to dead grandparents, uncles, fathers, mothers, and sisters, sons, and daughters. I take a deep breath and let the scent of marigolds, burnt candle wax, and incense travel up my nose, into my body.

"I lost my first tooth today."

Someone pulls on my skirt. I look down and see a little girl smiling at me. I can see the empty space where her tooth once was.

"It fell out this morning," she says. "I almost ate it with my cereal!" She giggles. She takes the tooth out of her overalls' chest pocket.

I can't move. My eyes take in the sight of her. Her curly black hair, her big brown eyes, the dimples in her cheeks. Her gap-toothed smile. The tiny tooth nestled in her palm.

"Lucía, get back here!"

The little girl turns to look behind her, then she looks back at me. She reaches into her pocket to put her tooth back in. She waves and runs back to her mother. I glance down at the floor, and that's when I see the tiny white object by my foot. The little girl's first tooth. I pick it up and look around me, but she's nowhere in sight.

"Miss, I'm ready."

I turn to see Fernando standing there. I nod and guide him out to the exit, past the altars. The smell of the flowers and candles now makes my head hurt. I walk quickly to my truck. Fernando walks beside me. A rushing in my ears makes my head feel as if it's going to explode. My heart thunders against my chest.

We exit the parking lot and almost crash. I didn't see an oncoming car. As I wait for the light to change I have to wipe my eyes a few times to clear them. The lights are blurry. The street signs are blurry. The road in front of me is blurry. Only the little girl's face is sharp and clear in my mind. I hold her tooth in my hand.

A car honks behind me. The light has been green for some time. I step on the pedal and go. Another car honks. I swerve to the side and stop.

"Miss, what's wrong?"

"Forgive me, Fernando," I tell him through the tears.

I know I'm not supposed to let him do this. I know I'm supposed to tell him no. But Fernando's arms pull me to him, and I allow myself to cry on his shoulder.

"It's okay, Miss," he whispers in my ear. I feel the heat of his embrace, feel his fingers gently taking off my glasses, then wiping the tears off my cheeks. Then his lips, like a feather, on my lips.

"Fernando, don't—"

His lips are upon mine, so soft and gentle. I hold on to him, afraid he might disappear if I let go.

I'm the first to break away. I start the truck and merge back into traffic. The windshield has steamed, and I turn on the A/C at full power. Cold blasts of air hit me in the face like a slap.

We enter the 110 South in silence.

"Miss?" He turns to look at me. I keep my eyes on the road. My lips are throbbing.

"I'm okay," I say.

He nods and is quiet for the rest of the time it takes us to get to his house. When I pull over, he turns around to look at me. "I'm not scared, Miss. I know what I'm doing. You probably think I'm just a kid, but I'm old enough to know what I'm feeling. I really care for you, Miss, and I wouldn't do anything to hurt you."

"This isn't right," I say. "You're so young, Fernando. I know it's hard to accept that, but you're still a kid. I shouldn't have done this. I'm really sorry, but I can't see you anymore."

He caresses my cheek and cups my face. He leans his forehead on mine. "Don't push me away," he says. He kisses my forehead and gets out of the truck. He goes inside his house, and I sit there, in the darkness. My fingertips glide over my lips, remembering Fernando's kiss.

I come home and sit on the couch for a long time, too drained to sleep. I hear the sound of the rain beginning to fall outside. It's a hypnotizing sound. It takes me back to the day I picked up Fernando at the bus stop, and then tonight's events come to my mind, the kiss I shared with him.

What have I done? I wipe my mouth with the back of my hand, as if that gesture could erase what happened, turn back time. I didn't have my guard up, that's what happened. It was a moment of weakness. It won't happen again. If it hadn't been for that little girl . . .

I see her again, her black curls, the dimples on her cheeks. I put my hand in my pocket and search for her tooth. When my fingertips don't feel anything, I panic, thinking that I lost it. But then I come upon it, tucked into the corner of my skirt pocket. I pull it out and it sits in my palm like a pearl. I close my fist and hold it there.

When the rain stops and sleep still seems to be an impossibility, I go outside, sit on the patio and watch the bright lights of the airplanes as they fly noisily over my house. In contrast, a snail crawls across the wet bricks in silence. I lean over and pick it up. Its head moves sideways, as if trying to figure out what's happening.

"So you're the one eating all the plants?" I ask it. Soledad's words come to mind telling me that her grandmother would get rid of snails without poison by gathering them in a container and taking them to an open field where they could be free to roam and eat as they pleased, far away from her garden. I go in search of a container suitable for the task.

I find a large plastic jar, place the snail inside and close the lid. Armed with a flashlight, I begin the hunt. Some are easy to find, crawling out in the open atop the wet leaves. Others are sneakier, crawling underneath, hidden by the branches. It's like hunting for Easter eggs. I pick them up with my bare hands, and soon my fingers are coated with slime.

When the container is full, I stand in the patio, not really knowing what to do with them. Soledad's grandmother would take them to the fields. The area I live in is called Green Meadows, but there are no meadows, green or otherwise, anywhere around here.

Feeling defeated, I open the lid of the container telling myself that it doesn't matter if they eat my plants. One way or another the plants will die anyway, from disease, neglect, from not being loved. I watch the snails slither little by little out of the plastic container.

Creatures so tiny, so fragile. How many times have I stepped on a snail that went unseen until it was too late?

They make their way across the brick patio toward my plants. So tiny. So fragile. Like my daughter.

No, not like Xochitl.

These creatures have more life in their disgusting bodies than my daughter has in her little pinky. These useless things that have absolutely nothing to live for, with no purpose in their lives, are living, moving, breathing the same air as I am.

I rush at them, and they don't have a chance. I crush them, crush them, crush them under my feet. *One, two, three, ten.* The moon shines for them but not for my Xochitl. *Fifteen, seventeen, twenty.* The wind blows kisses on them but not on my Xochitl. *Twenty-five, twenty-eight, thirty.* God has allowed them to live but not my little Xochitl. Not her, not her, not her. Crush, crush, crush, until they're all dead.

Soledad

Because Lorenzo and I are leaving soon, I decide to treat us to a trip to El Rosario Sanctuary to see the monarch butterflies. They're all home now, and it's sad for me to think that if my grandfather and father hadn't died crossing the border, they would have been home, too. They always brought enough money from America to take me, Lorenzo, Ma, and Abuelita Licha to the oyamel forest and welcome the butterflies home. I remember seeing all the colors, the movement of their wings— nothing comes closer to it than seeing dancers performing Folklórico.

The sanctuary is open to the public, now that the butterflies have had time to nest. Lorenzo says the children have never been there. It's only an hour bus ride, but he's never had enough money to buy the bus tickets, pay the admission fee, and buy all the other necessary things that a trip requires. It'll cost money, but I can't leave without seeing the butterflies, and it's the least I can do for Malena and the children.

We wake up very early in the morning, before the sun comes out. Malena and I prepare a meal of bread and dry cheese and a can of jalapeños. We fill up our canteens so we won't need to buy water bottles there. We take some oranges and mangoes for snacks. When we get to the town of Angangueo at nine o'clock, it's already alive with people doing their everyday chores. The children admire the beautiful Gothic church in the town, so different from our little adobe chapel.

No sooner have we gotten out of the bus in the center of town than the children start asking for the candied fruit and the cajeta sold by the vendors. My mouth waters at the thought of that sweet caramel sauce on my tongue.

"Maybe if you behave yourselves today Tía Soledad will give you a treat," I promise.

It's ten fifteen when we arrive at the entrance of the sanctuary. In the later months the monarchs will gather closer to the entrance, but now we have to walk more to reach them. Lorenzo carries Lupita on his back because she's small and gets tired right away. The first part of the journey, we climb up concrete steps. I'm glad Lupita slows us down. It was easier for me the last time I came, when I was twenty. I wasn't too fat then and I was used to the walking. The years driving in America have made me lazy. When I start to feel dizzy, I stop to catch my breath.

Lupita cries when she sees dead butterflies and broken wings on the trail. She says maybe one of those butterflies was Abuelita Licha, and now we won't see her anymore.

"Abuelita Licha isn't here," we say to her. "If we keep going we'll find her."

It's an overwhelming sight, to see the butterflies perched on the oyamel trees. At first the branches seem to be covered by what looks like bundles of dead leaves, but when you look closely you can tell they're butterflies. Millions and millions of them weighing the branches down. We stand in a small clearing by the trail, surrounded by the fir trees. The air is like ice-cold water. I'm glad I brought a sarape to wear over my sweater and long-sleeve shirt underneath.

Because it's Sunday it's crowded with visitors. I wish we had come here before the weekend, but right now it's time to harvest the corn and Lorenzo has had much work. He's happy for the work because he can make more money now, save some of it for Malena and the children to live on once we leave. Because it's November the sight isn't as beautiful like it is in January or February, even early March. I remember when I came with Abuelita Licha the butterflies were everywhere. The ground looked as if covered by a flaming orange carpet. The sky was as if covered by stretched layers of coral charmeuse. The trees wore their butterflies like a quinceañera wearing her princess dress. I remember the sunlight falling on the butterflies and they would fly off the branches in swirls. They would fly around us so close I could hear the pat-pat-pat of their wings. And Abuelita Licha and I stood so very still the butterflies landed on our hair and our bodies and blessed us with their magic.

I remember looking at the butterflies mating. A male chased after the female as if they were dancing Folklórico, and when he caught her in the air he took her to a tree where they mated. I remember telling Abuelita Licha that I wished one day a man would love me like that. Catch me in the air and carry me somewhere safe, to love me. Abuelita Licha didn't laugh at me when I said that. She didn't say I was dirty for thinking that. She didn't remind me that I have an ugly mark on my face and that no man would ever want me, like Ma sometimes says. She just grabbed my hand and squeezed it and said someday I would find someone to love me the way I wanted to be loved.

Now I'm here again, and I know that Abuelita Licha, my father, both my grandfathers, my Abuelita Dolores, my dead uncle and aunt, are here. I close my eyes and I can hear them, the wings of the butterflies fluttering like a beating heart, like a susurro, like the sound of someone whispering words of love in your ear.

I hear you, Abuelita. I hear you.

Adriana

A donde quiera que voy, me acuerdo de ti.
A donde quiera que voy, te estoy mirando.
El viento me trae tu voz, no hay música que oiga yo,
Que no me deje llorando . . .

I lie on my couch listening to this song over and over again. Thanks to the repeat button on my stereo I can lie here until the cows come home, and "Corazoncito Tirano" will keep playing and playing even after they do.

I stare at the empty tequila shot glass in my hand, wishing it had a repeat button so that I wouldn't have to keep filling it.

I tell myself I should stop drinking. I close my eyes for a moment, feeling the room spinning around. Or maybe I'm spinning around it, like a Folklórico skirt that twirls around and around on the stage.

Estoy sola. A-L-O-N-E.

Ben left to spend Thanksgiving with one of his sisters, and Emilio, where the fuck is he? He comes and goes like diarrhea, when you least expect it. I touch the fading bruise on my cheek and tell myself I shouldn't care that he isn't here, but I do.

Laura invited me to her place, bless her little dancer's heart. She didn't want me to be all alone on this special day of Thanksgiving. But man, what's there to celebrate anyway?

Besides, I don't fit in at Laura's house. I was there last year, and I can still remember all those cousins, aunts and uncles, nieces and nephews, and the cute white-haired abuelitas you just want to cuddle with. And I remember her mom, the way she smiled at me and put her hand on my shoulder and pulled me away from the little corner where I was hiding. I still remember the softness of her hand.

I told Laura I already had plans. And I do, I guess. I plan to stay here, on this couch, surrounded by my dripping candles and Frida's art.

Viva La Frida bigotona! Que Viva!

Elena thinks I like Frida's mustache and that's why I have her artwork all over my apartment, but that's not the truth. She thinks that just because I'm not e-du-ca-ted like her I can't think deep thoughts, or feel hasta adentro, in the deepest part of my heart. But I can. Te lo juro.

I remember the first time I saw a print of *The Two Fridas* at Olverita's Village. I stood there, thinking, How did Frida know? How did this woman know this is how I feel?

The Two Adrianas. I struggle to understand them. They share the same heart, yet they don't think the same thoughts. One Adriana wishes she was free, free of those memories that hurt her, free to live her life in a better way, and to love and be loved in the purest way possible. And the other Adriana . . . ? That's the one that's fucked up in the head.

Completamente loca.

The thing that struck me about the painting was their hands. The two Fridas holding hands, as if they're trying to reassure each other. And that's what the two Adrianas do. Because one can't live without the other. Both are so vulnerable. Especially the Adriana that wants her mommy and daddy. She's like a baby that wants to be sung to and told she is loved. But who will sing little Adriana to sleep when she's afraid of the dark? Who will sit by her side and reassure her that there are no monsters in the closet eating her dance shoes and waiting to eat her, too? Who will tell little Adriana she's their estrellita, their little sky, and their moon?

244 ■ REYNA GRANDE

No-bo-dy.

That's why I sit here and wrap my arms around my legs. My right hand holds my left and won't let go, won't let go because if it did, little Adriana would be lost. And the cows would come home, and "Corazoncito Tirano" would keep on playing, and the candles would keep shining their little lights, but Adriana would be like this empty shot glass. This empty shot glass with no one to fill it with that holy tequila that burns your throat and turns you inside out.

Elena

This evening I go to Adriana's place to celebrate my twenty-seventh birthday. My sister's made mole con pollo and flan. It's a shame she's such a bad cook. Before I left home I made sure to grab a bottle of Pepto-Bismol, just in case.

"Pásale, mujer, it's freezing outside," Adriana says when she opens the door. She reaches out and pulls me inside, commenting on the fact that I neglected to wear a jacket and if I'm not careful I'll end up with pneumonia. I don't remind her this is L.A. and it's nowhere near "freezing" outside.

She ushers me through the Frida Kahlo curtain into her small kitchen. I walk over to the stove and look down at the red liquid in the pot. I take a deep breath and smell it. Hmm. It actually smells like mole. I breathe in the pungent smell of the chiles and the sweetness of the chocolate. A pot of Mexican fried rice is on another burner.

I wonder how my stomach is going to take it. As if she's reading my thoughts, Adriana says, "Don't worry, mujer, I'm getting better at cooking."

I look at her and raise an eyebrow. "Is that Frida cookbook I gave you doing wonders for you?"

"No. You know I'm not good at following recipes. But Fat Pancho, at La Parrilla, taught me how to make mole con pollo. He actually taught me a lot of stuff about cooking."

"It looks good," I say, glancing back at the mole.

"Yeah, I kinda liked that job."

I ask where that bruise on her cheek came from. Adriana tells me she hit herself on the door. "You know, stupid me, don't look where I'm going."

I feel ashamed of myself then, because I wish I could be a good older sister and give Adriana advice, tell her she shouldn't be letting men abuse her this way. But instead, I tell her to be more careful, hoping Adriana understands I'm not referring to the door.

"So how does it feel to be twenty-seven?" she asks.

I shrug. "Same as being twenty-six." Adriana waves my answer away.

"You'll feel different tomorrow," she says. "It always hits me the following day." We sit down at the dining table and Adriana sets a plate in front of me. Mole con pollo. I don't know why she insists on making this every year for my birthday like Mom used to do.

She doesn't seem to understand how painful it is to remember her.

The mole feels like silk in my mouth. I tell her that it tastes wonderful, and it's the truth. For the first time, Adriana has managed to make a great mole. I imagine her working hard to learn to make it. Things don't come easy for Adriana. The thought that she learned to cook this for me pleases me.

Adriana talks too much, too loudly, as if she's trying to cover up for my silence. She talks about the group members, about who just got married, or divorced, or who's cheating on whom, who's having babies, who's leaving, who just joined, and Eduardo.

"What's the matter with him?" I ask.

"I don't know. Sometimes he just looks so miserable."

I agree. We both wonder how Yesenia's strange behavior is affecting their marriage. Eduardo has always been good to us, and Adriana and I both hate to see him suffer.

We stay quiet after that. The spiciness of the mole now burns my stomach. I'm glad I brought the Pepto-Bismol.

"I'm sure things will be all right," Adriana says after a while. She gets up and goes to prepare us two margaritas. I tell her I can't drink because I have to teach tomorrow. She waves the words away and comes back with the margaritas.

"It's your pinche birthday today, mujer. Enjoy it."

I sip the drink reluctantly. I don't like alcohol. I watch as Adriana takes a big drink from her glass, not even bothering to enjoy the taste of it. My sister needs to stop spending time with borrachos. But just like I can't tell her she needs to stop letting men beat on her, I can't tell her she drinks too much. She finishes her margarita before I do and gets up to make another one—no, two.

"I'm not done with mine," I say.

"Then you should hurry with it."

"Mrs. Rodríguez gave me two tickets to *The Nutcracker*," I tell her. I feel the alcohol begin to flow into my head, my tongue loosening up.

Adriana makes a face. "Mujer, I would go with you but you know I hate those things. Laalaaalaaa. Laaalaaalaa. Yuck." She does a horrible pirouette. "I mean, if it was a Folklórico show I'd go." She sets down the margarita glass in front of me. "Take Fernando," she says.

I stop the glass midway to my mouth and look at her. Ever since the other night at Olvera Street, things have been awkward between Fernando and me. "It'd be too complicated," I say. "I would probably need to ask my administrator for permission, fill out a bunch of paperwork, trip slips, insurance forms—"

"He's not in kindergarten, come on. Plus this isn't a school trip. Just ask his mom. It's not like you don't drive him around already."

"I have his mother's written permission for that. I also have a form that releases me from any liability in case something happens to him."

Adriana shakes her head. "Just take him. Or what, don't tell me you don't want to?" She leans over from across the table and looks at me.

I try to shake my head. Maybe it's the alcohol that's gotten to me, because the answer I give Adriana scares me. "Yes, I do."

Adriana bangs her fists on the table. "Ajúa!" she yells and then quickly makes more drinks for us.

Yesenia

At first I think it's a dog, or a cat, or something creepy lurking in the darkness of the garage. I look around, at the Folklórico costumes hanging on racks. The giant papier-mâché heads hang on the rafters, looking menacing in the dark. When I turn on the light the costumes hanging on the rack to my right move for a second. I pick up one of the machetes for the dances of Nayarit and walk slowly to the rack. My heart is pounding. What if it's a thief?

I quickly part the costumes, machete in front of me ready to strike, and then the thief yells, "Don't hurt me!"

I let the machete drop to the floor. "Stephanie? What in the world are you doing here?"

Stephanie quickly sneaks a paper bag into her backpack. "I don't know."

"What do you mean you don't know? What are you doing hiding in the costumes?"

"Nothing. This place reminds me of Soledad, that's all."

"Is everything okay with her? When is she coming back?"

Stephanie shrugs and gets up and heads to the door. She looks at me, hesitating, her backpack hanging from her shoulder. I walk over to her and take her hand.

248 ■ REYNA GRANDE

"Come. I was about to make hot chocolate."

I take the young girl into the house and busy myself by pouring milk into a pan and putting it to boil. I look for the Chocolate Abuelita carton and take out a bar of chocolate. I toast some bread and smother it with Nutella. Stephanie watches me in silence. I suddenly don't know what to say to her, but I can see she needs someone to talk to. It's been so long since I needed to soothe a child. I place the sandwiches in front of Stephanie and pour her a cup of hot chocolate.

"Does it hurt?" Stephanie asks. "The surgery?"

"Oh," I say, my hand automatically reaching up to touch my face. "The surgery itself didn't hurt. I was asleep then. It was when I woke up and the anesthesia went away that the pain came. Now it's not so bad. I'm healing."

Stephanie smiles. "Good, maybe once I get my money I can get my nose fixed. And maybe I can get breast implants, too. My boobs are so small. The boys at school don't . . ."

She stops talking. She looks down at her hands. I feel ashamed all of a sudden. I was staring at the finger with the missing tip. Stephanie puts her cup down and curls her hand into a fist.

"Stephanie, having plastic surgery isn't—"

"But you did it," she says. "I'm sure it's fine."

I'm suddenly ashamed. The thought of Stephanie on a hospital bed, her body covered in bandages, fills me with dread. "So tell me, why were you hiding in my garage?"

Stephanie shrugs and looks down at her feet. "I stole some money from my mother."

"Why did you need money?"

She sighs. "I wanted to buy some shoes. Some of the girls at school make fun of me because I wear shoes from Payless."

"So did you buy them?"

She nods. She takes her backpack out and shows them to me. A pair of black and pink Jordan shoes. "They're very beautiful," I say. "But I'm sure they were expensive."

Stephanie nods and puts them away.

"Well, since you've already worn them you can't return them and get the money back. So what are you going to do?"

"I don't know, but I can't tell Ma I took the money, and she'll know I did it if she saw the shoes . . . that's why I was hiding them here. She thinks my dad took the money to buy beer for him and his friends, and she was saving it to pay for the smuggler to bring Soledad back."

"Well, Stephanie, the right thing to do is to confess to your mom and not let someone else be blamed for what you did."

Stephanie shrugs again but says nothing.

"How is the dancing going?"

"It sucks. Eduardo won't let me dance the regions I want. I want to do Jalisco, but he says my muscles aren't trained yet for that because Jalisco is always the last region we do and by then the dancers are so tired you have to be strong to be able to do proper skirtwork and footwork. He says I don't—"

"Well, if that's what he says . . . But don't let that discourage you, Steph. You just moved up to the professional group not too long ago, and you still have much to learn."

"I think I'm ready," she says. "I know I'm ready. Maybe you can talk to him."

"I can't do that, Steph."

"But you guys are my godparents! Why do I need to prove myself?"

"You know that Eduardo and I have never had favorites."

"When I have my own group I'm going to dance whatever I want," Stephanie says, standing up. "Thanks for the chocolate. I won't bother you anymore."

"Stephanie, wait," I say, rushing to her side. "Don't be angry. Tell me, how much does your mom need?"

"Just forget it, okay?"

"But what about Soledad?" I'm suddenly awash with shame at the thought that I just spent thousands of dollars on my surgery, and Soledad is stuck in México with no money to come back. "You should've told us sooner your mother was struggling to pay for the smuggler. Tell her I'll have Eduardo ask for donations from the dancers, maybe then she'll have enough." I walk her to the door and say, "Take care, Steph."

Stephanie walks out of the house, down the street, her backpack hanging from one shoulder, her ponytail swinging angrily side to side. I stand there for a long time, until she finally disappears once she turns the corner. I go back into the house, and as I pick up the mug with the chocolate she didn't finish drinking. I wish Memo were here.

Eduardo gets home at midnight. I hear him open and close the door. He goes to the bathroom and pees for a long time. Then I hear him brushing his teeth. He doesn't come to the room. There's no reason to. He's been sleeping in Memo's room for over a week now. I hear him close the door to the bedroom and then the noise of the TV seeps through the thin walls. I get out of bed and stand outside the door, but I can't get myself to knock. Someone on the TV laughs. Then I hear snores, and I know that the TV made him fall asleep. It always has that effect on him.

I go to the living room and see the jacket he wore tonight thrown carelessly on the couch. He knows I hate it when he doesn't hang things up. But my guilt doesn't allow me to get mad at him this time. I pick up the jacket, and, just like I've seen women in soap operas do, I hold it under the lamp and look for strands of hair. What would I do if I found a hair that belonged to another woman? Would I care?

I sigh. There are no hairs or lipstick stains. Nothing. I hate to admit that my sigh was one of relief. Eduardo would never want anyone else but me.

I put my hand inside his pockets and find receipts. One is for a $200 withdrawal at the Bank of America somewhere in Boyle

Heights. Another is for a Chevron gas station for $50. Another is for a coffee and doughnut at a Winchell's Donuts from two days ago. And then I find another withdrawal slip from an ATM at the Commerce Casino. What the hell was he doing at a casino? He's never been a gambling man. I gasp at the amount he withdrew, $500. What was Eduardo doing at a casino?

I put the receipts back in his pocket and throw his jacket back on the couch where I found it.

Elena

The pearl buttons of my silk blouse slip from my shaking fingers. I look in the mirror and reprimand myself for my nervousness. There's no reason to be nervous. Finally, the last button slips through the hole and I take a step back to admire my reflection. My lavender silk blouse and black pants are neatly pressed. My black pumps are polished, and my brown hair is pulled back into a French twist. I look as if I'm ready to walk into my classroom and begin the first lesson of the day. I look like a teacher.

I don't want to look like this tonight.

I sag onto the bed atop a pile of discarded pants and blouses. I should cancel. I glance at the phone, wondering what excuse I could give Fernando. The two tickets to *The Nutcracker* are on the dresser.

I tell myself that I look fine, but I head to the closet and for the hundredth time, glance through my clothes. As always, I look toward the end of the rack and see the red dress Adriana gave me on my twenty-fifth birthday.

The stereo rotates to the next CD, and now Nina Simone's voice drifts into the room. I remove the dress from its dark corner and take it out. The red fabric shimmers under the light. I toss the clothes I'm wearing on the bed, and soon the silky fabric of the dress is caressing my skin like a lover's kiss. It glides over my thighs, the curve of my waist, and hugs my breasts in a tight embrace.

I turn to look in the mirror. I remove the pins from my hair and let my curls cascade down my shoulders. I take off my glasses and go in the bathroom to put on contacts. When I come back to look at myself in the mirror, I don't recognize the woman standing before me.

Fernando is sitting on the front steps of his house. As soon as he sees my truck pull up he stands and walks over to me. He's wearing tan slacks and a wine-colored dress shirt. He's holding a red rose. I blush as he hands me the rose through the truck door window.

"Hello, Miss," he says, then walks around and gets into the passenger seat.

"Where is your mom? I should let her know we're leaving now."

"She's at the Laundromat."

"But—"

"It's okay, Miss. You talked to her earlier today."

"Yes, I know, but—"

"It's okay."

I close my mouth. I'm making a fool of myself and I know that. I nod and start the engine. In silence we make our way down to the freeway. I become drunk with the scent of his cologne.

"You look beautiful, Miss." He utters this as a whisper. A warmth spreads throughout my body and I quickly reprimand myself. But the warmth doesn't stop.

I turn on the music and pretend I didn't hear him.

Fernando smiles. He lowers the volume.

"So," I say. "Have you thought about what career you want to pursue in the future?"

His smile broadens. He leans his seat back and looks straight ahead with half-closed eyes.

"I want to be a Folklórico dancer," he says.

"But Fernando, dancing Folklórico is not exactly a career. I mean, Folklórico isn't like ballet, where a dancer can make a living dancing with a company. Not in this country, at least."

"Look, Miss, I know that. But I also know that since I don't have papers I don't have a lot of options, so what's the point of thinking about careers and college?"

I try to find something to say, but I understand too well how he feels. This is how most undocumented students feel. Can he dream about being a doctor or a lawyer, knowing that without legal residency, he can't be either? But I'm sure that soon enough lawmakers will finally pass the DREAM Act and give undocumented students, like Fernando, the chance to pursue their dreams. He says he doesn't think lawmakers care about the dreams of illegal students. I argue that he shouldn't give up on college or a degree because of his lack of legal residency. There are ways to get help to pay for college.

"Say I do go to college, Miss. But then what? I still wouldn't be able to get a job and put my degree to use. Anyway, I don't need papers to be a Folklórico dancer," he says matter-of-factly. He turns and looks at me. "You *do* look very beautiful tonight, Miss." He says it loudly, and this time I can't pretend I didn't hear him.

"Thank you, Fernando," I say. The look of desire in his eyes frightens me.

When we arrive I place a shawl over my shoulders. Fernando offers me his arm, and I take it. We walk out of the parking garage and head over to the theater. We go to the bar and order drinks while we wait for the show to begin. Fernando orders a Coke. I order an apple martini. Before I can open my purse Fernando takes out a twenty-dollar bill and pays for our drinks. The gesture pleases me, although I think about the hours of work—cutting people's grass with his uncle on the weekends—he had to put in for that money.

We find a quiet corner. I tell him a little bit about the story of *The Nutcracker*, just enough to give him an idea of what it's about. He looks around at the people eagerly waiting for the performance to begin. He smiles at me and my lips instantly respond.

"One time," I say to him as I point to the can of Coke in his hand, "Alegría performed at Fremont Adult School in an evening assembly. That same day, in the morning, they had waxed the stage floor. We, of course, didn't know this. So we just showed up and got ready. Then the assembly started, and no sooner had we stepped on the stage than a dancer fell, and then another. The floor was unbelievably slippery. Instead of the usual clapping the audience was laughing and waiting for the next dancer to fall."

"And what did you do, Miss? That sounds terrible."

"Well, Eduardo asked for an intermission and got someone to go to the student store and buy some Cokes. Then we walked around the stage sprinkling the floor with soda and mopping it up to dry. The floor got nice and sticky, and we were able to continue our performance."

He laughs at this. I think about that night, of how much effort it had taken to keep my balance. Then I find myself laughing with him.

When the curtains open and the performance begins, I try to lose myself in the ballet. Unlike ballet, Folklórico is more forgiving when it comes to body mass and height. How can it not be? Mexican women are rarely super thin and tall (although Amalia Hernández, who single-handedly put Folklórico on the map in México and abroad, always did choose the tall and thin dancers for her group). Ballet doesn't forgive the extra pounds. There's no superfluous flesh allowed. The body must be perfect. Perfect lines and movements. But both types of dance must have grace; grace of the head, the hands, the arms. Perfect carriage.

Despite the beauty of the show, I find myself unable to relax. To forget that Fernando is sitting right next to me. That our elbows touch. Our knees graze against each other. Our lips brush up against each other's ears when we whisper in the dark.

Intermission saves me from my nervousness. I stand up even before the lights go on. We go out to look at the souvenirs. I purchase a T-shirt, and Fernando buys a pin of a nutcracker for his mother.

"I like ballet, but nothing beats Folklórico," Fernando says.

"Ballet provides a good foundation for any kind of dance," I tell him. "If you want to be a well-rounded dancer, you need to take not just ballet classes, but jazz, hip-hop, modern dance. Every dance style has its own beauty. And they're all connected in some way." I suddenly remember one of my favorite Folklórico stories. "Did you know that it was a Russian ballerina who made El Jarabe Tapatío famous?"

He shakes his head in disbelief as I tell him that in the early 1900s El Jarabe Tapatío, the Mexican Hat Dance, which is now México's "national dance," wasn't well known or well liked in México. But when Anna Pavlova visited México and did her own rendition of several Mexican dances, including El Jarabe Tapatío—on pointe, no less—both the dance and the China Poblana costume became incredibly popular.

We stand in line to purchase water bottles when I hear the familiar laughter. I turn around and see Richard standing in front of the souvenir counter. Perhaps he felt my gaze on him, for he turns to look in my direction and stops laughing. I see him inhale, and then he walks toward me. I hadn't noticed her at first, but when I peel my eyes from him I take in the magenta dress, the skin the color of cocoa, and the black thick hair flat-ironed into a stylish bob. Richard, with a black woman.

"Hello, Elena," he says.

"Hi."

His eyes slowly travel up my body, questioning. I know he's never seen me dressed like this. He glances at my cleavage. Desire flickers in his face for a second, then it's instantly replaced with a look akin to anger. He glances at Fernando.

I make the proper introductions, although I omit the fact that Fernando is a student at the school where I teach.

"This is Tamika," Richard says.

A friend? A lover? A girlfriend? He does not say. I wonder if he met her before or after we separated.

I excuse myself and Fernando, claiming we must get back to our seats.

Richard looks at me, then briefly glances at Fernando at my side. "Can I talk with you in private?" he asks.

I shrug and he takes my arm and guides me to a quiet corner.

"I see you haven't wasted any time," he says. "But I'd be careful if I were you."

"What do you mean?"

He glances at Fernando. "Do you really need me to spell it out for you? I'm a teacher, too, Elena, remember? And I just want to make sure you're aware what the consequences are—"

"I don't need a sermon from you," I say, using one of Adriana's favorite things to say to me. "And look at the woman you're with. How old is *she*? Is she one of your students at UCLA? And did you meet her before or after you moved out?"

"Please, Elena. Don't turn things around. This isn't about me. It's about you, about the choices you're making."

The ushers announce the last call to get to our seats. "You no longer have the right to tell me what to do," I say.

I walk away, and Fernando and I hurry back to our seats. I'm thankful for the dim lights that let me hide from him and all those around me.

On our way back, Fernando waits for me to say something, and when I don't, he asks me if I'm okay. My stomach is hurting, and I wish I had an antacid tablet to help stop the pain.

"Was it seeing your husband that made you feel sad?"

"Soon-to-be-ex-husband," I say. "And yes, I guess that has something to do with it." I pull over two houses away from his house. He takes off his seat belt and turns to look at me. He reaches out for my hands. Since they're cold, he brings them up to his mouth and blows warm air onto them. I feel a shiver as his lips brush against my skin. How can I tell him about this conflict within me? How could I explain to him that although I care for him, I'm ashamed about my feelings? Love shouldn't come with shame. And fear, this fear buried deep within me at the thought of going to jail, at being labeled a criminal.

"This isn't easy for me," I tell him.

"I know," he says. "Soon I'll turn eighteen, and things will be different then." He pulls me against him and holds me. I breathe in the scent of his cologne and let myself fall into his embrace. "I understand how you feel, Miss, I really do. And I'm sorry it's this way. But I know that things will change. Just give it another four months."

I think about what he says. Soon he'll be of age, and although people might scorn me because I'm almost ten years older than him, at least I would no longer be afraid of being arrested. I run my hands over his shoulders, feeling his muscles contract at my touch. He has the body of a dancer. Of a man.

I'm the first to make a move. My lips fall upon his with an intense hunger. He presses me against him and a groan escapes his mouth. It never felt like this with Richard, never. I grab him and press him closer, feeling my hunger for him growing. It frightens me. His lips slide down, and he nibbles on my neck, my ears, all the while whispering how beautiful I am. When his hand brushes against my breast, I open my eyes and pull away, frightened.

With shaking fingers I reach for the keys in the ignition and say, "I think I should be going."

"Okay, Miss. Have a good night." He leans over and kisses my cheek.

"Good night, Fernando."

I start the truck and wait until he disappears into his house before pulling out into the street. My breathing is agitated, and I feel dizzy. I wait at the stop sign for a while, trying to get a grip on myself. Then a car pulls up behind me, and I have no choice but to continue driving. When I get home I immediately take off the red dress and put on my pajamas. I wash off the makeup, take off my contacts, and brush and brush my teeth, trying not to think about Fernando's kisses.

CHAPTER EIGHT

If I cannot dance, I shall die!

—ANNA PAVLOVA

*Y*ou *pull off your clothes and stand naked in front of the mirror. The hated girdle is buried deep in one of your dresser drawers, for now no longer needed, not until you have your tummy tuck. You trace your face with your fingers. It's still your face, minus the wrinkles, the disgusting double chin. Why can't he see that? Why can't he appreciate that, instead of giving you the silent treatment* *and looking at you as if you had a hideous birthmark? If he only knew that at work you've been getting hit on by your male customers more and more, even by twenty-something-year-olds!*

You grab your abdomen. So many years after having given birth the stretch marks can still be seen, silvery, like a spiderweb, and the skin still crinkles and sags, now more than ever after having lost all that fat. The Cesarean scar is a dark, ugly line against your skin. Soon, you'll have a nice stomach. No more stretch marks. No more sagging skin. Now that the swelling from lipo has completely disappeared you're a size seven. Who would've thought! Ah. Thank God for plastic surgery.

You lift up your droopy breasts, cup them in your hands.

"Your turn will be next," you tell them. Yes, why stop with a tummy tuck? Why stop now that you're looking so good? Now that you can walk into Forever 21, Express, The Gap, knowing that there's something in there for you. How good it feels to be able to walk around the mall, to see the displays at the windows and know that if you want to buy that pretty dress the mannequin is wearing, you can! You can walk into Victoria's Secret and buy silk lingerie and actually wear it instead of burying it deep inside your underwear drawer like a dirty secret, like something to be ashamed of.

Yesenia

I stand outside the room that once belonged to Memo but is now Eduardo's. I can hear the TV on, and I wonder what show Eduardo's watching at this hour. Doesn't he know what time it is? Has he forgotten it's Sunday?

I open the door and go inside. Clothes are thrown carelessly around the room.

He's lying on the bed, his ankles crossed, his hands put together as if in prayer. He's looking up at the ceiling, his face completely devoid of any kind of emotion.

"It's ten thirty," I say. I walk over to the bed and sit down on the edge. I put my hand over his praying hands. "Aren't you going to practice?"

"No."

I grab the remote from the dresser and turn off the TV. "Why aren't you going?"

"I just don't want to go."

He turns around and faces the wall.

"But the dancers need you there. They won't know what to do if you're not there."

"They'll know. Besides, Emilio will be there."

"So what? Alegría is not Emilio's group."

"It isn't my group, either," he says.

"What's that supposed to mean?"

"I never wanted this," he says. "You knew that since the start, I never wanted to have a group. It's your group."

"Don't you know what I would give to be there again?"

"Then do it. Go and teach the dancers. You don't need to have a good knee for that."

"If I go there I'll want to dance."

I sit on the bed beside him and run my hand over his shoulder, hesitantly at first, afraid he might push me away. When he doesn't, my hand moves down to his chest. He's so still. I muster the courage to unbutton his shirt. At the touch of bare skin my nipples become hard. It has been so long.

He doesn't move.

I lie down beside him, in a spoon position, and rub myself against him. My hands move down, resting over his hardening penis. With more confidence now I begin to undo his belt, and that's when he stops me.

"Don't."

"Why?"

"You know why."

"No, I don't."

He turns around and looks at me. "You know why," he says again.

"Goddamn you. Then tell me again. Tell me why you don't want to touch me anymore!"

He grabs my arm and drags me off the bed. He digs his fingers into my flesh and doesn't let me go. He takes us to the door, turns on the light, and pushes me in front of the closet mirror doors.

"You see that?" he says. "That person is not the woman I married."

I look at my face, the swelling practically gone, and just like the doctor promised, the clock has been turned back. I look so good, and yet he looks at me with so much disgust, so much loathing. I try to yank my arm from his but he grabs it harder, hurting me.

"Let me go!"

"What have you done to my wife?"

I push against him. "It's still me, don't you see that? I'm still here."

"No, my wife was kind. She was a good mother. A loving wife. A true Folklorista who wouldn't allow anything to stop her from loving Folklórico. And you, I don't know who you are . . ."

Tears well in my eyes. My hands reach out to grab him, to hold him, but he takes a step back. "If you don't want me, I know other men who do," I say defiantly.

He lets me go suddenly and leaves the room. I run after him. He puts on his jacket, grabs his car keys, and opens the door.

"Where are you going?"

"Away from here."

"Where, back to the casino? Yeah, I know all about it. You accuse me of wasting money but you're throwing our money away, too."

He stops for a moment and looks at me as if he wants to

say something. He shakes his head instead and walks out of the house. I stand on the porch and watch him drive away.

I walk back to Memo's room, fighting the tears. I stand in front of the mirror, trying to figure out what Eduardo was talking about. I'm still here. I'm not some stranger, like he claims. It's still me, Yesenia.

"You don't know what you're missing, baby," I tell Eduardo's ghost. I look in the mirror and slap my butt. *You don't know what you're missing.* I go to the bathroom and turn on the faucet in the bathtub. I pour bubble bath into the water, light some candles and place them around the bathtub and the sink. Then I turn on the CD player.

The water is warm and inviting. I undress and lower myself slowly, sink into its silkiness, its warmth. It caresses my legs, then my butt, my hips, my waist, my breasts. I close my eyes. Sam González's face appears out of the darkness. His eyes look at me with so much hunger, so much want, my nipples become hard. I remember that day in Spanish class, his light brown eyes like honey dripping slowly over my body. My skin gets covered in goose bumps. My hand moves down my stomach, down, down, to that place Eduardo no longer cares for.

When I touch the tip of my clitoris, I open my eyes, suddenly embarrassed. What am I doing? When was the last time I needed to do this myself? High school? I take a deep breath and close my eyes again, letting Luis Miguel's sexy voice hypnotize me once more, and my fingers begin to move. I think of Sam again. I think of his smile, imagine his mouth on my breast. I moan.

Because I've never been able to get myself off with my fingers, I let the bath water go until the bathtub is empty. I turn on the faucet again, and I scoot all the way down and put my legs up on the wall. I lean back down, letting the water do what my fingers were doing before. The electricity comes in waves, spreading all over my body from the center of my being. Slowly, slowly it builds, and I think of Sam, of his mouth down there, of his hands on my breasts, my butt, everywhere, but suddenly it's Eduardo's face that comes up before me. My need intensifies then, and my body convulses in a wave of pleasure. When it's over I push myself back up and turn off the water.

As the pleasure fades, I'm suddenly overcome with loneliness so immense, my body becomes cold. I pull up my legs and hug them against my chest, trying to hold off the tears, telling myself not to cry, not to cry. But I do.

Soledad

Finally I get a call from Ma. Don Agustín's son, the owner of the store that Ma calls us at, comes running to the house to say there's a call from America. I'm washing the dishes when he comes, and I'm so excited I take the dirty pot I was washing with me. Lupita, who now follows me everywhere, laughs at me and takes it from me before I go into the little room where the phone is kept. I sit on the wooden chair and say, "Bueno?"

Ma says she finally has enough money to pay for the smuggler because the Alegría dancers made donations. I say to Ma it wasn't right to ask the dancers for money. They have their own expenses, too, like paying for school or caring for their families. She says I do so much for the group the least they can do is to help me. She says now with the holidays coming, she's selling lots of toys, too. With that, and the rest of my savings I left behind in my shoe box, we'll buy the bus tickets to the state of Chihuahua and pay the smuggler. All the money I saved is now completely gone.

"You aren't leaving, are you, Sol?" Lupita says. She holds my hand as we walk back to the house. I wait until Lorenzo comes home from the fields to tell him the news. Then I let him tell his family.

The next few days pass by us quickly. Malena cries day and night. The children cry, too. Lupita holds on to me, and she even wants to sleep with me on the old couch so that I can hold her at night. I cry so much when she's sleeping. I hide my face in her silky hair, and I wish with all my heart I could take her with me.

Lorenzo and I take the bus to Chihuahua. Because he rarely gets to ride in buses, he gets carsick and has to go to the bathroom many times, and on the fourth time he says to me that he's been vomiting. I pat his hand and give him a box of gum I bought from one of the little children outside the bus terminal. To get Lorenzo's mind off his carsickness, I entertain him with stories about Folklórico that I have learned from Eduardo during all my years of watching him teach the Alegría dancers. He doesn't just teach them the dance steps, but also the history of the dance, even though some of the dancers don't care to learn the history or meaning of the dances, like Stephanie. Just like Lorenzo, I have never traveled anywhere in Mexico. I went straight from Michoacán to the U.S. and never got a chance to see more of my country. But it is through costume making that I have been able to "travel." As I feed the pieces of the costumes through the sewing machine, I think about the events in history that have shaped them, the people that have preserved them, the dancers who will wear them.

It takes two days for us to get to the border. When we get to our destination, we take a taxi, and I give the driver the address Ma gave me last night. It's the address of the coyote they found to take me and Lorenzo across the border.

The driver lets us out in front of a little taquería. When we go inside we order some tacos and sodas and then sit in a corner, not knowing what to do. After an hour of sitting there, a man walks in the door. He walks over to us and whispers, "Soledad?"

I nod.

He sits down and calls the waitress over. He orders some tacos and then grabs a handful of the chips Lorenzo and I didn't eat.

"My name's Lucio," he says. His mouth is open as he chews, and I can see the chips being ground by his teeth. "I'm going to take you across the river."

"Is it dangerous?" I ask. I know how to swim, and Lorenzo does, too, but I have heard stories about the river.

"Ay, Dios mío, hasta la pregunta es necia," the coyote says. My cheeks get hot. I know it was a stupid question.

"Vámonos," he says as he takes a last swallow of his Squirt. We follow him outside, and he tells us to keep up. We take the bus for about twenty minutes, and then we get off on this little street. Lorenzo and I walk behind him. I know that Lorenzo is thinking what I'm thinking. Someone killed our grandfather and father while crossing the border. What if we have the same bad luck?

Lorenzo doesn't talk much, which is okay because I don't want to talk. My stomach hurts with worry. We go to a motel. I look at Lorenzo. I stop walking, and I don't want to follow the smuggler anymore.

"Come on, I'm not going to do anything to you," the coyote says, but I shake my head, and I hold a skinny little tree outside the motel. Lorenzo holds me, and he feels just as skinny as the tree.

"Wait here," the coyote says. He goes inside the motel and doesn't come out for a long time.

Lorenzo sits on the curb. "Are you nervous?" he asks.

I nod.

"Was it like this when you crossed the first time?"

I remember thirteen years ago when I crossed the border. Ma paid a friend to let her borrow her daughter's birth certificate. A lady smuggler drove me through the border inspection station using the birth certificate. It was easy but very expensive for Ma. The less dangerous the crossing is, the more it costs. I tell this to Lorenzo.

"Do you regret coming to México?" he asks.

I tell Lorenzo about the butterflies, the whispers of their wings, and I tell him no, I don't regret it, because I got to say good-bye to Abuelita Licha.

He nods and says he understands.

Finally, the coyote comes out with four more people. "Let's go," he says. We follow him. We take another bus that takes us to the river. Nobody says anything. No one looks at each other. Eyes to the ground. Hands in a fist. Lips pressed together. Pale and sweaty skin. Prayers under one's breath.

The coyote has a little boat, the kind you inflate with a pump. It's made of rubber, and he has two little paddles for it.

"I'll take two people at a time," he says. First he takes the two young girls in the group. He's very fast, and the river doesn't seem dangerous at all. The water is very brown and looks dirty, but it's calm. He gets to the other side and lets the girls out. He comes back and takes the other two people, an older lady and a man.

Lorenzo and I are last. All this time I bite my nails, my eyes looking everywhere for la migra. There's nothing out there but a few trees and lots of shrubs and bushes. I pray to God that la migra doesn't come this way.

"Get in," he says. I get in first. Because I'm fat, the little boat dips down more in the water on my side. We hold hands, Lorenzo and me. We know how to swim, I tell myself. We know how to swim. We're almost at the other side when la migra surprises us.

"Hold it right there!"

I turn around and I see them walk out from the bushes, and I wonder how long they've been there. They're dressed in green, big brown sunglasses, white hats. Behind them, a white truck is driving fast, coming this way. The four people waiting for us start to run everywhere, screaming.

"Hijo de la chingada," the coyote says.

He starts rowing back, paddling quickly, but because the

weight isn't the same, the little boat flips over, and I go into the water first.

At first I can't move from the shock of the water's icy temperature. I feel needles stabbing me everywhere. I flap my arms to come up for air. The coyote is next to me, and he pulls me up and tells me to hold on to the little boat. But Lorenzo is not anywhere. I yell for him, but I don't see him. The coyote starts to swim, pulling me along with the little boat.

I put my head in the water but I can't see anything.

"Lorenzo!"

I let go of the little boat and start to swim.

"What the fuck are you doing? Hold on to it!" the coyote yells.

I hear water splash and I see two of the officers dive in the water. One of them swims toward me, the other swims somewhere else. I try to kick and kick and start to feel something pulling me under.

I feel hands grabbing me and I hold tight. I kick with my legs and go back to the surface.

We come up to the bank. I cough up water, my body is numb, and I can't feel my trembling hands.

"You're okay now," one of the officers says. "You're safe."

Farther down on the bank, another officer has Lorenzo, who is coughing up water.

"Look at that coward running away," I hear one of the officers say. I turn around and see the coyote on the other side of the bank.

The officer helps me get up and they walk me and Lorenzo to the truck. They turn us around and put handcuffs on us, then they put us inside the truck.

"Are you okay?" I ask Lorenzo. He nods. His eyes are red.

They catch the older woman and the man, but not the two young girls. They look for them but can't find them. They drive us away, and through the bars of the truck I can see the river, and the water so calm. I shiver.

They take us to the immigration office. Lorenzo and I sit and wait to be called. The air conditioner is on very high, and we're shaking with cold. Our clothes are still wet, and I'm afraid we'll get sick.

"You don't tell them your real name," I tell him. "Make something up, anything."

"But why?"

"Because we're going to try it again, and if we get caught again and they have our real names, we could get in big trouble."

Lorenzo is very quiet. He looks around at the people being brought in by la migra. Some look sad, some look angry, frustrated, afraid, but I know that they think like me—we will just have to try again.

We get called up. I go to the officer calling me. When he asks me my name, I suddenly forget what name I was going to give him. He asks me again, and the name that comes up in my head is my grandmother's name.

He writes it down. "Okay, Alicia, I need to take your fingerprints." When he calls me by my grandmother's name I start to cry. I came back for my grandmother, I tell him in my broken English. She died. He nods. He takes the prints of both my index fingers and when he's done with me another officer takes me to a line. Lorenzo is already there, his face so serious. They take us out and load us inside a bus.

"We'll try again the day after tomorrow," I tell him on our ride back across the border. "Maybe not the river this time, but another way."

Lorenzo looks at the woman sitting next to us who's crying so hard it makes me sad. "I gave them my name," Lorenzo says.

"What do you mean?"

"La migra. I gave them my name."

"But why?"

"Because I'm not trying it again, Soledad. I'm going home."

"But Lorenzo, I told you it wasn't going to be easy. I told you it—" He puts his hand on my shoulder.

"Listen, Sol. When I was in the river and I thought I was going to die, I suddenly realized one thing: By being in México at least I know that I can give a little food to my children, even if I have to steal it from the fields. But I'm no good to them dead, do you understand?"

I get choked up and my eyes get wet with my tears. I nod because I can't speak. I understand what he says, I do, but still, I don't want to make this journey all alone.

Adriana

"How was your trip?" I ask Ben. It's a dumb thing to say, considering that he's been back for two weeks now, but I've been avoiding him as much as he's been avoiding me.

"Fine," he says, opening the door to his apartment while holding a grocery bag from Trader Joe's in the other.

"So are you doing anything today?"

He shrugs. "I'll probably go hear Dave play tonight."

"That sounds good," I say, following him into his apartment.

"Yeah."

Yeah, but he doesn't ask me to come with him, and I don't have the guts to ask him if I can. He busies himself putting his groceries away. After a couple of minutes I decide to head to the door.

I notice the Scrabble board he has under the coffee table and remember the few times he asked me to play. I always said no, not wanting him to see how dumb I am.

"Hey, maybe we can play Scrabble. I'm up for learning how."

He comes to the living room and glances at the red box. I see a little spark in his eyes, but then it's gone and he shakes his head.

"Not today. I actually have a painting to finish before I leave for Wisconsin for Christmas. I should try to get some work done right now."

Christmas is three weeks away, I want to say, but instead I sigh. "All right, dude, I guess I'll see you when I see you."

I head to the door slowly, waiting for a word from him, waiting for him to tell me not to go. I pause at the door and nothing comes from him, only a sigh. I walk out into the cool December day. I turn to see Ben standing by the door. "Have a good day, Adriana," he says to me, and then he's gone.

How did I manage to fuck this up so bad? I miss our movie nights, the hours of sitting together, sometimes not even talking but communicating just the same.

I go up to my apartment and lie on my bed. I dial Emilio's cell phone, even though the asshole hasn't been answering my calls. I hear his voicemail, listen to the throaty, rough voice. Then I hang up and call again, and listen to his voice again, and again, and again, until I've heard it enough times that it's recorded in my head. The gentle sounds of the piano start to drift up from Ben's room. He always plays this music when he paints. I get up and lie down on the floor, my ear against the thin carpet. I fall asleep to the *Moonlight* Sonata.

I dream that I'm covered in maggots crawling all over me. When I wake up from my nap it's already dark outside, even though it's only six o'clock. I sit in the darkness of my room, remembering the years with my grandparents. Things had gotten so bad with my grandfather yelling at me for everything, that eventually I stopped coming out of my room. I would come straight from school and lock myself up and not come out because if I did, he'd pounce on me and tell me how worthless I was. I'd lie on my bed, listening to Folklórico music, or watch soap operas, trying not to think about how hungry I was and how badly I needed to pee. If I couldn't hold it and they were still in the living room, I would pee in a bucket I had stolen from Grandma's garden supplies and empty it in the toilet in the morning. Once everything was quiet and I pressed my ear against the wall, listening for the snores in their bedroom, then I would sneak out, like a thief, on tiptoe. I got quick at this right away: grab a plate, load it up with whatever my grandparents had for dinner, and then run back to my room to eat.

By then I was too hungry to care the food was cold.

And one day, Grandma made chile verde, and I forgot to take out the dirty dishes I hid under the bed throughout the week. When they left for church the following Sunday and I was all alone, I took out the dirty dishes from under the bed. The pieces of pork I didn't finish eating were now maggots, maggots crawling all over the bowl. I ran to the bathroom and threw up. And that day I began to hate Elena. That day, I finally started to believe what my grandparents said was true: if Elena really loved me, she wouldn't have left me behind.

I dial Emilio's number again but he doesn't pick up. Everything is quiet. I grab my shawl, put on my shoes, and head out the door. I walk by Ben's apartment and notice the light in his living room. I stand outside the door and almost knock, but instead, I walk away and head to my car. The damn piece of crap rattles all the way to Emilio's apartment building. It's like I'm a newlywed dragging a long string of cans behind me. It's the axles, I think Ben told me, many weeks ago.

Emilio's truck is parked across from the building, so I know he's home. I park behind his truck and run across the street. The door to the building is locked, and because I don't have a key there's nothing for me to do but sit outside on the steps and wait for someone to come.

My shawl is too thin to keep my body from being so damn cold. And what the fuck was I thinking wearing sandals tonight?

I keep forgetting it is winter now. I miss the heat of L.A. summers. I don't do well in the cold, although Ben claims that this cold is nothing compared to Wisconsin's.

I pull my peasant skirt as far down as it will go. The wind ruffles the trees around me, dogs bark somewhere close, music drifts from a window up above. Adolfo Urías singing about loving two women, a dark-skinned one and a light-skinned one, just like me and Elena.

What the fuck am I doing here anyway?

Just as I'm about to leave, I hear footsteps behind me. A man opens the door and walks out. I ask him to hold the door for me and I run up the stairs.

"You live here?" he asks.

"Yeah," I said. "But I forgot my key." I go inside and walk quickly down the hallway. Emilio lives on the second floor. The curtain of the living room window is slightly open. I take a peek inside and find Emilio on the couch, asleep. With one hand he hugs a pillow and with the other he holds a beer, which is on the verge of falling. I stand there for I don't know how long, watching him sleep. Then I finally have the guts to knock.

"It's you," he says when he opens the door. For a second I think the asshole is going to slam the door in my face, but instead he steps aside and lets me pass.

I stand in the middle of the living room like an idiot, waiting for him to ask me to sit down. But then I remember that he isn't Ben, and so I head to the couch and let myself fall on it. He stands by the door, his hands in his pockets.

"Want a chela?" Emilio asks.

I sigh, relieved. "Yeah."

He comes back with two beers. He sits next to me and we drink our beers in silence. He turns on the TV and flips through the channels. He finds an India María movie and I ask him to leave it. I love la India María, but he tells me he finds her ridiculous and keeps flipping channels, stopping at a horse race.

"You ever been to a horse race?" he asks.

I shake my head no.

"Maybe I'll take you one day," he says. I lean against him. For a moment he hesitates, but then he puts his arm around me. I soak up the heat of his body.

"I'm hungry," he says after a while.

"Do you want me to cook something?"

"Nah, I don't think I have anything in the refrigerator but chelas. Let's go get some tacos."

We stand up and he grabs his keys. He drives us down Soto Street to a taco stand. I wish we'd gone to King Taco instead. I love the sopes there. Besides, it would be nice and warm in there, whereas here, out in the street, I know I'm going to freeze my ass off. But I keep quiet and I let him order our tacos while I wait in the truck. When he returns he tells me to go to the back. He puts the gate down and sits on it.

"Why can't we sit inside?" I ask.

"Don't want to get my truck stinking of onion," he says. "Eat."

I munch on my carne asada tacos. They're actually very tasty, but I'm too fucking cold to enjoy them. My feet are like frozen tamales.

"You done?" he asks.

I nod.

He takes the paper plates over to the trash can and then we get back the truck. He blasts Vicente Fernández songs all the way back to his apartment. The guy isn't big on conversation.

He pulls over two cars away from mine. We get out of the truck and wait for the street to be free of cars before crossing. I look over at my car. Maybe I should go home. But to what?

"Are you coming or not?" he asks, ready to cross the street.

I nod and cross with him.

Yesenia

Today after work, I decide it's time to return to Sam's house. I make a quick stop at the mall and buy a dress for this special occasion. I still can't believe how good I look, and that now I can shop in the misses section and find something nice that'll fit me. On my way to Victoria's Secret I stop at the hair salon. There are two hairdressers inside. One is dyeing a woman's hair and the other is sitting at the counter reading a magazine.

I ask how long the wait is to get my hair dyed, and I'm told it'll be at least forty-five minutes.

"But if you just want a haircut I can help you with that," the hairdresser at the counter says.

I look at the picture of a woman up on the wall. Her hair is cut a little below her ears and styled in soft waves. I always wondered how I would look with short hair. Of course I always had long hair because of Folklórico, but now . . .

"Can you cut my hair like hers?" I ask, pointing to the picture.

"Yes, of course," the hairdresser says. "Have a seat."

I ask the woman to turn me away from the mirror. I don't want to look. If I look, I'll hate myself for cutting off my hair. So many years of having it almost down to my waist, buying expensive shampoos and conditioners to keep it healthy, and now it piles around me on the floor. I hear the snipping of the hairdresser's scissors, like the hissing of a snake.

I close my eyes, and I'm thankful that the hairdresser isn't the talkative type. The last thing I want to do is make small talk.

Finally, the snipping comes to an end. The hairdresser begins to style it with the curling iron. When she turns me to face the mirror, I reach up to touch my short hair. It feels so final now. I'll never again wear braids and ribbons in my hair.

"Do you like it?" she asks.

I manage a nod and a weak smile. I pay for the cut and leave the salon as the hairdresser begins to sweep my hair into the dust pan.

After a stop at Victoria's Secret I change in the public restroom and put on a fresh layer of makeup.

Now I'm ready.

On my way to Sam's I chew on the inside of my lip because I'm trying really hard not to chew on my acrylic nails and ruin them. But my teeth bite too hard, and soon I taste blood in my mouth. The pain distracts me from my nervousness, and I keep gnawing on my lip all the way there.

With one more glance in the mirror I'm ready to see him. His motorcycle is parked in the driveway, and I sigh in relief knowing he's home. But what if he has company? No. Nothing can go wrong tonight.

I'm a hot momma. I'm Yessy the hottie. My hips sway side to side. I told Eduardo that if he didn't want me I knew someone else who did. Well, Sam might not know it yet, but as soon as he sees me, he's going to want me.

I knock and after ten seconds I'm ready to turn around and run away. But I force myself to knock again. I reach up to touch my hair, make sure that I do have some. I feel bald. I never thought about how heavy my hair actually was!

Nobody opens the door. I peek through the curtains and see a light in the kitchen. I start to make my way down the steps, disappointed and yet relieved. I hear the door open, and he stands there wearing pants and a muscle shirt, drying his wet hair with a towel. "May I help you?" he asks.

"Hi, Sam. It's me. Yesenia," I say. "Yesenia Alegría."

"Yessy? God, what are you doing here? How did you know where I live?"

"You aren't that hard to find," I say with a laugh.

"I can't believe this. It's been so long. Don't just stand there. Come inside."

All of a sudden, I'm afraid. What if he doesn't like what he sees? I wish I could stay outside in the dark, but he pulls me into his house. We both speak at the same time. "I'm sorry about—"

"I was taking a shower and—"

Then we start to laugh, followed by an awkward moment when neither of us knows what to say to the other.

"So, here you are."

"Here I am," I say, forcing myself to smile, to hide my shaking hands behind me.

He stands there and puts his hands inside his pockets, his eyes roaming over my body. "You look wonderful," he says. "Look at you. Haven't changed a bit since high school."

"You don't have to lie," I say. "I've gotten older."

"Don't look a day over twenty," he says. His words give me all the confidence I need. I stand up straighter and stop shaking. He excuses himself to go finish getting dressed. I look around the tiny living room. There's hardly any furniture except a couch filled with junk, a large plasma TV, a floor lamp. The kitchen is on the opposite side, just a hot plate and a small refrigerator, a table with two chairs.

He returns wearing a T-shirt with the sleeves rolled up to show off his bulging biceps. He offers me a drink and quickly goes to the kitchen and comes back with two black cherry Smirnoffs. He asks me what I've been up to, and I tell him briefly about my marriage with Eduardo, Memo, Alegría, the fact that I no longer dance.

"That must be hard, Yessy. I remember how much you loved to dance."

I wave the words away and lean back on the couch and cross my legs. "It was probably time to move on," I say. "Try new things." I take a few more sips of the Smirnoff. "And what about you?"

"Well, I'm just here, you know. No responsibilities. Just chilling and having a good time, doing a little arm wrestling here and there."

"Really? How long have you been doing that?"

"Just a year or so."

"Wow, I never pictured you doing that!" I say. "What about kids?" I'm thinking that at forty-three the man has got to have at least one.

"I've got three," he says. "But don't see 'em much. You know how it is."

"So where are they now?"

He finishes his Smirnoff in one big gulp. "One is in San Diego. And I think the youngest is in Arizona, or New Mexico, or Colorado. I don't know where his mom took him to. And the oldest, my daughter, lives here in L.A. She visits me sometimes, usually when she needs money." He laughs at that. "Not that I have any, but you know how kids are."

He stands up and offers me another drink. I shake my head no and he disappears into the kitchen to get one for himself. I wish I could ask him if the young woman I saw last time I came is his daughter. But then he would know I was spying, so I keep my mouth shut. I stand up to look at the pictures he has on a shelf behind the sofa.

He comes back with a beer this time. A Budweiser. "Those are my kids," he says. I look at the daughter. I know it was dark the other time I came to look for Sam, but I'm quite sure the young woman who was here that night wasn't his daughter.

I look at the clock and tell him it's time for me to leave. I have twenty minutes before Eduardo comes home.

"Yessy, Yessy, Yessy," Sam says, his voice slurry. He puts his hand on my waist as he walks me to the door. "You come back and visit me again, you hear?"

"Of course," I say. He presses me against his hard chest and bends to kiss my cheek, except his lips land right at the corner of my mouth. My knees weaken and I hold on to him, feeling his muscles contract under my hands. He's so hard and strong, and all I want is for him to hold me and protect me. I feel the tickling of desire, and as I rush out of his house, I realize my panties are wet.

"What's going on with you two, Mom?" Memo asks over a cup of coffee. He tells me about his father's new habit of showing up late to practice, or sometimes not even showing up at all. He's worried, he says. About me. About Eduardo. About Alegría.

"Your father just doesn't understand me. He's pulled away from me. I hardly ever see him anymore."

Memo looks at me for a while. I fidget under his gaze. "Don't get mad at me for saying this, Mom, but you've—you've changed a lot."

"What do you mean I've changed? I'm still the same person."

Memo shakes his head. "No, you're not. You look different. You act different, too. Like you don't care about us anymore. About the group."

I stand up and pick up the empty coffee mugs and carry them over to the sink. "You're just like your father, trying to pin everything on me. What about you? Huh? You don't want to live with us anymore. You hardly ever come visit or call us. Half the time I don't even know where you are. You left us, so don't come and try to put the blame on me—"

"Mom, stop—"

"Maybe you're the reason Eduardo's been behaving so strangely. Maybe he's feeling abandoned by his only child—"

"Goddammit, Mom—"

"Don't you dare come and curse at me, Guillermo. I'm still your mother and I demand some respect around here. First your father, and now you. Who do you guys think you are?" I stand with my hands on my hips, breathing heavily.

Memo stands up and rushes to the door. He pauses there as

if to say something, then turns abruptly and dashes out of the house. I stand there in the kitchen, part of me wanting to run after him. Did his eyes suddenly get glossy with tears, or did I imagine it? I turn around and let my head hang over the sink in resignation.

Adriana

I'm walking aimlessly around the Starlight swap meet in Montebello. It's a busy Saturday for the vendors. The weather is nice and sunny, and it's now time for Christmas shopping. But I'm not here to shop. I've come searching for memories. Mom liked coming to this swap meet. I remember walking from booth to booth with her. She'd stop at one that sold perfumes and spray herself with them. I'd breathe in the perfumes she would test on her wrists and make myself dizzy with their scent.

I stop to look at the birds and parakeets inside cages of different sizes. Mom would stand for a long time at booths like these, looking at the colorful birds, making funny noises at them, or trying to teach a parrot to say, "I love Folklórico."

I keep making my way from line to line toward the other side of the swap meet. Families pass me by, women dressed in tight jeans and high heels, men wearing Wrangler pants and Tejanas, and their little girls dressed in pink puffy dresses and the little boys wearing cowboy boots and plaid shirts. Most people carry big black plastic bags full of Christmas gifts, mainly toys.

I stop in front of a toy booth. The female vendor is trying to help three people at the same time. Sweat soaks on her forehead and dampens her hair. She clumsily puts batteries in a remote-control car. Her customers gather around, asking for prices as they point at different toys. Some people walk away, not wanting to wait around until she is less busy. When I get closer to her I realize who she is. Stephanie and Soledad's mom.

"Buenos días, Señora Valentina," I say in Spanish. "Do you need help?"

Valentina sighs in relief. "Ay, Adrianita, you have fallen from the sky." She tells me to walk around the piles of toys in the front. I join her in the back and she hands me a screwdriver and tells me to put batteries in the three cars on the table. She rushes to help her customers, and I bend my head down and begin to unscrew the cover underneath a car.

"Any news from Soledad?" I ask her once the rush of customers starts to slow down. She tells me that Soledad got caught and was sent back to México.

"She's lucky she wasn't arrested," Valentina says. "There are parts in Texas now where they're arresting people instead of sending them right back to México. But she's on her way to the Arizona border now, where she'll try again."

I think about Soledad. I don't know her that well because I try to avoid her. She's always talking about those stupid butterflies that come to her town in México. But I have to admit, she's always been nice to me. She knows how much I love embroidered blouses and peasant skirts, and she would sometimes surprise me by making me a blouse or a skirt with the fabric from the costumes she'd have left over.

"Well, I hope she makes it this time," I say, and I mean it.

Valentina sighs. "I hope that God is kind to my Soledad. I already lost my father and husband that way. I hope He remembers that and lets my Soledad come home."

Lately, Eduardo has been coming late to practice. On those days Emilio has been the first to get up and get the group going. Everyone is getting used to him. Except Memo, who refuses to follow any of Emilio's instructions. Emilio is changing some of the choreography we learned from Eduardo. The changes are small, but I think this is just the beginning. Like, for example, he wants us to lift our legs higher, and instead of one turn he makes us do three. And Memo, being the calm person he is, leaves the room, and through the glass doors I see him on his cell phone, dialing and dialing again. When Eduardo finally shows up, he stands by the door and waits until Emilio acknowledges him. Then Emilio steps down and hands the group over to Eduardo.

But Eduardo is not the same anymore. He looks like a stick, for starters, and he seems to forget the dances we're practicing. He doesn't correct us anymore. Half the time he doesn't even look at how we're dancing. He says, "Good job, good job," even if we fuck up all the way through the dance.

Some of the dancers turn to Emilio for help. Emilio smiles and pulls on his mustache. Throughout practice he whispers things to the dancers. Some nod. Some shake their heads. Others only stare at their reflections in the mirror.

". . . a new group . . ."

". . . Alegría's time has passed . . ."

". . . things are not the same anymore . . ."

". . . Eduardo is becoming irresponsible . . ."

". . . a waste of time . . ."

Whispers.

I go stand beside Emilio, and sometimes I'm bold enough to put my arm through his. Or to lean against him. Or to get so close as if we are about to kiss. He doesn't move away.

Soon we'll both have our own group, and everyone will know that he and I are together. That he's mine, and I'm his, and that the group is ours.

One time I'm bold enough to kiss him while practicing "Jesusita," my eyes daring him to say something. I'm not hiding our relationship anymore.

"Cabrona," he says to me, but he smiles anyway.

Yesenia

I ring the doorbell and stand on the porch. I lick my bottom lip and give my hair a gentle tap. I look at my reflection in the window, and when Sam opens the door my confidence is up 100 percent because the image in the windowpane is real. I'm one hot lady.

"Yessy," he says as he leans on the door. "What a surprise." He ushers me inside the house, and I'm surprised at how messy it is. Worse than last time I saw him. He coughs an apology for the mess, then throws the stuff on the couch onto the floor so that I can sit. "You look . . ." He pauses for the right word. Stunning? Beautiful? Gorgeous? He shakes his head and leans over to give me a kiss on the cheek. "Stupendous."

We sit on the couch with two cold drinks in our hands. He asks me about my job at AAA, and then tells me that he hasn't had a job in a year. "I'm on disability."

"What happened?"

"Nothing to worry about. Just got hurt on the job and now I'm taking a vacation. You know, we're still young. We work so damn much and by the time we get to retire at sixty-five—or is it seventy-five now? With this fucking government you never know—anyway, by then we're old farts and can't enjoy retirement anymore. But at this age, taking a nice break from work is the best thing to do. I can relax, get up if I want to and if I don't then it's okay, too. I've got nowhere to go, nothing to do."

He puts his arm around me. A well-defined muscular arm that makes me feel safe. Protected from the outside world. He's right. Why wait until we're old and decrepit and can't enjoy life anymore. This is the time to enjoy. To make the most of life.

"Society is always trying to tell us what to do. How to live. But I say, screw society. I'm going to do what I want."

"I know what you mean," I say. I tell him about my last two

surgeries. About Eduardo and Memo not understanding or respecting my decisions. "Who are they to judge me, right? I mean, it's my body. I can do whatever I want with it."

He pats me gently on my lap. "Atta girl, Yessy." He pulls me to my feet and says, "Now, let me see that new, sexy body of yours." He spins me around and I laugh, the alcohol already making me a little dizzy. And when I stop spinning, he stands before me, grinning that boyish grin that takes me back to my adolescent years when I would lie awake at night fantasizing about kissing him, about feeling his hands on me. Maybe it no longer has to be a fantasy.

I cup his face in my hands and draw his head down. My lips fall hungrily on his. He picks me up as if I were weightless, like a corn-husk doll. How strange it feels, how good it feels to be in the arms of a man who's two inches taller than me, who weighs more than I do. His legs so thick and strong. I wrap my legs around his waist and feel his lips all over my neck. I moan. My body is trembling with desire.

When he slips my dress down my shoulder and his lips make their way down the valley between my breasts, I stop him. "I—um—I'm, I think I should go," I say, pulling myself away from him.

He grabs my hand and gently pulls me back into his arms. "Not yet," he says. "Let's go for a ride."

He grabs his keys and two helmets and says, "Ever been on a motorcycle?"

I always thought nothing would ever make my heart beat fast and my body pulse with adrenaline the way Folklórico did. But I was wrong. I wrap my arms around Sam's waist, and my nipples tingle as I push my breasts against his back. We zip through the streets and by the time we get onto the freeway, I'm wishing for the ride to never end.

When we return to his house it's dark already. I go inside to get my purse, but when he leans down to kiss me good-bye, I turn so that his lips fall on my lips. His kiss is hard, demanding, and when I break it off I hold him by his shoulders, feeling dizzy with too many emotions. What the hell am I doing? What about Eduardo? My marriage? What would this do to it?

"I have some condoms in the bathroom," he says, "should we use them?"

He releases me and looks at me. I stand there in the living room between him and the front door. I could leave and walk away from this. Eduardo would never know. But I've wondered what it would be like with Sam. And now I don't have to wonder anymore.

"Let's go get one," I say, and we walk hand in hand to the bathroom.

Even though I'm thin now, thinner than I've been in ages, I can't help feeling self-conscious when Sam begins to undress me. With Eduardo it isn't like that. Eduardo knows every inch of my body. But Sam, what's he thinking now as his lips make their way down my stretch-marked stomach? Does he find my breasts too big, too small? And how do I compare to all the other lovers he's had?

Eduardo loves it when I kiss his neck, and I wonder if Sam feels the same as I gently nibble on his jawline. The smell of him, so different from Eduardo's. Sam is sweaty, and his skin is salty and gives off a smell that reminds me of steamed rice. Eduardo bathes twice a day sometimes and always smells like Irish Spring, his favorite soap. And their bodies, so different, too. Sam is so much hairier. His entire chest is covered in hair, as is his back, whereas Eduardo has only a sprinkle of hairs on the upper part of his chest, and his back is smooth and soft. The hair on their head, too, is different. I've always loved to run my fingers through Eduardo's hair while we make love, but with Sam it's impossible to do so. His curly black hair is so hard and stiffened with layers and layers of gel, and every time I try to touch it he moves out of reach so I won't mess it up.

286 ■ REYNA GRANDE

Stop it! Just focus. Enjoy it. Isn't this what you wanted? I try to push all my thoughts from my mind, and just when I begin to enjoy the rocking motion of our lovemaking Sam's breathing intensifies and suddenly he lets himself fall on me.

We lie there in silence for a while, and when his breathing becomes regular I wiggle from under him and begin to get dressed. He lies there on the bed watching me.

"Well, you're officially the second guy I've had sex with in my entire life," I say, feeling stupid as soon as the words come out.

Sam laughs.

He puts on his boxers and walks me to the door. He kisses me one last time before I leave, and as I walk out to my car I wonder why his mouth tastes like coffee even though he isn't a coffee drinker. I sit in my car fighting the disappointment beginning to creep up. Our lovemaking was an anticlimax to that motorcycle ride. I always thought that sex with Eduardo wasn't good enough. But I've always had an orgasm. Eduardo never comes without satisfying me first. And now, my body feels teased, unsatisfied, empty, desperate.

It was the first time! Isn't that how it was the first time with Eduardo, too, clumsy and uncomfortable? On our first time together neither of us had an orgasm because we had been too nervous, too self-conscious, too scared. *Yes, next time it will be better.*

When I get home I take a shower and scrub myself hard and long. When I turn off the water I hear the sound of the TV and realize Eduardo is home. I spray on perfume, two, three times, making sure that if there's any lingering smell of another man's body the perfume will cover it up.

When I come out of the bathroom Eduardo is sitting on the couch taking off his work boots.

"How was your day?" I ask. "Are you hungry?"

"Don't worry about me," he says. "I'll make myself something."

"No, no, I'll get it." I rush to the kitchen, wondering what I can give him. I didn't have time to make dinner. Inside the fridge I find a container of the cocido I made two days ago, so I pour it into a bowl, heat it in the microwave, and call Eduardo to the dining room. I find myself not being able to look at his eyes. I put the bowl of beef stew in front of him, heat up a few tortillas, cut a lemon in half, ask him if he wants anything to drink. I place a glass of lemonade by his bowl and sit across from him. I nibble on a wheat toast and eat the green salad I quickly tossed together, in silence. Now that I look this good, I'm not going to let myself get fat again. And the doctor warned me I could gain weight again if I don't watch what I eat. His assistant said she had lipo twice already, and now she's more careful about eating healthy and exercising.

"How was work?" I say, making a feeble attempt to start a conversation.

"Busy."

Silence.

"Have you finished the choreography for Tamaulipas? How are the preparations going for Alegría's tenth-anniversary performance?"

"Fine. Emilio says he's got some ideas."

"I see."

He puts his fork down and looks at me. I force myself to look at him. *Don't look away, don't look away.* His mouth opens and closes, as if he's debating whether or not to tell me what's in his mind. Finally, he says, "You know what Memo suggested to me yesterday? That we take a vacation."

"We?"

"Yeah, as in you and me."

"Where to?"

"México. We haven't been there in a while. Maybe we can go visit your family in Jalisco and then swing by Nayarit to visit mine."

"But what about work?"

"That's the beauty about having my own business," he says. "And you have plenty of illness days—despite, you know, the surgeries."

I think about Sam. I can't be away from him, not when whatever it is we have is just beginning. Not now.

"We can go to Cancún like we did for our honeymoon," Eduardo says. He takes my hands in his, squeezes them gently. "We have to try. We can't let our twenty-one years of marriage go down the drain like that. We have Memo to think about. He isn't doing too well. Our problems are affecting him. Right now what he needs is to focus on his studies, not to be worrying about us. What do you say, Yessy? If not for us then let's do it for him."

I pry my hands from his, trying to think of an excuse to give him. What would Sam do in this situation? Hasn't he told me that I need to do what's best for me? Not to let anyone else tell me how to live my life? What would he say? What would he do?

"I need to think about it," I say, finally, feeling like a coward. Eduardo nods and tries to smile.

Elena

Beginning December 16, some of the Alegría dancers will be performing at La Golondrina restaurant at Olvera Street for nine days, ending on December 24. It's time for las posadas, the re-enactment of the journey Joseph and Mary took as they sought shelter.

Fernando is one of the dancers performing. Eduardo will pay them $50 a night, and Fernando is beside himself. It's his first paid performance.

"With this money I can actually buy presents for my family,

and even have some left so my family can have a decent Christmas dinner," he says.

I smile, knowing what getting paid will do for him. It'll make him feel like a real dancer.

There are only six couples performing. The dance space in the restaurant is fairly small, only enough for one or two couples at a time. Fernando goes upstairs to the dressing room and I sit at a bar. I order a virgin margarita.

Fernando is first. He's dancing "Jesusita" with Stephanie.

The music begins and they both spring into action. Their faces light up as they execute the intricate footwork and percussive heel stomping as their feet imitate the prancing of a horse. As I look at them dance, I wish I hadn't ordered a virgin margarita. Fernando twirls Stephanie around, holding her close, his hand on her waist, their faces so close. He flings her away and then pulls him to her. They press their cheeks against each other's and he pulls her even closer, their legs almost intertwined. I tell myself that this is the way the song is danced. Someone in the audience whistles; others cheer them on by clapping to the beat of the music. When Fernando twirls her around, Stephanie's mid-calf skirt spins, revealing the white petticoat and lacy bloomers underneath. The sight of him dancing "Jesusita" with Stephanie fills me with an intense jealousy. I've never been the jealous type.

I throw a ten-dollar bill on the bar and walk out of the restaurant, the sounds of the accordion and the bajo sexto following me. I appreciate the cold air that hits my face. I go to Olverita's Village thinking about doing some Christmas shopping, but nothing interests me, and when I look up at the Folklórico costumes displayed on the walls I can't help but think of Stephanie and Fernando dancing together.

I give up on the shopping, unable to concentrate on anything but the event at La Golondrina. I make my way back to the restaurant. Adriana is dancing Veracruz with José. They finish "El Canelo" and start "La Bamba." I watch them tie and untie the long red scarf on the floor with their feet while doing a zapateado. They danced this at my wedding; the bow they're making with their feet represents the union between two people. The jealousy toward Stephanie I was trying to suppress is still there. As I watch Adriana, I make myself feel better by taking pleasure in the fact that wearing a beautiful costume isn't enough to make you a true dancer. "Ay arriba, ay arriba por tí seré, por tí seré. Bamba, bamba, bamba. Bamba, bamba, bamba . . ." Just as the song is ending, they hold up the scarf they've tied into a bow. It isn't a perfect-shaped bow: one side is bigger than the other. I wallow in the thought that unlike Adriana, I would always make perfect bows.

I order another margarita, with alcohol this time.

Fernando comes down the stairs still wearing his costume. My heart quickens at seeing him. The cowboy hat makes him look older, mysterious. And his jeans hug his dancer's legs.

He sits next to me and orders a Coke.

"How did we do?" he asks.

I take a drink of my margarita before answering. There's too much alcohol in it. "Fine, fine," I say, wanting to sound more encouraging but being unable to.

Stephanie heads over to us. Even though it's cold, she's wearing a short, thin blouse with spaghetti straps, revealing her flat stomach. Her navel ring glitters under the light. I take another drink of my margarita.

Since there are no more stools available Fernando offers her his. She sits down and orders a Corona.

"I forgot my ID," she tells the bartender.

"Then I can't give you the drink," he says.

She bats her eyelashes at him and whines, "C'mon, I'm twenty-one, I swear. You can even ask her," she says, pointing at me.

The bartender looks at me. Stephanie pinches my leg from under the counter.

"Ouch!" I say. I shake my head at the bartender.

He goes to wait on another customer.

"You're so mean," Stephanie says. "Now I have to wait for him to get back so I can order something. I'm so thirsty." She turns around and asks Fernando if she could have a sip of his Coke.

Fernando blushes but gives it to her.

The dancing begins again. Eduardo brings out his drum, except that it's Memo who stands behind it with the drumsticks in his hand. Eduardo heads to the center of the stage carrying a sahumerio in front of him; the flames bursting out of the sahumerio illuminate his face, the bags under his eyes. For a moment I forget about Stephanie and Fernando, remembering how much I enjoyed seeing Eduardo dance "La Danza del Fuego Nuevo." It always amazed me as a child to see him put his bare feet into the flames and hold them there for a long time, alternating from one foot to the other.

Memo points at the piñata hanging above the stage and motions to Eduardo to be careful with the sahumerio. Eduardo looks up and nods. Then the drumming starts and Eduardo begins his magical dance in honor of the Aztec fire god.

As he dances I notice the weight he has lost. He does not look good with the costume, which leaves his torso and legs completely bare. He looks like a skeleton, not a fearless Aztec warrior.

Eduardo should be mesmerizing the audience with his graceful movements, but something about the way he dances looks forced. It's as if his heart isn't in the dance at all. He has a faraway look, there's a frown on his face, and when he sets his foot into the flames he takes it out right away. He's not concentrating at all. This dance requires deep concentration in order to withstand the pain.

He dances around the sahumerio on the floor, the flames casting an eerie glow. Memo pounds away at the drum, and it amazes me how good he's gotten since I last heard him play. His father has taught him well. Eduardo picks up the sahumerio and holds it above his head, raising it higher and higher, and then it happens so quickly that nobody really has time to react: the streamers of the piñata catch on fire, and within seconds the piñata is engulfed in flames.

People get up from their seats. Memo drops the sticks and runs off the stage yelling for a fire extinguisher. Eduardo yanks down the burning piñata with his bare hands, throws it on the floor, and stomps out the fire with his feet.

By the time the fire extinguisher comes the fire has been put out. The manager of La Golondrina comes to the stage to calm down the customers, who are whispering and pointing at Eduardo. They all look shocked.

An employee comes to clean up the mess. Memo puts an arm around Eduardo and gently ushers him upstairs to the changing room. Eduardo's head hangs low, ashamed. I stand up and walk after them.

"I'm all right, mi'jo. I'm fine. Go get ready for Jalisco. We need to finish the show," Eduardo is saying to a frazzled Memo.

Adriana and Laura are standing beside him, asking what happened.

"Are your hands and feet okay?" I ask.

He looks down at his hands. "I'll be all right," he says. I ask him to show me his hands, and I wince at seeing the blisters.

I look around for a first aid kit but don't see one.

"I'm okay," he says. He gets up and takes off the headdress of feathers. He grabs his pile of clothes from a chair. Memo stands by the door, now dressed in a charro outfit.

"Go on mi'jo. Don't worry about me. Show 'em what you got," Eduardo says before going into the restroom.

Laura takes Memo's hand and pulls him out of the room. A few moments later, I hear "El Gavilán" playing.

"What happened?" Adriana whispers.

"He burned the piñata. I think he was too distracted."

She nods. "Yep, he's been like that lately."

Eduardo comes out of the room fully dressed. "Well, have a

good night, mi'jas. Thank you for coming." He makes his way out of the door and leaves.

Adriana and I look at each other.

"I think we need to have a talk with Yesenia," I say. "Eduardo doesn't look too good."

"Yeah, I know. Maybe it's time for him to step down and leave someone else to take over the group," Adriana says.

"What do you mean? Eduardo is a wonderful director. He's just going through a rough time. I'm sure he'll be okay."

"Maybe, or maybe not. Either way, Emilio and I have been talking about starting our own group."

"Really?" I say. I hear the applause of the customers, and then "La Negra" begins. Adriana is busy packing her gym bag.

"Uh-huh. Can you imagine that? Me—a director?"

As a matter of fact, I can't. "And how are you and Emilio going to do this? How are you going to rent a studio? And where are you going to recruit dancers?"

"From Alegría, of course." She throws her gym bag over her shoulder and turns to leave. "Many of the dancers aren't happy anymore."

My stomach gets queasy at the thought of Alegría breaking apart. And Adriana having a hand in its downfall.

"Adriana, please think about this, okay? If Emilio is onto something, you don't have to do it, too. Alegría is our family."

"What the fuck do you know about family?" she says, suddenly becoming angry. She takes a step toward me. "You broke up ours without a second thought. Why should it matter to you if I break up Alegría? Besides, Emilio knows what he's doing. And he's right—Eduardo has become a shitty director. We lost the Mariachi Festival at the Hollywood Bowl next June, did you know that? They gave it to another group. And why, because Eduardo's too fucked up in the head to make the phone calls he's supposed to make. And Yesenia is too fucking into 'sculpting' her body to care."

"They're going through a rough time, Adriana. That doesn't give you the right to move in and destroy what isn't yours."

"I don't know why you get so high and mighty about it. Besides, isn't that what Eduardo and Yesenia did nine years ago when they started Alegría? They left México Lindo and started their own group—and they took some of México Lindo's dancers with them. Anyway, I'll keep you posted." She opens the door just as "La Negra" comes to an end. People clap. "Maybe we'll take Fernandito with us. He's an awesome dancer." She winks at me and leaves.

I return to the dining area. Stephanie and Fernando are still sitting at the bar. When he sees me, Fernando stands up and comes to meet me.

"Ready?" I say.

He nods and turns to wave good-bye to Stephanie, but she stands up and comes over to us. "Elena, would you mind giving me a ride home?"

I look at Stephanie, not knowing what to say. Then I wish Soledad were here, taking care of her sister. I tell myself I'm being foolish. But the looks Stephanie gives Fernando are not figments of my imagination, and though it might be childish of me, I can't help feeling how I feel.

I swallow my jealousy and say, "Of course."

Stephanie sits in the back and talks too much during the ride to her house. She directs her conversation to Fernando, completely ignoring me. She asks him if he wants to go to her friend's party with her next weekend. When he fails to respond right away she asks him if he has a girlfriend. Fernando glances at me, and then he answers no.

What else is he supposed to say? I ask myself. I'm not his girlfriend, after all. And it's not as if he can admit to her there's something between us. But still, I grip the steering wheel as I feel my body begin to be engulfed by raw, bitter jealousy. Stephanie's voice is like an ice pick. I try to ignore what she's saying, and even though the ride lasts only fifteen minutes, it feels as if an hour has gone by. I feel a headache coming on, and my eyes are beginning to water.

Stephanie reluctantly gets out of the truck. Fernando rolls down the window to say good-bye. She leans in and gives him a kiss on the cheek. My eyes water even more. My headache intensifies.

"Bye, Elena," she says.

Once she's gone, Fernando turns to me and sighs.

I busy myself by looking in my purse for a tissue to wipe my eyes. I wipe a little too hard.

"Shoot." I lean back on my seat, frustrated.

"What happened?"

"My contact fell out." I hold it on the tip of my finger and try to decide whether or not to put it back in. I don't have any saline solution to wash it, but I can't drive without my contacts. I put it back in my eye, and just as I knew it would happen, the dirty lens irritates my eye. I take it out.

"Let me drive, Miss."

"But you don't have a license."

"It'll be okay. My uncle lets me drive sometimes."

"It's not a good idea, Fernando. I still have one contact on." I turn on the truck and start to drive. Too soon, I realize that I feel disoriented with my vision. Everything looks askew, and this headache of mine only makes things worse.

"Let me drive," he says again. "This is dangerous."

The thought of us in a car accident, and me being responsible for Fernando getting injured, makes me pull over and give up the wheel. As we switch seats, just thinking that I could get in big trouble for this worsens both my mood and my headache.

"You're sure you can drive?" I ask.

He grabs my hand and squeezes it. Then he puts the truck into gear and merges into traffic. I direct him to the freeway, and within five minutes we are on the 110, on our way home. I begin to relax. Fernando is a careful driver, and I'm glad that at ten o'clock on a Saturday night the 110 South is not too heavy with traffic. Everyone is going north, on their way to the Hollywood freeway.

Fernando and I don't say much during the drive home. I tell him he should concentrate on his driving. He tells me I worry too much. I decide to take off the other contact, and the pressure in my eyes eases off. In the silence of the truck, and in my blindness, I think about Stephanie, about the navel ring on her flat, unmarked stomach, her youth, her eyes looking longingly at Fernando. Her flirtatious smile.

"Stephanie has become quite a good-looking girl," I say.

Fernando does not reply. He keeps looking at the road ahead and once in a while glances at the rearview mirror.

I repeat my comment and ask him what he thinks of her.

He turns to look at me for a second, and then his eyes are on the road again. "I don't want to talk about Stephanie, Miss. I hardly know her."

"And do you want to get to know her?" I ask, hating myself for doing this. How immature I'm behaving, but I can't stop. I can't.

He glances at me again, his face becoming serious. "There's only one person I'm interested in."

I clear my throat and look away from him, my cheeks becoming hot with embarrassment. I got what I wanted, didn't I? But how ridiculous I must have seemed just now. Acting like a teenager. I decide to change the conversation. "So, are you nervous driving?"

"A little. Driving my uncle's beat-up car isn't the same as driving your truck, Miss. I wouldn't want to wreck it."

"Forget about it being wrecked," I say. "That would be the least of my worries. I would be sent to jail."

"Just for letting me drive without a license?"

"No, Fernando, not for that."

He's quiet for a moment, but being the intelligent boy that

he is, he says, "It's not a sin, Miss. If we were in México, nobody would care. I mean, in México, there are tons of men who marry young girls who are underage. Even my aunt married a fifteen-year-old guy when she was twenty-two. And nobody went around pointing fingers at them."

"We aren't in México," I say.

"Yeah, I guess not."

He exits the freeway and I give him directions to get to my house. He pulls over and parks in the driveway.

"I'll just grab my glasses and go," I say. He nods and follows me into the house. My three cats are on the couch, sleeping. They wake up and come to me, meowing. I grab my glasses from the bedroom dresser, sighing in relief as everything comes into focus. I think about the ad I received in the mail two days ago, about Lasik surgery. Perhaps it's time that I do it. But the thought of someone messing with my eyes scares me.

I come back to the living room. He's holding one of the cats in his arms.

"That's Canelo," I say. "And the black one there is La Negra, and the other one is Jesusita."

He smiles. "Your favorite dances?"

"Some of my favorite," I say.

He looks around the living room. It feels so awkward to have him here, in my house. His presence makes everything small; even the space between us feels not like six feet but one. I go to the kitchen and pour food into my cats' bowls and give them fresh water. I go back to the living room, then the bathroom, the bedroom, until I finally find Fernando in the nursery, standing by the crib Richard tried to disassemble.

"Maybe we should get going," I say.

He turns around and looks at me. "I'm sorry, Miss." He runs a finger along the edge of the rail. I come to stand by him, touched at his sadness.

"There's no need to feel that way. I'm doing better. It doesn't hurt as much as it used to." I leave the room and hear him walking behind me.

"Miss?" I turn around and face him. "I could help you take it apart, if you want."

I take a deep breath, and say, "Yes, I think it's time." I look down at my feet and then I remember that his aunt is expecting. "Maybe your aunt might want it."

"I think she would like to have it, but don't get rid of it just because my aunt needs it."

"It's time to be rid of it," I say, choking back the tears. He nods and then pulls me to him. I melt into the warmth of his embrace. Then, his mouth seeks mine, and I welcome his kiss. His right hand moves up and down my back, and then it begins to move in another direction. When it grazes my breast a moan escapes my lips, and when I try to push him away he holds me even tighter.

"Don't," I say, but his hand is cupping my breast, and he presses me against the wall. "Fernando—"

"Shh." He kisses my neck while his hand unbuttons my blouse. I make a feeble attempt to stop him again. But instead, Fernando holds me even tighter. "Elena," he says. Chills go up and down my body at the sound of my name on his lips. He wants me. Not Stephanie. Not Adriana. Not Becky. Me.

"Elena," he says again, and when we both drop down to the floor, I stop pushing him away.

Soledad

I'm somewhere near the Arizona border now. This coyote seems nicer than the other one, but coyotes are not to be trusted, this I know. I keep my eyes wide open. The dirt under our feet is full of small rocks. This way we go, the coyote says, so la migra doesn't see our footprints, so the desert doesn't betray us. It's hard to walk, and even the men aren't safe. Sometimes they lose their balance and struggle to not fall.

I'm too slow, and I get slower as we keep walking. I ask for them to wait for me, but the coyote keeps walking fast. He waves at me from way up ahead and makes a sign for me to hurry. I fall and scrape my hands. Another time I hurt my elbow. They get farther away, even the other women move quickly over the loose rocks, but I'm having trouble breathing. I wish I was a dancer. Esperen, por favor. Don't leave me.

I tell my legs to move faster. But they want to become earth, rock. Sweat gets in my eyes and it burns. I take more quick steps, but then my legs bend under me, turning into sand, and I fall. I try to get up, but my ankle hurts so much it makes my eyes water.

"Espérenme!" I say.

They see me on the ground, and only the coyote comes back. He moves so quickly and his feet are so sure. He reminds me of a goat.

"What happened?" he asks.

"I hurt my ankle."

He says a bad word and shakes his head. He looks toward the sun. The sky is streaked with a fiery orange like the wings of a monarch butterfly. "We don't have much time before it gets dark," he says. He helps me get up and I hold on to him. He calls one of the men over and they help me up. Every time I put my right foot down I feel the pain. But I don't cry; I know if I cry, the coyote will know how bad it is. I bite the inside of my lips, and I taste blood. I bite more and more, feel the pain there so I don't think about the pain in my ankle.

We take a rest among the shrubs. I drink my warm water. The coyote looks out again at the brown vastness that is the desert. It's getting dark now that the sun is going down. He shakes his head and spits many times on the ground. The seven men and the three other women talk in quiet voices, but I know they're talking about me. They look at me sometimes, and I think they hate me. If we get caught it'd be my fault.

My ankle is swollen now. It feels hot in my shoe, but I can't take it out and look because the men will see me. So I undo my braid because it is loose, and I braid my hair again, pretend I am fine. I feel good. Yes, I am ready to continue. No, it doesn't hurt much. I can walk.

"Órale pues, let's go." The coyote spits again, and then everyone gets up. I lean on my good leg and I try to get up, too, but it's hard. We start to walk. They go first and I'm at the end. We are careful not to step in the rattlesnake holes in the ground. I tell myself we're safe from the snakes. Before our journey started we rubbed garlic on our tennis shoes to keep them away. The pain in my ankle gets worse with each step. *Come on, Soledad. You can do it.* The group is leaving me behind. My eyes are wet and I wipe them, but more tears come out. I stop walking and take deep breaths. The coyote turns around and he tells the men to stop. He walks back to me.

"It's bad, isn't it?" he asks.

I shake my head. "I'm fine."

"Listen to me, Soledad. If you are hurt I need to know. We're almost at the meeting point where a car is waiting, but we can't slow down now."

The way he looks at me scares me. He knows I am lying, but still I stand up straight and I shake my head again and again. "I can do it. I can."

He spits. "Look, there are thousands of dollars at stake here. If I lose you, that's fine. I can deal with not getting paid for you. But if I lose everyone, then I'm really fucked. Me lleva la chingada, Sol, entiendes? If you can't make it, you need to say it now."

I start crying this time. I don't care if he sees me cry. I don't care if my nose is runny and I need to wipe it. I don't care.

He puts his hand on my shoulder. "I'll take you as far as the dirt road up ahead. Then you will stay there and wait. La migra always drives by and they'll pick you up in less than an hour."

I shake my head and cry harder. "Don't leave me here, please. I don't know where I am. The darkness is falling and then what will I do all by myself?"

"I'm sorry, Soledad. But I'm not going to risk getting caught. Come on, let's go."

He grabs my arm and puts it around his neck. I start to walk, leaning all my weight on my left leg. And between crying and begging, I can't help thinking that this is the first time I'm so close to a man. It is different from being close to Rubén or Lorenzo. I try to pretend that I'm not at the border, that he isn't a coyote. I try to forget he's about to leave me in the middle of nowhere. I imagine we're at the plaza in my town. That we're in love. I feel the muscles on his shoulders, feel his breath on my face, smell his sweat.

"Please, don't leave me," I say. "It's my birthday today. Don't leave me."

He doesn't say anything. He is quiet the rest of the time. We get to the group and he tells them we will walk a little farther to the dirt road and that I'll wait for la migra there.

The others in the group tell me they're sorry. They say it's best this way. They look sorry, but I know they're just pretending. Inside they're happy. I won't hold them back anymore. The women look away from me, and I want to yell at them and tell them they should be ashamed. I'm a woman, too. Do they not care?

Because I'm too scared to have pride, I get down on my knees and beg the coyote again. For one moment I think he'll change his mind, but then he shakes his head again and tells me no. Punto. He tells the men to start walking. He bends down in front of me, takes off his backpack, and gives me a flashlight.

"There's nothing out here that can hurt you," he says. "As long as you stay here and don't go anywhere."

He puts the flashlight in my hand and then kisses my forehead. I stop crying then. I take a deep breath and I tell him to leave. He takes a few steps, then comes back and gives me his jacket. I already have one, and a rebozo and a sweater in my backpack, but I take his jacket and hold it in my hands, feeling the heat from his body.

It isn't long before I can't see them anymore. I keep looking at the place where I stopped seeing them, and I imagine that maybe God will change their minds and they'll come back for me. I stare and stare, and I wait to see them return. I begin to pray. But then everything is completely black, and after many prayers I can feel this knot in my stomach at the reality that I'm here alone, and they won't be coming back for me.

I shiver. With the darkness, the cold becomes cruel. I put on the coyote's jacket and take out my second sweater from my backpack and wrap it around my legs and feet. I undo my braid and I wrap my long hair around me, trying to keep warm. Up in the sky there are hundreds of stars. They remind me of the China Poblana costumes I made for Elena's group at the high school. The dresses were made of black velvet and were decorated with silver and gold sequins. I turn on the flashlight and I point it into the bushes. I move it around, and I pray that la migra will see this light.

But no one comes.

I think about Ma and Tomás and Stephanie inside the house. Stephanie lying on the bed, maybe watching TV or talking on the phone with her friends. Tomás and Ma in the living room watching the soap operas, eating chile verde or milanesa con papas, or maybe even tamales that Tomás's sister had left over from today's batch. And I think about Alegría, and how I wish I was sitting in my little corner, watching them do dances from Sinaloa because that is the region I love best.

Something moves in the dark, and I close my eyes. My body is shaking, and my teeth rattle like maracas. I think about Lorenzo, at home now with his family. I think of the butterflies sleeping soundly in clusters in the safety of the fir trees. And I hate myself for not listening to Lorenzo. I could be there, too, at home with him and Malena, and the children, celebrating my thirty-fourth birthday with them. I could be braiding Lupita's hair and smelling the sweet scent of her breath like warm milk.

Why did I want to go back to America? Go back to the apartment full of roaches? Go back to the constant whining of Stephanie. Back to trying to get my mother to make the right choices, to plan for the future. Back to dreaming dreams that will never come true. Why go back?

"Go to America and do something great with your life," Abuelita Licha said to me. "You can do it, Sol."

My tears are like ice on my face. Something in the bushes moves again, and this time I make my shaking hands point the flashlight in that direction. There's nothing there, but I remember the coyote telling us that the snakes come out at night.

Dear God, I'll do anything you want me to do but please don't leave me here. I don't want to die here. Not on my birthday. I want to see my mother again, and I want to make my beautiful dresses. I want to have my dress shop, God, and buy a nice little house somewhere, and one day I want to meet someone and fall in love, and have children. I know I can be a good mother, I know I can. Just give me a chance. Please, God. Give me a chance and save me. Save me from this place, from this place, from this place, from this place. God, please. God. God. God. God.

The flashlight begins to die. The yellow beam little by little disappears. And then only the tip shines.

I hear a noise again, and in my mind I picture a thousand rattlesnakes coming out of their nests to get me.

I scream. I scream and I scream and I scream and I can't stop. Can't stop until God hears me.

When I wake up it's bright. I crawl from out of the bushes to get warmed by the sun. My stomach hurts from hunger, and my throat is dry. I sip my water because there's only a little left. I eat

304 ■ REYNA GRANDE

the last can of tuna and crackers. I save the orange for later. I lean
against the bush and look around. There's nothing here. Only the
blue sky, wispy bushes, prickly pear cactus, tumbleweeds, and
trash left behind by other immigrants. I wonder if they had better luck than me. My ankle is swollen and it throbs with pain. If I
don't move it doesn't hurt too much. I don't know how long I sit
there, but no one comes. The sun moves little by little, and I watch
my shadow move, too. My stomach starts to hurt again and I eat
my orange. I have no more food and only a little water.

I see a cloud of dust not too far from me. I see a white truck
with a green line through the bushes. It's la migra. I grab on to
the bush and stand up. I yell for them to help me, but they can't
hear me.

"Here, here!" I say. I wave my sweater up in the air. I hop on
one foot and try to get to the dirt road, yelling for them. But they
don't come this way. They turn and go to the left. How can they
not see me?

I keep hopping. Maybe they'll come back the same way. My
eyes water at the pain. When I get to the turn, I sit down and
drink the last of my water. Please, God, let them come back soon.

Time passes, and my stomach begins to growl. I get up and
I begin to hop down the road. I pick up a stick to help me walk,
and this way it is easier. My throat hurts from being dry, and
my scalp is burning from the sun even though the air is chilly,
although not as cold as last night. I wrap my shawl around my
head and keep going. Up ahead, out of all the brown colors of
the desert, something blue sticks out. It's a barrel, and a white
flag flies above it. I make my way to it, and when I get close I
can see big white letters that say "Agua. Water." I try to hop
faster, but I am too tired and dizzy, and my throat hurts even
more now, with the thought of getting some water. When I get
to the barrel I have to take a minute to catch my breath. Then I
look inside it and see plastic gallons of water. I take them out,
but they are empty. I look around and see other gallons scat-

tered in the bushes, flattened like if someone stepped on them. I keep walking with my stick, dizzy with thirst and hunger.

It's almost dark when I see a little house made of wood next to a mesquite. There is a metal fence around the property, and a black dog starts to bark as soon as it sees me, but I don't have a choice. Maybe someone there can help me. My ankle is hurting too much from the walking, but I tell myself soon someone will help me. Finally I come to the house and I call out. "Hello?" I say. "Hello?" My lips hurt when I open my mouth to speak. They are so dry. "Hello?" I say, and the dog's barks are louder and I think maybe whoever is in there can't hear me.

But then a man comes out. I wipe the sweat that's burning my eyes and I try to smile, the skin on my lips breaks. What is that he's holding? A rifle?

"Get out of here before I shoot you," he says in English. He picks up his rifle and points it at me.

"Please, water," I say.

I hear the rifle click.

"I said get out. I don't help wetbacks."

I'm too dizzy with hunger and fear, tears begin to fall down my cheeks. "Please, sir. Please give to me water. I have thirsty."

He points the rifle at me and shoots. I drop to the ground. I look at myself and there is no blood.

"That was a warning," he said. "I won't miss the next time."

My heart is beating fast, like the needle of a sewing machine when I make dresses. I hold on to my stick and I lean on it when I get up. So much pain in my ankle, I cry more. I am afraid to turn away from him. What if he shoots me? But I don't want to look at his rifle, at his angry eyes. I turn, feeling that at any moment he will shoot, I struggle to walk away. One step. Two steps. Three steps. I bite my lips so I don't cry out from the pain. Four steps. Five steps.

"What's the matter with you?"

Six steps. I stop to catch my breath.

"Qué pasa?" he says. At hearing the Spanish words, I turn around to look at him. He points at me and asks again, "Qué pasa?"

I try to think what the English word is for "ankle." I try to remember my ESL class, the lesson my teacher gave us on health and the body, and I can't remember, I can't remember even though I got an A+ on the test she gave us. "Tobillo," I say. "Tobillo is hurts."

"Tobillo?" he asks.

I turn around and keep walking. Maybe there are other people living around here. Maybe I can find help. My stomach growls, and I lean my weight on my ankle to keep my thoughts away from food. The pain in my ankle is too much, and all my energy is gone from me. I fall to my knees.

"Jesus Christ!" I hear the man say. I hear his footsteps, then he's in front of me, his rifle pointing up to the sky.

"Show me," he says. That I understand. I try to take off my tennis shoe, but my ankle is so swollen it is hard to take it off. I leave it alone. If I take it off, I won't be able to put my shoe back on.

"Jesus," he says. He stands up and looks around. I don't know what he is looking for. He puts his hand up on his forehead and looks and looks. "No sign of 'em," he says. "Maybe later they'll pass by."

I think he's talking about la migra, but I don't ask him. My English words are locked in my brain. How easily they come to me in the safety of my classroom. But now, looking at the man's rifle, hearing the harsh sound of his voice, my English words hide deep inside me.

He turns to look at me. He spits and pulls on his graying beard. "Goddammit," he says. Then he reaches out for me. "Come on." I want to say no. I am afraid of him. He will hurt me with his rifle. But I'm so thirsty and dizzy with hunger, I let him help me get up. He grabs me tight as we head back to his house.

When we go through the gate the dog comes and sniffs me. The man tells it to leave me alone, but the dog smells and smells, even my private area it wants to smell and it makes me get hot with shame. I sit on the steps of his porch and he goes inside. He comes out with a tin cup filled with water. I lick my lips. I sip on the cup, savoring the coolness of the water. The dog lies down at the man's feet.

"You from México?" he says.

I nod.

He spits and says, "Damn Mexicans, won't you people ever quit?"

I drink my water quicker now, thinking he might take the cup from me and tell me to leave.

"So how is it you speak English?" he asks. "Were you deported?"

I shake my head. I open my mouth to speak, but the words don't come out. You are a great student, Soledad, my English teacher said to me many times. But now, I feel ashamed. What would she say to me now, not being able to use the English she taught me? I feel I've failed her. I open my mouth again, "I go México," I say. "My grandmother sick."

"Hmm. So you went to see your grandmother?"

I nod.

"And what happened? She get better?"

My water is finished, but I keep putting my lips on the tin cup. It's cool on my lips. I shake my head.

"She died?"

I nod. I feel so stupid. Can't talk.

He clears his throat and says. "Border patrol passes by here in the mornings or in the afternoons sometimes. You can sleep here on the porch. Tomorrow I'll try to get them out here so they'll take you away. I don't think you're going anywhere with that ankle of yours."

I nod and I give him back his cup. He turns around and goes

inside his house, and I can hear him saying, "Goddamn Mexicans. They never learn." The dog stands up when the man goes inside the house, but now it lies down again on the same spot by the door.

I look out there, at the desert, thinking maybe I can leave here and hide somewhere in the shrubs. I don't want la migra to take me. But the thought of being out there in the dark, alone, scares me. In the distance, I hear a coyote howling. The dog stands up and barks at the darkness. I think of my father and grandfather, out there alone, getting killed and left for the coyotes to eat.

The man comes out with two fleece blankets and two pieces of beef jerky, and then goes back in again. I have my two jackets on and now I wrap my feet with my shawl. I use my backpack as a pillow and I lie on top of one blanket and wrap myself with the other one while I chew on the jerky, taking tiny bites to make them last. The dog comes to sniff me, and I can feel its wet nose on my cheek. It lies down next to me, and I fall asleep knowing I'm not alone here.

CHAPTER NINE

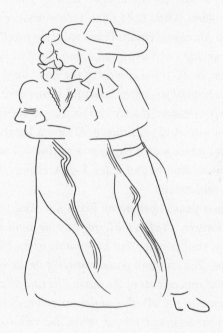

She danced the dance of flames and fire, and the dance of swords and spears; she danced the dance of stars and the dance of space, and then she danced the dance of flowers in the wind.

—KHALIL GIBRAN

YOU enter the Home Depot garden center with tentative steps. What were you thinking driving all the way out here for flowers?
   Xochitl.
   Flowers won't ease the pain. Flowers won't make her absence

more bearable. But the desire to dig into the earth with your bare hands, to surround yourself with life, beauty, love, pumps through your body and makes your legs go forward.

The colors blind you. Table upon table of plants and flowers of dazzling colors. White calla lilies, their elongated stems like a dancer's neck. Ah, what beautiful carriage of the head! Ranunculus sitting atop curving stems like a spine running from the tailbone to the base of the skull. What control of the spine line! Cyclamen in red and white remind you of the beautiful Veracruz dresses and the red silk shawls. Alyssum, dainty and delicate as a frilled petticoat lined with fine lace. And you think of "El Jarabe Tapatío," a courting dance, a lover's dance with a happy ending. The woman holding up her skirt between thumbs and index fingers, coquettishly revealing the petticoat underneath.

Tulips, their petals opening up like a fan. And you remember dancing "El Canelo," the fan fluttering in your hand as you smiled flirtatiously at your partner. The blossoming irises, like the unfurling of a shawl. The fountain grasses swaying in the breeze remind you of the fluid movements of the skirts. The camellias, the fuchsia colors as vibrant as the silk-thread flowers embroidered in a Chiapas dress. Primroses in red, purple, white, and yellow, like the floral print of Alegría's Nayarit skirts, with their overlapping ruffles. You remember dancing to the violin music, pulling the skirt above your head, the ruffles cascading down. The snapdragons standing tall and still. What poise!

You close your eyes and give in to the mystical power around you. The flowers dance and you become part of their cosmic rhythm.

Elena

For the first time in many, many months, my hands finally dig into the earth. I sigh, smelling the fresh scent of flowers. A butterfly passes by and I can't help but smile. When was the last time I saw one of those? Dead plant after dead plant makes its way into the green bin. Fernando finds me trying to dig up a dead hibiscus tree behind the house. He apologizes for showing up without calling. At seeing him, reality sinks in and I'm torn between crying and laughing, between sending him away and pulling him close.

"Fernando, about the other night . . ." He leans forward and presses his lips against my own to silence them. He takes the shovel from me and continues the job I started. He digs holes with a shovel, once in a while stopping to wipe the sweat off his forehead. We work in silence the entire morning. I finally finish planting the snapdragons, the impatiens, and the marigolds; the advantage of living in a sunny place like L.A. is that flowers abound year-round. I go into the house to grab two cold water bottles.

I come back and Fernando has pulled off his shirt and is wiping his face and neck with it. He stands there wearing his undershirt, which is soaked in sweat. My stomach clenches and unclenches. I blush under his gaze. I hand him the water and he quickly drinks it. He continues to work, replacing the dead plants with new ones—azaleas, ferns, and fountain grass, camellias, a blue hibiscus tree, and jasmine to climb on the pergola. While I finish planting the calla lilies, he asks me what I'm doing for the holidays.

"I'm having dinner at Yesenia and Eduardo's house on Christmas Eve," I say.

He invites me over to his house on Christmas Day. I neither accept nor decline, unsure how I would feel being in that tiny house, so close to him, exposed to his mother's eyes. What if she can see through me?

By the time we are finished, my patio has come to life once more. New flower pots hang on the hooks of the pergola. Rosebushes line the walls of the garage and the house. The fountain, once full of leaves and stagnant water, is now flowing with fresh water. Fernando and I lie together on the hammock, listening to the purring of the water in the fountain, the birds singing.

He grabs my hand and holds it in his. I tell him that every time I'm with him, it feels so right. But when we're apart, I let all my doubts and fears come to the surface, let them paralyze me, choke me up inside. He listens and doesn't say anything. He only squeezes my hand even harder, and then begins to undress me.

Before he leaves, he helps me take the crib apart and put it in the truck. I drive him home, and when we get there, he unloads the crib. "You sure about this, Elena?" he says.

I nod and then he takes the crib inside his house, piece by piece. He pulls out the swing and the rocking chair, and from the backseat he gets all the bags of clothes and baby gifts I once tried to give away to Goodwill.

From the rack on top of the truck he unties the walker and the stroller, the changing table which miraculously didn't fall off. I sit there watching him take all those things to the porch, wishing I could help him but unable to move. I concentrate on making the tightness in my stomach go away. When Fernando is done unloading the truck, I feel as if a weight has been taken off of me.

"That's it. I think my aunt is going to go crazy with all these things. She'll think Santa Claus came to town!"

I smile. "I'm glad I was able to help out," I say. "I know how expensive those things can be."

I return home and sit on the floor of what used to be a nursery. The wallpaper with teddy bears and balloons is the only trace left. I wonder if my daughter thinks I'm forgetting her, letting her go.

Yesenia

I sit on the porch and wait for Sam to get home. Because he doesn't work it's hard to know when he'll be here. I've gotten into the habit of dropping by on him. Usually I call to tell him I'm on my way. Sometimes I like to surprise him. I dial his cell phone again and get his voicemail. About an hour later, he finally gets home.

"Yessy," he says. He opens the door and I follow him into his house.

"Where were you?"

"At the gym."

I pull him toward me and say, "You must be tired." I tell him to sit on the floor, between my legs, and I rub his neck and shoulders, feeling his muscles contract and relax under my fingertips. He tells me I'm as good as the masseuses at Glen Ivy.

"What's that?" I ask.

"A spa I go to sometimes. Maybe I'll take you one of these days."

"You hungry?" I say.

He shakes his head.

"I could make you something to eat if you are."

"No, I'm fine." He turns around and hides his head under my dress and starts to kiss my leg. "I'll just eat this yummy leg."

I laugh and squeeze his head between my legs, trapping him there. Then I stop laughing.

Afterward, we lie in bed, and I don't know if it's the aftermath of our lovemaking that makes me think of Alegría. There is something similar about the way I always felt after a performance and the way I feel after making love.

"I miss it," I tell Sam. "I miss it a lot."

He turns to look at me. "What about it do you miss?"

"I miss the euphoria, the rush of adrenaline right before stepping onto the stage. I miss being limber and agile. Since I stopped dancing my body feels heavy, rusty even. I miss seeing the audience out there, hearing them cheer, feeling admired. Empowered."

Sam doesn't say anything. He just stares at the ceiling as if he were trying to find the right words he should say to me written up there.

"I should just get over it, right? I mean, it wasn't all that great. It wasn't. Having to be responsible for all the dancers, making sure they had their costumes, that they knew the steps and choreography. And putting up with their bullshit." I move closer to Sam and play with his chest hair. "You know what they would do? Some of them would get involved with other Folklórico groups and then, when our performances coincided, they had to choose between that other group and Alegría. And some of the girls, they're so dumb, you know. They would stop coming to practice because their stupid boyfriends would tell them that Alegría was getting in the way of their relationship. And once Olivia—one of the dancers—decided she wanted to run a marathon, and she returned to practice with blisters on her feet and feeling so damn sore she couldn't even lift her skirt up or do a proper zapateo. I mean, do I really need that stress in my life?" I look at Sam and realize he has fallen asleep.

Because Eduardo is going to be home soon, I force myself out of bed and go into the bathroom to take a shower. Sam is snoring softly. I tiptoe out of his house and take a deep breath outside, feeling light and free. On the drive home, I think about our lovemaking. This time I hadn't felt so self-conscious and I almost had an orgasm. I just need to stop thinking about Eduardo. Stop thinking and just let myself be immersed in the moment, enjoy Sam's awesome body. God, what woman wouldn't want to be in my place!

My stomach contracts painfully when I spot Eduardo's truck in the driveway. *Shit, he's early.*

I go inside the house and find him sitting in the living room watching the news.

"Hey," he says.

"Hi."

"How was work?"

"All right."

I walk over to the kitchen and open the refrigerator door. My stomach is growling. Sam and I never did have anything to eat.

"You hungry?" I yell from the kitchen.

"I ate some leftovers," he says.

I grab two eggs from the batch I boiled yesterday and my usual salad. When I sit at the table Eduardo comes over and sits with me. I hate eating when someone is watching me.

"I called you," he says.

I put the fork down, my appetite gone all of a sudden. "I was at the gym and my cell phone died. I forgot to charge it."

He looks at me for a while, and I try not to look away. When you look away people can tell you are guilty. But I can't hold his gaze. I feel my cheek begin to get hot, and I end up looking down at the eggs and start to stab them with my fork.

"Have you given any thought about going to México?"

The egg yolk feels like sand in my mouth. I take a drink of water, wishing he weren't bringing the subject up again.

"I . . . I just don't think it's a good idea."

"Is there a reason?"

"Well, Christmas is coming up, and we can't leave Memo to celebrate on his own, can we? Besides, don't forget it's tradition that we always have Elena and Adriana over on Christmas Eve, and how would they feel if we tell them not to come this year?"

"They'll understand."

"Besides, I had scheduled my tummy tuck for after Christmas." I don't tell him that I decided to give up on the tummy tuck. Maybe I don't need it, after all.

"So you're still going to go through with that?"

"That was my plan."

"That's sheer stupidity, Yessy, and you know it. You still haven't replaced the money you borrowed from Alegría, and now you want to have another surgery? Where are you going to get the money this time? I won't let you take another penny out of Alegría's bank account."

"I won't touch your precious account," I say, my voice rising now. "I'll find another way."

He takes a deep breath, the way only a dancer would, and calms down. He walks to me and puts his arms around me. "There's no need to keep having surgery. I've always loved you just as you are. I never wanted you to change anything about yourself."

"And what makes you think I do any of this for you?" I say, tearing myself away from him. "I don't care what you think of me. I want to be able to look at myself in the mirror and love what I see."

"But, Yessy—"

"But nothing. Why can't you respect my wishes? Stop trying to tell me how to live my life." I get up from the table and dump the uneaten salad and eggs into the trash. "And forget about that trip to México. I'm not going anywhere in México except Tijuana."

I run to the room and lock myself in. A few seconds later, the front door slams shut and a truck pulls out of the driveway.

Sam's gift to me for Christmas is to take me to Glen Ivy Hot Springs Spa in Corona. He has a season pass, he says, and usually goes at least one a month. We spend a long time in the heated pool. The air is chilly but the water is very warm and inviting. As I glance at all the young girls walking around in bikinis, I wonder if I shouldn't go through with the tummy tuck after all. I would look just as good as them. Sam's eyes follow a skinny blond girl as she makes her way to the bar. Her nipples are erect and poke through her bathing suit. I move in front of him to block his view, and when that doesn't work, I playfully splash water at him and pretend to make a joke of it, but suddenly I think it was not a good idea to come here.

Sam convinces me to have a massage. He claims the masseuses

here are the best and the massage will take all my stress away. He doesn't offer to pay for it, of course, and when the cashier rings me up for $125, I want to cancel it, but I'm too embarrassed to do so. Besides, it'll just be a Christmas present to myself. I leave Sam at the mineral baths. The sulfurous water smells like rotten egg, and it grosses me out. As I make my way to the masseuse I can't help but wonder if this is how rich people live. Surrounded by palm trees and beautiful buildings. Lounge pools where all you do is just lie on your back with a drink in your hand and do absolutely nothing. How easy it is to tune out all one's troubles—all the world's troubles, in fact—and do nothing but relax and enjoy being alive.

My massage is a combination of pain and pleasure. She starts with my head, and I'm reminded how the head, the eyes, arms, and hands aid a dancer's balance. As the masseuse's fingers dig into my muscles, I remember how each muscle in my body, each ligament and tendon, each limb, was used to execute a specific movement. She massages my feet and I think about the intricate footwork I was able to do, the heels and the balls of the feet producing rhythmic staccato sounds. Toe, heel, stamp. Toe, heel, stamp. Clear, sharp, precise sounds. Toe, heel, stamp.

"You're so tense," the masseuse says. "Try to relax."

I do slow inhalations and exhalations and try to do as I'm told. As she does my arms, I'm taken back to the studio, where I'm standing in front of my dancers. *Always keep control of the arms. Do not fling them about. Do not let the elbow drop.*

After the massage, I tip the masseuse and go back to the mineral baths to find Sam. He isn't there. I check the lap pool, the lounge pool, the beverage bar, and finally find him in Club Mud. He's in the brownish red pool, surrounded by four young women, one of whom is in the process of lathering his back with the clay mud.

"Sam!" I yell.

"Hey, Yessy, get over here and let me put some mud on you!" Sam says, moving away from the girl.

318 ■ REYNA GRANDE

The girls get out of the pool and say they're going to the sauna to let the clay dry up quicker.

I stand there with my hands on my hips, feeling my eyes sting with tears. Sam doesn't bother to call me over again. He grabs a handful of clay and lathers his forearms and chest with it, longingly looking in the direction the girls disappeared to.

Today is Christmas Eve and Memo, Elena, and Adriana are coming over in about an hour. But, since I won't get to spend Christmas with Sam, I sneak out of the house to go see him. I tell Eduardo I forgot to buy the sugar cane for the fruit punch I'm going to make. I run out to the car, where I've hidden the sugar cane, before Eduardo offers to go to the store. As I make my way to Sam's house, I think about calling him but then decide it's best to surprise him. The present I bought for him is in the glove compartment in an envelope. Two tickets for a seven-day cruise in Hawaii. A getaway for the two of us. AAA was having a special on cruises, and even though I got a pretty good deal I had to use one of the checks from Bank of America I just got. The interest isn't very high (1.99 percent for the life of the loan) and I'll pay it. I know I haven't worked hard to meet my goal; Sam is a constant source of distraction. But if I focus I know I can sell more policies than any of the other agents at the office and be top agent again.

Now, about the cruise . . . all I have to do is tell Eduardo I'm going to visit Susy and my mother in Phoenix for a week and get them to lie for me. How I am going to do that, I still don't know; I'll deal with it when the time comes.

I hum the tune of "Jingle Bells" all the way to his house. If it weren't for Sam, Christmas this year wouldn't have been the same. I always participated in Las Posadas in Olvera Street. Those nine days leading up to Christmas Eve were always so much fun, so by the time Christmas Eve came around I was really into the Christmas spirit, doing gift exchanges with the dancers, throwing a big party a few days before Christmas Eve so we could celebrate together. But this year I told Eduardo no pre–Christmas Eve party. It wasn't hard to get him to give up on the idea; he knows we don't really have that much money to spend on big parties. Granted, I'm mostly to blame. My spending has escalated with buying all kinds of clothes and shoes, plus the little gifts here and there I've gotten Sam, not to mention the surgeries. But I'm making at least the minimum payments on those loans, aren't I?

To hell with Eduardo's complaints.

I take a deep breath and concentrate on letting go of all those thoughts. I pull over and park in front of Sam's house. I check my lipstick and mascara before making my way to the back, carrying the envelope in my hand. Before I knock I can hear music playing inside. "Europa." The sensual sounds of the guitar make me feel sexy. I love Carlos Santana's music—and his line of shoes.

A woman opens the door. I'm taken aback. I look at her and wonder if she's Sam's daughter. But she can't be. She doesn't look like the girl in the picture Sam has in the living room. "Can I help you?" she says.

"I, ah, I . . ."

"Who is it, Marcia?" Sam says from inside the house. He opens the door wider and stands next to the woman. "Yessy, what are you doing here?" he says. He asks the woman—Marcia—to excuse us and she goes back inside the house. Sam steps outside and closes the door. He's wearing the shirt I bought for him a week ago.

"Who's that?" I say. I grab the railing on the porch, trying to keep steady. My teeth clench in my mouth as I look at Sam. He doesn't look at me; he looks past me, at some invisible thing behind me. I reach out to him, to hold him. I want him to tell me everything is fine.

"I can't do this anymore," he says.

"Can't do what?" My hand stops in midair and I let it drop to my side.

"You—me. This has to end."

"What are you talking about? Everything is going great. You and I, we belong together, Sam." I grab his shoulders and try to pull him to me, but he pulls away.

"I'm sorry, Yessy. I don't want to hurt you. For the sake of our friendship when we were kids, let's not make it harder than it needs to be, okay? Go back to your husband. Your son. They need you and I don't."

Suddenly, I can't control myself. I remember the young girls at Glen Ivy, the way Sam looked at them, and I explode with rage. "Is it because she's younger than me? Does fucking young women make your ego feel better, is that it?"

"Stop it."

"Are you feeding off of their youth? You're forty-three years old, Sam."

He goes back inside the house and slams the door shut.

I beat my fist on the door, yelling his name. "You fucking ass-hole! How could you do this to me? How could you?" He never opens the door again, and I crumble to the ground, still holding the tickets in my hand.

Adriana

Olvídate de todo, menos de mí.
Y vete a donde quieras, pero llévame en ti.
Que al fin de tu camino, comprenderás tus males.
Sabiendo que nacimos, para morir iguales.

She stands at the doorway and doesn't say hello. She just says, "I'll wait for you in the truck," turns around, and doesn't even wait for my ass to get off the couch, get dressed, blow out my candles, put my guitar back in the case, comb my hair, put on my shoes, spray my favorite perfume on (Haiku, from Avon), grab my keys, pick up the plastic bags with Christmas presents and go.

That's Elena for you. I run down the stairs toward her truck. She already has the motor running.

"Well, hello to you, too!" I say as I get in. "Glad to know you're alive."

She fans the air in front of her and says, "I told you to be ready by six thirty. And I show up to pick you up and you're still in your bathrobe, your hair dripping wet while you play borracho songs." She rolls down the window. "I've waited for you for twenty-five minutes now."

She glances at the clock in the car. It's 6:55. Eduardo and Yesenia invited us for Christmas Eve dinner. It's tradition that we spend it with them. Yesenia's going in for her tummy tuck and is taking off for TJ the day after tomorrow.

We don't talk for another five minutes. Elena zips down the 5 freeway to where Eduardo and Yesenia live, just a few minutes from the studio. Real soon the singer in the stereo gets on my nerves with his stupid "starry, starry, night" shit. I mean, this is L.A., hello. Are there any stars around here except for the concrete ones on Hollywood Boulevard? I switch from the CD to the FM button and search for a Spanish station. El Recodo comes on, blasting their trombones and clarinets.

Yeah, that's more like it.

Elena says nothing about the music. "How are you and Emilio doing?" she asks, as if she cares.

"Fine."

"Are you still working at the fish market?"

"No."

"Oh? Where are you working now?"

Is this the Inquisition or something? Jesus. "I'm working at the swap meet."

"Really?"

"Yeah. Since Soledad isn't around, her parents need all the help they can get, especially right now during the holidays."

"You know, Adriana, any other person who is a U.S. citizen would be working elsewhere."

"What the fuck does that mean? That I'm worth shit because I'm working at the swap meet? For your information I saw Valentina at her booth swamped with customers who wanted to buy toys, and out of the kindness of *my* heart I volunteered to quit my job at the fish market to help her. But you wouldn't understand that, so fucking perfect that you are."

"I didn't mean it like that, Adriana. I just meant you should take advantage of the opportunities you have. You were born in this country, stop acting as if you don't have any choices but low-paying jobs."

"And what gives you the right to tell me what to do? You gave up those rights a long time ago, sis."

"When are you going to get over that, Adriana? What I did to Dad—"

"You are so fucking blind," I say. And as soon as we pull over in front of Eduardo's house, I get out of the car. I take deep breaths and try not to rub my eyes because then she'll know I want to cry. Dammit. She'll never understand what she did. If she hadn't left, I wouldn't be so damn pissed.

I turn around and look at the house, my jaw dropping in amazement. The house is beautiful. Candy canes light up the walkway to the house. All the windows and the roof are outlined with lights. Santa Claus and his reindeer are resting on top of the roof, by the chimney. And every tree in the yard is decorated with lights shaped like snowflakes.

"Wow!" Elena and I say at the same time. We look at each other and smile, our anger melting. She and I have always loved Christmas since we were kids. I remember how we both would save every penny we came across, and when Christmas would come along we would buy decorations from the 99 Cents store and decorate the house. Like two little girls we walk slowly toward the front door. When I look at her, the sadness in her eyes is gone, the tightness around her lips replaced with a smile. And I feel we are back to being young, before Mom died, before Dad was sent to jail, before she walked out on me, before Xochitl. Back, back, to the time when we cared for each other.

Before we can knock we hear rattling inside, and the door swings open. Eduardo stands there. "Hi, beautiful ladies, come in, come in." He lets us in to the living room where a huge Christmas tree lights up the whole room. A fire is crackling in the fireplace. I look around but Yesenia is nowhere to be seen.

"The lights are awesome," I tell him as we sit down. Eduardo shrugs and says it was Memo who did it all. "He still believes in Santa Claus," he says, trying to smile, but it's like smiling is too much for him so he stops halfway.

I fidget in my seat, my guilt beginning to creep up at the sight of Eduardo's tired eyes. When he looks at me, I wonder if he knows what Emilio and I are doing.

Yesenia comes home fifteen minutes later. Her eyes are red and swollen, as if she's been crying.

"What took so long?" Eduardo asks her.

We stand up to hug her and wish her a Merry Christmas. Memo arrives with Laura, and then we move from the living room to the dining table.

The dinner is fucking weird. Eduardo is quiet for the most part. And Memo and Laura keep giving me hateful looks, which I'm trying to ignore. Yesenia is drinking too much. Corona after Corona goes down her throat. What the hell is wrong with her?

When Elena gets up to get another soda in the kitchen, Yesenia asks her to bring another beer and Elena tells her maybe she's already had enough. And man, I've never seen Yesenia get so pissed off before.

"If I ever need advice from you I'll ask you for it," she says. She waves her empty Corona bottle at Elena and says, "And who are you to be giving anybody advice? If you aren't careful you'll end up in jail like that teacher that ran away with her student to México, or worse yet, like that other teacher, what was her name? LeTourneau?"

Elena's face turns red, like a damn chili pepper.

"I mean, you do remember that fiasco, don't you? Getting pregnant by her twelve-year-old student. Disgusting. And she didn't stop there. As soon as she was released from jail she saw him again and got pregnant a second time. Can you believe it?"

Eduardo leans across the table and puts his hand over Yesenia's, not in a loving gesture but in a way that's meant to say: *You better stop this shit right now.* "That's enough," he says.

Yesenia yanks her hand from him and stands up. "What do you mean? Someone's got to tell her what's right and wrong." She walks toward Elena and asks, "Have you slept with him?"

Elena stands there looking at Yesenia as if hypnotized, her face becoming redder by the minute. I feel like walking over and pinching her, telling her to wake her ass up and start defending herself.

"Oh my God," Yesenia says, "you have, haven't you?"

Elena excuses herself and runs to the bathroom. I get my glass of water and try to swallow the damn ham in my mouth, which now tastes like shit.

But Yesenia laughs and laughs. Eduardo shakes her to get her to stop.

She laughs even more, as if the fucking devil has possessed her or something. Who is this crazy bitch standing in front of me? That ain't my friend.

"Just like Cecilia," she says. "She didn't care how old or young the guys were. If she had an itch all that mattered to her was who was around to scratch it."

"That's enough, Yesenia. If you want to throw dirt around, then let's go on with you," I say, all of a sudden getting defensive. I ain't going to let anyone talk shit about Mom. "I mean, what the hell's wrong with you? Getting a face-lift and shit. You're getting old, girl. There's nothing you can do to stop it. And you look so damn different, nobody recognizes you. Not even your husband sitting next to you knows who the fuck you are."

"You're one to talk," she says. "Letting a man beat the shit out of you. Don't you have any respect? Your mother was right when she called you a moth. You like getting too close to the fire, but one day it is going to burn you."

I stand up, ready to kick some ass. The other Adriana tells me it's Yesenia, my friend, my second mom, and she is drunk, but I had some beer, too, and now it's heating up my blood real good.

"Who are you to talk about respect?" I say, going up to her, my fists in the air. But then there's Elena holding me back, and Memo and Eduardo come to stand between us. Memo holds Yesenia back. Eduardo takes me to the corner of the dining room, mumbling apologies.

"I think it's best if we went home," Elena says. She takes my arm and guides me to the living room, picks up both our purses, and heads to the door. Eduardo walks us out, carrying the presents they bought for us. He gives us the biggest hug I've had in years, and tells us he loves us and that he's sorry.

"Take care of her, Eduardo," Elena says. "It will pass, I'm sure."

I'm not as kind as Elena, but I tell him to watch her. I think Yesenia left her brain on the damn operating table!

When we get home Elena and I sit in the darkness of her car.

"Elena," I say into the darkness, "el amor no tiene edad." So what if the kid she's in love with is ten years younger than her? Love has no age. After all is said and done we all die anyway, sooner or later.

Elena is quiet the whole time. She just sits there and stares at the steering wheel.

"Do you want to sleep over?" I ask. She doesn't move. I wonder how much truth there was to Yesenia's accusations. Has Elena slept with Fernando? I just can't picture Elena being reck-

326 ■ REYNA GRANDE

less. No, Elena thinks things through all the time. She always follows the rules of society and doesn't defy authority. I'm the crazy impulsive one. I ask the question again, and Elena only manages to shake her head.

"Okay, well, I guess I'll see you around. G'night."

I sit there for another minute but Elena is still out of it. I grab the door handle and open the door slowly, trying to find the right words to say.

"I'm another LeTourneau," Elena says under her breath. And I don't know who the hell this woman is they keep mentioning, but before I close the door I tell her that love is love. And love is never simple.

Soledad

The man said my ankle had a bad sprain but it wasn't broken and it wasn't so bad that I would need surgery. He said he would fix it. "Just because it's Christmas time," he said to me. I wished he felt like that before he made me spend the night dealing with the pain. He isn't a real doctor. He said he was a veterinarian some years ago. But he fixed it. He made the swelling go away and gave me medicine, and now it doesn't hurt as much. He wrapped an elastic bandage on it and gave me a cane, but he said it'll take at least four to six weeks to fully heal.

Every day I look out the window and my stomach hurts when I see the border patrol pass by his house. I hide away from the window. I don't feel safe, even in the house. I feel as if the walls were made of a sheer material like organza or tulle—and la migra could see right through and find me in here.

The man says his name is Jerry and he's sixty-one. He lives here alone with his German shepherd, Tucker, because his wife died five years ago. The house is one big room with a small kitchen and a small bathroom. There's a bed, and for the days I've been here the man has let me sleep on it and he sleeps on the couch.

"The bed's too soft anyhow," he said to me. "And it's almost Christmas," he said again.

I didn't let him see the sadness that came to me then, knowing I was spending this Christmas season with a total stranger. But I wonder if he's lonely, if the thought of spending Christmas alone is why he's being kind to me.

The bed smells of his sweat. But it doesn't bother me. I wonder if that's how my bed would smell if I was married. The smell of my husband's sweat and my own. There is a Singer sewing machine in the corner of the house, covered in dust, and on it, there's an unfinished man's shirt.

"The old lady passed away before finishing it," he said. He pointed at the shirt he was wearing and said that was the last shirt his wife made for him. Died of cancer, he said.

Many times I've looked at the sewing machine. When he is not here, I walk up to it and wipe it clean with a soft rag. It's the only familiar thing. I touch the unfinished shirt, feel the softness of the flannel, and I fight with myself to not sit down, to not put my foot on the pedal. I miss the clicking sound of the needle and the feel of the cloth under my fingertips. I know sewing. I know the different stitches and what they're for, I know how to thread and place the needle. I know how to hold the scissors and cut with no hesitation. But this world, Jerry's world, I do not know. His blue eyes are like iridescent taffeta—like the dress Stephanie tried to steal at Macy's. They change colors depending on his mood, and I don't like trying to guess what kind of mood he's in all the time.

When I hear footsteps outside on the porch I hide behind the bed, thinking it might be la migra. Then Jerry calls out, "It's me, Soledad." I come out and see him carrying a paper bag of groceries. I am not too afraid of him anymore, but still, I wonder when he will finally call la migra and be rid of me.

I think he sees the fear in my eyes because he calls me to the kitchen, where he's heating up a can of noodle soup. I sit down on one of the two wooden chairs and smell the soup. Even though I'm hungry, my stomach doesn't growl with anticipation. Jerry makes canned soup every day. I wish I could tell him that if he buys fresh vegetables, chili peppers, meat, and beans I could make him something good. But I don't say anything. My grandmother taught me to be grateful for the things I have. And for now, a steaming bowl of chicken noodle soup that is too salty is what I have.

"Border patrol found a dead person this morning not too far from here," Jerry says. "They say he died of exposure."

My hunger disappears at the sound of Jerry's words. I force myself to swallow the noodles I was chewing. Last night was so cold Jerry kept getting up to throw more wood into the black woodstove in the corner.

"Damn Mexicans just don't get it," he says as he takes a big slurp of his soup. "Even animals know to stay inside when the temperature drops like that." He looks at me and tells me he thinks I'm different.

How? I want to ask, but at this moment I don't care what he thinks of me. At this moment all I want is to be home with my mother and Stephanie and Tomás. All I want right now is to be far away from this man that seems kind one minute and cruel the next.

"You remind me of my wife, Soledad," he says, putting the accent on the "O" instead of on the "A," like we do in Spanish. "She also had a birthmark, right there by her cheek like you do."

My hand goes up to touch the area where my birthmark is.

I want to ask Jerry that the next time he goes to town if he can call my mother and tell her I'm fine. But I'm afraid he might get angry and call la migra instead. Today I'm about to ask him, but I'm a coward and the English words in my mind don't come out. I hear his boots hit the wooden steps, then I hear the engine of his old truck. I watch the cloud of dust the truck leaves behind as

Jerry drives away. He says sometimes he gets hired by the ranchers nearby to take care of their sick animals, and that's where he's going now.

I limp on one foot using the old cane Jerry gave me. I sit on the bed for a long time, not knowing what to do. I don't cry anymore, not like the first few days, now I just sit there, and sit there, and wait. Tomorrow, I tell myself, I'll ask Jerry to call my mother.

Because it's too much temptation, I finally sit down at the sewing machine. I turn it on, and soon my mind becomes hypnotized by the humming of the motor. I start to feed the cloth through it, and the sound of the needle coming up and down, up and down, fills me with warmth.

Yesenia

I sit in the garage looking at the costumes stored in the green garment bags hanging on metal racks. Each bag looks like the pupa of a butterfly hanging from a branch. Since Soledad is always talking about the monarch butterflies that come to Michoacán, once, for her birthday, Elena bought her a book about butterflies. I remember Soledad cried over the book.

I stare at the bags, trying to visualize the beautiful costumes inside, waiting to emerge, to be free, to be seen and admired. My fingers itch to reach for the zipper, to open one of the garment bags and watch a Chiapas dress emerge in all its flowery splendor. I could just picture a Veracruz dress emerging out of its bag like a white butterfly. But I don't move. I glance at my wristwatch and realize I've been sitting there for half an hour and it's time to leave.

I go back inside the house, and Eduardo is standing in the living room, his hands in his pockets, the suitcase I packed last night for my trip to Tijuana by his feet.

He stands there waiting for me to decide. He has given me an ultimatum. And I know there will be no going back once I utter these words: "Please put it in the trunk for me."

Eduardo looks at me. His face reveals no emotion, but I know that if I were to look into his eyes I would see the pain, the disappointment, the heartbreak of my betrayal.

"All right," he says, and then walks past me and heads to the front door. I pick up my purse, take the car keys from the key holder on the closet door, and then go outside.

I'm always amazed how getting to México is so easy. Nobody asks you for your papers. You just drive right through and no one cares. I think about Soledad and wonder where the heck she could be. Surely nothing has happened to her. Surely she's fine, maybe on her way to Los Angeles at this very minute. Eduardo has been trying to find out her whereabouts. He even called the police department and border patrol in Arizona but found out nothing. He told me I should be more concerned about Soledad, and I have to admit I haven't been a good friend to her right now in her hour of need. But what can I do? And worrying about it won't help.

I pull into the parking garage underneath the clinic and park close to the hotel's entrance. I sit there for a while resting my head on the back of my seat. My eyes hurt from all the crying I did during the trip, and the saliva in my mouth feels sticky and thick. There's a bitter taste in my mouth and no matter how much I swallow I can't get rid of it.

He told me he will not be there when I come back.

I head to the hotel and check in. I sit on the bed, fighting the urge to leave. Would he still be there?

I don't think I can go through this alone. Why didn't I call Elena? She would've forgiven me for what I said that night. Elena easily forgives.

If only my sister, Susy, didn't live all the way in Arizona. But she'd probably give me a long speech about the dangers of cosmetic surgery. Being overweight doesn't bother her, so she probably wouldn't understand my motives.

Anyway, who needs her? I don't need her, or Elena, or Eduardo. I don't need anybody.

I dry the moisture in my eyes and head over to the clinic next door. I'll go through with the surgery, even if it costs me my marriage and makes the last twenty-one years of my life mean nothing. What else can I do? My body has betrayed me. It's taken from me what I loved most. So what else can I do now but transform it into something else?

Under the doctor's knife it'll morph into something beautiful. Like a butterfly.

By now, I'm familiar with the procedure. I put on the robe and the white stockings the nurse gives me. Dr. Salas comes in and with a black marker circles the area on my abdomen he'll work on. He explains to me again what he's going to be doing—making an incision from hip bone to hip bone, separating the skin from the abdomen, tightening the muscles underneath, and cutting off the extra skin before stitching me back up.

After one last trip to the bathroom two other nurses come in for me and wheel me into the operating room. They transfer me to the surgical bed and insert an IV into my wrist and hook me up to a monitor. The anesthesiologist gives me a sedative, and when I see the doctor and his assistants above me, with masks on their faces, I'm already groggy. Yet despite the anesthesia I'm fully aware of the panic that suddenly seizes me. I tell myself I've done this before. Two times already. I'm a pro. Things are fine. He's a good doctor. He's a magician.

I'm not yet totally out when they begin cutting. It doesn't hurt, but I can feel the knife cut into my flesh. They stand above me, their faces covered in masks, and just before I succumb to the darkness I think of Adriana gutting fish.

༄

When I come to four hours later, I'm in the recovery room feeling drowsy. A nurse comes in to check on me.

"How are you feeling?" she says.

"Not bad," I say. "I thought it would hurt."

"The anesthesia will wear off in about six hours," the nurse says. "I'll give you some medication for the pain after that."

I tell the nurse about the throbbing and tightness I feel in my swollen abdomen.

"That's normal," the nurse says, "nothing to worry about."

"I'm really thirsty," I say, but the nurse gives me only enough water to wet my mouth, telling me more water will make me want to throw up.

Because I'm spending the night at the clinic I'm transferred to another room, and the same nurse who attended to me the last time I was here is assigned to take care of me.

I feel uneasy under the nurse's care. I keep expecting her to say something, to look at me with contempt like she did last time. But the nurse says nothing to me now; if anything, she looks at me with something akin to pity as she goes about her business of taking care of me, rearranging the pillows behind me, checking the drainage tubes and emptying the reddish fluid from the collection bulb and recording the drain output, helping me get up to walk around for a few minutes every hour.

Dr. Salas comes later that day to check in on me.

"Listen, Ms. Alegría, there was a small problem you need to know about," he says after checking my vital signs.

"What?" All of a sudden the room feels very cold and I wish I had an extra blanket to cover myself with and that I was wearing more than just a hospital gown and stockings on my legs.

"Well, it seems that I underestimated the amount of skin I had to work with, and well, I'm afraid I cut too much."

"I don't understand."

He sits down on the chair next to the bed and explains to me that when it was time to sew the skin back together and bind the wound at all points there wasn't enough skin no matter how much he stretched it, and so he had to put back a little bit of the skin he had already cut off. "What do you mean? You can't just put back skin you already cut off. What do you think I am, a goddamn quilt you can just patch up? I mean, weren't the nerves severed? What about the veins?"

"Please, Ms. Alegría, calm down. Let me explain."

I look at my hands, at the IV inserted into my wrist as he tells me that for now all we can do is wait. "If the piece of skin I sewed back on reattaches itself, then everything will be fine. And if it doesn't, then we will have to redo the surgery in a few months, once the swelling has gone down, and see if we can stretch the skin farther."

"Let me see it," I say.

"Ms. Alegría—"

"I want to see it."

He goes out and calls one of the nurses. Little by little they unwrap the bandages. *Oh, God, please, don't let it be as bad as it sounds.* The nurse holds a mirror over my abdomen so I can see what the doctor is talking about. According to the pictures I saw before the surgery, I'm supposed to have one horizontal cut across my pubic area from hip bone to hip bone. But I have three cuts. One horizontal and two diagonal lines.

"I have a fucking triangle on my stomach!" I yell. "I can't believe this. How could you do this to me? How could you mess up this badly?" Tears start streaming down my cheeks. "It looks disgusting."

"Ms. Alegría, it's going to be fine. I'm sure the skin will heal back and your stomach will look just like you wanted it," Dr. Salas says. "You'll even be able to wear a two-piece swimsuit if you want!"

My crying, by now, is uncontrollable. I think about Sam. About those girls he was ogling at Glen Ivy. Frankenstein. Frankenstein. That's what I look like. Frankenstein! The nurse gives me a sedative and they both stand beside the bed, trying to calm me.

Elena

When the phone rings, I hesitate to answer. What if it's Fernando? I can't go through this again. Ignoring his calls. Locking myself away in my room, hiding from him, from everyone. I need to face this someday.

I peel myself away from my computer, rubbing my tired eyes. How many articles have I read about teachers who have had relationships with their students? LeTourneau, LaFave, Feil, Geisel, Firkins, Johnson . . . I've lost count, but all the printed pages sit in a pile around me.

I let the answering machine pick up. "Elena, are you there? Elena?"

I rush to the phone. "What's wrong, Yessy?"

Whatever Yesenia says is muffled by her weeping. "Franken-stein," she says, over and over again. I ask Yesenia to calm down, that I can't understand her, but she only cries more. Finally, after several minutes, her weeping subsides and then I can hear her better. "Can you come down to Tijuana?" she asks. "I really need somebody right now."

"What's wrong?"

"The surgery went wrong. The doctor cut me up like a damn quilt and my stomach looks so disgusting."

"Have you called Eduardo?"

"No. He and I aren't doing too well right now. He left me."

She starts crying again, and this time, I know she isn't crying over the surgery. I glance at the clock. It's already noon. Why is she calling *me*, after what she did? What she said?

"I'll understand if you don't want to come, Elena. I was a real bitch to you the other day. I shouldn't have called—"

"Yessy, wait," I say. "I'll be there as soon as I can."

As we hang up, I can hear her starting to cry again.

It takes me half an hour to get out of the house. How could

the surgery have gone wrong? I remember hearing on the radio that more and more people in the U.S. go to México for plastic surgery, the price being almost fifty percent less there than in this country. But how much greater are the risks?

It takes me almost three hours to get there. It's almost four o'clock when I cross the border, and because I can't quite remember how to get to the clinic, it takes me another hour to finally find my way and pull into the parking garage.

I make my way up the elevator to Yesenia's room.

"It's unlocked," Yesenia says.

I find her lying down on her bed, and as soon as she sees me, she bursts into tears again. I sit by her side and wait until her tears subside. Then she tells me how the doctor misjudged how much skin to cut and had cut off too much.

"What's going to happen now?"

"He says I have to wait until the swelling goes down before he can do anything. But how can he ever fix it?"

"He's a plastic surgeon. That's his job."

The crying begins again, and I sit there feeling helpless. When she's well enough I call to order room service. Yesenia refuses to eat anything, although she confesses she hasn't eaten the whole day. I tell her she needs food to take her medication, and after a while, she finally allows me to give her some soup.

At night, although Yesenia insists I sleep in the bed with her, I decide to sleep on the floor instead. I'm afraid that in my sleep I might hurt her. I wrap myself with the comforter and curl into a ball, like a cat.

"Elena, I'm sorry about what I said to you the other night."

I stare at the shadows in the room. "There's nothing to be sorry about. You told me the truth. And the truth hurts."

"I don't want anything bad to happen to you. It's a dangerous thing, and the consequences aren't pretty."

"Yes, you're right." I turn to face away from her bed, hating Yesenia for being right. "But the same thing could be said about you, too, Yesenia. Time after time we all told you that you were treading on dangerous ground, and look at what's happened? You went through with the surgeries because of your knee. But the thing is, you ignored your body's warnings. You decided to dance with pain and as a result caused further injury. What did you expect was going to happen?"

The silence grows heavy in the room. I wish I could slap myself for what I said, but part of me felt good uttering those words. I'm not the only one making mistakes around here. Why should I be the only one to feel dirty?

"You're right, Elena," she says, breaking into a sob. I'm about to get up to hold her hand and tell her everything is going to be all right. But at the moment, my cell phone rings. Fernando's phone number appears on the screen. And my anger for Yesenia and her accusations comes back again. Even the simple pleasure of answering the phone and hearing the voice of the person I love is ridden with shame, guilt, and self-loathing. I let the phone ring until it stops, then I flip it open and turn it off. Why torture myself?

I spend two days of my winter vacation at Yesenia's side. On the third day Yesenia finally allows me to call Memo. Someone needs to drive her car back to Los Angeles. He takes the Greyhound bus and I pick him up at the Tijuana bus station.

Memo insists on driving his mother back. Yesenia looks beseechingly at me, as if afraid to be in the presence of her own son. I shrug. He's her son, why shouldn't he drive her back instead of me? I help take Yesenia's luggage to her car while Memo helps his mother.

"It hurt this much when I had you," Yesenia tells him. "Cesarean section because you were breech."

Memo says nothing to this. Finally, they get to the car and I wish them a safe trip.

"Aren't you leaving, too?" Memo asks.

I shake my head. "I have four more days before I go back to school," I say. "I think I'm going to go to Rosarito. Would you mind going to my house to feed my cats? I'm sure the food I left behind must be running out. I wasn't expecting to be away this long."

Yesenia holds my hand tight, and even though she doesn't say it I know she's forgiven my harsh words. I smile and tell Yesenia to take care.

I get in the car and begin to make the journey south. I really have no destination. Perhaps if I kept driving I would end up in Chiapas, in the place where my mother was born. I would search for her family. The grandparents I never met. The uncles and aunts whose names I no longer remember. I wonder if they would welcome me with open arms. If I could take my mother's place in the family and never leave.

What must it be like to have a grandmother tell you stories about your mother's childhood? To make you hot chocolate and buñuelos, to sing a bolero under her breath while teaching you to pluck a chicken or to embroider cloth napkins, to tell you the history of your ancestors, to give you roots, to help you feel as if you belong to someone. That you are someone's grandchild. Someone's daughter. That someone out there loves you.

On my way down south, I stop at Puerto Nuevo for an early dinner. I walk through the streets, politely declining offers from the street vendors to purchase trinkets, jewelry, clothing, and papiermâché flowers. As I walk by restaurants, employees tell me they have the best lobster around, best prices. They call me güerita. I wave their offer away. *I have Mexican blood*, I want to tell them. But I know they won't believe my words. They will look at the whiteness of my skin, at my brown hair, my caramel eyes, and see the truth my father always knew. That I am someone else's child. An Anglo my mother spent a night with.

She told me his name was Matthew, but she couldn't remember his last name; she'd been too drunk, she said. "When I met your father I didn't know I was pregnant," she said. "And when I found out I didn't know what else to do but to tell him you were his. I had nobody, Elena. You understand? I was alone in this country, pregnant at nineteen. What else could I have done?" She made me promise never to tell Dad about this, as if Dad didn't have eyes and couldn't see I wasn't his.

I remember the way Yesenia looked at me, the disgust in her eyes made me feel like a child molester. A sexual deviant. A pervert. That night after the Christmas dinner a memory of my childhood came back to haunt me.

I remember my father calling me from his bedroom. He took my hand and sat me on his lap, something he'd never done before, and at thirteen years old I wondered why he was doing it now. I was no longer a little girl, but because he never showed any tenderness toward me, I allowed him to sit me on his lap, and I pretended I was five years old, and that my father loved me.

"You're getting so big now," he said as he caressed my hair. "The color of brown sugar." He smelled it and said, "And it smells so sweet."

I fidgeted on his lap, part of me wanting to get up and run out of his room. The other part wanting to stay, to be held by him, to be told sweet things. This was better than the yelling, the hitting, the insults.

"You're a big girl, now," he said. Then he asked me if he could take a peek down there. Just a peek, he said.

I tried getting off his lap but he held me there, and I could see the veins bulging under his brown skin, smell the alcohol on his breath. I wanted to scream but couldn't. Adriana was in our bedroom, listening to Folklórico music. And my mother, where was my mother? Out somewhere, with someone. If I called for Adriana, wouldn't he try to do something to my little sister, too? I kept my mouth shut, trembling with fear.

"You have hair down there already?" he asked. "You must have. How old are you now? Twelve?" I shook my head but couldn't speak. "Is it the same color as the hair on your head? Let me take a look."

I struggled against him, but he was too strong for me. He managed to pull down my underwear, to leave me exposed to his gaze. I tried to bite him, push him, and when he put his hand on my private parts I managed to yank my wrists from his hands, push him with all the strength I had, and I freed myself from his grasp and ran out the door.

"You shouldn't be scared of your dad!" he yelled after me.

As I make my way down to the beach I think about that frightening moment. It was never repeated and my father never brought it up. But I felt dirty after that, and wondered if *I* had done something to make him behave that way. The day I picked up the phone and called the police, I thought about that day, about the many times he hurt Mom, with me not doing anything about it. I had stood aside, time after time, and not helped my mother; even though she said she didn't want me to get involved, I should've done something. The anger and the hatred, the guilt and the shame I carried inside me, surfaced at that moment. It gave me the courage I needed to finally make that call—for my mother it was too late, but I thought I could still save Adriana.

Have I harmed Fernando by loving him? I hadn't meant to hurt him, to take advantage of his innocence. I never wanted to use him. But do I love him? Do I truly love him, or have I clung to him for the wrong reasons? Used him to fill the void Xochitl left behind?

Soledad

Jerry liked the shirt I made for him. He put it on and wore it the whole day, even the next day, too.

"I'll be damned," he said when I held it up for him to see. "I didn't know you could sew."

He unbuttoned his shirt, right in front of me to put on the new one. I tried to look away, but my eyes wandered back to him. I saw the silver hair on his chest, and was surprised to see the muscles on his shoulders. I thought a man his age wouldn't have muscles. Jerry, he saw me looking at him, and I turned away right away. I played with the button of the dress he gave me some days before. It was his wife's, and she was skinnier than me so the dress fits tight, mostly on my chest.

Ever since I gave the shirt to him, Jerry has been much nicer to me. I hear him whistling outside when he's cutting up firewood for the woodstove. He even brought some flowers yesterday and put them inside a large glass. And for the first time today, he didn't make soup.

It is New Year's Eve today and he went to town to the store. Finally, I had the courage to ask him to call my mother. I handed him the phone number on a piece of paper I tore off a newspaper.

"Say to her I'm good, please."

He took the number and said he'd call. He came back with pork chops and fresh vegetables for a salad. I haven't eaten pork chops for such a long time, so it didn't bother me they weren't seasoned how I'm used to.

"No one answered when I called," he says after dinner. "But I left a message telling your mom you're alive and well." Jerry tells me to come outside with him. I don't want to. I shake my head no, and my insides start to hurt. I feel as if I'm going to vomit the pork chops we ate earlier. La migra is out there.

"Don't be afraid, Soledad," he says.

I go to where he is, and when I get to the door he puts his hand on my back. I shiver. Except for when he bandaged my ankle, he's never touched me, and my cheeks get hot because underneath the fear there's something else. A tingling at his touch. He gives me my jacket to put on and a thick wool shawl that belonged to his wife.

As we step out, I inhale the cold night air, and when I look up at the stars shining like sequins I feel a pang of sadness thinking about Alegría.

Jerry takes me to the side of the house where a fire is burning. Tucker comes with us. I see Jerry's guitar lying against a large log. He tells me to sit and gives me a beer, and Tucker comes to lie down by my feet. I reach down to scratch his ears. I never had a pet, and I think I'm getting attached to him.

I hold the beer in my hand and I don't tell Jerry this is the second time I drink in my whole life. We sit around the fire, and Jerry picks up the guitar and starts to play music he says is called country. It reminds me of Calabaceados from Baja California Norte and norteño music from Coahuila and Chihuahua.

I keep looking around, peering into the darkness, wondering if la migra is nearby. I'm so nervous I decide to take a sip of the beer, just to have something to do. Jerry takes a big drink of his and then keeps playing. The beer helps me to relax. I wrap myself in his wife's shawl and listen to him play. He's now playing a slow song.

When I finish my beer I take another one from the bucket. Jerry's voice moves me. When he speaks it's very rough, but when he sings his voice turns softer, sensual. Through the fire I notice his eyes staring at me the way I used to wish Rubén would look at me. I see his lips moving. I never noticed that his bottom lip is fuller than the top one. And something about his beard makes me want to touch it. What kind of cloth would it feel like? Would it be soft like cashmere? Coarse like hessian? Wiry like tailor's canvas used for interfacing?

Even though the air is cold, I begin to sweat at the back of my neck. I take another beer from the bucket. The ice has melted now. I put a little bit of the ice water on my forehead and my neck. Jerry puts down the guitar and just sits there looking at me. Then he stands up and comes to sit next to me.

"Nice night," he says to me. "Not too cold. In January the temperature can drop to the low twenties."

We look up at the stars and I tell him that in L.A. I forget how many stars there are.

"I love it here. Been here for eight years now. My wife and I moved to the city for a while but we didn't like it. Too many people there. Too much noise, you can't even hear yourself think. It ain't like that here. It's peaceful, and so quiet you can even hear a mouse piss on cotton."

"How much time you are marry?" I ask.

"How long? Our twenty-fourth anniversary was coming up when my wife got sick. Took her to so many doctors and none of 'em could figure out what was wrong. Kept telling her to take antacid tablets for her stomach pain, that it was just heartburn. I said to the doctors, 'Doc, my mother may have raised ugly bastards but she didn't raise no dumb fuckers. If my wife says there's something wrong, then there's something wrong and your job is to find out what it is.'

"Anyhow, eventually they found out what she had. By then it was too late. She had stage 4 intestinal cancer. I brought her here to this place to die in peace. One time damn wetbacks broke into the house while I was away, and they tied her to a chair and ransacked the house. Those sons of bitches. Couldn't they see how ill she was? She died shortly after that."

He puts a stick in the fire to move the logs around, and the light of the flames shows the sadness and the hurt on his face. "My wife and I, we knew each other since we were kids. My old man used to say we were like flies on dog shit."

I surprise myself when I reach out to touch his shoulder and tell him I'm sorry she died. Jerry grabs my hand and takes it off his shoulder. I think he's mad at me for touching him, but then he puts my cold hand up to his mouth and blows warm air on it. He leans closer to me, and I can smell the beer in his breath, and the scent of cigar smoke.

He looks at his watch and tells me it's one minute left for midnight. For the New Year. We sit there watching the little hand of the watch move, second by second. Then, when it is twelve, Jerry says to me Happy New Year and kisses me on my mouth.

I don't move back. When he pulls me up from the ground, and we walk hand in hand inside his house with Tucker at our heels, I don't pull away from him. I feel his hands on my body, and my breasts push against the fabric of his wife's dress.

"Soledad, Soledad," he says to me, the accent on the "O." And I think maybe I'm no longer Soledad with the accent on the "A." I'm a different Soledad. I'm the Soledad whose body is being caressed by the hands of a man—a white man. I'm the Soledad lying down on the bed that once belonged to another woman, wearing another woman's dress, smelling of alcohol and sweat. I'm the Soledad who pushes buttons through their holes and lets her breasts spill out, eager to be touched, kissed, squeezed like fresh dough between callused fingers.

Jerry leaves in the morning and comes back with bags filled with all kinds of fresh fruit, vegetables, and meat. This time, when he's in the kitchen preparing the meal, I push him aside and take the meat away from him. I look through the cupboard for spices and he turns to peel the corn instead.

He doesn't say anything when we sit down to eat, but when I see him close his eyes and take his time chewing the steak, I know he's pleased.

After the meal he goes inside and brings in another bag. He gives it to me and when I open it I cry out in surprise. Inside are yards and yards of different kinds of fabric: calico and flannel, rayon, poplin, some yards of dark brown corduroy (but I don't wear this fabric because it makes me look fatter). There are also a few yards of woven cashmere, which is expensive, but soft and warm.

"So you can make yourself some new clothes," he says.

I thank him and while he sits on the rocking chair by the window, smoking a pipe, I look at the fabric, run my fingertips across it, and try to imagine what kind of dresses to make myself. I choose the poplin because it reminds me of the practice skirts I made for the Alegría dancers.

Jerry watches me the whole time I make a pattern out of newspaper sheets, lay out the fabric on the bed, smooth out the creases, cut it, and sit at the sewing machine. As I feed the cloth through the machine I glance at Jerry once in a while. I wonder if this is what it's like to be married. For me to sew while my husband smokes a pipe and watches me. I forget where we are. What we are to each other. What lies outside the door. I concentrate on my sewing. When I'm finished with the dress Jerry asks me to try it on. I want to ask him to go outside so I can change, but the way he looks at me makes me blush. And then the thought of last night, in bed with him, makes me blush even more.

I look outside and wish it was dark. I can't have Jerry look at me in the daylight. He'll see my fat body, the ugly stretch marks.

"Come here, Soledad," he says to me.

I walk to him and he pulls me down on his lap. I tell him I'm too heavy for that, but he only puts his arms around my waist and tells me I'm beautiful.

"You've got nothing to be ashamed of," he says.

He holds me tight, and I lean against him. I could stay here with Jerry. I could learn to love the desert the way he loves it. I could learn to live without Alegría. Forget my dream of having my own business. Yes, surely I could.

I don't know how long we are like this but Tucker begins to bark really loud. We run to the window and what I see frightens me.

Five or six immigrants running, some crawling under the bushes. And two of them are heading straight to the house, a man and a woman. I notice the big bulge under the woman's dress, see her hand clutching it tight as she runs.

Tucker barks and barks, but the man and woman are so afraid of la migra they don't stop running. They run up the steps of the house and start to knock. Tucker keeps barking but doesn't get close to them. Jerry says he's never bitten anyone.

"Abran, por favor, abran la puerta!"

Jerry moves away from the window but I stay there paralyzed and peek through a hole in the curtain. I see them knocking, see the woman looking desperately at the door. See la migra lining people up farther down the dirt road.

"Abran, por favor, abran!" They knock and knock. I see the desperation on their faces. The woman clutches her bulging stomach.

I put a hand on the knob, and then Jerry says to me, "If you open the door they'll get you, too."

I turn to see him, sitting on the rocking chair again, smoke coming out of his pipe. I go back to the window, see two border patrol guards running toward the house.

The woman lets out a cry. The man holds her and she sobs. They look toward the spot where I'm standing, and I think they can see me because they say "Ayúdanos," help us, help us, but instead I move away and I cover my ears so I don't hear them ask me for help, so I don't hear la migra running up the steps and taking them away.

When it's quiet again, I look outside. All I see now is bushes, cactus, and dirt, and the sky a deep blue against the brown land.

"You did the right thing, Soledad," Jerry says to me. He stands and comes up to me, holding the new dress I made for myself. He puts it in my hand and says, "Now let's see how this dress looks on you."

Yesenia

Getting out of bed has taken on a new meaning. First I roll on the side closest to the edge of the bed. Then I let my legs drop over the side of the bed as I push my upper body upright with the arm underneath me. Then I stand still for a little bit, slouching, as I try to catch my breath.

After I give myself a warm shower, I stand naked before the mirror and stare at my abdomen. The scars are like a living, breathing thing, red, thick, raised, quivering as I breathe in and out. The bruises like melting wax. I feel numbness in some areas, soreness in others.

Soreness.

So different from the kind of soreness I felt when rehearsing for a performance. That was a good soreness, satisfying even, at knowing I had worked for it, I had earned it. But this soreness that comes from lying on a hospital bed while being butchered, brings me no satisfaction.

What is this worth? The itchiness from the tape covering the incision, the excruciating pain that comes with a cough or sneeze, the hassle of getting in and out of a car, or a couch, or a bed. The uncomfortable tightness of the skin, tight and taut like Eduardo's drum. And the lower back pain and neck pains from slouching so much, and the muscle spasms in my back, as if an invisible hand was squeezing my muscles over and over again.

What is this worth? To have done this to my body after the years of joy it gave me. To have defiled its sacredness so that now I feel like a monster, hideous, revolting. Instead of a butterfly something else has emerged. Something I don't quite recognize.

Eduardo shows up to drive me to Tijuana for my follow-up visit with Dr. Salas to have some sutures removed and the drainage tubes taken out. He finds me on the recliner putting ice packs on my abdomen, over the compression garment. The doctor said it would help with the swelling.

"Where's Memo?" I ask as he helps me to get up from the recliner, where I've been sleeping these past two days. Elena suggested it might be better to sleep there than on the bed, and she was right. The recliner helps me to keep my head elevated and my torso semi-flexed, like I was told to do.

"He has to study. I made him stay home. There's no need for him to be sacrificing his grades for your problems.

I bite my lip and say nothing, thinking about the long drive to Tijuana. I wish Elena hadn't gone back to work already and had been able to take me. I take small steps to the car, slouching and wincing with every step.

Eduardo looks at the overalls I'm wearing but says nothing. It isn't my typical style of dressing, but they're comfortable and easy to get into, and I can put my drains in the pockets.

Eduardo is quiet for the first half hour, glancing at me once in a while. He's distracted, too. Usually he's a very careful driver, keeping his distance from others, looking both ways at a stop sign, obeying speed limits, stopping when a light is about to turn red. But now he gets too close to the car in front of him and brakes suddenly, as if he hadn't realized there was another car there.

"Go ahead, spit it out," I say, tired of the tight shooting pains through my incision site every time he brakes suddenly.

"What are you talking about?"

"Tell me I deserve it. Tell me, 'I told you so.' "

He moves to the right lane and slows down. I breathe a sigh of relief. Finally he's going to stop speeding like a reckless teenager.

"It isn't about that," he says. "I'm sorry things turned out this way. But . . ."

"But what?"

"There was no need for you to do this, Yessy. There was nothing wrong with you. You're beautiful just how you are. You put yourself in danger for what? I told you those doctors are just butchers."

I feel my eyes stinging with tears and look out the window, at the blue of the ocean as San Diego passes us by.

When we cross into México, I think about Soledad. "Any news about Sol?"

"I was just thinking the same thing," he says. "Valentina received a call from a man named Jerry. He left a message saying Soledad is alive, but he didn't leave a number where he can be reached."

"Isn't there a way to find her?"

"I don't know. The last time she crossed was in Arizona. Maybe you can call your sister and see if she can find something out."

"You think she's okay?"

"I hope so, Yessy. I really do."

I look out the window and think about Soledad, about how important she was to the group and yet I never told her I appreciated her dedication to it. Seamstresses are a dime a dozen. But Soledad isn't a seamstress. She's a costume designer, and what is Alegría without her?

After removing the outer stitches and the drains Dr. Salas looks at the little patch of skin he re-attached. The color of that piece of skin has been turning darker. He says it's dying. He scrapes the top part to see the bottom layer and tells me there's a possibility the tissue underneath will regenerate itself. "Come back next week to see how it's going," he says. "Make sure you keep rubbing it with silvadene cream, and keep taking the antibiotics I prescribed."

"Why can't you fix it now?"

"There's no extra skin to pull. The only thing to do is wait and see if that piece is going to make it or not."

"And if it doesn't?"

"We need to wait until the swelling goes down to see if we can stretch the skin a little farther."

I glance at the door and wish I'd allowed Eduardo in here with me after all. Last week I let Memo come in with me, and he almost punched the doctor in the face. I look at Dr. Salas and wish I had the strength to punch him myself.

On our drive back I tell Eduardo I want to see another doctor, here in the U.S. He agrees but doesn't offer to go with me. He's quiet after that. I want to ask him how long he plans on staying away, how long before he returns home. But I don't. We drive in silence for the rest of the way. He helps me out of the car, puts me in bed and places three pillows behind me, gives me the pain medication, and then tells me he's leaving. I lie in bed staring at the ceiling, fighting back the urge to cry.

"Don't go!" I yell when he starts to close the bedroom door. "Goddammit, Eduardo. Don't go!"

For the next few days I go for a short walk around the block, then come home completely exhausted. Eduardo goes to work in the morning, then comes to check on me during lunch. He helps me change the dressings, and I can't help remembering how things were between us when I gave birth to Memo. Because of the Cesarean section it took me a while to heal. And Eduardo was there the whole time, helping me to recover, taking care of Memo as best he could, waking up throughout the night to get Memo from the crib so I could breast-feed him in bed. Our dancer friends would come and go, checking in on me, help Eduardo so he could get some rest. But this time it's just me and him. There's no baby to cuddle or tend to.

When the bandages come off I try not to look, but I always do. I see the ugly incisions, one horizontal, two diagonal to form a triangle. The patch of skin has turned black, and a dry crust is forming on it. I bite my lips to keep from crying. "It could've been worse, Yessy," Eduardo says. I nod, not saying anything. Sometimes I lie on the couch, watching him read article after article in the computer about cosmetic surgery horror stories.

"Look, this woman here had liposuction on her stomach and the doctor accidentally cut her intestine but didn't realize it. And two weeks later she was feeling so sick she went to the emergency room and it turned out that feces had been leaking out. She was in really bad shape. Lost both legs." As he reads the articles, I can see him shake his head, his mouth open in disbelief. He says, "My God. My God," over and over again. "This woman's husband sued the doctor for malpractice because she died two days after her tummy tuck," he says.

Moments later he says, "Look at this one. A woman goes in for a face-lift and eyelid tuck and the doctor severs a nerve that ends up destroying her corneas."

"Eduardo, please."

He looks at me and then comes over and takes my hand. "Forgive me. I just don't know how to make you see that it could've been worse. Memo and I could've lost you. But we didn't. You're here, and we're going to get through this."

The first thing Dr. Peters does after looking at my disgusting abdomen is to lecture me on Tijuana clinics and tell me it was irresponsible of me to go down there for surgery. "You could've died, and all for what, to save a few dollars?"

I want to tell him it was more than a "few" dollars, but instead I lower my head in shame.

"At this point I'm not going to tell you I can fix it and make it look better. Skin necrosis is one of the risks of these kinds of surgeries, but it wouldn't have happened if he'd done things right. All we can do now is to make sure the area doesn't get infected and then wait."

"Wait? For what?"

"Ms. Alegría, the most beautiful thing about the human body is that it can heal itself."

"But I'll have this terrible scar, and a hole the size of a football field on my stomach!"

"We'll wait and see how your body recovers. In about a year, we can look at it again and then decide what to do. We might be able to do revision when the scar softens and the swelling is completely gone."

He leaves the room so I can change back into my clothes, and I sit there on the bed, repeating his words again and again: *The most beautiful thing about our body is that it can heal itself.*

Adriana

Tonight, Emilio and Memo got into a fistfight at the beginning of practice. Now that the holidays are over, we have to get serious about preparing for Alegría's tenth-year anniversary performance at the Ford. Eduardo hasn't put anything together, and Emilio has done a half-ass job teaching us new dances because he's positive that Alegría won't be having a tenth-year anniversary. He's already sentenced the group to death.

I wonder what it'd be like without Alegría. But I tell myself Emilio and I will start our own group, and it'll be better than Alegría. So much fucking better that I won't miss it. I won't think about Elena, or Eduardo, or Yesenia here in this room together. I won't think about the good times. Only the bad times. That's what I'll think of. Bad times such as the one tonight.

The fight started because Memo told us that Eduardo won't be coming to rehearsals for several weeks, and that he'd be taking over until his father returns. Of course this didn't suit Emilio at all. So Memo gave us the list of the regions we will be dancing.

Some dancers even groaned at hearing the list. We've done these cuadros so many times already.

"There's no money for new costumes right now, and there's no time to prepare anything new," Memo said.

"Then why don't we just cancel the performance?" Emilio asked.

"We can't cancel. It's our anniversary," Memo said.

"And let people pay good money for a show that's going to suck?"

"This is Alegría we are talking about," Memo said, flexing his fingers as if trying hard to control his anger.

"Is that supposed to mean anything? The last time I checked, Alegría's director hasn't been around, letting *me* do all the work, and there's hardly any money left in the budget to pay for the musicians and everything else that needs to be paid for. And that is what I don't understand, because these past few months we've been dancing our asses off. Where's the money going to?"

Memo fidgeted under Emilio's stare, and his face got as red as our practice skirts. I've known Memo since he was born. We are practically brother and sister. And I knew, just by looking at him, that there was some truth to Emilio's accusations. But how could that be?

"I'm right, aren't I?" Emilio said, immediately sniffing Memo's weakness. "Your mother, with all her plastic surgeries, has been using Alegría's money, hasn't she? Hasn't she?"

The dancers looked from one to the other, whispering, shaking their heads. Olivia and Memo looked at each other for one brief moment. Memo's face got redder and redder.

"Is it true?" the dancers asked Olivia. As the group's accountant, she would be the one to know.

"I'm telling you it isn't true," Memo said. "Leave Olivia out of this. Look, Emilio," Memo said, taking a step toward him. "I—I've had enough of this. If you don't like the way things are run here, then why don't you get the hell out of my dance studio!"

Emilio lunged at him as quick as a panther. The dancers froze, watching Emilio pummel Memo. It was Laura's scream that got everyone moving. Emilio was on top of Memo, and it was a strange thing not to be the one on the receiving end of Emilio's fists. I didn't move. I stood there and stared while some of the guys rushed over and held Emilio back. Fernando and Laura helped Memo to get up. Blood was gushing from his nose, dripping on the wooden floor.

"I'm getting the hell out of this group," Emilio shouted, "and if you know what's best for you, you should do the same. There's nothing here for us anymore," Emilio said as he gestured around the room. "And I'm not going to sit here and let a college boy who doesn't know shit about teaching Folklórico tell me what to do. Nor am I going to be working my ass off to pay for someone else's surgeries." Emilio grabbed his gym bag and then turned around to look at me. "You coming or what?"

I stood there in the middle of the room, everyone looking at me. I looked at Memo, remembering the times we played together when we were little kids, practicing our steps together. Memo wiped his nose and smeared blood on his cheek. *He's your brother,* the other Adriana told me. But what if it's true that Yesenia has been using Alegría's money? And me here, always broke, always on the verge of getting kicked out of my apartment, devoting all my time and energy to the group without pay—while she's spending the group's money.

"Is it true?" I asked Olivia. She moved from one foot to the other, like a skittish horse, ready to bolt. "Tell us the truth. No more of these bullshit lies."

Her eyes swept across the room, looking at all of us frozen in place, holding our breaths, waiting, demanding the truth. She turned to Memo and said, "I'm sorry," and when she nodded nobody knew what to do, what to say. We were stunned into silence.

Finally, I walked over to my gym bag, picked it up, and took Emilio's hand and together we walked out of the glass doors. We didn't say anything. We got in his truck and watched as one by one the Alegría dancers exited the studio and drove out of the parking lot.

I toss and turn the whole night, this scene replaying in my dreams. But in my dreams I rush over to Memo's side and help him up. In my dreams, when Emilio holds his hand out me, I don't take it. There must be an explanation for what Yesenia did. Surely, if we give her a chance to explain herself . . .

I don't go to the swap meet. Instead, I stay home watching videos from all of Alegría's dance performances. The phone rings a couple of times, and I don't answer. No one leaves any messages, and I am glad because I don't want to know who called or what they want. Fuck.

I stand up and rush to my dresser and pull out the bathing suit Ben gave me. I grab a towel and get the hell out of my house as if something was chasing me. I run the four blocks to the Roosevelt pool, pay the fee, and then I don't know what to do. I stand against the wall, watching women and young girls going in and out to the pool area. Some change right in front of me, and once in a while they look at me with a weird look on their face. I've been standing there for ten minutes now.

I go to the restroom and change into my bathing suit, then I sit in the women's dressing room for a long time, wanting to go home. I play around with the price tag still attached to the bathing suit underneath my T-shirt. I sit and watch a trail of ants going back and forth from a piece of candy on the ground into a tiny hole on the wall. I wish I were an ant.

From here I can see a little piece of the pool, the water like the color of Ben's eyes. Finally, I stand up and go outside. There are only a few teenage boys and girls swimming around the shallow end. Others are on the other side, swimming laps. I enter the pool and stay in the shallow end, where the water is up to my waist. I feel the water pulling me toward the deep end. I take a deep breath and sink into the water. I've always been afraid of drowning. But now, as I sink into silence, the water protecting me from the outside world, I think that drowning is not the worst way to die, after all.

Elena

I open the door and he's standing there. His hands inside his pockets, a baseball cap on his head. Behind him, lying on the grass, a bicycle.

"Hi, Elena," he says.

I press my robe tighter around me, my eyes hurting from the brightness of the morning.

"What are you doing here, Fernando?"

"Can I come in?" he asks.

"I think you should go home. I have tons of papers I need to grade."

"Just let me come in for a little bit. I promise I won't take up all your time."

"All right, come in."

He picks up his bicycle and brings it onto the porch before coming inside. He stands in the living room, his hands in his pockets again. I hold the door open, afraid to close it. I look at my bare feet.

"I brought you this," he says, holding out a present.

I look at the small package, afraid to get too close to him. I don't move. He walks over to me and puts it in my hand.

"You shouldn't have—"

"Open it."

I peel the golden wrapping paper and open the small box. Inside is a gold necklace, the charm in the shape of a ballet dancer.

"I looked everywhere for a charm of a Folklórico dancer. It seems they don't make them."

356 ■ REYNA GRANDE

"You shouldn't have spent your money on me," I say. "This necklace must have been expensive." I hold it out for him to take back.

He doesn't take the box. Instead, he grabs me by my elbows and tries to pull me to him. "Why don't you tell me what's bothering you? I've called you a bunch of times. And at school you avoid me." I feel the heat of his body radiate against my own. His lips so close to mine. If I move three inches closer, they would touch.

"I'm sorry, Fernando. I know how I've been acting lately. I feel ashamed for being a coward. But the truth is that I can't see you anymore."

He lets me go and takes a step back.

"Did I do something wrong?"

"No, it's not you. It's me. It's this situation. I just can't do it anymore. It's wrong, don't you see? It's wrong. I'm sorry I didn't call. I just needed time to think. To—"

"Elena—"

"Please, Fernando. Just go. This thing between us must end."

I take off my glasses, not wanting to see the expression of pain on his face, the hurt in his eyes, my betrayal.

"I love you," he says, coming to stand beside me.

"You are seventeen. What can you know about love?"

"And you are twenty-seven, how can't you not recognize love?"

"You need to leave," I say. "And I'll understand if you've told someone about what happened between us. I'm ready to pay for what I've done."

"Can you please stop talking like that? First of all, I haven't told anyone and I never will. Second of all, what happened between us is not something you have to pay for. And third of all, who the hell cares what you and I do, what we feel? This is between you and me, no one else."

I shake my head. "You're wrong, Fernando. There are rules in this world, rules we must abide by. Just like in a classroom. Once you're eighteen and no longer a minor, I would still have to fight every single day to be with you. And I don't have the strength or the courage to fight. I'm a coward." I open the door and stand beside it. I try to give him back the gift, but he doesn't take it.

"You aren't a coward," he says softly.

"I'm sorry I haven't been taking you to practice anymore. I'll try to find someone else who can do it."

He pauses at the door and says, "I won't be needing a ride anymore. Alegría broke up."

"What?"

He nods and tells me what happened. Then he gets his bicycle, and I close the door shut and lock it. I put my glasses back on and go to stand by the window and open the curtain a crack. I see him walking away with his bicycle, once in a while wiping his eyes.

I rush to my phone and turn it on. I have twelve unheard messages from Laura, Memo, and other Alegría dancers telling me about what has happened.

Adriana

"So what's next?" I ask Emilio as soon as we finish eating our shrimp tacos from my favorite taco truck, Los Cuatro Vientos, on Olympic Boulevard.

We get in his truck and start heading over to my place. "I've found a nice dance studio for rent. I have an appointment tomorrow to look at it," he says.

"What time are you going? I'll tell Valentina I need the day off."

"You aren't coming with me." He grabs a toothpick from his shirt pocket and starts picking his teeth.

"What do you mean?"

He stops at the red light and waits. He leans closer to me,

the toothpick between his lips. Two inches closer and the fucker would poke my eye. I press myself against my seat.

"Stephanie is coming with me."

"What?"

"I've been working on her ever since you told me about all that dough she was going to get on her eighteenth birthday. Now that she turned eighteen, she's got all that money sitting in the bank. I got her to commit to taking care of the expenses."

"Are you serious? She's going to pay for the studio, and the costumes, and all that?"

"Yup."

I punch Emilio on his arm, laughing. "I can't believe you. I mean, she'll be our little piggy bank."

He starts driving again, smiling, and then gets serious. "In return, she's going to be the co-director of the group."

"What the fuck are you saying? You told me *I* was going to be the co-director." I hit him hard on his shoulder. "You promised me."

He spits the toothpick out and it lands on the windshield. He slaps my hand away. "Stop that shit right now," he says. "Truth is, she's the one with the dough and you don't got a penny to your name. What did you want me to do, huh? If I want my group to get going I need cash. Lots of it. Besides, I don't care if she wants to be the co-director because I'm not going to let her do shit. I'm the one who's going to make all the decisions. She's got money. But she ain't got no brains, like someone I know."

"You fucking asshole!" I push him as hard as I can and the truck swerves to the left.

"Stop that shit right now!" he says.

I hit him again, and again. What the fuck does he think I am? When his fist comes at me and hits me square in the face, I hit my head on the window. I lie against the seat, blood seeping out of my nose. Who the fuck does he think he is? What do they all think I am? Someone they can just fuck over, again and again? I grab the empty Corona bottle at my feet and break it on his head.

The truck swerves to the right into the oncoming traffic. Cars honk. Tires screech. "Emilioooooo!"

I close my eyes right before the truck crashes against a tree, and I remember I'm not wearing a seat belt. I hear the glass shatter even before I feel the impact of my head slamming into the windshield.

Something wet starts to slide down my forehead.

"Fucking bitch," he says, massaging the back of his head. He looks at me with horror. "Fuck, fuck." He opens the door and gets out of his truck. "Mierda," he says. I hear myself groaning. I see my hand reaching out for him, asking him to help me. And when he takes off running I can't make my mouth yell for him to not leave me.

I move my head slightly, just enough to see the tree trunk so close to me, the front of the truck smashed up against it. The broken windshield.

When my fingers touch my forehead I know right away that it is blood. My body shivers with cold.

Elena.

She isn't here to call this time. She isn't here to help me, to keep me from falling into darkness.

Yesenia

It isn't from Memo that I learn about what happened the other night. I learn of it from Laura. I'm out the door before we hang up. My anger is so intense, it helps me to deal with the pain in my abdomen. I wipe my eyes, visualizing the scene in the studio. How dare that asshole hit my son? My son. Even I never raised a hand to him. And how did Emilio know? How could he have possibly known about me using Alegría's money to pay for my face-lift?

I get lost on the way. All the apartment buildings look the

same—I can't remember which one is his. I came out only once, when he first signed the lease to rent it, but I wasn't here to move him in. In the five months he's lived here never once have I come out to visit him. What kind of mother have I become?

Finally, I spot his car and I recognize the white oleander in front of his building. I get out and make my way slowly up the stairs, slouching a little to keep my torso bent. I knock on the door and no one answers. I knock and knock. I hear footsteps behind me and I turn to see Memo walking up the stairs with his book bag hanging from one shoulder. His face, so similar to how my own face looked after my lift—bruised and swollen. I had forgotten how much he looks like me.

"Mom, what are you doing here?"

"I'm going to kill that bastard!" I say, and the tears immediately start flowing. "I'm going to kill him!"

"Mom, don't say those things." He comes to unlock the door. I reach out to hug him and I cling to him, my child. I cling to him and I want to tell him how sorry I am. I want him to forgive me, to say that he loves me still. But Memo just pats me on the back, as if I were a child, and says nothing.

I follow him into the apartment. He brings me a glass of water and sits on the couch opposite me.

"You didn't have to drive all the way out here, Mom. I was going to visit on Sunday. Besides, I have a lot of homework to do—"

"I won't stay long," I say, finding it hard to swallow the water. "I heard about what happened. I'm sorry, Memo. It's all my fault."

"Don't worry about me, Mom. I'll be okay. I'm more worried about Dad. About the group. What's going to happen to it? I tried. I really tried, but I couldn't keep it together." His voice breaks, and I can see how hard he's trying to hold back the tears.

"Mi'jo, it's not your fault. Please, don't ever, ever think it was your fault. It was my responsibility, and I'm the one who failed the group—who failed *you*, Memo."

"I didn't know how to lie, Mom. When Emilio brought up your surgeries, and about the money, I didn't know how to lie—"

"It's okay, mi'jo. It's okay. You shouldn't have had to lie to cover up my mistakes . . ." I struggle to stand up, to go to him. There's so much I want to tell him, but just then his two housemates and their friends come home, and the moment between us is lost. They are a boisterous bunch, and I have to waste the little energy I have left talking to them, smiling when I don't feel like smiling.

"Will I see you on Sunday?" I ask as he walks me to the door.

He nods and wishes me good night. But he doesn't give me my usual kiss. And I'm too afraid to ask him for it.

"Mom?" he says as I'm walking out the door. "There's something I want to tell you."

"What is it?" I say, pausing halfway down the steps.

"You know how Dad went to the casino?" I nod. "Well, he was just trying to win some quick money so he could replace what you took from Alegría. He realized how stupid it was, to gamble, and that was the only time he went to the casino. I just thought you should know that."

I grip the rail tightly. "Good night, mi'jo," I say. He closes the door and I stand there for a long time, feeling nauseous. I remember when I first learned to spot, how dizzy I would get doing it. One time I had even thrown up. This is how I feel now. When the feeling subsides I make my way to the car, wondering how in the world my life came to this.

CHAPTER TEN

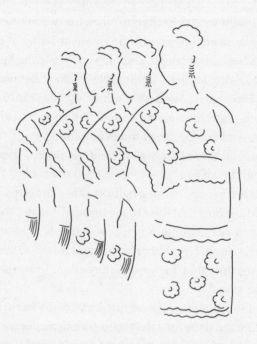

We're fools whether we dance or not, so we might as well dance.

—JAPANESE PROVERB

Every day you stand by the window, looking out at the brown land outside. You're tired of all the brown; you want to see bright colors, like the vibrant colors of Alegría's costumes. The cloth Jerry bought for you is on the chair. You made only that one dress the other day and haven't touched it since.

Shame spreads like poison inside you. You don't help Jerry with the cooking anymore, and now he's bringing chicken noodle soup or split pea soup to eat. You don't feel hungry. Now Jerry's wife's dress fits you fine. It's not too tight now.

The thing between you and Jerry doesn't happen again. Not because Jerry doesn't try. But because you turn away from him; his hands don't make you feel the way they did before.

Jerry says you did the right thing. La migra would've gotten you, too. But his words don't help you forget the fear in the woman's eyes, or her husband knocking on the door, begging you to open it.

When you open the door and stand on the porch, Jerry stops whistling from inside the house. You feel the cold air on your face as you stare at the desert outside. Your feet refuse to take a step, and even though your ankle is feeling better it begins to throb. You walk backward, into the safety of the house, and close the door.

Jerry keeps whistling while he shines his shoes. You sit on the edge of the bed.

"Why don't you make yourself another pretty dress?" Jerry says.

You pretend you didn't hear him.

Jerry gets up and goes outside to chop wood.

You sit there for a long time, not moving, the woman's screams ringing in your ears. You take off the new dress you made and put on your old torn one, grab the cane and your sweater, put on your jacket and the one the coyote gave you, and fill a water bottle and put it in your backpack.

When you step into the sunlight, you don't look back. Not even when Jerry calls out and asks where you're going. Not even then. One thing you've learned as a seamstress is that sometimes when one makes a mistake, that mistake can't be fixed, and the best thing to do is to start from the beginning.

"They'll get ya, Soledad!" he yells. "They'll get ya!"

You head to the gate, Tucker at your heels. He whines when you close the gate behind you; you force yourself to not look at him. You walk and walk, listening to the sound of Jerry's ax get softer, Tucker's barks following you until you can't hear them anymore.

When la migra finds you, you realize you're not afraid of them. You keep your eyes on the cloud of dust rising above a dead agave that fell over from the weight of its stalk. Its seeds are scattered around, promising new life. A new beginning. A second chance. You hold your head up and walk as straight as you can, trying to not limp.

Soledad

When la migra releases me, I go to the hotel to look for my coyote. He isn't there. I sit and wait for more than three hours. My head hurts; my stomach growls with hunger. I don't have a cent to my name and I'm too embarrassed to beg for money. So I sit and wait. I wish I had a rosary to pray with, to have something to do to take my mind off my hunger.

The coyote comes finally and when he sees me, his eyes open wide in surprise. "You," he says. He looks down at my ankle, sees it's wrapped with a bandage.

At that moment my stomach lets out a loud growl, so loud it sounds like a monster is eating my insides. The coyote bends down and says, "Come on," and helps me to get up. He holds my arm as we walk out of the hotel, around the corner, down a block to a little taquería.

He orders tacos and a drink for me and then comes back carrying them to the table. He sits there and watches me eat. When I'm finished the coyote says that with my hurt ankle he can't take me across.

"I need to call my mother," I say. I don't tell him I don't want him to take me anywhere. He would leave me again, and I don't blame him. I did the same thing, didn't I? I didn't open the door, and instead I saved myself.

He buys me a calling card and takes me to a pay phone. He walks away to give me privacy, and I can see him leaning against a wall down the street, smoking a cigarette. The smoke of the cigarette reminds me of Jerry. My eyes burn, and I wipe them and take a deep breath before dialing my mother's cell phone number.

When she answers the phone I start to cry. I don't mean to cry. But at hearing my mother's voice it is like opening a faucet inside my eyes and now the tears are pouring down, and I tell myself I have to stop crying, I have to tell my mother what I need to say, before my calling card runs out.

"Soledad? Is that you? Soledad?"

My sobbing gets louder and louder, and I take deep, deep breaths until finally my throat opens up. "Sí, Ma. Soy yo."

"Soledad, where are you? What happened to you, mi'ja? How could you leave your poor mother worrying like this for you?"

I tell Ma about spraining my ankle, about the coyote leaving me behind. But I don't tell her much about Jerry except he helped me with my ankle, and la migra caught me and arrested me.

Ma says she's spent most of the money she saved for a coyote. "I had to pay the rent and the bills, Soledad. Especially right now that Christmas is over, you know the money is going to be hard to come by, so I wanted to make sure I started the year with no debts."

"What am I going to do now?" I say.

"I'll wire you some money so you can buy a ticket to come to Tijuana. When you get here, I will go down and see you. Maybe in the meantime you can stay at a cheap motel while I try to borrow money. There'll be no more donations from Alegría now that the group has fallen apart . . ."

"What? What are you saying, Ma?"

But the line is dead now. The money on the calling card all spent. My crying begins again, thinking about the journey ahead, about how complicated this trip turned out to be, about everything going wrong, about Alegría. What did Ma mean about the group breaking up? That can't be possible.

The coyote comes and I tell him what Ma said. He walks me back to the hotel and tells the receptionist to give me a room and he pays for it.

"I'll come pick you up tomorrow and take you to the bank where your mother is wiring the money. Then I'll take you to buy your bus ticket to Tijuana."

I nod and watch him leave. He has had the chance to make things right with me. But I'll never have the chance to ask the man and the woman for forgiveness.

Elena

I walk into the hospital room carrying a bouquet of calla lilies, Adriana's favorite flowers. She glances my way and then looks away, at the TV hanging on the wall.

"Hi," I say. She doesn't reply.

I pull up a chair and sit next to her. "How are you feeling?" I hold her hand. She doesn't pull it away.

She snorts. "Never been better."

Her head is wrapped in bandages and I cringe to see her like that. The doctor said she was lucky her injuries weren't more serious, just a grade 2 concussion and a cut above her forehead that required some stitches. I wish my mother had been as lucky.

"Emilio has disappeared."

"It doesn't matter," she says.

"Of course it does. He needs to be held accountable for what he did. He just left you there, bleeding and unconscious."

"It's my fault. I hit him on the head and that's why we crashed."

"But it isn't your fault that he ran and left you there. He's a coward, and I hope they find him." We sit there for a minute not knowing what to say. We look at the TV instead, pretending we're interested in what Rachael Ray is cooking.

"Elena?"

I turn to look at her. She looks so young without all that makeup, the big flashy earrings. Young and vulnerable.

"Yeah?"

"Alegría has fallen part. And it's partly my fault."

"Yes, I know. But it can be put together again. It can heal, just like you."

"I don't know what's wrong with me. I don't know why I hurt so much, inside."

I take a deep breath and then reach for her hand. "You've been through a lot. You and I both. But we can help each other heal."

"Right before I lost consciousness I wished I wouldn't wake up. I thought, 'This is it. This is death,' and it didn't bother me. It didn't scare me at all. But then, in the last split second before I fell into the darkness, I suddenly wanted to live, I wanted it so badly, thinking it was too late."

"I don't want to lose you, Adriana. I know I haven't been the best of sisters, but I love you and I don't want to lose you."

I tell her that when Ben called to say she was in the hospital, I was seized by a fear so great it took my breath away. The first thing I thought was that she was dead and I hadn't told her that I loved her, that I was sorry I'd left. I realize now it was a mistake. She was right to be angry because the truth is, I did it out of selfishness. I ran away to San Jose to escape a life that was unbearable. I lied to myself that she would be fine without me. Once I was there, so far from Los Angeles, so far from my grandparents, from Dad, I felt as if I could finally breathe, and I didn't regret leaving. But when I returned to Los Angeles, I knew there was a price I had paid to get my college diploma—the love of my sister. In this moment, as I sit here holding her hand, wondering if she's listening to me despite the fact that her eyes are glued to the TV screen, I realize the price was too high.

〰

I find the envelope in my mailbox at school, "Ms. Sánchez" written on it in small black letters. I throw it on top of the pile of mail and office memos and head to my classroom to prepare for today's class. I don't recognize the writing, but even though the letter isn't signed I know right away it's from Fernando. As I read, I can't help thinking about the missing commas. Fragmented sentences. A misspelled word. A missing period. I put the letter down and tell myself I'm not reading someone's class assignment. I pick it up again and reread it several times. I fold the letter in half and stand over the trash can, wanting so desperately to throw it away, to rid myself of the evidence. I glance at my classroom door, and even though it's closed I wonder if someone out there saw me read the letter, if someone out there knows about Fernando, about the words of love he's written in a clumsy, childish way. I fold the letter again and then put it in my coat pocket.

I see Fernando during lunch. He sits with other kids from the Folklórico group, and when he sees me out by the lunch area supervising he stands up and starts to make his way toward me. I hide behind a cluster of kids, and then Mrs. Rodríguez comes to stand beside me and begins talking about her new ideas for a show. Fernando makes his way back to his group of friends, his head hanging low in disappointment. Our eyes connect for a few seconds, and then I tear my eyes away from his and pretend to listen to what Mrs. Rodríguez has to say.

Adriana

I leave the hospital with Ben, who has volunteered to keep an eye on me until I recover completely. Elena wanted me to stay with her, but I think she has enough problems of her own to deal with. The only bad thing about going home with Ben is that now I have to listen to the Beatles. I've failed to get him to listen to my kind of music. Ben tells me I could change the music if I'd like, but I don't feel like listening to depressing Mexican songs. I lean back on the seat, and after a while Ben starts to sing along to the song. I wonder what's so great about a song about some yellow submarine. So unlike Mexican ranchera songs, full of sadness and despair, passion and hate, love and betrayal. There will never be a song in Spanish written about a damn yellow submarine, I tell you.

But Ben starts to sing even louder, and I realize that I missed his smiles. I missed his blue eyes looking at me.

We go home and Ben starts to make tomato soup. I tell him what I really want is pizza. Pepperoni and jalapeños, please. He shakes his head no and says I just got discharged from the hospital and the last thing I need is to eat greasy food. He continues stirring the soup. I sit in his living room and realize how much I've missed this place. How long has it been since I've been here? Ben's paintings are all over the living room. I forgot his art exhibit is in a few weeks in a gallery down in San Pedro. I stare at the painting of his older sister, see her sitting by the window, leaning all her sadness on her elbow. Her eyes looking out at the world with fear, sorrow, and even a little bit of hate. She looks so much like Ben, but Ben would never have that look in his eyes.

"What's the deal with your sister, Ben?" I ask him.

"It's a long story," he says from the kitchen.

"Well, I'm not going anywhere. So, c'mon, spit it out."

He sighs and then comes to sit next to me. "She got raped when she was sixteen out in the woods. Nobody knew who did it, and she stopped talking and no one could get her to describe the man. When she realized she was pregnant, she tried to kill herself. My parents sent her to live in Green Bay where no one knew her—so she wouldn't tarnish the family name. They're fairly wealthy and their reputation matters very much to them. But as soon as my sister gave birth she put rocks in her pockets and drowned herself in Lake Michigan."

"Jesus, Ben, why didn't you ever tell me about this?"

"Because it hurts, Adriana. She was my sister, the sister I never knew. My parents never talk about her. Nobody does. I always paint her because I feel that through my art, I can keep her memory alive."

He leans back on the couch and we sit there leaning against each other, the nasty tomato soup thankfully forgotten. "Now it's your turn," he says after a while, his fingers reaching behind me to trace my tattoo.

I tell him about Mom calling me a moth. I tell him about the day that motherfucker Héctor took my virginity and then didn't want anything to do with me. But first, he told half the school what an easy lay I was, and from then on I became an outcast. The girls at school kept me out of their circles, and because I couldn't stand being alone I hung out with all those losers who were just like Héctor, looking for an easy lay. But it was either them or nobody. On my eighteenth birthday I got the tattoo. I was so drunk I hardly remember it.

Ben squeezes my hand and says, "I think moths are just as beautiful as butterflies. And they've been around for millions of years longer than butterflies. They're survivors."

The next day while Ben is at work I go to Olvera Street and walk around the kiosk, have tacos de carnitas, a churro, a mango with chile, and a cup of hot chocolate. Eventually I find myself inside Olverita's Village and look at all the Folklórico costumes they have displayed on the walls. I touch the shawls, look at the expensive Miguelito shoes, the beautiful earrings, the braids. I stop and listen to the mariachi song playing from the stereo. I close my eyes, my head reeling with the colors, the beauty of everything that is Folklórico.

I come to the charro suits they have toward the back of the store. Female charro suits. I always wondered what I would look like wearing one of those, singing in front of an audience, filling them with the essence of mariachi music. To make people cry, and laugh at the same time, just with my voice.

I'm at home, still thinking about how I can join a mariachi, when Stephanie comes banging on my door. "Where is he?" she asks the minute she walks in. Her eyes are swollen from crying. She goes into my bedroom, the bathroom, the kitchen, all the while screaming Emilio's name.

"What the hell's up with you?" I say.

"Where is he?"

"Well, obviously he isn't here. So how the hell should I know?"

She runs her fingers through her hair, then lets herself drop on the couch and starts to cry. Seriously cry, snot and all, and I don't even have any tissues to offer her so I go to the bathroom and bring back my last roll of toilet paper. "What happened?" I say.

She just cries even more, and I throw my arms up in exasperation. Jesus, the girl watches too many telenovelas. Or where else would she learn how to cry like this? She's bawling now, wasting my toilet paper, and I'm thinking I'm going to have to go to El Pollo Loco nearby and steal some rolls from the restrooms. I don't have much money left, and whatever I have I'd rather spend on food. Finally, Santa Magdalena here turns off the faucet and blows her nose for the last time. "He took my money."

"What?"

"He said he needed money for the rent and deposit for the studio, plus paying some people to start making costumes and I don't know what else."

"And you gave it to him?"

She glares at me.

"How much did you give him?"

"Fifty thousand."

I whistle, then she looks at me as if she wants to slit my throat. Fuck me. I could use that kind of money right now.

"I went to his apartment and all his things are gone. I talked to a friend of his, the one with the pimples, and he told me Emilio was hiding because he thought the police would come after him because of what he did to you."

"Well, he isn't hiding here, I tell you."

She sniffs and then blows her nose again. "And I called the people who own the studio and they told me Emilio called a few days ago and told them he's changed his mind and won't be renting it anymore."

She breaks into tears again, and this time, I go sit by her and put my arm around her. "He didn't take all your money, did he?" I ask, seriously concerned now for her. I mean, she's been talking about this money since I've known her. And yes, she always sounded like a little conceited bitch rubbing all that money in our faces, going on and on about everything she was going to do once she had it, but still, she didn't deserve this shit.

"No, I still have more, but how could he do that to me?"

"Look, Steph, I don't know why he did it, but I know there's no point in asking why. That's how Emilio is, and honestly, thank your lucky stars that he's gone because he would've taken it all at some point, trust me."

She stands up and heads to the door. She looks at me and says, "I feel so stupid."

"That makes two of us, sister."

She leaves me wondering where the hell Emilio is and what he's doing with that money. For Stephanie's sake, I hope they find him. I close the door and head over to my guitar, which has become my only companion, besides Ben. And honestly, I ask myself, do I need anything more? It's just me now and my music and Ben's friendship. I stare at the poster of a female mariachi based in L.A. I taped on my wall. They're having a performance in a few weeks, and I wonder if they might have space for one more group member sometime soon.

⤜⤛

Elena comes to visit me in the evening. She says she's surprised at how well I'm doing. She's even more surprised when I tell her about my idea to audition for a mariachi.

"What about Folklórico?"

"You know, I've realized that all this time I've danced for the wrong reasons and that's why my heart was never really in it. I tried so hard to learn so that Mom could love me the way she loved you—"

"Adriana—"

"Wait, let me finish. And then when she died I had to keep dancing because that was my only connection to her. I know now I'll never be as good as you are. And honestly, I don't even care. It doesn't matter anymore."

"You were born with a different gift, Adriana. A gift you haven't fully embraced. If I could dance as beautifully as you can sing, I would be a very happy woman, believe me."

I smile and lightly punch her on the arm. "Well, I don't know what you're waiting for, girlfriend. You've taken a long 'leave of absence,' and it's time to get back to dancing."

"I don't know if I'm ready."

"Of course you are. You know, all these months you've clung to Fernando because of Folklórico. You've danced through him, and now it's time to let your own feet do the dancing."

She looks at *The Two Fridas* hanging on the wall. The two Fridas holding hands—one Frida with a damaged, broken heart, slowly bleeding to death from a cut vein, while the other Frida is alive, her heart intact. "You know, I realize now why you love this painting so much," she says.

"The question is," I say, looking at the two Fridas, "which of the two do you want to be?"

Yesenia

Today I drive by Sam's house and notice his Harley parked in the driveway, and a second, smaller motorcycle next to it. My foot automatically presses on the brake. I pull over and sit there for a minute, and I'm surprised to realize the hurt I felt before is hardly there. Now, only the anger is there. The anger toward myself.

I drive away as the tears start to slide down my cheeks. Why was I such a fool? Why was I willing to give up my marriage for this loser?

When I get home Eduardo isn't there yet. He hasn't officially moved back in. He's still living at one of the apartments his family owns and won't say when he's coming back to stay, although he's still talking about that trip to México he wants us to take. He doesn't know how much I want to go with him. I wish I could erase all the mistakes I've made—especially with Sam—and start over. I could keep it to myself, couldn't I? Eduardo doesn't suspect anything and he would never find out. But wouldn't the knowledge of my betrayal eat at me for years and years to come, make my soul die little by little, the way the skin on my belly died from my ill-fated tummy tuck? He would never know. He need never know.

When Eduardo comes he finds me sitting in the dark in the living room. He turns on the light and asks me what I'm doing there.

"Just thinking," I say.

"What about?"

I take a deep breath and tell him what I needed to tell him a month ago, because after all, if I'm going to clean up the mess I made it has to start with my marriage. And he deserves the truth. "There was someone else."

"What are you talking about?"

"There was someone else in my life, but it's over now."

"You mean you had an affair? Is that what you are telling me?"

I nod and keep my eyes down.

"I can't believe I'm hearing this. I can't believe it. How could you do this to me? What were you thinking? Didn't our marriage vows and our twenty-one years of marriage mean anything to you?"

"I'm sorry. I'm sorry."

He stands up and starts to pace the room. "Who was he? Do I know him?"

"It was Sam."

"What Sam?"

"Sam González, from high school."

He drills me for the details, and I have to re-live every minute I spent with Sam. "I'm sorry, Eduardo," I say again, feeling stupid every time I utter those words. I tell him I was wrong . . . that I was afraid and lonely, resentful toward him for having Alegría whereas I had nothing; even though it wasn't his fault, I resented him.

He heads to the door and stops, his hand on the knob. He doesn't look at me, he looks at his shoes. "I'm sorry, too, Yessy. I'm sorry things had to end this way."

"It's over, then?" I ask, feeling as if I just took a drink of ice-cold water and it's now slowly traveling down my throat before settling in the pit of my stomach.

"I'm going to México, as I've planned. After that, I don't know what's going to happen to us, but for now, I don't want to see you. You think the scars of your tummy tuck are hideous, but that isn't what *I* find revolting."

He slams the door shut and leaves. I sit in the darkness, knowing the pain I've inflicted on him can't be taken back. I thought I loved Sam, that I secretly loved him all these years. But it wasn't love, just some foolish dream I clung to. I let myself get caught in a whirlwind and let common sense go right out in the trash. And by doing so I destroyed a part of my life—my marriage—that I will never get back.

I head over to the dance studio and sit outside in the car for a while before I have the courage to get out and walk through the glass doors. I walk slowly around the room, running my hand over the large mirrors, the barre. I close my eyes and hear the feet tapping, the music vibrating against the walls, the laughter. So many years of memories in this place. And now it is empty. Silent, but for the scuffling sounds of my feet.

I stand there in the silence looking at myself in the mirror. So different now than last year. I touch my face and realize how different I look.

Alegría.

Not too long ago I hadn't cared about its fate. But now, as its death looms before me, I shudder with pain, with regret. Can I really bear to see it end? To spend so many years loving it, nurturing it, feeding it with my very soul so that it would come to this?

If only . . .

How I hate those words. And yet, I keep telling myself, if only my knee hadn't given out on me. If only I hadn't become obsessed with Sam, with my looks, if only I hadn't messed up my marriage, my relationship with my son. If only . . . I stare again at the woman in the mirror.

The most beautiful thing about our body is that it can heal itself, Dr. Peters said.

I wonder if the same could be said about Alegría.

I go to Elena's house and the first thing I say when she opens the door is this: "You will be the new director of Alegría."

"What are you saying, Yessy?"

"I'm saying that I'm going to save the group. I might not be able to save my marriage, but I'll save Alegría. To do so we need a director who's talented and smart. Who loves the group. And you are that person. Just think, Elena," I say as I grab her by the shoulders. "You as the director."

Elena sits on the couch. I remain standing. "Do you really think the group can be put back together?" she says. "You've broken the dancers' trust. And trust is the hardest thing to earn back. You put the group's money to personal use, and that's something that won't be easy to forget."

"I know that, Elena. I know that. I should have never, ever, used Alegría's money to pay for my surgery. But believe me, that was the only time—the only time—I ever did such a thing. Believe me—"

"I believe you, Yessy. I do. But I'm not the one you have to convince."

"You're right. But I think once the dancers know you're taking over, they'll come back. They like you. They trust you. I can't do this alone, Elena. Please." I continue to share my vision for the group. Maybe Olivia can co-direct. She's been around for a long time now; she deserves the promotion. And Soledad can continue making the costumes.

"But Soledad isn't here, Yessy. And we don't have the money right now for that."

"We'll bring Soledad back. And about the money, there are some grants I've looked into that we might still be able to apply for and hopefully get."

I sit next to her and I tell her about my plan to bring Soledad, which is to smuggle her through the border inspection station using my sister's passport.

"It's too dangerous," Elena says. "Why would you take that risk?"

"Because of me, Alegría is where it is now."

"But what about Stephanie? She has her money now. I'm sure she would use it to pay someone to bring her sister across."

"I know that, but you see, getting Soledad back—and facing those risks—will be my first step to bring Alegría back together, and then I can look at the dancers again and feel no shame."

"Do you really want Alegría back?"

"Yes! I want my group back, and I'm going to do whatever it takes to put it back together again. Look, Mariachi Alma Mexicana is doing a concert at the performing arts theater at the Tijuana Cultural Arts Center this Saturday night. They want to have six or eight couples from Alegría to perform with them. I've already talked to the dancers—the ones who are staying in the group—and they've agreed to do it. And that's where we come in. When the mariachi and the dancers cross the border to come back to the U.S., we're going to cross with them, and Soledad is going to be with us and we'll pass her off as one of the dancers. So, what do you say, Elena?"

Elena

After school, the sound of a harp penetrates the classroom despite the thick walls. The music is barely perceptible, yet I can hear the song so clearly in my head. As I tidy up my desk, I hum along to "El Canelo," the sound escaping from my mouth like a lament.

I collect my briefcase, lock the door, and head downstairs to the main office. The music becomes louder as I approach the auditorium, the sound echoing against the walls.

After I sign out, I stand outside the auditorium, my feet refusing to enter but at the same time refusing to stay outside. The music ends and now "El Tololoche" comes on. The only one there is Fernando, and I wonder why he's alone.

Fernando stops dancing when he sees me.

"Hi," I say.

He stands there above me on the stage. "Hi," he says. He doesn't smile.

"Where are the others?"

"The girls are in Mrs. Rodríguez's room, helping her with the decorations for the assembly in a few weeks. The other guys went home. They didn't want to practice with me."

I can detect the disappointment in his voice. "Not everybody is as devoted to Folklórico as you are," I tell him. He holds his hand out to me and helps me get onstage. He doesn't let my hand go, and I gently pull it away. We are at school, after all.

"We need to talk," I say.

"El Tololoche" ends and is followed by "Jesusita," one of my favorite polkas. "Not right now, Miss," Fernando says. He grabs my hand and begins to dance. "Wait!" I say. But it's too late.

I look into Fernando's eyes, and I feel the awakening taking place in my body, like a bolt of lightning—beginning at my feet, shooting up my legs, through my stomach, chest, neck, up to my head. The yearning for movement is too great to contain; the desire to dance bursts out of me.

Fernando twirls me around and around to the music. He doesn't let me stop. He doesn't give me a choice. He puts his arms around me and guides me around the stage. I give in to him; I allow the music to flow through me, the notes of the accordion reverberating inside my heart.

I hold on to him, afraid that if he were to let go, my feet would go back to not feeling anything. I feel the energy running up and down my body, my heart beating hard against my chest as I'm dominated completely by the dance, everything around us out of focus except for Fernando. I feel his breath on my face, the heat of his body radiating against mine, enveloping me. I give in to the wonder, the excitement, the forgetfulness that comes from being completely absorbed in the inner workings of your body, the miracle created by the movement of even the smallest bone, muscle, joint.

"Jesusita" ends and is followed by "Chicha," then "El Circo." When the CD ends, he holds me for a few seconds as I struggle to catch my breath. He smiles at me, and at that moment all I want is to have him hold me in his arms again. All I want is to lay my head on his chest and listen to the rapid beating of his heart as we breathe in and out together. I'm exhausted, overwhelmed by the reverence I feel for Folklórico, for life, for love.

He lets me go and goes to turn off the stereo. He wipes his neck and face with his handkerchief. My heart is pounding against my chest, and I feel the blood rushing through my veins. This sudden release of energy suddenly grips me with a newfound joy of being alive. My mind feels brighter, clearer, and I'm overwhelmed by the sudden rediscovery of my body. For the first time in a long time, I feel whole.

We make our way out of the auditorium and leave the school. I'm glad the parking lot is almost empty when we get there. I tell myself I have permission to allow him in my car, but still, I guiltily glance around as we get in the truck, and my eyes dart to the glove compartment where the permission slip is safely stored. Mr. Mendoza walks out the back door, and we drive by him as he makes his way to his car. I hope he didn't see me. I pull over a block away from Fernando's house and we sit there for a long time not really saying anything. He talks about the new dances Mrs. Rodríguez is teaching them. He expresses his impatience with how slowly she teaches. Now that he's been part of a professional group he's not at the same skill level with the high school students. He tells me he's gotten a job in the evenings bagging food at a supermarket and is getting paid under the table.

"I won't earn much, but at least it'll help buy some things we need around the house." We finally run out of things to talk about and, to my shame, he's the one who brings up the chasm that has grown between us. "I don't regret anything," he says. "I know it's hard for you to understand that what I feel for you is real."

"Fernando, you're so young. I know you think you feel something, but believe me, sometime down the line, when you get older, you'll realize—"

"Please, Elena, don't."

His face blurs in front of me, and I wipe my tears with my sleeve and look away from him. The image of my father comes to my mind, and I wonder why I think of him at this very moment. I remember his cold eyes and the way they looked at me as if I didn't exist. I look at Fernando, and in his eyes I see things that make me reach out to him and hold him. He wraps his arms around me, and we hold each other for a long time.

"Don't think that I don't love you, Fernando. It's because I do love you that I'm ending this. I'm just not ready for this. I'm going through a divorce. I'm grieving for my daughter. Maybe my feelings for you are influenced by my situation right now, and if that's the case it wouldn't be fair to you. I'm just not seeing straight. Maybe you're the love of my life; maybe you're not. But right now I'm not in a place where I can make a decision. Do you understand?"

"I do, Elena. I do. And I just want to say that I'm not going anywhere. My feelings for you aren't going to change. And I'll be right here, for when you're ready."

He kisses my cheek and then opens the door.

"Thank you, Fernando," I say when he gets out of the truck.

"For what?"

"For the dancing."

He leans in through the window and pulls my hair back behind my ear and smiles. "You're amazing," he says. "Maybe one day, I'll get to dance with you onstage. With Alegría. When it gets back together."

The next time we return to Tijuana, it isn't for a doctor's visit.

Yesenia is here to redeem herself. And so am I. We all are.

"This is crazy, isn't it?" Yesenia says under her breath as we make our way through the México–U.S. border. She glances at me from the corner of her eye. I smile and stop biting my nails.

"Everything is going to be fine," Adriana says from the backseat. "We'll just get Soledad so drunk that by the time we bring her across she'll be so knocked out the border patrol agent will just have to let us through."

Yesenia weaves her way in and out of the chaotic traffic. Here in Tijuana nobody seems to obey driving laws. She brakes just in time for a car that's run a red light. "Crazy bastards," she mutters under her breath.

"I don't think getting her drunk is a good idea," I say. "They're bound to become suspicious."

"Would we really go to jail if we got caught?" Adriana says.

"Yes," Yesenia says. "We will go to jail." She pulls into the parking lot of the motel where Soledad has been staying, and we get out of the car. "Adriana," she says. "If you have a change of heart we'll understand. I'll drop you off and you can cross the border on foot with your passport and I'll pick you up on the other side."

"That's if you don't get caught," Adriana says.

"You're such a pessimist," Yesenia says.

"I'm just being realistic."

"Well, that's a first," Yesenia says.

Adriana shrugs. I remember our conversation yesterday. Adriana came over to my house and asked if she could come with us. "It's partly my fault Alegría is where it is," she said. I couldn't contradict her.

Soledad is waiting in the room. Her ankle is well enough that she doesn't limp anymore, which is a good thing because otherwise the lie we're going to tell the officer won't be as believable. She starts crying the minute she sees us.

"I can't believe this," she says. "Dios mío. I can't believe you're all here." We all take turns hugging her, crying and laughing at the same time. She's thinner now, and her eyes are red and swollen as if she's been crying for days on end.

"What happened out there, Soledad?" Yesenia asks.

"I just had bad luck, that's all. But you're here now, that's what matters. I didn't know if I'd ever see you again." She starts to cry harder now.

I put my arms around her and hold her.

We head over to a restaurant on Calle Revolución and have lunch. We have to wait until eleven at night to attempt the crossing. We order margaritas, even Soledad, who seems to be even more nervous than the rest of us. She's constantly fanning herself with her hand, and keeps looking around as if afraid she's going to get arrested any minute now.

We sip the margaritas and try to keep our minds off what we're about to do. Adriana brings up her audition for an all female mariachi group next week and says she's keeping her fingers crossed that she gets in.

"Will they let you audition from jail?" Yesenia asks.

Adriana tries to laugh, but we can tell it hadn't occurred to her that she might miss her audition if things don't go as planned. "Shit," she says. "Well, I guess since ranchera music is so damn depressing, maybe auditioning from jail would add something to the performance." She laughs and downs her margarita. She motions for the waitress and orders a shot of tequila.

"We can't get drunk," Yesenia reminds her. But Adriana waves her words away, and when the tequila shot arrives she picks it up and says, "Here's to us crazy bitches."

"I don't think this is a good idea," Soledad says. "If you get arrested it'll be my fault and I'll never forgive myself. Never. Please, I think we shouldn't do this. I'll find another way, but please—"

"Stop, Sol. Stop. Nothing you say will change our minds," Yesenia says.

"Alegría needs you, Sol," Adriana says.

"I don't understand how it fell apart," Soledad says. "And to think my own sister had something to do with it."

"Let's not talk about that now," I say, glancing at Adriana. "What we need to do now is think about the future. Alegría is strong. The dancers love the group, and they'll come back."

"And you? Are you coming back, Elena?" Soledad asks.

I think about Fernando, about how good it felt to dance again. "Yes, I am," I say. "I am."

Yesenia reaches across the table and squeezes my hand. "And I'm going to continue taking care of all the other stuff," she says. "Like trying to get some grant money so we can keep our award-winning costume designer working."

Soledad smiles, but there's a sadness in her smile, and I wonder what she is keeping from us. What happened to make her so sad? I'm awash with guilt at seeing her like this, thinking about how self-absorbed I was with my own problems and didn't do anything to help her. Sure, I donated $300 to help Valentina pay for the smuggler, but that wasn't enough. But I'm here now. And this time, I won't abandon my friend.

"Damn, I'm going to miss dancing," Adriana says.

"You have another road to follow now," Yesenia says. "You're on your way to becoming a famous ranchera singer."

"You'll be like the female version of Vicente Fernández," Soledad says.

"Just remember us little people when you are famous," Yesenia says. Adriana blushes and then yells to the waitress to bring us another round of margaritas. She stands up and starts to sing "Acá Entre Nos" at the top of her lungs. Everyone turns to look at us as if we were crazy, but because no one can resist Adriana's voice, we all stop talking. Even the music from the speakers is lowered, and all you can hear is Adriana's beautiful voice resonating against the walls of the restaurant.

When her song ends, applause breaks out, mingled with people's voices yelling "Otra! Otra!" Adriana takes a bow and then sits down, laughing.

"I could get used to the applause," she says.

When it's time, we head back to the motel, the reality of our situation setting in. We're quiet as we make our way inside the room. We all take out the supplies from the car and get busy. Yesenia and I decided to dress up as if we were going to a jarana dressed in our exquisite and elegant Yucatán Ternos de Lujo, white satin dresses embroidered with flowers of dazzling colors.

"We're about to give the performance of our lives, ladies," Yesenia says. We take turns using the mirror. I help Soledad put her hair up into a bun and then attach the hair ornaments.

"I'm going to shit my pants," Adriana says as she puts on her eye shadow. I bite my tongue and don't remind Adriana to go easy on the makeup. I glance at Yesenia and know she's thinking the same thing. If it were a real performance, Yesenia would've said something. She hates it when girls overdo the makeup, saying they look like transvestites.

When I do Soledad's face, I put extra layers of pancake makeup on her birthmark until it's nothing but a dark shadow. Soon, we all look the same: blue eye shadow, black eye liner, pink cheeks, red lips, fake eyelashes, large golden earrings, golden rosaries, and hair ornaments of flowers and combs. Soledad keeps looking at herself in the mirror, not being able to believe that she looks as if she's ready to step onto a stage. Her rebozo is wrapped around her arms, and she raises her hands and twirls the fringes of the shawl above her head, the way jaranas are danced. She covers her mouth and giggles.

"It's never too late to learn to dance, Sol," I say. I remember Soledad at my wedding. That was the first and only time I saw her dance. She was standing by the cake, looking at the pink swirls that looked like roses, at the little doll dressed in a wedding gown, the groom by her side. Just then the DJ began to play "La Negra Tomasa." Soledad's body began to move to the rhythm of the song. Her eyes closed, and I knew she was somewhere else, in another place where we did not exist.

Her bulbous hips moved side to side; her arms rose up into the air, hands turning gracefully around and around. She reminded me of a belly dancer. Up and down, up and down her hips moved, her breast bounced gently, her thick braid circled around her body like a feather boa. Under the blue, red, green colors of the disco lights flashing on her, Soledad looked sensuous, voluptuous.

The four of us stand in our gala dresses. We hold hands trying to suppress our fear. "Bomba!" Yesenia yells. "Bomba!" Adriana, Soledad, and I yell back. We raise our shawls above our heads and begin to dance, letting our love for Folklórico give us the courage we need.

We get a call from Laura. "The performance is over now and we're ready to go," she says. "We'll see you at the meeting point."

"We'll be right there," Yesenia says. We check out of the motel and make our way to the car.

"What's your name?" Adriana asks Soledad.

"Susana Alegría."

"When were you born?"

"I was born on October 24, 1970."

"What were you doing in Tijuana?" I ask.

"I dancing."

"I *was* dancing," Adriana says.

"Maybe she should say 'I was performing traditional Mexican dances,'" Yesenia says.

I shake my head. "Let's keep it simple."

We pull into the gas station where the rest of the dancers and the mariachi members are waiting. There are six cars total. Our car is last in line.

"How did you injure your ankle, Sol?" Yesenia asks. I was wondering the same thing myself, but I could sense this is something Soledad doesn't want to talk about.

"I fell."

"And the man who called your mother—Jerry, I think was his name—Who is he?"

I want to tell Yesenia to take pity on poor Sol. Because she's driving, she can't see the expression on Soledad's face at the mention of Jerry.

Soledad starts to cry, and my first instinct is to tell her not to, because she's going to ruin her makeup. But I can sense her sadness, and I know that nothing will stop her tears from flowing now.

"There's nothing you could have done," I say when she's done with her story. "Jerry sounds like a complicated man, Sol, but he was right. If you had helped those immigrants, they would've taken you, too. There's no shame in what you did."

"She's right," Adriana says. "They were fucked either way, Sol. Whether you opened the door or not. I mean, c'mon. It's not like the border patrol was going to stop chasing them just because they went inside Jerry's house. It's not like his house is a damn church or something . . ."

"Jerry would've gotten in trouble," Yesenia adds. "For aiding illegal immigrants."

"But—"

"No buts, girlfriend, no buts," Adriana says. "Sometimes you gotta do what you gotta do. Sometimes, you have to think about yourself, even if it hurts others, and that is okay."

Adriana and I look at each other briefly. She smiles at me, and without the need for her to tell me, I know she's saying that to me, not Soledad.

It's an eternity to get to the border patrol agent. We all start sweating, our anxiety increasing minute by minute.

"Maybe this wasn't such a great idea," Adriana says.

"You still have time to get out of the car," Yesenia says. "Nobody is forcing you to do this."

"Fuck!" I hear Adriana play with the door latch. For a second, I think she's going to get out. "Fuck!"

"Just stop, okay? Stop. You're making me nervous," Yesenia says.

"Well, *excuuuuse* me."

Soledad starts crying. "She's right. She's right. We're going to get caught and you will all get into trouble and it'll be my fault . . ." She rubs her eyes to dry off the tears and one of the eyelashes falls off.

"Oh, shit," Adriana says. We have three more cars in front of us and then we're next. Adriana grabs her gym bag and desperately looks for her glue. Yesenia moves to turn on the light, but I stop her.

"They'll be able to see what we're up to," I say. So in the dark Adriana has to find her glue. One by one the cars in front of us pass the checkpoint. Adriana takes the glue out of the bag and tells Soledad not to move while she tries to fasten the eyelash back on.

"Hurry!" Yesenia says.

"I'm trying. I'm trying."

Finally it's our turn.

"Good evening, officer," Yesenia says as she pulls to a stop. She hands him our four passports.

"Reason for visit?" he asks.

"Dance performance," she says. "We're with the performers that were in the five cars in front of us."

He peeks into the car and looks at us. "Names?" he asks.

We all take turns telling him our names. When it's Soledad's turn she pauses for a second too long and then finally says, "Susana Alegría."

"Where were you performing?" he asks.

"At the Tijuana Cultural Center, with Mariachi Alma Mexicana," Yesenia quickly responds. "I'm the director of Grupo

Folklórico Alegría from Los Angeles, and we were invited to participate in the event." She hands him her business card.

"Are you bringing anything back with you?"

"No. We didn't buy anything."

He looks at her for a moment, then he looks at me sitting in the passenger seat, and at Adriana and Soledad in the back. I wonder if we look suspicious, clad in our beautiful satin dresses. Can he see our fear hidden beneath the stage makeup?

"Please pop your trunk," he says.

Yesenia releases the latch, and from the side mirror we watch him make his way to the back. The car shakes a little as he rummages in the trunk. Yesenia turns to look at me, and I notice that her eyes are opened a little too wide. I imagine what he must be seeing. Four pairs of black boots, red shoes, and white shoes. Four sets of costumes from Jalisco, Veracruz, Chiapas, and Nuevo León. A plastic box with braids, fans, earrings, hairpieces, shawls. Yesenia and I were careful to pack as if we really were going to do a performance.

Suddenly, the reality of what we're doing hits me. All this time I've been having nightmares about going to prison because of Fernando, and now I'm only seconds away from becoming a criminal. I could lose my teaching credential, my career. Everything I have worked for.

He closes the trunk and then comes back.

He hands Yesenia the passports and then waves us away.

"Are we free to go?" Yesenia asks, looking shocked.

"You aren't smuggling any illegal aliens, are you?" he asks.

"Of course not!" we all say at the same time.

"Welcome back to the United States," the officer says. And just like that, with the wave of his hand, we enter the U.S.

Not even thirty seconds later, we start to cheer. I sigh with relief.

"Ajúa!" Adriana yells.

"Ajúa!" we yell back.

Adriana sings her favorite borracho songs and we all sing along with her. I put the window down, and I breathe in and out and let out another sigh. The knot forming in my stomach slowly begins to unravel.

"I can't believe we did it!" Adriana says.

"God has blessed us," Soledad says between tears. "And He will bless Alegría, too."

I close my eyes and try to picture myself as the co-director. What regions would I teach? What choreography would I create? I wasn't sure before, but now I know, with every fiber of my being, that I want to direct the group. There are things we can do to raise money for Alegría. We can launch a campaign. Do silent auctions, go from door to door and ask for donations. Do a car wash. Maybe we can organize a benefit concert. Alegría will come back. And it will be better than it's ever been.

Yesenia picks up her cell phone. "Let's tell everyone the good news," she says.

I look at the dark road in front of me, looking forward to tomorrow. Yesenia grabs my hand. In the back, Adriana and Soledad are deep in conversation, and I'm glad for the friendship that seems to be forming between them, right here in the car. As I listen to them closely I can't help but smile.

They're talking about, of all things, butterflies.

ACKNOWLEDGMENTS

I could fill another book with the appreciation I feel for all the people who have contributed to the creation of this novel. This is merely a preface to the thanks I owe.

My most sincere thanks to:

Erica Ocegueda, for introducing me to the beautiful world of Folklórico in my junior year at UC Santa Cruz, for showing me how to do a huachapeado in your kitchen, and for your careful reading of the manuscript.

Grupo Folklórico Los Mejicas of UCSC (1998)—for the good times, and the bad times.

Marta Navarro, Diana Savas, and Micah Perks, my wonderful teachers and friends, for encouraging me to pursue what I love most.

Luis Felipe, for bringing Folklórico back into my life. You were the most talented and passionate dancer I've ever known.

José Vences, artistic director of Grandeza Mexicana Folk Ballet Company, for your invaluable suggestions and the numerous hours sitting in your dining room talking about Folklórico. Also, Erica Bawek, and all Grandeza members, for inspiring me to write about dancing.

Elías Roldán, for sharing your passion for and expertise in Folklórico costume design. Congratulations on the grand opening of your shop, and for receiving the Lester Horton Award for best costume design. Your talent is inspiring.

Adriana Astorga Gainey, director of Pacífico Dance Company, for sharing your vast knowledge of running a dance company.

Benita Medina, costume maker, and Sam Cortez, director of Mexican Dance Emsemble, for meeting with me at such short notice.

Bridgette Colleran, for sharing your expertise in fabrics.

Leonard Chang, and all my instructors at Antioch University, for pushing me to go above and beyond my own expectations. My classmates, for your insightful suggestions (such as Neal Bonser's agave image).

Leslie Schwartz and her writing group, for being there from the first draft.

Margo Candela, Rigoberto González, and Melinda Palacio, for seeing what I couldn't see.

Malín Alegría, for sharing your love of Azteca danzas with me.

Ruby Vásquez, Teresa Rodríguez, and Eduardo Granados, for your feedback on the novel and your endless cheerleading on my behalf.

Dr. Mónica Lugo, for all the lunches we shared to discuss knee ailments.

My sister, Magloria, for letting me steal all the juicy parts of your life.

Roberto Cantú, for making me believe in my work; when I'm around you, I feel like a real writer.

My wonderful editor, Malaika Adero, for believing in this novel and sticking with me until the end.

My agent, Jenoyne Adams, for being there from the beginning.

My husband, Cory, for the endless hours you dedicated to the reading and re-reading of this manuscript, and for listening to my nonstop talk of Yesenia, Elena, Adriana, Soledad, and butterflies.

DANCING WITH BUTTERFLIES

REYNA GRANDE

A Readers Club Guide

INTRODUCTION

Folklórico, traditional Mexican dance, brings together four women in Los Angeles. Yesenia and her husband lead Alegría, a successful Folklórico dance group, but Yesenia's arthritic knee keeps her offstage and restless in her marriage. Sisters Elena and Adriana grew up dancing in Alegría, but bitterness over their difficult childhood has soured their relationship. And Soledad, the group's costume designer, is determined to open a dress shop in L.A., even though she is in the United States illegally.

Tragedy strikes each of these four women, leaving Alegría's future in doubt. Yesenia tries to reshape her body through cut-rate plastic surgery in Tijuana. Elena's new marriage breaks up after her baby is stillborn, and instead of dancing through her grief, she lusts after an underage dancer. Adriana, missing her abusive father, chases oblivion through a series of dangerous relationships. Soledad sacrifices her career dreams to bid good-bye to her ailing grandmother, but, trapped on the Mexican side of the border, must risk her life to return to her family, to her passions, and to Alegría.

These four women, bonded by their passion for Folklórico, will learn to heal together, to keep Alegría dancing another day.

QUESTIONS AND TOPICS FOR DISCUSSION

1. What does Alegría mean to each of our narrators: Yesenia, Elena, Adriana, and Soledad? For whom is the group a family, a dream, a connection to roots, or a painful reminder of the past?

2. Discuss the symbol of the butterfly in the novel. Why does Soledad love butterflies? What do they mean to Adriana? Why does Adriana choose a moth tattoo instead of a butterfly?

3. What do we learn about Cecilia, Elena and Adriana's mother, from their conversations about her? What kind of relationship did she have with her daughters? If she were alive, what sorts of challenges might she be facing?

4. Discuss Soledad's attempts to cross the México–U.S. border. Which attempt seems the most dangerous? What drives her to keep trying to cross, again and again?

5. Why is Adriana only a mediocre dancer, unlike her sister Elena? What motivates Adriana to keep dancing? What finally inspires her to pursue her greater talent for singing?

6. Soledad's friend Rubén undergoes a very dramatic change in the novel. How does Soledad react to her friend's surgery? How do Rubén's reasons for radical surgery compare to Yesenia's motivations?

7. Adriana tells Elena, "You know, all these months you've clung to Fernando because of Folklórico. You've danced through him, and now it's time to let your own feet do the dancing" (page 373). Do you think Elena was attracted to Fernando's talent for Folklórico? Or was there a deeper passion between them?

8. Yesenia's second plastic surgeon tells her, "The most beautiful thing about the human body is that it can heal itself" (page 351). Why are these words so important to Yesenia? Is Alegría able to heal itself as well? Explain your answer.

9. Although each section is narrated from one character's point of view, there are many scenes in which two or more main

characters interact. Find one of these scenes and imagine it from another character's point of view. How does this switch of perspective change how you read the scene?

10. At the end of *Dancing with Butterflies,* all the romantic relationships are up in the air: Eduardo is traveling without Yesenia, Fernando is waiting for Elena to change her mind, and Ben's crush on Adriana continues. As the four women cross the border in the final scene, why are all the men out of the picture? What is the mood at the end of the novel?

ENHANCE YOUR BOOK CLUB

1. For your book club meeting, turn your host's living room into a butterfly sanctuary! With colored paper and scissors, use this website's template to make paper butterflies that can perch anywhere in the room: http://www.marthastewart .com/good-things/party-idea-wing-it.

2. View *The Two Fridas,* Adriana's favorite Frida Kahlo painting, and discuss your impressions of this famous work with your book club. You can find it here: http://www.frida-kahlo-foundation.org/The-Two-Fridas-large.html.

3. Folklórico is not the only type of dance in *Dancing with Butterflies,* Elena also appreciates ballet. Take your book club to a performance in your town—folk dance, ballet, or any other type of dance.

4. In the spirit of the novel, take your book club out to your local Mexican restaurant. Or if you prefer, go out for sushi, Adriana's least favorite food. Just be careful not to mistake wasabi for guacamole, like Adriana did!

5. Yesenia is able to fulfill her lifelong dream of leading a Folklórico dance group. What were your earliest dreams? Have each book club member write down a childhood "dream job" anonymously. Pull the answers out of a hat, and let your book club guess whose dream is whose.

A CONVERSATION WITH REYNA GRANDE

1. *Exquisite details about Folklórico appear throughout* Dancing with Butterflies, *from specific dances to the challenges of directing a group. How did you research Folklórico?*

Researching Folklórico was one of the hardest things about writing *Dancing with Butterflies*. The public library had shelves upon shelves of books written about ballet and other popular dances here in the United States, but there were only three booklets about Folklórico, and they weren't much help. They were about how to choreograph a dance, but they didn't contain specific historical details about Folklórico. At first, the two biggest sources for me were José Vences, artistic director of Grandeza Mexicana Folk Ballet Company, and Elías Roldán, its costume designer. Mr. Vences spent hours with me talking about the history of the dances, his experiences of starting his own dance group, and the trials and tribulations of running the group. He was also kind enough to read the 500-page manuscript and point out things that only a dance director would know. (This was very helpful in developing Yesenia.) Mr. Roldán shared his passion and knowledge of Folklórico costume-making, and I especially loved talking about cloth with him.

Books about Folklórico just aren't available in the U.S., but very late in the writing process, I was lucky to get my hands on three books that helped me. The first is a self-published book called *La Danza y el Traje en Mexico*, written by Dr. María Guadalupe Castro y Páramo, created especially for the Danzantes Unidos Festival which I attended in February 2009 in San Jose, California, a month before the final draft of this book was due! In June I got my hands on an anthology called *Dancing Across Borders*, published in May 2009 by University of Illinois Press. One of the contributors (and an editor) of the anthology was Olga Nájera-Ramírez, my Folklórico teacher at University of California, Santa Cruz. The third is a book called *Music and Dance of México* that a Folklórico teacher, Andrés de la Garza, wrote but hasn't yet been able to publish. He was kind enough to share it with me.

2. *Four distinct voices lead us through* Dancing with Butterflies: *each woman has her own, unique style of narrating. Please tell us about the experience of writing from four different points of view. How did you develop their separate voices? Was one narrator harder to envision than the others?*

My first book, *Across a Hundred Mountains*, is told from two points of view. It gave me the training I needed to tackle four different characters. I used the same techniques I had learned in that book—pay attention to the voice, the way the characters talk, the way they see the world around them. I also worked on each character individually, spent a lot of time trying to get to know each woman, without the distraction of the other three. Having said that, writing from four points of view was a lot harder than I imagined! I think for my next book I will try just one. The hardest character for me was Yesenia. Since she's ten years older than I am and is going through a different stage in her life, I was having a difficult time getting into her head. I ended up using my older sister as a model for Yesenia, and sometimes, when I was stuck, I would call my sister and say, "So tell me again about the time you . . ." Adriana was the easiest for me because I understood her. I grew up with an alcoholic father who physically abused me for many years, and later on, in my twenties, I too was looking for men who were like my father (not physically abusive, but controlling). Luckily I escaped those relationships and got over that very fast, and I found a wonderful man (like Ben!) to marry.

3. *Each chapter opens with one of your graceful line drawings of Folklórico dancers. Why did you choose to include these drawings? Have you ever felt you had to choose between two art forms, as Adriana struggles to choose between dancing and ranchero singing?*

The drawings came very late in the process, right before I turned in the final draft. I had thought about it for a long time. Because I was writing about such a visual topic—Folklórico—I felt that the drawings would complement the story. I couldn't find someone to do them, and I didn't feel confident enough to do them myself. But one day I said, why not? Why not at least try? So finally I decided to do them myself, just to see. And I ended up liking them enough, and when I showed them to my editor she liked them, too. Like Adriana, I felt torn between the passions I had. I loved music and from seventh grade up until my first year of college, I was a member of the marching band (I marched in the Rose Parade three times). From middle school to college, I took drawing and painting classes because I loved doing that, too. I also started writing when I was thirteen years old. At UC, Santa Cruz, I met a teacher who once told me that even though it was a good thing that I had many passions (I was also doing film and dancing at the time I met her), I needed to choose one thing that I really loved, above all others, so that I could focus on it and be great at it. Otherwise, as the saying goes, I would just be a jack-of-all-trades. So I chose writing. I'm glad I listened to her, because otherwise I wouldn't have been able to complete my first novel, which required a lot of discipline and commitment. Once in a while I still dance Folklórico and I still draw. Having my drawings included in *Dancing with Butterflies* was, what can I say, extremely fulfilling—to see two of my passions come together, at last.

4. *Sibling rivalry is a prominent theme in the novel, with Elena and Adriana's constant conflict, as well as Soledad and Stephanie's less explosive rivalry. Why did you focus on siblings in this novel?*

How can you write about siblings and not have rivalry thrown in the mix? I have four siblings, and there is always some drama going on. The only time we are drama free is when we avoid each other! The rivalry between Elena and Adriana was inspired by my relationship with my older sister—not the way our relationship is, but how it could have been if things had turned out differently. Like Adriana, my older sister left me in a hellhole—my alcoholic father's home. She didn't take me with her when she left, and the two years I was at my father's without my sister were two of the worst years of my life. To this day my sister apologizes for not taking me with her. I forgive my sister. But Adriana isn't as forgiving. When I wrote about Adriana and Elena, I asked myself: how would my relationship with my sister be if I had held a grudge and not forgiven or understood my sister's choices? (She was only twenty-one and could barely take care of herself, but at the time all I thought about was that she had left me and saved herself.)

With Soledad and Stephanie, I wanted to write about siblings who belong to two worlds. Most immigrant families have siblings who were born in this country and others born in other countries. Even in my own family, my two youngest siblings were born here, but the three oldest (myself included) were born in Mexico.

5. *Soledad faces enormous challenges in her efforts to cross the México–U.S. border. What inspired Soledad's story?*

Soledad was the last character to make an appearance. One day when I was at Mr. Vences's house (the director of the dance group I researched), Elías Roldán was there, showing Mr. Vences a costume he was designing for the group. As I watched them talk about the costume and what changes needed to be made, I realized that I was missing a crucial part in my novel—the point of view of Alegría's costume designer! Mr. Roldán was very generous with his time, and I visited him at his house to interview him several times. Like Soledad, he used his dining room to do his sewing, and every corner of the living room and dining room was covered in bolts of cloth. In the interviews he not only talked about costume-making and cloth, but he shared with me his dream of having his own shop and everything that was keeping him from making his dream come true. But now I'm happy to say that Mr. Roldán has his own shop in East L.A., and his business is thriving. Although *Dancing with Butterflies* ends before Soledad makes her dream come true, this is the kind of future I envision for her. In terms of the challenges she faced crossing the border, it was inspired by all the stories I hear from immigrants who have had to make the dangerous journey north (myself included).

6. *Despite all the challenges that your characters face, there are many light-hearted moments as well. How did you manage to balance serious subjects and humor? Do you have a favorite humorous moment in the novel?*

I tend to write depressing stuff, and writing funny isn't my strength. Whatever funny moments appear in the novel were not planned. But a little humor goes a long way, and it gives the reader a break from all that sadness, so I'm glad I managed to have a few funny moments here and there. One of my favorite humorous moments is when Adriana and Ben go out for sushi and she mistakes the wasabi for guacamole. I was twenty years old when I first had sushi, and like Adriana, I was very ignorant about what wasabi was. I put a lot of it on my sushi, and, boy, did that hurt!

7. *Frida Kahlo is featured prominently in the novel, as Adriana's favorite artist. How does Kahlo's work affect you?*

Frida Kahlo is an inspiration to many Latinas. She was a fighter. For most of her life she was in deep physical (and emotional) pain. Yet her passion for art helped carry her through the toughest moments of her life. Writing has been my salvation. When things got bad at home, I wrote. Writing kept me sane. Kahlo painted herself many times. When I write I use myself as the starting point for my characters. Elena, Adriana, Soledad, Yesenia, they are all facets of me. They are not self-portraits, no, not like Kahlo painted her self-portraits. My self-portraits (my characters) are drawn in a style like Picasso's, very distorted, but somehow recognizable. Like Adriana, my favorite Kahlo painting is "The Two Fridas." When I lived with my father, I developed a second personality, another Reyna, so to speak. One Reyna was afraid, depressed, and lonely. But the other Reyna was strong, brave, and smart. When things got tough, that second Reyna was the one who would give me the push I needed to keep going. I could hear her in my head telling me, "Things won't always be like this. One day they will be better." When I saw "The Two Fridas," I saw my dual personality represented in that painting, and I fell in love with the painting and with the woman who painted it.

8. *Although the main characters in* Dancing with Butterflies *are Mexican or Mexican-American, they face many of the same problems as women from other backgrounds and cultures. Which of the characters' challenges do you feel are the most universal? Which feel more culturally specific to you?*

Just a few weeks ago, my older brother asked me why I don't write books without Latino characters or themes. He said that I am "limiting my audience" and therefore (or so I read between the lines) I will never have a bestseller. At first I felt furious about his comment, especially because I was showing him the advance copy of *Dancing with Butterflies* and instead of just saying, "Good job, Reyna," he asks me that question! (Sibling drama? Yes!) But the thing is that even though I write about Latino characters, ultimately I am writing about human beings. No matter what ethnic background we come from, first and foremost we belong to the human race. The problems the women in *Dancing with Butterflies* face are universal. Like Yesenia, who hasn't thought about aging and being frightened by it? Who hasn't thought about the body's limitations and what it can and cannot do as we get older? Elena gave birth to a stillborn baby. What mother, at some point during a pregnancy, hasn't feared the worst? And for some, no matter their ethnic backgrounds, the worst has come to pass. What culture hasn't had sibling rivalry, dead relatives to mourn, dreams that haven't come true, obstacles to overcome, marriages that fail, illicit love affairs, forbidden love?

9. *At one point, Elena realizes that her ex-husband never understood her passion for dancing. Do you think artists need to connect with other artists in order to share their passions?*

I think that it is very hard for nonartists to understand an artist's inner world, needs, and thoughts. But it doesn't mean you can't try! I think it is very important for artists to build friendships with other artists. I have been lucky to have made many writer friends, especially female writers. We get together sometimes for coffee, or communicate through email or phone calls. We critique each other's works, talk about our goals, our dreams, our troubles with our respective partners, our children, our editors, our publishers, our readers. I think that artists need to have a support network and spend time with those who understand, those who are walking the same difficult path. I have made it a point to reach out to other writers. For example, this year I am helping to organize the Latino Book & Family Festival in Los Angeles to reach out to other writers and have us come together, for at least one weekend, to share our passion for the written word, not only with each other but with the community. I love my writer friends. They understand me in a way my own family never will.

10. *Your first novel,* Across a Hundred Mountains, *also centers on immigration and families. Do you plan to continue these themes in your future work?*

I like to write about things that are important to me. My older sister once asked, "Why are you always writing about Mexico?" My father once said, "Why don't you just forget about the past and move on? Why do you need to write about it?" I write about things that I care about, that matter to me. The immigrant experience is one of them. Right now, I am working on a memoir, in which I write about my childhood in Mexico, living in poverty, being raised by my grandmother because my parents were here in the United States working. I write about what it was like to come here as an illegal immigrant and the difficulties of trying to close the gap created by eight years of separation between me and my father. So to answer the question, yes, I do plan to continue writing about immigration and families, among other things. I am always looking for new ideas and topics. One has to grow as a writer, and one way to do that is to take chances and try new things.